Introduction

I hope you enjoy the unique twist this book presents. I have written each and every story; I do "research" with some of the people in the stories, and have certainly asked questions regarding thoughts and feelings to gain a better understanding of both sides of the story. These stories are a mixture of experiences I have had. All are based on fact, at least concerning the person(s) involved. Some are true to the letter and some are the way I wished things worked out, these being total fabrications built around someone I've met. As the reader, you will have to decide which is which. If you are looking for a romance novel, put this book back where you found it. This is a book about classy adults doing erotic things. This is a nightstand book more so than a coffee table book. Enjoy the stories one or two at a time, whether by yourself or with someone you are close to.

As an advocate for safe sex, I strongly encourage you to take the necessary precautions in your own adventures. Although I do not make reference to the use of condoms in every story, I assure you I do my part to protect myself and my partner. You should be sure to do the same.

Please log onto my website at www.flipside-erotica.com and let me know what you think of this project. Enjoy the free preview of the audio downloads that is offered. Some of the voices in the audio files are the actual people in the stories; some are just friends of mine. Again, you will have to decide for yourself who's who. ☺

Jennifer

"The door is unlocked, come inside. There is a blindfold hanging on the doorknob, put it on and wait for me." I push send on my phone delivering the text message to her. I know she is still ten minutes away, but I want her thinking about it for ten agonizing minutes. One of my favorite things in life is the anticipation of sex. The actually sex itself is mind-blowing, and always has been for us; but the excitement we both feel beforehand is a delicious torture that makes life worth living.

After I send the message I begin to wonder if, in fact, I can get her undressed without removing the blindfold. I guess I will figure it out later. I go to the bedroom to make sure I have everything ready. The candle is lit, and wax is pooling around the sides. I put the new silky soft sheets I had just purchased on the bed and three ripe strawberries in a small bowl sitting on the nightstand. Everything is set, and I am already showing signs of my excitement. I am practically shaking with anticipation and the growing bulge in my linen pants is becoming more than a little obvious. I love when I have the time to set up an elaborate scenario like this; it is such a turn on to break from the routine and get creative. I know she likes it as well; she has told me many times how encounters like this get burned deep into her brain.

I hear her car pull into the driveway, and I peek through the blinds to see her. I am as excited as if this is our first time together, but it is far from it. We have been lovers for a long time, and are quite familiar with one another, and yet my desire for her has never waned. She is still dressed from work; her business casual attire the perfect framing for that firm and fit body of hers. She is wearing her favorite Jimmy Choo heels, adding three or four inches to her height. I hear them clicking on the driveway as she walks to the door. I am bursting; I want to tear her clothes from her body and ravage her against the door. She would love it, but it has been done before. Besides, I want to use all of the props I have set up, so I will have to contain my desire as best I can. It won't be easy.

She opens the door..."Hello?" she asks. I do not answer. I wait for her to follow her instructions, knowing she will. I hear her keys hit the table and her purse land on the floor. I am hiding in the bedroom, but can picture the scene perfectly. She announces that she is ready, and I quietly enter the living room to find her leaning against the door, blindfold in place. I walk over to her as quietly as I can. "I'm ready!" she says loudly, obviously not hearing me approach. I am standing directly in front of her, and breathe gently against her face to let her know I am there. She jumps at first and then smiles, knowing it is about to begin. I push her gently against the door and lean forward to kiss her, stopping just short. I hold my face in front of hers, making her feel my proximity. I trace my lips against her cheek, and across her mouth, but do not let her kiss me. She leans forward, her mouth wanting mine, but I make her wait. I very gently kiss her neck, and she leans her head to the side giving me access to her favorite spot. I sink my teeth into her flesh right where her neck curves into her shoulder, biting slow and deep. I hear her moan a delighted sound, and her hands reach for me. I grab her wrists, and push her hands back to her sides. I continue to tease her, nibbling and kissing all the flesh I can access while she is still clothed. I begin to gently unbutton her blouse, one button at a time. I am proceeding agonizingly slow on purpose. I tell her I have something special planned today, and I know she is aching to get to it. But as I said, the buildup is half the fun.

I push my hands inside her shirt and back over her shoulders, removing her blouse from her. She has chosen a wonderfully sex bra, lacy and black. It accentuates her breasts, amplifying her cleavage under her conservative business shirt. She loves the feeling of a sexy look cloaked under business attire; it's the feeling of hidden sexiness that is so appealing. I resume kissing her skin, traveling between her breasts and down her stomach. I can't keep my hands from her any longer, and firmly push her breasts against her body. She sighs heavily; I love the feel of her soft, supple flesh in my hands. I knead and caress them feeling her through the sheer lacy material. I can feel her rosebud nipples harden under my touch. They press into the material, and I strum my fingers across them like I am playing a guitar. She is biting her lip, and I know she loves my touch. I am so into this; the whole world collapses and there is only this moment in time shared by the two of us. I pull one of her breasts free from its confines, and flick my tongue across her nipple. She shudders, and grabs the back of my head, pulling me into her. I grab her wrist once more, pushing her hand back into place by her side. I know she is growing frustrated by my tactics, and I smile in front of her blindfolded face.

I pull her away from the wall, and slide my hand up her back. I feel the hooks in her bra, and I pinch the two ends together, unclipping it. They are free, and I worship her lovely breasts the way they deserve. I press them together, and put both her nipples in my mouth at the same time. I drag my tongue across them both, alternating between the two. I suck and bite them playfully, teasing and taunting her with my mouth. Her groans encourage me, and I continue as my hands find their way to her pants. I trace her curves through her clothes, feeling the subtle change from her stomach to the groove in her thigh. I can feel the heat emanating from her, and I gently brush the back of my hand across her pussy. She is growing hotter by the second, and I love it. She is dying for me to touch her, and when I finally do, it brings sweet relief. I place my palm flat against her hot mound, pressing up and into her. She lets out a loud moan, and I can feel how wet she is. I slowly move my hand around, rolling her own folds against her. She reaches for me again, and this time I grab her wrists and trap them together. I lift them, pushing them against the door above her head. She arches to meet my mouth, still working over her breasts. I can feel the moisture soaking through her pants, and decide they need to be removed.

I release her hands, and undo the belt in her pants. I unhook the clasp, and pull the zipper down, increasing my pace for the first time today. I am glad to see she is wearing baggy pants because I want her to leave the heels on. I pull them down, and she steps out of them, now standing in front of me in only her black thong and the heels...those sexy-ass heels. I take a step back, just to take it all in. I hope she can feel how much I am enjoying the tour of her body I am taking, and how difficult it is for me to go so slowly. I want to tear her clothes from her and smash her into the door with my thrusts. We have done it like this before and loved every minute of it, but today is all planned out, and I want to stick to the agenda. I get on my knees in front of her, drawing her musky scent into my nose. I love the smell of her. I kiss her thighs, feeling the smooth skin against my face. I push my palm into her again, and this time she pushes back, leaning into me. Her desire grows and her patience diminishes. I love it. I grab the thin material of her panties, and pull them aside. I take one finger and pierce her waiting folds, going as deep as I can in one motion. She moans loudly, finally getting some form of relief to the pent up feelings deep inside. I stroke it in and out of her, seeing her glistening wetness clinging to my finger as I slide it in and out. She grabs her breasts, squeezing them roughly as I work her sopping pussy over.

My own desire is mounting, and in an undisciplined burst I reach up and tear her panties off of her. I yank them right to her feet, and I plunge my face into her. I shoot my tongue in and out of her, and she groans loudly, calling out. "Oh Jesus!...oh my God!" echoes through my house. I can tell it's coming, and I want is as much as she does. I push two fingers into her again, and rub my tongue as hard as I can against her clit. She is clutching at the wall, trying to find a way to brace herself for the coming storm. I am unrelenting, and lash her swollen clit into submission. Her orgasm bursts forth, flooding her senses and practically buckling her knees. I put my hands on her hips, pressing her against the door to keep her balanced in her heels. Her cries of ecstasy continue, as her orgasm vibrates all through her. She is shuddering, seizing in pleasure, and I am loving what I am doing to her. She slowly comes down from the high it produces, and is panting heavily from the output of mind and body. I am far from done with her, but I know she will need a more stable foundation for any more activity. I look at the high-back bar stool across the room and think this will solve our dilemma.

I leave her where she is standing, and hurry across the room. I return with the high back chair, and set it in front of the door. I can see her peeking under the blindfold, eager to see what is next. She is cheating, and I love it. I lead her to her new location, and sit her down on the chair. I sling one of her legs over the arm, exposing her waiting pussy to me. I return to my knees in front of her, her naked pussy staring back at me, beckoning. I want more, as does she and I get right to work. This time I can reach more of her, and I slide my tongue over every inch of her mound. I tease her by going dangerously close to her most private hole, flicking over the sensitive skin in between. I see her peeking at me again, and I love it. I return two fingers to their rightful place; stroke them into her, twisting as I go. I gently seal my mouth around her clit, and tenderly begin to suck her love button. She loves it, and is quickly building towards another fierce orgasm. Her voice strengthens, her cries growing louder with each passing second of my mouth on her. I continue, bobbing and weaving in order to match her unconscious movements. She explodes in a huge, wild orgasm. Her hands grip the arm rails of the barstool, her knuckles white in exertion. I move with her, riding the storm out as she shudders and wriggles under my tongue. It is awesome, and she is left spent, slumped in the chair.

I stand, giving her a moment to regain her composure. It also gives me the chance to remove my clothing. I am at full stride, stiff from the action thus far even though it was all focused on her. Nothing pleases me as much as pleasing her. I reach for her hand, and place it on me. She grabs it, stroking the hardness in her smooth hands. Desire fuels her recovery. She falls to her knees, wanting it in her mouth as soon as possible now that she has touched it. She pushes me towards the barstool, and we trade places as well as trading roles. Her mouth is hot on me, and her tongue wet. She glides her hand up and down the length of it, her mouth following close behind. They work in tandem, complimenting one another, completely different sensations yet both wondrous in their own right. I sit back, looking down at her. I love to watch her go to work on me, and the sexy, fevered look on her blindfolded face only adds to my own delight. I brush her hair aside, making sure nothing interrupts her. She continues slurping and sucking it, and I am building to my own wild explosion. The internal debate of what to do begins.

She continues her task, loving what she has undertaken. She loves to have me in her mouth, almost as much as I enjoy being there. She is good at it, and there is no substitute for enthusiasm. I am going to have to make a decision really quickly if I want to stop; I am about 30 seconds from the point of no return. I decide that today's events are going to continue to require some restraint, so I push her away from me. I catch myself just in time, and find myself gripping the arm of the bar stool in effort to collect myself. If she wasn't blindfolded she would be proudly giggling at me. She hates and loves the fact that I exhibit so much self control, so when she gets the chance to make me squirm, it is especially delightful to her. "You alright?" she asks, smiling up at me. She could sense my dilemma, and despite the blindfold she knows she has pushed me to the brink.

His Eyes

I stand up and grab her wrists, helping her to her feet. I turn her to face the barstool, place my hand in the middle of her back, and firmly push her forward over the stool. I place my hand under her right leg, and lift her knee up onto the seat. She is angled perfectly, and I am going to fuck her from behind. I brush my cock against her clit, rubbing it, teasing it. She wants it inside her, and moves to try and let me enter her. "You in a hurry?" I ask, full well knowing the answer. "God yes, fuck me...fuck me hard" she blurts out. I oblige, ramming the full length of it deep into her. She is so hot and wet the feeling is amazing. I pull all the way out, and ram it home again. I grab her hips, and repeat this process over and over, slamming into her. She grabs the barstool, bracing for the impact of my body into hers. She arches her back, wanting...needing more. Fuck she feels so good I already find the need to start containing myself, and I begin the process of delaying my own desires to prolong this experience.

I slide my hands around her, grabbing her breasts from my position behind her. They hang soft and free, and I knead them against her body. I pinch her nipples, causing her to squeal in delight. I am still pushing and pulling slowly in and out of her, each of us loving every stroke. I reach up and grab her shoulder, and she knows what is coming. She tenses, bracing herself for it, but I wait. After another few long, deep strokes she relaxes, and then I catch her off guard. I clamp down on her shoulder and thrust deep into her in one sudden motion. I hold myself there, penetrating her, touching her deep inside as the barstool rocks back to a still position underneath us. She turns to look back at me, even though she cannot see. I know the look that is in her eyes despite the blindfold concealing it from me. That look, God that look in her eyes is one of my favorite things about this. It is so....hungry. The passion is fiery, and the sex is bone-charring. It is why I have to hold back so early in the process, otherwise these sessions would last about one-tenth of the time that they do. Her face expresses how much she loves me deep inside her like this. I grab a handful of hair, holding her head firmly in place as I finally withdraw just a little, only to slide it back into her just as deeply as before. "Oh God...fuck yeah!" she growls at me. She has never been one to hide her exuberance for a great fuck session. She arches her body and pushes back into me, wanting more.

14

Releasing her hair and sliding my hands back to her waist, I begin to pound into her as fast as I can. I fuck her hard, slapping my body into hers. She moans loudly, and I know it is coming. As she increases her moans, I increase my pace. Or maybe she is following my lead; it is difficult to tell at this moment. Either way, we are quickly mounting the crest of another explosion, and there is no stopping us before we reach our goal. "That's it, take my cock you dirty little whore" I command her. "Oh yes, fuck me....FUCK ME!!!" My voice acts as a catalyst, and she explodes into a huge orgasm. She seizes again, spasming and writhing underneath me. I am unrelenting, continuing to hammer her into the barstool. We continue, drawing it out as long as possible until she slumps forward, breathless once again.

It is time for a change in venue, and after giving her a moment to collect herself, I grab her hand and I lead her to the bedroom for phase two of today's plan. I am deliberating whether or not to remove her shoes, wondering if they will be a help or a hindrance for the upcoming events. I glance at the strawberries, and decide to start there. I lead her to the edge of the bed, guiding her to sit down. I keep one hand on her, while the other reaches for a strawberry. I take a small bite, releasing the sensual smell of the ripe fruit to her. She brittles at first, not placing the smell immediately. I wave it directly under her nose, and her she smiles, recognizing the sweet scent. "Open your mouth" I tell her. It's as if I am going through the process of seducing her all over again; I tease her with the berry, touching it to her lips but not letting her bite into it. I rub it across her lips, and touch it to her extended tongue. She grows impatient with this game too, and bites down the first chance she gets, nearly taking my finger with it. "Hey! You cheater" I scold her. She laughs defiantly, and I can't help but smile at her. She is never one to back down or give in, so these little games we play are ever the challenge.

For the next strawberry I have a little different idea. I bite into the new one once again, exposing the soft flesh inside. I feel the juice run onto my fingers, and I taste the combination of the strawberry and her pussy juice on my hand as I run my tongue over my own fingers. I move closer to her, and she reaches for me. Her hand finds my stomach, and she slides it down until she has my cock in her grasp once again. Her mouth is on me, and she slides her tongue up and down my shaft. She moans in delight, enjoying the taste of her on me. I grab her hair and

15

pull her away from me, and then take the strawberry and run the exposed flesh of it all over my cock. I release her hair, and she returns her mouth to it, only to find the surprise I have created for her. She tastes it, and begins sucking me feverishly. "MmmohhGod...you taste so good" she says between mouthfuls. She sucks and slurps my cock until the taste is gone, and I have to replenish the juice. As she journeys downward, taking my balls in her mouth I smash the rest of the strawberry against the stiffness of my cock. It squishes the remaining juice out of it, and it runs down my shaft to the base. She begins sucking it off of my balls, loving the taste once more. She works me over like never before; using more tongue than I can remember her ever doing before. The feeling is amazing, and I never want it to end.

I am about to burst when I finally have to make her stop. I grab her wrists and lift her back to the edge of the bed, pushing her backwards onto the silky sheets. I reach for the last remaining strawberry, and plan on putting it to good use. I bite the top off, tossing it back into the bowl. Kneeling down in front of her, I position myself right in front of her aching hot sex. I can see her trying to peak under the blindfold to see what I am going to do next, so I reach up and push her flat onto the bed. I pull one of her legs over my shoulder, and spread her pussy lips open. I push the strawberry just inside her, and begin eating her out in the truest sense of the word. I go to town on her, the juices of her and the strawberry smearing all over my face. She is loving every suck and flick of my tongue on her, and begins to buck her hips in anticipation of another explosion. She grabs the back of my head, pulling me into her. She is quickly on her heels and shoulder blades, bucking frantically as she rises to another toe curling orgasm. I keep after it, relentless as I run my tongue all over her. I rub her until she can't take any more, and begs for me to stop. Only then am I satisfied and relent.

She is paralyzed by her orgasm once again, but I am not in the mood to wait for her any longer. I climb onto the bed, once again throwing her leg up over my shoulder. I position myself between her thighs, entwining my other leg with hers. She is trapped beneath me, and is going to take the pounding I want to give her. I am so hard I do not need my hand to guide myself into her, the moist folds giving no resistance to the rock hard cock penetrating them. I drive deep in one motion, impaling her with it, making her feel my excitement all the way to her core. Her mouth opens in a silent scream; she looks at me through the mask, wanting more but unable to ask for it. I withdraw and plunge again, this time hitting bottom. I feel it, and hold myself there, stretching her, escorting her to the line between pleasure and pain. I withdraw again, and she braces herself for another thrust. I wait, teasing her, taunting her pussy by stroking just the tip inside of her. When I feel her relax, I drive again. I catch her off guard once more, and this time she moans loudly in approval of my tactics.

I begin to fuck her hard and fast; she is trapped in my leg lock and couldn't get away from me if she tried. From the sounds of her cries, getting away from me is the last thing on her mind. I stroke her juicy hole with my stiff rod over and over, varying the speed after a few minutes of the same thing. Her nails dig into my arm, her breath echoes in my ear. I love fucking her like this; it is raw and primal, and we both love it this way. She comes again and again, her voice echoing throughout the house. I pound and pound her until I literally feel sick to my stomach from the impact and have to stop.

I climb off of her, and move to the foot of the bed. She feels for me, and knows what I want her to do. I want her to do her favorite thing: ride me. She climbs on top, and guides it into her. Still so wet, it goes deep without hesitation. She presses downward, taking all of it inside. She begins to slowly grind on me, her shaved pussy reddened from desire and friction. I let her work; fully engrossed in watching the look on her face beneath the mask. I have seen it a hundred times and still never get enough of it. Watching her is maybe the best part of this for me; pleasing her to this level is the biggest turn on I know. I look to my left and see our reflection in the TV screen, and now I watch her ride me from a third person point of view.

Her hands are on my chest, and her head is tilted back in deep moan after deep moan. I reach up and place my hands under her breasts, lifting and squeezing them. I pinch her nipples which have hardened once again under my touch. "Oh God...yes...put your mouth on them" she moans in request. I sit up underneath her, and she cradles my head, holding my face in her breasts. I take one in my mouth, sucking it hard and nibbling gently. I clamp it between my teeth, and slowly apply pressure until she winces just a bit. "Eeeasyyy" she cautions, but I know better. If it doesn't hurt a little it isn't enough.

I reach back with a free hand, wind up, and drop my hand down on her ass. I feel the sting in my hand, and I know that my hand print will own her for a few moments to come. She moans aloud once again, and it is the catalyst she was waiting for. She hits another gear, and her hips grind into me like she is riding a horse. I lift into her, going deeper, and then lay back. She digs in, her jaw set in determination as she takes control of her own climax for the first time today. She rides me; getting what she wants, taking what she needs. I place my hands on her hips, encouraging her motion but not controlling it. This part is her show, and I let her do as she pleases. She is getting close, her breathing shortens and her nipples grow hard without any contact from me. Her hands find them, and she squeezes her own tits as she reaches the top of her orgasm. She bursts, crying out loudly and clutching her tits. Her hips find a mind of their own as she spasms on top of me, screaming in delight. She always comes the hardest when she is on top. She manages to keep her rhythm fairly intact despite the lightning storm in her head, but I decide to add a helping hand. I grip her hips and yank her back and forth on my cock to extend the pleasure just a few moments more. She collapses forward onto me. I can feel her heart pounding in her chest.

I have exhibited about as much self control as I can muster today and am ready for my own. I roll her over onto her side, and lay down behind her. I lift her right leg, exposing her to me once again. She is lying on her side, her elbow on the mattress and I mirror that right behind her. I reach around with one hand and slide the blindfold off of her eyes. I plunge into her, rubbing hard against her by not taking a straight angle into her. The feeling of rubbing against the inside of her pussy is almost too much to take in my heightened state. It is a feeling almost too intense to describe and I love every slow and deep stroke. I stare deep into her eyes as I slide in and out of her over and over. She reaches back with one hand, placing it on the back of my neck. I can feel my cock slide in and out of her, glistening with her wetness. Mine is building and building, and my cock strains in its own skin. I increase my pace just a little, and that is all it takes. I can feel it well up inside me, and I wrap my arms around her body and pull myself towards her. I close my eyes as my orgasm explodes inside of her. My cock pulses again and again, releasing torrents of my seed into her. I swear we are floating above the bed as I finish, and then slump almost lifelessly down next to her.

We lay there motionless, and eventually she falls asleep in my arms. It was yet another epic round of afternoon sex, and it still amazes me after all this time how we still manage to find ways to stretch our boundaries and keep things so new and exciting. In spite of barely being finished from a great session, I am already looking forward to our next time together. For now, I am content to fall asleep right next to her, dreaming of what just happened, and what is still to come.

Chloe

The first thing I am sure everyone notices about her is the accent. When I look back on that week, it is that very accent that is burned in my brain like it was yesterday. It was another whirlwind adventure, and the story unfolds like this:

Standing in the lobby of the hotel waiting to check in I hear a lovely woman's voice with a heavy accent. It is deliciously thick and different, and I turn to see who is responsible for catching my attention. I look around the crowd of people standing behind me and she looks right at me as if she knows I am looking for her. Her crystal blue eyes shoot right through me, and I smile a bigger smile than I have in a while. "Wow, I think we have a winner" I mumble to myself. I was wondering if I would meet someone to hang out with this week, and the return smile confirms my hopes. I turn back to the front desk attendant to realize she had been standing there waiting on me. "Oh, sorry about that" I say to her. "Yes, she likes you, in case you were wondering" she informs me. I chuckle a little and sign my receipt.

It is now about 7:30pm and I am hungry. On my way to my room I walk passed the bar in the hotel and find it to be fairly empty. I turn down the hall and head to the room to drop off my stuff. I hop in the shower and throw on a pair of jeans and my favorite t-shirt...black on black design with a dragon on the front. I always joke that my wardrobe is very subtle since my personality more than makes up for it. Even though only about twenty minutes has passed, I am really hungry now. I walk quickly to the bar in hopes of a decent steak and a beer. I turn the corner and enter the bar, finding it less busy than before. "Well, at least the service should be quick" I think to myself. I do prefer to not eat alone, but do I really want to talk to the bartender or just sit at a table by myself?" my internal debate continues right up until the moment the hostess asks me where I would like to be seated. "That table in the corner should be just fine" I tell her. We walk over to the corner, and I sit down on the opposite side of the table with my back to the wall. I take the menu from her and jump right to the bottom where the steaks are listed. I am happy to see a variety of choices. The waiter comes over and I tell him I would like the 12 ounce Ribeye medium rare, a baked potato with everything on the side and a Killian's Red. I settle back in

21

my chair, straining to see the TV at the bar from where I am. I am just about to reconsider my choice of seats when she walks in.

The woman with the accent I saw in the lobby earlier has entered the bar; she stops at the hostess stand, scanning the bar as if looking for a place to sit in a sea of open chairs. She sees me, and I wave hello to her; she waves back in the rolling finger wave that girls do. I stick my foot on the chair in front of me and push it backwards in effort to offer her a seat. She leans towards the hostess and tells her something and then begins to walk my way. I stand up to introduce myself and extend my hand; "Hi, my name is Darren. I'd love for you to join me." "Chloe...and I would be delighted" she says in her heavy accent. I have never been very good at placing where someone is from, and I am sure she gets asked that question all the time, so I decide to wait before asking. The conversation is just getting started when the waiter stops by and interrupts us. "I have already ordered, so please, go ahead" I let her know. She scans the menu quickly and then places her order. "A Ribeye steak medium rare, a bake potato with everything on the side and a Corona with a lime" she says. The waiter glances at me quickly and then turns to leave. "Corona? They have that crappy Mexican beer where you're from?" I ask with a playful smile on my face. "I happen to like a bit of the amber nectar, and I can't always get that one where I live" she retorts. "Speaking of which, where are you from anyway?" I ask. "I am from just outside London in the UK" she tells me.

Two beers arrive at the table and I ask one more question before making a toast. "What brings you to St. Louis?" I inquire. "I am here for a conference my company has sent me to" she answers. "Well" I start, raising my beer for a toast, "then here is to...the fun that lies ahead." She smiles a big smile, understanding my thinly veiled message, and raises her bottle to meet my glass. There is a long, almost uncomfortable yet exciting pause as we stare into one another's eyes after the toast. She finally breaks the connection, glancing downward in a shy response to the burning stare I am throwing her direction. "How is it you find yourself here today?" she asks, breaking the brief silence. I have to laugh a little at her "proper English" and how what she says seems so different. "I am here for a conference as well; maybe we are here for the same reason...where are you headed tomorrow?" I inquire. "My company's headquarters is here, and I am going for some sales training" she answers, and I start to laugh a little. "Me too" I tell her. The waiter comes over to the table and has two of the exact same dinners in his hand. He sets them down and walks away, and she notices the second coincidence in the last ten seconds and bursts out laughing, and I follow suit. We are sharing a good laugh; two people half a world apart ending up in the same place at the same time for the same reason. Add in the food order and our apparent mutual attraction and it seems fate has brought us together.

Over dinner we exchange ideas and information, thoughts about the world and preconceived ideas about each other's culture. Being a huge tennis fan, I ask if she has ever been to Wimbledon. "Oh yes, everyone goes to Wimbledon if they have the chance. It is difficult to get tickets, so we usually just wait in Que for ground passes to open up" she tells me. "Que? You mean wait in line?" I ask, smiling at her as if to make fun of her for saying something incorrectly. "Yes, you snobby American...*in line*" she throws back at me in jest. I love a girl with a sassy attitude and am really enjoying the banter exchange between us; it is a great mental turn on. I laugh at her willingness to verbally spar with me, enjoying her feistiness. I notice a remnants if the lime still clinging to the outside of the bottle, it is slowly sliding down the glass side which is dotted with perspiration. She sees me looking at it, and turns the bottle to see what has caught my attention. She lifts the bottle like she is going to take drink, but then sticks her tongue out, wrapping it around to the other side of the bottle to reach the lime fragment. Her tongue is long and grooved down the center, which for someone like me who has a near fetish about such things is a huge turn on. She seems to notice me watching her, and it suddenly embarrassed, most likely by the look that is probably on my face. A moment of silence passes before she finally breaks it with an obvious switch of "So...how long have been with the company?"

Dinner passes quickly, and I am two beers behind her. I was only planning on one to start with, but we are really enjoying hanging out and getting to know one another and I don't want it to end just yet. I order another, as does she. It is getting late but I am concerned whether or not we have covered enough ground to ask her to my room. I decide one more beer and we'll see where we are at. She has been leading the conversation for most of the night, eager to ask questions and answering

23

without hesitating when I return the favor.   She begins to bend the conversation towards dating and customs here in the U.S. and I decide to try and stack the cards in my favor a little bit. "What would you like to know?" I ask her. "OK, so when two people are dating, how long is it before they, um...you know?" her thoughts trail off. "Know what?" I ask playfully, wanting to make her say it to me. "How long do you wait before people kiss?" Apparently I did not know what she was thinking after all; I assumed she was going to ask about spending the night together. "Oh, well, usually no more than about 20 minutes if you like someone....so I guess you are not really that interested in me" I throw at her. She misses the joke at first, stumbling over the words to finally spill out "no, no...I like you. Er, I mean,... bullocks! Full on blush; she grows red as she realizes she has just shown her hand. My laughing at her discomfort only adds to her embarrassment. "It's ok...I am really digging you, too" I confess. Another moment of silence. We look at one another nervously, trying to decide the next thing to say. Finally the waiter comes to check on us, and I laugh in relief. "Just the check, please" I tell him.

"Well, at the risk of misreading you, I am going to ask you a question. I would love for you to come back to my room with me, would you be comfortable with that?" She looks at her empty bottle, swirling it around the table for a moment, thinking. "I would like to..." she began. In effort to save her from actually saying the words, I jumped in "but we just met and it's too soon." I didn't want to hear her say no to me anyway, so I figured this would be easier on both of us. "You didn't let me finish" she said, almost scolding me. "What I was going to say is that I would feel better if you came to my room instead." "Hahhahaha...what's the difference? They are the same rooms!" I point out to her. "Yes, but if you leave my room in the middle of the night, you'll be the one spotted in the hallway with your shoes in your hand" she fires back, smiling at me the whole time. I notice the time stamp on the bill reads 11:25pm; I pay the bill and we head for the stairs.

As we climb the stairs to the second floor, my mind begins to race with thoughts of how to begin this whole process, how to transition correctly from strangers to lovers. We reach the top of the stairs and turn down the hall, and I notice I am really kind of nervous about this. I wonder what she is thinking; and since I misread her earlier if we are really headed to her room for the reason I think we are. Another moment of silence passes as my internal conversation continues. She has not said anything to me for a moment either, and I am beginning to perceive a little tension in the air. We get to the door, and she slides the keycard into the lock. I grab the door handle, holding it closed for a moment. "Wait...I want you to kiss me before we walk through this door" I tell her. She looks at me quizzically for a second, and then leans towards me. I join her half way, our lips meeting in a deliciously soft and warm kiss. It was gentle and soft. I think it sort of set the tone for what she was trying to figure out how to say. "I can't sleep with you tonight" she finally just blurts out, her accent as prevalent as ever. "I mean we can have fun, but I don't want to sleep with someone I just met. I never have slept with someone on the first date, and I don't want to break that" she said, the words pouring out of her as if to escape her mouth while she had the nerve. "HA! What makes you think I am that easy?" I retort, breaking the tension of the mood. She laughs at me, knowing full well that is a lie. I fling the door open; she pushes me in, and I grab her wrists, pulling her into me as we fall back onto the bed.

We land in the middle, and I immediately roll her over, gaining position on top. I put my hands on the comforter, holding myself over top of her as I look down at her. She is beautiful; her nearly platinum blonde hair and her accent and her piercing blue eyes are all such a turn on. My thoughts flash back to her tongue wrapped around the longneck beer bottle, and I hope that I get to see what she can do with it to me. I lean down to kiss her, and she wraps her arms around me, pulling me down onto her. I settle my weight on top of her, and sink into the kiss. We start slow at first, tenderly kissing and exploring one another. I always try to take note of the speed of progression when kissing someone new; it usually mimics the same they prefer when it comes to sex. It appears that Chloe will want to start slow and take our time as we build up speed. Another thing I am becoming aware of is the fact that we are rolling around on the comforter in a hotel room. I have heard the same horror stories that everyone else has, and am trying to figure out how to suggest we remove the comforter before continuing. Finally, I just break from her kiss; I grab her hand and pull her to the edge of the bed. I help her stand and then rip the cover off, letting it fall to the floor. "Hold your knickers...we are going slow remember" she cautions. "I know, I don't know how it works where you are from, but here we do not trust that the comforters in hotels are clean". For some reason I began a lengthy explanation of the process of how sheets and towels are washed daily but since the comforters were so much more expensive they are only cleaned once a month. About half way through she rolls her eyes and tells me she was kidding, and starts to kiss me again.

I reach down and grab the sheets without breaking away from her kiss, and yank the sheets down to the bottom of the bed. I reach down sliding my hands behind her knees, and suddenly lift her up in my arms, settling her down on the bed in one quick move. I realize too late that I have set her right on the edge, and now I have to practically hurdle over her to join her in bed. She laughs at my lack of foresight, and instead of jumping over her I sit down on top of her, pinning her beneath me. I begin to tickle her, and to my delight she is very ticklish. She is begging me to stop as soon as I start, and I laugh at her expense. I am relentless, not letting up for a second until I have had my fill. A little unintentional foreshadowing of things to come. She is gasping for breath between bouts of laughter.

Finally I let her catch her breath before diving into her for another long and lingering kiss. She is a great kisser, and we seem to find comfort and ease with one another right away. I love to make out, and am more than happy to spend a long time doing just what we are doing at this moment. It is sensual and intimate, and I am reminded of how much I miss this closeness with someone. I relish the moment; feeling her body underneath me, her hands slowly beginning to explore me and her delicious mouth in mutual exchange with mine. I shift my position on top of her just a little bit, settling down in between her legs. I can feel the heat from her emanating from inside her thighs, and I very, very slowly begin to grind into her. She breaks from our kiss, and puts her lips next to my ear, letting a very quiet moan escape from her. That noise is one of my favorite sounds in life, and I press harder into her, wanting more. She wraps her legs around me, clamping me where I am and also giving her leverage to grind back into me. Our kisses grow harder and deeper as the passion builds between us. Her hands find their way down to my ass, and the thin material of my well worn jeans is barely a barrier between our bodies. She squeezes it, digging her nails into my flesh. She throws her other leg around me, and now we are really going at it. She is groaning louder by the moment, and grinding hard against me.

I slide over just a little bit and start to bite her neck, pushing her hair out of the way. She gasps loudly, and squeezes her legs around me to the point of it hurting. She bucks her hips and digs her nails into my ass, and I suddenly realize that she is about to cum. I smash her into the bed, bearing down on her and bucking my hips just enough to create a little friction. "Yes, keep doing that....just like that...." she cries out. I slide down and thrust upward, putting direct pressure on her mound. That did the trick; she exploded in a long and intense orgasm, grinding herself into me as she went. She went completely limp after a moment, shaking slightly as she lies beneath me. She seems to need a minute to recover, and I oblige. I kiss her tenderly, waiting for her to signal me for what comes next.

"Wow, that was...unusual" she whispers. "Hmm, not exactly the statement I was looking for" I thought to myself. "Um, thank you?" I say to her, pulling away to see her face. "Hahaha, what I meant was I have never had an orgasm like that before, you know, without someone...touching me" I smile down at her, realizing that what she said is a huge compliment. "That was quite cool" I tell her. I am kind of guessing that we may be done for this evening; the momentum of the moment is completely broken and we are sort of back at square one in my eyes. I roll off of her and get out of bed, heading to the mini bar to retrieve a bottle of water. "Where are you going?" she asks, sounding like she thought I may be leaving. "I am thirsty" I reply without turning around. I crack open a bottle of four dollar water, confirming the hotel industry's believe that convenience has no price limit. I take a huge slug of water, rehydrating from the drinks and our rather torrid make out session. I turn around to find her standing in the middle of the room completely naked. I nearly spit out the mouthful of water in surprise.

I look her up and down, smiling at the sexiness of her curves. She is not model thin, and thank God for that...I love a woman with some curve to her shape. "I wanted to make sure you weren't going to drink my expensive water and just walk out of here" she says with a devilish smile. Being the smart ass that I am, I fire back with "And you thought this would do the trick?" but I broke into a laugh halfway through, showing my hand. I take a step backwards, and lean against the wall. I signal for her to come over to me, and she does. But she adds an element to it that hadn't even crossed my mind. She bends down, and then proceeds to crawl across the carpet towards me on her hands and knees. I am not one to push for subservience from a woman, but her doing it of her own accord made it that much hotter. She arrives at my feet, and I am throbbing hard already. Chloe gets on her knees and reaches up for me, grabbing my zipper. She pulls it down slowly, reaching into the folds to release my cock from its confines. She pulls it out, unzipping far enough to get my balls out too. She looks at it for a second, and then looks up at me. She takes my cock in her hand and slowly begins to work it. I love the scene looking down at her; totally naked, on her knees in front of me. I am fully dressed, exposed through my jeans for her to please. Completely, totally fucking hot.

My knees almost fold underneath me as she smashes her nose into my stomach. I lean over, arching to meet her, putting my hand behind her head. I knew she could take it, and hold it there, I just knew it and so I did what I wanted at that moment. The feeling is amazing, and I hold her there until I feel her try to pull away. I release her, not wanting it to end but certainly wanting her to do as she pleases to me. She draws in a deep breath, her eyes watering just a little as she looks up at me. She goes back to jerking it from the base, and sliding that glorious tongue of hers up and down my shaft. It is just as I pictured sitting in the bar and I watch her every move as she works it over. I lean over again, this time reaching down and squeezing her breasts in my hands for the first time. She moans, and the vibrations tickle as they travels down my cock. I love her small, perky tits, and I knead them in my hands as she continues to suck my cock. Her nipples jut out in excitement and I rub the back of my fingers over them, teasing her with the smooth skin of my hands.

I stand upright again, and take more delight in watching her beneath me. I grab the bottom of my black t shirt and slowly pull it up over my head. She reaches up and touches my stomach, tracing the muscles with her fingertips. She didn't say a word, but her look said plenty. I put a lot of time in the gym, and certainly don't mind being rewarded for my efforts. She keeps after it, her tongue doing a majority of the work. I feel the pressure inside building, and I hate the thought of making her stop, but I am going to have to give in before it is too late. I finally push her away from me and help her to her feet.

We walk to the bed, and I lose my jeans on the way. I am so hard it almost hurts when I walk, but certainly not enough to keep me from following her. She arrives first, and lies down on the bed on her back, barely spreading her legs as if shyly welcoming me. I am not sure what she had in mind, but I know what I want to do, I want to go down on her. Her neatly trimmed pussy is beckoning me, and I want to answer the call. I get down on my knees beside the bed and lean into her, drawing her musky scent into my nostrils. She smells of vanilla, and I can't wait to taste her. I start at her knees, kissing and nibbling my way upward. I am moving agonizingly slowly by design, and making her squirm in anticipation of my mouth on her. I reach the cleft in her leg, right where her hip joins and skip right over her pussy, kissing my way up her stomach. She groans in disappointment, and so I decide to release the fire inside her. I slide two fingers into her molten flesh, twisting and turning them as I push in and pull out. She arches almost instinctively, her fingers bunching the sheets up in effort to hold still. She lifts her hips up, and I gently flick my tongue over her swollen pearl. She gasps, and her mouth opens in a silent scream.

I continue to plunge my fingers in and out of her sopping wetness, and rub the full width of my tongue up and down over her clit. I only get to do this for a brief moment before she explodes. She arches even further, lifting herself off the bed. I am almost standing up to stay with her, and I put my hands underneath her back trying to hold her there. I shove my tongue into her, replacing the stiff invasion of my fingers with the languid softness of my tongue. She tastes as good as she smells, and I hold her in place so I can eat her pussy. Her hands are gripping the side of the bed, and she is balanced on her shoulder blades as I lash her into submission. Her legs clasp together behind my back, the back of her legs rubbing over my shoulders. I vacuum seal my mouth to her, sucking and prodding, bring her to another explosion after only a minute or two. Her cries grow louder and louder, and although I am fully engrossed in what I am doing, and can't help but wonder if the people in this hallway can hear her. Finally she collapses away from me, falling back into the bed. I stand there looking down, admiring what I have done to her, relishing the thought of fucking her every day of the week we are here.

His Eyes

I climb over top of her, letting her recover just a little longer. I lay there next to her on my side, looking at her, grinning from ear to ear, watching her heavy breaths slowly return to normal. Her eyes are tightly shut, and she seemed to be in a world of her own for a bit, not really even conscious of me next to her. She opens her eyes and finds me looking at her. "Wipe that smile off your face, you arrogant Yankee" she jousts. I just laugh a little, and say back to her "Why don't you try and wipe this smile off my face." My challenge empowers her; she springs to life, rolling over onto me and quickly gaining position on top. I am still rock hard despite the gap in time of direct attention to me. She reaches down between her legs, grabbing it at the base, and guides herself over top of me. Now it is my turn to groan in pleasure as she slowly pushes herself down over the length of my cock. She wriggles back and forth on top of me, making sure I am as deep into her as I can go. I can tell I am filling her completely, touching her deep inside. She leans forward, and puts her hands on my face. "Let me do it" she whispers to me. I smile, brushing her hair out of her eyes. She kisses me tenderly, and slowly begins to grind into me.

We are in this same position for a while; she seems very happy to be shouldering the work load at the moment. Our bodies slide easily over one another's and her grinding movements begin to gain more and more length to their strokes. Her kisses grow harder, and she is moaning and groaning more by the minute. The time is drawing near once again, and I can't wait to feel her cum with me inside her. She suddenly pushes herself downward, planting me as deep inside her as I can go. I reach up to grab her hips, but she grabs my hands and places them on her breasts instead. I pinch her delicate nipples firmly, and her pace increases accordingly. She puts her hands in the middle of my chest, and her hips continue to grind into me faster and faster. She is so close, and I want to help her over the edge, but I am doing as I am told and letting her do it. Suddenly she freezes in place; her nails dig into my chest, her breath trapped inside of her. Her eyes are shut again and she seems poised to explode. After a few seconds, everything happens all at once. She cries out, her hips sputter back to a blinding speed and she releases her death grip on my chest. Her face contorts into a sexy combination of pleasure and relief. I can feel her juices run out of her onto my leg, and her whole body convulses several times before it ends. She melts onto me, her quivering flesh now supported by mine as she lies on top of me.

I look at the clock across the room; it is already almost one o'clock in the morning. We are catching the bus to company headquarters at 7:00AM. I decide instead of continuing deep into the night, that I will roll her over and take her from behind, finishing myself off in the process. I peel her off of me, and slide out from under her. She drops down onto the mattress as if unable to move on her own just yet. She is on her stomach, and I position myself behind her. I bend one of her legs forward, exposing her to me once again. I line up, and guide myself into her slowly. She lets out a growl-like moan, and arches her back to meet me. I grab her hips and quickly build up speed. I am thrusting in and out of her, and the angle is perfect for me. It is making me strain into a very slight downward angle, and the tension in my cock is growing to uncontainable heights. I pump away at her, pounding my thighs into her ass. Skin slapping on skin echoes through the room, and my hardness is growing inside her. I know I am about ten seconds away, and I grip her hips and shove forward, pushing her down into the bed. I hold myself above her, gritting my teeth, holding....holding...and then finally releasing full force inside of her. I pump every ounce deep into her, and she pushes back, accepting every drop of it. Now I am the one shaking; barely holding myself above her as I lean forward and kiss her on the cheek. She turns into me, and I kiss her tenderly as the buzz of my orgasm slowly fades. I pull out of her, and lay down next to my new lover. She is facing away from me, and makes no attempt to move. I settle in, deciding that I may not sleep my room this entire trip. And that is just fine with me.

The wakeup call comes in at 6:00AM, and we both jump to reach for the phone. I laugh at how much it startles us, and she hangs up the receiver. She heads for the shower, and as much as I would like to join her I know we will miss the bus if I do. I kiss her goodbye, and head for my room to shower and change clothes. We meet in the lobby, and I am uncertain how much she wants to hide our immediate association with one another. She strides over to me hand extended, introducing herself to me in a loud voice. I shake her hand, staring into her eyes, smiling a knowing smile. We get on the bus, sitting side by side. I can hear two people behind us talking, and one of them is complaining that she couldn't sleep last night. "Why not?" her new friend asks. "Oh my God, you should have heard the people next to me going at it...they were having a good old time." Chloe and I both looked at one another and do our best to contain our laughter. We are giggling like school kids on the bus on our way to the first day of a weeks' worth of visits to company headquarters. This trip is going to be way better than I could have ever imagined.

Chloe

Deidre

I walked into the room, just like I do every hour of every day to see another client. Then our eyes met and my whole world stopped. In the midst of another busy day, my mind on a hundred things to do, and suddenly someone pulls the rug out from under me. My focus zooms in on her, and suddenly I see nothing but her face, her smile. She has beautiful brown eyes and a becoming smile, soft and warm. She stands when I enter, introducing herself to me. She extended a hand, and tells her name...Deidre. How appropriate I thought; she has a different look to her, and an uncommon name is the perfect compliment. She has short dark brown hair and is about 5' 3". What appears to be a body filled with luscious curves is hidden under her tastefully conservative outfit. I am cognizant of the fact that in my eyes everything she says, every little move she makes, seems to be amplified. I am refreshingly captivated by her, and the moment is magical. I am rarely infatuated with someone any more. My life riddled with attractive women; the job, the gym, and of course the occasional club; no one really phases me any more...until now. It is almost visceral, like I took one look at her and somehow I knew she was going to be someone special in my life.

Two months later, our business together finally concludes. I have grown addicted to the feeling her presence has on me. The only vague similarity I have for comparison is the time I was on a ski trip and came down one last run right before dark. The scene was perfect; the setting sun in the distance, the cold air and the stark landscape. I was nearly numb, and walked over to my friends who were waiting for me with a celebratory shot of Cinnamon Schnaaps. It burned right through me, warming me from the inside out. This is how she makes me feel. I was nervous to see her that day; afraid it may in fact end, that she would walk out of my life forever. Over the past few weeks the professional atmosphere of our relationship slowly disintegrated and our interactions became much friendlier. I looked forward to seeing her at every appointment, clearing my schedule after her hour in case we ran over. I drank in every moment with her, savoring it. She was showing signs of attraction lately, but I am still nervous about asking her out. The transition from business to personal is not always easy. I glance at the clock, ten minutes until she gets here. The suspense is killing me.

His Eyes

She enters in her usual fashion, gracefully gliding into a room like she not really touching the ground. Or maybe it's just me. My stomach knots and I feel the air leave my lungs. She turns and shuts the door behind her, striding across the room beaming a huge smile at me. "Today is the last day, huh?" she asks, already knowing the answer. "I believe it is" I reply, thinking now was not the time to ask, we still had an hour to go before we were technically finished. The look in her eyes changed, and suddenly she looked sad. I felt it; it shot through me like a lightning bolt. "Don't worry, I have a feeling we may be seeing more of each other soon" I tell her. "If you were to agree to that" I followed. "Are you asking me out?" she asks, tilting her head an arching an eyebrow. For a brief moment I was about to buckle, but her smile signaled me to press onward. "Yes, I am asking you out. I would love it if you joined me for dinner sometime" I stated to her. "I would really like that" she says, accepting my offer. I stand there for just a moment, staring into her eyes, wondering if she knew the impact of this simple offer would have on our lives. Finally she turns and walks towards the table where we normally meet. She tosses her purse onto the chair behind her, and sits down like nothing just happened. I walk over to her, pulling her file out and laying it on the table between us as I pull my chair into the table.

I am much more relaxed now that I know we will see one another again. We laugh and joke as usual, finishing some busy work and bringing her case to completion. I sit there for a moment, staring into her eyes. As much as I want us to move forward, I have become so happy and comfortable with what we have been doing that part of me is hesitant to leave this familiar spot we are in. The fleeting moment in time passes, and we stand at the same time. I extend my hand, shaking hers as if in one last symbolic closure of our time with her as my client. As she releases my hand, the nature of our relationship has officially changed. Suddenly I am nervous again.

It is an agonizing two days before I think the time is right to call her. I dial her number from my cell phone instead of my office line...this is personal. She didn't recognize the number, but she knows my voice right away. She sounds happy to hear from me. I dispense with the formalities and ask her out for Saturday night. She accepts, and I ask if I can pick her up at 7:30pm. She agrees, and the date is set.

36

Saturday night I pull into her driveway right on time, and park the car. I get out, drawing in a deep breath to try and relax. I button the top button of my jacket and walk around the car to retrieve the flowers from the passenger side. I ring the doorbell, and take a step back from the door so she will be able to see me through the window. I hide the flowers behind my back in as obvious a fashion as I can muster, and wait. I hear her approach the door, her heels clicking on a hardwood floor. She opens the door and I smile at the site of her. She is wearing a slinky black dress and stiletto heels. Her look was different from how I am used to seeing her; the nature of our relationship has changed.

I wait to enter until she invites me in, and I follow her into the kitchen. I am still hiding the flowers behind my back, and when she turns around I produce them in grand fashion is if I were a magician. Her eyes light up and the look on her face was worth ten times the purchase price. "Roses...they are beautiful" she says tilting her head to the side in the charming fashion that she does. After putting the roses in a vase, she gives me a brief tour of her home. It is quaint and tastefully decorated, and the house is filled with the music of Mark Anthony. I am not a huge fan, but I have heard enough of his music to recognize it. We head for the door, and walk by a photo of her singing on stage. I stop in front of it. She looks so powerful, like she has such a commanding presence. "Doing your best Pat Benetar impression?" I ask playfully. She spins on her heel. "How did you know that?" she asks in shock. The look on her face is one of disbelief. "I don't know...just a feeling I had" I tell her. "I was singing Fire and Ice in this shot. That is freaky that you knew that" she says, looking at me kind of sideways. She looked almost uncomfortable with me suddenly, and turns towards the door.

We get in the car and head to the restaurant where we have reservations. Dinner is a nonstop parade of hostesses and servers, and I am trying to hide my annoyance for the interruptions. We have a great dinner, and the conversation flows between us. She laughs just a little too loudly at my jokes and stories, and I find even that charming. It seems every time we get going on a topic someone comes to the table with water or to check on us. "Would you two care for some dessert?" the waiter asks. I jump in and ask for the check. I look to her and say

His Eyes

"How does ice cream strike you?" She just smiles back at me. I pay the bill and we leave.

I drive down the street, pulling into the parking lot in front of an ice cream shop. We walk in and the smell of sugar and empty calories hits us like a wave. She stops just inside the door. "I don't really eat ice cream" she states flatly. "You don't like ice cream?" I ask her incredulously. "That is not the problem, I like it too much. If I want to fit into this dress, I don't eat ice cream" she informs me. "Well you're already in that dress, so come on" I say, grabbing her hand and pulling her with me. "You can get a child size if it makes you feel better. Besides, you ate like a pound of pasta at dinner" I fire back over my shoulder, followed by a playful glance. "I did not!" she yells, smacking my arm in protest. We have a good laugh and then each order a cone to go. "Let's go for a walk" I suggest.

We leave the store and walk around the corner of the strip mall. The park next door has a small lake in it, and there are always open benches and tables. We meander along, talking and laughing together as we walk the well lit path that I run every other morning. We walk towards an empty picnic table, and I lean against the edge. She is standing next to me, looking up at me with those big brown eyes. I want to kiss her, but I am nervous about it. I decide to take a less than straight forward tactic. "Can I have a bite of that?" I ask, looking at the remnants of her cone. She complies, sparing a taste of her strawberry ice cream. I raise my cone as if to return the favor, holding it in front of her mouth. She leans forward, opening her mouth to take a bite. I pull the cone away just a little, making her move to meet the cold treat. She looks at me, and I do my best to reassure her that this time I will hold still with an innocent look. She leans in again, her mouth slightly open this time. I pull the ice cream cone away and lean down to meet her mouth with mine.

The moment is perfect; I lean into her, kissing her full tender lips in a soft kiss. I pull back to read her face, and she still has her eyes closed. I put my hand on her face, and pull her into my mouth for another kiss. This time she really kisses me back. Her delicate tongue flicks against mine. She wraps her arm around me, holding herself against me. The kiss seems to last forever as we melt into one another. I finally pull away from her. She opens her eyes, looking up at me. I toss the cone in my hand into the garbage can nearby and turn to her. I lift her up onto the table, sitting her in front of me. She follows suit, throwing hers at the can as well. She misses, and I can't help but slip in "nice shot" under a big smile. "Shut up and kiss me again" she says smiling back at me. I oblige, and take another taste of her strawberry flavored kiss. It is delicious, and we kiss for a long time, absorbing the moment for all it is worth.

We walk towards the car, seemingly getting slower as we close the distance. I want things to continue, but know that they will end soon. She seems to be thinking about something, and after a moment or two of silence she finally speaks. "Look, it's been a long time since I have been in this situation. I hope you can be patient with me as I get used to dating someone again." "How long has it been?" I ask, curious how this topic got avoided at dinner. We stop next to the car to talk. "I used to date someone who was in a band; he traveled a lot and I stayed home living my life around the brief visits from him. It went on like that for eight years, and I finally gave up and ended it. I haven't dated anyone since" she spills. "Wow, how long ago was that?" I ask, suddenly wondering if I am going a little fast for her. "Six years ago, hmmm, more like six and a half" she confesses. I pause, looking at her like I am thinking deeply. "How am I doing so far?" I ask, finally breaking into a smile. "Not bad....not too bad" she laughs, and turns to get into the car. I drive her home, kissing her good night at the door. I leave her house with an emotional buzz; I am so into this woman it is starting to scare me.

A few weeks have passed, and we are seeing more and more of one another. We have spent a lot of time together and my feelings and thoughts for her have only increased. I can tell this is different; by now I am usually finding the person I was enamored with not quite as exciting as I did at first. But with Deidre that is not the case. We have lead very parallel lives, and never seem to run out of things to talk about. We make dinner plans for Saturday night once again, including "dessert" as she put it. She is letting me know the time has come. We have been gearing up for it, teasing and joking about it, testing the waters. I know she is really cautious about it; it has been so long. I want to do everything just right, and make it the night she wants it to be. She tells me she is house-sitting for her brother, and that the home is beautiful. I should arrive at 7:00 and be sure to come to the door by the garage. "I have a surprise for you." she whispers into the phone. I can't wait to see what it is.

I pull into the circular driveway of a great house in North Scottsdale. It is far enough north of the rest of the city that it is quiet. I walk towards the twelve foot wooden double doors, and ring the doorbell. I hear "Shit!" followed by a pause and then "Be right there" from behind the door. I can hear her scrambling around inside, and am laughing to myself. I have no idea what she is up to, but I can't wait to find out. She opens the door, and literally squeezes out, making sure I can't see inside. "Change in plans...we're going out" she informs me. "Alright, where are we going?" I ask. She tells me where the restaurant is, and we drive to it. It is a very small little Italian restaurant; dark, with intimate tables. It is the perfect start to tonight's festivities. We have a great dinner, and when the waiter asks if we would like dessert, she looks right at me.....and blushes, fumbling for the right words. I jump in and save her, telling him we are fine and just the check will do.

We head for the house, and she is a little quieter than usual. "Everything OK?" I ask. "Yeah, I am just nervous" she shares. "Look, we don't have to...you know, tonight. It's okay, I understand" I offer up, really wanting to but certainly willing to wait until she is ready. She looks at me with those big brown eyes and says "Thanks." I am not sure what that meant, if we are not spending the night together or that she was just happy for the moral support. I guess I will find out.

We arrive at the house, and she opens the garage door. We walk in, and the kitchen is gorgeous. An island kitchen, Italian marble counter tops, and the works. "Wow...I've always wanted a kitchen like this" I said, genuinely. "Me too" she agrees. "Wait here" she instructs. I lean against the counter top, waiting for her to return. When she does, she has a towel and a pair of shorts in her hands. She leads me outside to the backyard and to the outdoor shower by the pool. "Change and I'll meet you in the Jacuzzi" she says, smiling at me.

I come out of the small bathroom located just off of the pool in a pair of shorts that are obviously not mine. I have the drawstring tied tightly or they would be around my ankles already. I head over to the Jacuzzi;

the backyard lights are on and the scene is perfect. It is a nearly calm night, a breeze slight enough to barely notice yet enough to move the leaves around in the trees above us. The steam is rising into the night, and the pervasive smell of chlorine fills the air. I ease my way into the water; the temperature is two degrees under too hot. I settle in on the other side opposite the stairs, and await her arrival. Only a minute later she appears with two bottles of beer and a sexy glint in her eye. She steps down onto the stairs, handing me a bottle. I stand to meet her, and with her two steps above me she is several inches taller than I am. She leans down to kiss me, and we kiss a long, deep and sexy kiss before parting. I step back from her, looking over her amazing body. She has always dressed conservatively, and I had only a vague idea what she has been hiding from me all this time until right now. Shapely legs, a flat stomach and perfect, full breasts compliment the pretty smile I have been seeing so much of lately.

I draw in a breath, catching myself before blurting out something overtly sexual. All I can come up with is "Wow." From the look on her face it seemed to be enough.

We sit down in the steaming water, letting the heat away any stresses of the week. She sits very close to me, and we hold hands under water. She is staring up at me with a look in her eyes that I have not seen from someone in a long time. It is innocent, loving, and seems to contain just the slightest hint of trepidation. I smile back at her, trying to put her mind at ease about tonight. I kiss her tenderly once again. We have only been in the water a few minutes, but are already feeling the effects of the heat. I stand to cool off just a little, and I catch her eyes drifting downward. She reaches for me, placing her hand on my stomach. I watch her hand touch my wet skin; she traces the muscles of my abs, rolling the drops of water around in the groove right down the middle. She leans forward, and slowly sticks her tongue out. She replaces her finger with her soft tongue, and runs the underside of it downward towards my navel. She looks up at me while she does it, and I can see the look in her eyes has changed. It is now one of pure desire.

I watch as she continues to explore my stomach with her tongue. Her hands are on my hips, and she is slowly kissing her way up my torso. She kisses my neck, and stands on her toes to reach my ear. I feel her tongue on it, and then I hear her raspy voice whisper "I want you to make love to me tonight." I was pretty sure that tonight was going to be that night, but I also loved to hear her say the words. It was magical, and they echo through my head over and over. "I have wanted you from the moment I saw you" I tell her, now looking deep into her eyes. We kiss again, embracing one another in the middle of the Jacuzzi. The air is cool on my skin, but I can feel the warmth of her body against mine. It is a delicious mix of sensation.

After a moment she takes my hand and leads me out of the Jacuzzi and towards the house. We wrap towels around ourselves to dry off, and she leads me towards the sliding glass doors into the living room. We walk through, and I follow her straight towards the bathroom. It has two doors and is huge; the frosted glass shower wall sits right next to the Roman style marble tub. The door on the opposite side is closed; it appears it leads to the bedroom. We walk into the shower, and I notice there are no shower heads. "Watch this" she says, pushing a button on the marble wall. She turns on the water, and adjusts the temperature. The shower has a built in rainfall style shower head, which amounts to basically just holes drilled into the marble ceiling. The water falls straight out of the ceiling, very cool. We get under the shower and stand in the water; it is different that a regular shower, it is just like being out in the rain. She leans back, wetting her hair and slicking it back. I grab her waist and allow her to hold herself there for a moment as she runs her fingers through her hair. She stands back up, and I spin her around so now I am under the water. I follow suit, washing the chlorine smell from my skin. I look at her as she watches me, and I want to take her right here and now. I resist the urge to grab her and press her against the wall, taking her straight away. I know better. I reach down and put my index finger under her chin, tilting her mouth to meet mine. We kiss, this time harder and deeper than before. She presses her body against me, and throws her arms around my neck. I lift her up for a moment, kissing her while she is suspended in the air. I set her back down on her feet, and turn her around to face away from me.

I pull her back into me, pressing my chest against her shoulders. I kiss her neck, biting and nibbling my way around to the other side. I reach between us, and grab the string on the top of her bikini. I pull it slowly, taking my time to undo the knot. I feel the material release and I reach around her with both hands at once, placing them on her flat stomach. I slowly lift them upward, my hands easing their way up her chest and under the front of her bathing suit top. I cup her beautiful breasts in my hands, squeezing them, feeling the soft flesh give under my touch. She leans her head back against my shoulder, and although I can't hear her over the water, but I can feel her moan. Her mouth opens, and I feel her breath on my neck as she responds to me touching her. I press her soft flesh against her; her nipples grow hard against my fingertips. I am growing hard in a hurry, and she notices it against her. She pushes into me and the pressure against it only expedites my growth.

My hands begin to travel over her, feeling every curve and nuance of her body. The water continues to cascade over us, splashing off of my shoulders and creating a mist around us. I sink my teeth into her neck like I was a vampire, biting her flesh. She leans her head back far enough for me to kiss her again, and I feel her hand slide around to the back of my head pulling me into her. She arches her back, grinding herself against my hard cock. Her other hand reaches down and grabs the string to the bottom of her bathing suit; she pulls it upward, and I feel it slide out from between us. I reach down and place my hands on her hips, and then slowly run my fingers down the front of her thighs. I tease her, brushing over her waiting pussy but not touching her there just yet. She reaches behind her, and begins to rub my hardness through the flimsy material of my over-sized swimsuit. She quickly finds the drawstring inside, and pulls it. The material melts off of me, falls into a heap around my ankles. I step out of the shorts, kicking them to the side.

We are both naked in the shower, our bodies pressing together under the water. It is warm, but her skin seems to radiate heat far hotter than the water temperature. She is rocking back and forth in effort to rub her ass against my cock, and the feeling is intense. I am becoming overwhelmed with desire, and in a fit of passion I spin her around, pressing her against the shower wall. I kiss her hard, my hands quickly traveling all over her body. I grab her tits, smashing them against her ribs. She reacts accordingly, gasping in surprise and then moaning in delight. I slide one hand between her legs, my fingers gently cleaving her soft folds. I curl my middle finger, and it slides into her slippery hole without resistance. She leans her head back, groaning as I penetrate her depths with a single digit. Her pussy clamps around my finger, and I cannot believe how tight she feels.

I lean down and take a nipple in my mouth, sucking the water from it. I am being rougher than I probably should, but I can no longer contain my desire. She grabs for my cock, squeezing its full hard length in her hands. I am so hard I don't think it gives a millimeter under her grip. I push her hands to her sides, and drop to one knee. "What are you.....?" I never let her finish. I plunge my face into her pussy. She gasps loudly, and then begins clutching the wall to brace herself. I grab her hips to steady her, and she throws a leg over my shoulder. Now I can really reach her, and shove my tongue deep inside. "Oh God!" she cries out, her voice echoing through the marble clad bathroom. I move my head back and forth as I slide my tongue in and out of her. I lick her pussy up and down, lapping her into a violent orgasmic explosion. She screams loudly, her whole body convulsing in pleasure. She slumps over top of me, finally releasing her grip on my shoulder. Only then did I realize her nails were buried in my flesh. She puts her arms around the back of my head, pulling my face into her stomach. She holds me there for a moment as she calms down, and I can feel her heavy breathing slowly subsiding.

Finally she releases her hold on me, and my knees are very thankful. I stand, relieving the pressure of the tile against my kneecaps. Her hair is slicked back, her makeup is washed away, and she has never been more beautiful in my eyes than at this moment. The expression on her face says it all; the hungry look in her eyes telling me she wants more. I shut the water off, and reach around the corner to grab the towels for us. We dry quickly, not wanting the moment to pass or the spell to be broken. I take her hand and lead her out of the shower to the closed door on the other side. I open it to find rose petals on the floor and candles burning in the bedroom. "When did you do this?" I asked in total shock. When you were waiting for me in the Jacuzzi" she replies beaming a smile. There was a trail of rose petals leading to the bed, and candles throughout the room, illuminating the bed where we are going to make love for the first time. And here I thought I was the one leading the proceedings tonight. She had it all planned out, and we ended up right where she had designed. I am stunned and flattered beyond belief. I couldn't believe the planning and effort she had put in; I only hope I can live up to my end of the deal and make this night as special as she wants it to be.

She steps forward and leads me to the bed. I follow behind closely, ready to make love to this beautiful woman who is presenting herself to me tonight. We reach the side of the bed, and she stops, turning to face me. She looks a tiny bit nervous, and I do my best to squelch her trepidation. I borrow a line from an old classic, and say "if I forget to tell you later, I had a really good time tonight." She laughs and smiles at me, and I think it did the trick. I put my hands on the sides of her face, holding her before kissing her tenderly. She seems to melt into me, her flesh pressing against mine, her hands clasped behind my back. I moan a little myself as I kiss her deeper and deeper.

We started slowly, but are quickly gaining momentum. I reach for the comforter, and pull it back without breaking our embrace. Next, the sheets, exposing the bed for us. I part from her kiss, and climb into bed. I lie down and hold the covers up for her to crawl in next to me. She does, and I drop the silky sheets around us, hidden from the world. She comes to me again, kissing me. We pick up where we left off, and the fervor of our desire grows. I wrap my arms around her, and roll to my back, pulling her on top of me. I love the feeling of her weight on top of me, her breasts smashing against me; her small body still seems to envelop me. My hands explore her smooth skin; it never changes regardless of where I touch her. She is whimpering soft sounds as we kiss and she grinds ever so slightly against me. She opens her legs just a little more, and I can feel her wetness on my stomach. I grab her hips, and rub her back and forth across my flexed abs. The ridges have the desired affect: half way through another kiss she tosses her head back in pleasure and surprise. She pushes herself up slightly, planting her hands onto the mattress on either side of me. She joins in, grinding herself on me, gaining speed. The tension in her thighs is climbing, and her stride growing in length. She begins to slide far enough to reach my cock, which is at full mast. It pokes into her moist flesh, prodding, teasing her with invasion.

As much as she is enjoying what I started, I want more. I put my arm over her shoulder and push her downward onto me. Her eyes widen and her mouth opens in a silent scream as I penetrate her depths. I push her down as far as I can, stuffing her full of me. She is slippery and snug, and the feeling is amazing. I pull her body down on mine, and we slide skin on skin in unison. She closes her eyes, burying her face in my chest. I can feel in building, and building, until she reaches her peak. Once again her body freezes for a moment, and then explodes in a violent shudder. I can feel it to her core, and her once rhythmic movements break down. It is delicious, and I move underneath her to help extend the moment as long as possible. She goes limp on top of me; surrendering.

I gently roll her over, taking position on top of her. I love this position because now I can stare into her eyes and see into her soul as we make love. I begin gently, teasing, taking short strokes before slowly thrusting all the way into. I withdrawal and repeat the process, making sure to never let her anticipate my next move. She wraps her arms around me, one hand on the back of my head, the other on my ass. She squeezes it, feeling me work. The thought of 'I could do this forever' echoes in my head. The moment is exquisite, and I never want it to end. We continue to kiss, seemingly never getting enough of the taste of one another. Her hips begin to move under me, and she wraps a leg around mine. Another one is on its way, and I increase my pace just a little to help speed the process. I am getting close myself, and I want so badly for us to come together. I release any restraints I have, no longer trying to hold out. She starts to tilt her hips up into me, taking me deeper into her. I dive deeper, pushing until even the base of it is inside her. I feel it coming, and I hope she is close too. I disappear inside myself, picturing me sliding inside her. I am barely conscious of the moans now escaping from my mouth. Her silent scream finally turns; a deep moan emanates from within her. I feel her nails in my flesh, and the pain releases the storm inside me. I thrust… hold…and explode. I can feel streams of it pumping into her. She explodes right behind me, her hips bucking against my weight, her voice echoing in the bedroom. It lasts only a fleeting moment in time, but it is so amazing it seems like forever.

We slowly settle back to Earth, resting on the cloud-like bed. I open my eyes and look at her, brushing the hair from her eyes. I am at a loss for words. "That was….." I drift off. "Yeah….." she replies, seeming to have the same problem I do at the moment. My brain is still; I have no thoughts running through. I only feel the lingering effects of the ecstasy we just experienced, and her lying beneath me. I never want to leave our moment, this bed, her arms. I kiss her gently once again, trying to convey my thoughts since I cannot articulate the words. She kisses me back, and somehow I know she feels the same. I wrap my arms around her, and we fall asleep together.

I wake first in the morning, her warm body still snuggled up mine. I look down at her; she looks so peaceful I hate to wake her. Deidre is snoring just a little bit, breathing through her mouth. I can't help but be playful, and I very gently touch her lips. She jumps in reaction, surprised more than I expected by my tender touch. She laughs at herself, and then buries her face in my chest. "Mmmm, I slept so good" she purrs, throwing a leg over mine and wrapping her arms around me. She kisses my chest, running her hands over my skin. I feel her hot breath on me, and I am very aroused at her touch, the memories of last night still fresh in my mind. Wriggling her way up to me, our mouths meet again. Her trepidation is gone, and it reflects in her kisses. She moans as our kisses grow deeper. She slides over on top of me, and her body melts into mine.....

Donna

"Oh, dude thanks. You saved me a long drive home!" I tell him. "Don't worry about it. My Dad's not even there. Go in through the door in the garage, it'll be open. I'll be there in about two hours" he says. I tell Paul thanks again and push the red button on my cell phone. I can't believe my plans fell through at the last minute like this. It is sheer luck that I reached him before he is out of cell phone range. I knew he was headed to his home town about two hours outside of Phoenix, and I am lucky enough to reach him before he left town. I was very fortunate this is the weekend he is headed to his Dad's place and that I can crash at there just like old times.

I pull into the driveway, and saw there was a light on in the den. That seems odd since Paul said no one would be home. I decided it may be a good idea to knock on the door, just in case Donna is home. I had spent many a summer hour torturing his kid sister, but I thought she was away at school. It had been quite a while since I had seen Donna, so I certainly didn't want to scare the heck of her by just walking in like Paul said I should. I knock, and I can hear someone approaching the door. She swings the door open, and I am quite shocked at who I see. Donna is no longer a little girl; although still shorter than I am, she has grown into a mature young woman. She now has jet black hair and multiple earrings in each ear, synonymous with the Goth look she obviously is going for. The shocked look on my face must have been somewhat of what she is aiming for with her new appearance. She recognizes me right away, and opens the door. "Wow, you look a little different since the last time we saw each other!" I exclaim. She laughs and says "In spite of what you must have thought, I did not remain twelve years old." She gives me a huge hug and invites me inside.

I follow her into the den and sit at the desk, leaving her the couch. We make small talk, catching up on the years that have gone by. "Six years! I can't believe it's been over six years!" she begins, losing the attitude she seems to be carrying these days, smiling and laughing with me. I find us clicking back into our old roles; me being like an older brother who liked to pick on his little sister all the time. I tease her about things like I used to when I would spend the summer weekends at their family's place. As the time passes, she keeps emphasizing the point that she is no longer a little kid. After a while the conversations taper off until we hit a point where we find ourselves just sitting and watching TV. We are watching FX, and the next show on was a new one called "Inked". It's hard to believe that an entire season's worth of shows can be extracted from something like a tattoo parlor, but then again it is the reality TV generation. I make a comment about not being sure that I would want a tattoo even five years from now, let alone for the rest of my life. She laughs, saying that she hopes she still likes hers when she gets to be my age. "Thanks a lot! Wait, you have a tattoo?" I ask, quickly changing gears. "Not *a* tattoo, three." she replies. "Really!?! Can I see them?" I ask inquisitively.

With that, she stands up and starts to lift her shirt. I have heard that most people who get tattoos enjoy showing them off, and I may be slightly guilty of using this information to my advantage. The location of hers seemed to pose a little bit of a problem, and I playfully offer my help. I am a compulsive flirt, and my assistance was more of a knee-jerk reaction than a true offer. She agrees, telling me to lift the back of her shirt. Donna begins to tell me about the black widow on her shoulder, and how the web runs down her side onto her lower back. I run my fingertips down the line on her side; her pale skin seems stretched over her ribs as she leans away from me. She pulls away from me, and the thought of "I shouldn't have done that" flashes through my mind. I have to admit, all of the sudden I found myself thinking about her in an entirely different light. I'm sure I had a weird look on my face when she turns around. She laughs, making me feel even more uncomfortable with the scenario. "Don't panic; it just tickled, that's all." she says, sensing my uneasiness. She stands there looking up at me. We have one of those awkward moments staring into one another's eyes. I can't believe I am even thinking about kissing her; she is so young she is still in college not to mention one of my best friends' little sister. This situation is riddled with problems. Is she really attracted to me enough to be thinking what I am thinking? Standing there in front of her, I have no idea if she would kiss me back or knee me in the groin. The voices in my head are beginning to consume my thoughts, and the longer I take to act the more uneasy I am getting.

She laughs a little, obviously also growing uncomfortable with the way we are looking at one another. I reach out and touch her face, running my fingers over the twelve rings in her ear. "Guess that little girl I used to know has grown up" I note. "That's true, and actually… that's not all of my piercings." She laughs as she sees my eyes light up. *My how you have grown up*, I thought to myself. "You wanna see?" she asks, giggling like the teenager that she still is. "I did them myself" she adds, turning away from me and lifting her shirt over her head. I can now see the full scope of the work she's had done on her back. I am not usually into this type of look, but for some reason I am really turned on by it. She turns around to face me, hiding her small, perky breasts under her hands. Donna stands there in front of me, smilingly shyly. I reach out and touch the design she has tattooed below her navel. Her skin is so soft and smooth, indicative of her age. She continues to hide from me, teasing and pulling away from my hand. "We shouldn't be doing this." she blurts out. "But…." she hesitates. "Yes?" I ask. "I've had a crush on you for as long as I can remember. How much time do we have?" I glance at my watch, thinking that Paul would be rolling in soon. This has ass-kicking written all over it. "Not much" I say, figuring this is about to come to an abrupt end. "Then we better get started!" she says laughing, freeing her breasts from the confines of her hands.

My eyes widen in approval, as she stands in front of me naked from the waist up. Her low rise jeans barely hanging on her bony hips, her pierced nipples rising to attention now that they are exposed. I lean in to kiss her, and she meets me half way. We embrace, kissing each other firmly. I grab her waist; pulling her into me, and I lean down to kiss her. We kiss and tongue one another standing in the middle of the den. I open my eyes and located the desk. We keep kissing as I lead her to the desk. I go to sit her down on the edge of the desk, but she spins me around and pushes me back against it instead. I lean against the desk as she fumbles with my belt. "Oh God, I have always wanted to do this" she states, her hands trembling with excitement. I am growing harder by the second just thinking about her mouth settling around my cock. I am aching to set it free, and she unzips my pants to set my burgeoning hard-on loose. She wastes no time and grabs it by the base, promptly swallowing me down to her fingers. I lean my head back, moaning in pleasure as she runs her tongue and mouth all over my now rock hard cock. She joins me in the moaning, enjoying ramming my hard cock into the side of her mouth and the back of her throat.

His Eyes

I love what she is doing, but I know we are pressed for time. I put my hands on her shoulders and push her away from me. She protests, but we have to keep pressing forward if we're to have any hopes of completing this dangerous tryst. I grab her hand and pull her up off her knees. We kiss again deeply; hands running all over each other's bodies. I reach down and begin pinching her pierced nipples, tweaking and pulling at them. "Easy now, they're more sensitive than ever since I pierced them" she groans. "Oh, I'm sorry; I'll kiss them and make them better" I whisper to her. I bend down and begin to slowly rubbing my tongue all around her nipples. She grabs the back of my head, tossing hers back in pleasure. I slide my hand into her waistband, and lift her jeans, pulling them tight up into her crotch. The pressure on her clit certainly gets her attention, and I hold it there by bunching her jeans up at the waistline. I relent, and reach down to unbutton her jeans as I switch back and forth between her breasts. Her jeans hit the floor, and I help her step out of them. No underwear and shaved slick, gotta love that I think to myself. All I say aloud is "Nniiccceeee!"

I pick her up and sit her on the desk. Spreading her legs as she settles back onto her elbows, she positions herself in front of me. I look down to see that she is ready, and I plunge my middle finger deep into her pussy. God it is tight; snug around my finger all the way up inside her. She opens her eyes wide with surprise, and then quickly shut them as she let out a loud moan. I begin working my finger in and out of her wetness. She smells like bubble gum, and I want a taste. I get down on my knees in front of the desk, and ready myself for a rare treat. There is nothing like eating pussy, but young pussy is even better. I leave my finger where it is and add to it by rubbing my tongue over her clit. She loves it, and really lets me know. Donna is moaning and groaning on top of the desk as I flick and rub my tongue all over her clit. I remove my finger from her, and shove my tongue as far up in her as it will go. That does it; she goes nuts. She is writhing and thrashing around on the desk, screaming my name at the top of her lungs. She arches her back and grabs the back of my head, pulling my face into her pussy. I think she is going to break my nose as she bucks her hips into my face. I have to pry myself out of her crotch; self preservation is an instinct I possess. I replace my tongue with my two fingers, and force them into her. She continues to ride the wave, extending her orgasm another few moments by clamping her pussy around my fingers. Her juices are practically running out of her onto Daddy's hardwood desk.

I stand up and remove my fingers from her. I position myself in front of her on top of the desk. I hold her legs up in the air, and ease my cock into her. God, she is so tight. It feels like her pussy is trying to keep me from entering her. I am trying to go slow, and make sure I don't hurt her. She plants her nails firmly into my ass, and pulls me into her. I take the invitation, and shove forward. Her pussy relents under my force, and lets me inside. She winces at first, but takes almost all of my length. She quickly gets accustom to me inside her, and begins to rock back and forth to meet my slow thrusts. We begin to pick up speed, and soon I am burying my cock all the way inside her. She is clawing my back, alternating between moans and screams. She is getting close again, and we are running out of time. I slide my arms under her knees and lock my hands around her back. I pick her up, and she flings her arms around my neck. She braces herself for what is coming; knowing this position is going to allow me to drive even deeper into her. She arches and lifts herself off of most of my cock, only to relax and slide back down. I lift her up again, and then slam her back down on my cock.

We are standing next to the desk, and I am holding her against me in mid air. I repeat this process about five or six times before she explodes all over me again. She throws her head back, digging her nails into my shoulders. She screams "Oh God! Oh Fuck!" over and over again. I do my best to keep fucking her, but I am close, too. She finishes and I have to put her down. I go to put her back on the desk, but she stands up instead. I look out the window and can see a car approaching in the distance. She grabs my cock and starts to jerk it furiously. "I'd better swallow the evidence" she says, smiling up at me. Oh, man, I can't believe this. She gets down on her knees and swallows all of me that she can. The feeling is phenomenal; I am so sensitive after fucking her that her mouth around my cock feels twice as good as before. I can't take much more. I grab her hair and pull her away from me. She opens her mouth and jerks me until I begin to empty my load into her mouth. Pleasure cascades through me, my knees nearly buckling from the release. Suddenly I am snapped back to reality; I hear a car door slam. I have one more pump left, and shoot the last batch into her mouth. She swallows it all with a smile. I hear the trunk slam. We finally snap out

His Eyes

of our orgasm–induced haze and come to our senses. I grab my pants as she runs for the bathroom, clothes in hand.

I zip up, wipe off the desk and sit down in the chair just in time to hear Paul open the door. I look up from the TV, and greet him. "How was the trip up?" I ask. "Traffic sucked, or I would have been here sooner" he grumbles. "Oh, don't even worry about it. You have no idea how much you helped me tonight!" I reply, smiling ear to ear on the inside.

Donna

Emily

God, what a crappy week. All I want to do is go to the gym, get in the steam room, and decompress. It is late Friday night, and I am expecting the gym to be pretty empty. Oh yeah, and Emily will be there; she is about as close to female contact as I have gotten in quite a while. Since the end of my last relationship, I have not had the time or the desire to date. Emily works at the front desk at the health club, and is probably too young for me anyway. But I do love the way she smiles at me when I arrive. Sometimes those three seconds are the highlight of my entire day. Her short, petite body and her shoulder-length dark hair are just the look I prefer. She also has at least one tattoo, and has recently gotten her tongue pierced. She didn't look like the kind of girl you would expect that from, which makes me find her even more appealing. She looks conservative, but apparently has a wild side as well.

The club is absolutely empty when I arrive. But there she is; that bright, smiling face and perky attitude that never seems to fade. She greets me warmly, but can tell right away that I am dragging myself in the door. "Rough day?" she asks. "Rough month" I reply. We continue with some small talk, and then as I am walking away I notice one of those sweaty romance novels lying open on the desk. I inquire "So, is that what you do with all your free time here." She blushes, and sheepishly looks up at me. I meant more along the lines of reading in general, but I think she took that comment a little differently.

I get to the locker room, and find no one around. Thank God, I thought to myself. I just want total silence, steam, and the smell of eucalyptus. I take off my clothes and stuff them in a locker, put a towel around my waist and head for the shower. I glance at the clock, and noticed it was later than I thought. The club closes at 10:00PM, so I have no more than 45 minutes. I hop into the shower, and then head for the steam room. I love the smell of eucalyptus, and when I open the door I am highly disappointed. No one has used the eucalyptus today, and the bottle that is kept in the steam room is empty. I walk back to the lounge area and dial the front desk. Emily answers and asks what she can do for me. I am trying to come up with something cute and funny, but instead just state the problem. She says she is the only one here, so she can't send someone back to the locker room. I ask if she can bring it to the

57

door, and I would meet her there. Emily agrees, and my problem is solved. I rewrap the towel around my waist and head for the door. She knocks, and I lean out to retrieve the bottle. She holds it out, and then pulls it away from me. I look at her, puzzled, and then realize she is having a little fun at my expense. She stands just far enough away that I have to step out into the club in my towel to get the bottle from her. I wasn't terribly amused; but I play along. When I reach for the bottle, I notice she is helping herself to a lingering look of me in my towel. I smile; a little embarrassed, and definitely surprised. The brief pause grows into awkward silence, and we both sort of turn and go our separate ways. I left wondering what she was thinking at that moment.

After the rush of the "Emily incident" wears off, I am back to feeling worn out. I grab a few extra towels and go to the steam room, spraying the eucalyptus oil into the steam vent. Finally, peace and quiet. I take a deep breath and lie down on the towels. I am out like a light. The next thing I hear is the sound of Emily's voice; I am caught in that in-between state of dream and awake. I may have imagined it, until I hear her knock on the glass door to the steam room. I sit up quickly, wondering what she is doing in the men's locker room. She opens the door and walks in. "Are you OK?" she asks. "It's almost 10:30! I was about to close up when I realized that you were still in here" she adds. I had fallen asleep, one of those really deep, relaxing sleeps. In fact, I was dreaming a rather vivid dream which left me quite aroused. The towel I am wearing isn't doing much to hide that fact. Emily notices it, too. She steps closer to me, and then seems to pull back. I got the impression she was coming over to me, and then changed her mind at the last minute. She has taken off her club uniform shirt, and the white tank top she is wearing quickly absorb the humidity, clinging to her shapely torso. The glasses she wears quickly steamed up from the heat, and she sort of giggles and says, "Hey, can I borrow your towel, my glasses are fogging up." I smile, and laughing, tell her "Sure, come and get it." And to my surprise, she does.

The next thing I know, she is on me. She straddles me in my seated position on the bench in the steam room. We begin feverishly kissing; her hands hold my face as we kiss and jam our tongues into each other's mouths. I pull off her glasses and set them aside. I look at her beautiful, young face, and begin to say "Are you sure you want to do this?" but I only get about half way through the sentence before she kisses me again, harder and deeper this time. "I have wanted to do this for a long time" she manages to squeeze out between kisses. She is grinding her hips into my lap, furthering the throbbing under my towel. I yank her wet shirt over her head. I am aching to see the rest of her and with one quick move unclip her bra and it falls to the floor. I have to catch myself; I don't want this to get completely out of hand, so I pause. I take a long, lingering look at her sitting on top of me. She obviously works out some; her arms are defined, her stomach flat, and her body well toned. I put my hands on her breasts, palms flat against her nipples, gently but firmly squeezing them. We begin kissing again, our tongues darting in and out of one another's mouths. I alternate massaging her perky, firm breasts and lightly pinching her nipples. They quickly became erect to my touch. I want my mouth on them.

I reach up behind her head, and grab a handful of hair, and tug firmly. I pull her mouth off of mine, and point her nose at the ceiling. I slide my tongue down her neck, pausing at the most sensitive spots. I nibble here, lick there, teasing her as best I can. I finally reach her breasts; I still have a handful of hair, and she is breathing much heavier now. The mild roughness excites her, which excites me all the more. I release her hair, and slide my hand down her back, wrapping my arm around her waist. I pull her body into mine, and then lean forward. She arches her back, molding her body into mine. She grabs the back of my head with her hands and pulls me into her breasts. "Oh please, yes!" she utters. I have her right where I want her…that fine line between pleasure and torture, too much and not quite enough. As soon as my lips meet her nipple, she lets out a deep moan.

I begin gently at first, cupping her breast and sucking playfully. As her grinding becomes more intense, I increase the force of what I am doing. I go back and forth between the two, following her rhythm; ebbing and flowing as she does. I look up at her, only to watch her green eyes roll back into her head and see the bottom of her chin. Her head is thrown back in ecstasy and she moans louder with each passing moment. I reach down and grab the top of her shorts, and give them a firm pull upward. The sudden tightness against her crotch makes her gasp. She looks up at me, and the look on her face is incredible. God, I love that part. She quickly stands, finally diminishing the pressure on my throbbing hard cock. It's almost too much to take, and for a second I am glad she got up. She quickly strips off her shorts and panties, standing completely naked before me.

She hops back on my lap, wanting more of what we have started. I look deep into her eyes, and the playfully but firmly said "Say please." She smiles, loving the way I was taking control of her. She coyly said "No!" I raise a hand and bring it sharply down on her bare ass. She lets out a squeal, part in surprise and part in delight. "OK, OK, you win, Pleeeaaasssssseee" she says. "Please what?" I ask. She laughs and leans forward like she is getting shy and hiding her face from me. Instead she bites into my shoulder, returning the favor of the slightly painful and exciting surprise. I wince a little, and plunge my middle finger as deep inside her sopping wet pussy as I can reach. She gasps, and throws her head back so hard I had to catch her to keep her from falling over backwards. She is close already, and I'm not going to make her wait any more. I curl my finger inside her, and rub right on her G-spot. She lasts through about three seconds of this and then tenses her entire body, clamping down on my finger. She lets out a loud yell, and then the waves of her orgasm rise within her. She comes very hard; slumping against me after about five or six trembling aftershocks.

Once she recovers, she stands up for a second. She surveys me; and decides to keep me right where I am. She pulls a towel off of the bench, and folds it up. Emily tugs at the towel I am wearing, which after all the bumping and grinding is all but hanging off of me. She opens it up and out jumps my engorged cock. She looks at it, smiling. Grabbing it with one hand, she slowly begins jerking it. She looks up at me, sticking her tongue out to reveal the piercing and says, "I have been waiting to try this thing out." With that, she swallows my entire cock. I can't believe it; she takes the whole thing in on swift move, all the way to the bottom. Rarely has anyone done that to me before. The sensation is incredible. She works her tongue up and down the shaft; the metal stud on her tongue rubbing on the taut skin of my cock. This is by far the best oral sex I have ever received. She continues with her task, pausing occasionally to run her tongue over my balls. She is good, I'll give her that. Emily teases me as I had done to her earlier. She now has the upper hand, and she knows it.

She takes my cock out of her mouth and asks "Do you like it?" "Oh yes", I state. "Do you want some more?" "Uh huh!" I say. "Say please!!!" she exclaims. Good for you, I thought. Turn-about is fair play. Nothing is more exciting than a woman who can take charge when it's her turn. "No", I say firmly. "OK" she stands up and shrugs her shoulders, smiling mischievously at me. "Alright, alright, PPPLLLEEEAAAASSSEEEEE???!!!!!" I say, and with that she leans forward and plants her nose on my stomach. I can't believe that she can take my entire cock down her throat like that. It is amazing. I slowly begin to reposition myself on the bench; I lay down on my side. She knows exactly what I am thinking, and as I roll onto my back, she climbs right on top of me. My cock is still deep in her throat as I begin to return the favor she is doing for me. I run my tongue all around the edges of her sweet young pussy, and only on the very top of her hood. She wiggles and squirms, trying to get me to go down farther, but I continue to tease her. After several minutes of this, I finally scoot down just a little bit and plunge my tongue all the way inside her. She arches, bending her body to meet my hot tongue. She lifts her head; moaning and groaning now became animal-like growls. I go to work on her clit, running my tongue up and down quickly over the swollen surface. I can tell she is getting close again; she is jerking and sucking my cock harder and faster than before. I do an old trick of mine that never fails. I shove my tongue back inside her, and rub her clit with my chin. She goes berserk! She comes three times back to back or has one long drawn out climax, it is difficult to distinguish.

Her body goes limp, she is spent. "Give me a minute" she says. But I have a better idea. I stand up and lift her up, placing her gently on the toweled bench. The smell of her body, the eucalyptus, and the overwhelming desire to bury my cock inside her is too much. I need her right now. She put her arms behind her, bracing herself with delightful anticipation, knowing she is about to be penetrated. I now kneel before her, using the towel to protect my knees from the hard tile floor. She spread her legs, opening herself for me. I oblige, and bury my cock deep inside her with one deep thrust. As wet as she is, I knew she could take it. The look on her face says it all; she has that surprised, pleasured look that makes life worth living. I start out slowly but soon gather speed, thrusting deeper and deeper inside of her. Her body resists a little, but she wants every inch of me inside her. I keep pounding away, our bodies slapping together, soaked from the steam and the sex. The thick, hot air fills my lungs as I breathe heavily from the excitement and effort. The waves of orgasm build within her again, and I reach down with my thumb and gently rub her clit. She throws her head back, wriggling and bucking with pleasure as she comes again. I have to slow down; I want this to last and I am getting to close to finishing.

After a minute or two, I regain control and am ready for more. I pick her up and spin her around. She gets on her knees on the towels and arches her back, sticking her ass in the air for the taking. I put one foot on the bench and one on the floor, positioning myself behind her. I guide myself into her again, her body accepting me in this position more easily. I bury it to the hilt, feeling her snug young pussy give to my intrusion. I reach up and grab her hips, pulling her body back into mine. Her skin is slick, and I grip her firmly to hold onto her. I push forward meeting her body with mine. My strokes are long and firm, smashing my body into hers. She loves it and pushes back into me, meeting my thrusts, encouraging my force.

I can feel my heart pound and my ears buzz from the exertion in the steamy hot room. Our bodies are totally slick with sweat, and the smell of eucalyptus is pervasive. She is so slippery I can barely hang onto her as we fuck. I reach up and grab a handful of wet hair again, pulling her head back, her ear next to my mouth. "Oh God Emily you feel so good. I have wanted you for so long" I growl into her ear. It seems as if my words release the hold she had on herself. She bucks her hips into me and erupts into a huge orgasm, her body convulsing and sliding against mine. It lingers, the effects overwhelming, and she falls forward onto her elbows breathless. She needs a moment to collect herself and for that matter so do I.

I sit down on the toweled bench of the steam room again. I tell her to turn around, so she is facing away from me. I grab her hips, and guide her down onto my cock. She is ready for anything at this point, and seems willing to trust whatever I am asking of her. Her pussy grips my hard cock, and she grinds her ass into me once again. I like this position because it gives me access to every part of her. I grab a handful of wet hair and turn her head to kiss me. We kiss just as hard and deeply as before, the intensity of our act has not subsided. I reach around, squeezing and fondling both her breasts, again gently playing with her nipples. She likes it when I lightly run my fingers over her nipples, so I oblige. When the moment is right, I send my right hand shooting down her stomach, pausing dangerously close to her swollen clit. I want her to want it....need it, before I actually do it. I hold my hand still, and wait. Finally, when I think she is going to absolutely burst, I relent. I rub her sopping wet pussy, from top to bottom. The firestorm in her thighs rises quickly out of control, and she screams my name loudly as she comes for the last time. I am right behind her. I hold off as long as I can, and then erupt into my own orgasm. I throw my arm over her shoulder, and ram her down on my cock as I come. She continues bucking into me, her sweaty body against my body until she is sure she had every drop of it.

After a few moments, we gather our strength enough to pick up our soaking wet clothes and walk out. I suggest we shower since I assume we are all alone; but then we hear a voice. "The cleaning crew!" she says. She dresses quickly and scurries out the locker room door. I meet her in the parking lot a few minutes later, most of my clothes still in hand. We laugh at the thought of getting caught by the cleaning crew, sharing a moment together under the lights. I kiss her good night and I head home, feeling a hell of a lot better than when I had arrived.

Holly

"Yes, that hurts but the pain is more localized here in the front" I explain to the physical therapist as I sit on the padded table. "Alright, we'll need to do some work on that, and finish each session with some massage work on your IT bands" he tells me. "My what?" I said, asking for clarification. "Your IT band is this right here, and it's way too tight" he says, grabbing the side of my leg just above the knee. I winced in pain and instantly understood what he meant. Fantastic, I thought sarcastically...I am guessing this is going to be a long and painful process. I sign the paperwork and give them my insurance card, scheduling myself for Mondays and Wednesday for the next eight weeks.

Twenty minutes later I look down at my legs as I sit on the table and laugh as I find wires coming out from everywhere, and the electrodes making my thighs twitch like I am freezing cold. The next treatment is some basic exercises for strength and balance and a few more for good measure. I think I am done, but I figure I should ask. "Anything else today?" I ask, hoping the answer is no. "Just one more thing. Holly, can you blast his IT bands for me? My next patient is here." the PT says as he walks away. Blast? I don't like the sound of that. And who is Holly?

Obviously in her early twenties, Holly turns out to be a cute college student here at the PT clinic on a summer internship. Athletically built and short blonde hair, she looks like the prototypical athletic college girl seeking a career in a sports related field. I smile at her and she smiles a warm smile back. I had no idea what I was in for. "Hop up on the table and lay on your side" she instructs me. I comply, curious to see what is on the agenda for me as the finishing part of my treatment. She puts a pillow between my knees, and then reaches under the table to grab a jar of some sort of white gel and scoops some out with two fingers. She starts rubbing it on her elbow, and I get a sudden flash of what is to come. "Try to hold still" she says with what appears to me to be an evil glint in her eyes.

She rolls my shorts up my leg, and feels around to find my hip bone. She rests her greased up elbow there for a moment, and then digs in. I think I am going to be sick from the pain. "Breath" she says as she begins a very slow and torturous journey from my hip all the way down the side of my leg to my knee. It is so tight and painful I am practically in tears by the time she reaches my knee. "Good, that's one" she says. "How many of those are we doing?" I ask, fearful of any answer that she is going to give me. "Usually six times...per leg" she tells me, and I think I can feel a tear well up. I brace myself for another round, and she begins the excruciating journey from top to bottom of my IT band. It is just as bad as the first, and I do my best not to squeal like a little girl while she does it. After six repetitions I flip over for the same on the other side. When she is finally finished, I sit up and am actually dizzy for a moment.

"OK, you are done. See you Wednesday" she says, smiling the whole time. This girl is doing her best to help me, and I hate her for it. "OK" is about as much as I can muster as I wobble away from her towards the door. I am not looking forward to my next session. My God that girl is strong.

Wednesday gets here sooner than I am ready for, and I arrive at the PT clinic at 5pm as arranged. I warm up and go through my strengthening exercises, the whole time dreading the last ten minutes of my time here. I am doing my best to mentally prepare for the coming torture, but to no avail. "Is it table time yet?" a voice asks from behind me. I turn to find Holly standing there smiling from ear to ear. "You enjoy your job a little too much" I tell her as I follow her to the PT table for my dose of "treatment". She follows the same routine as before, and although it is by no means comfortable, it doesn't seem as bad as the first go round. I am happy to see noticeable progress so soon. Holly seems to notice I am not grimacing as much as before, and digs a little deeper just to hear me beg for mercy. "You sadistic bi..." I catch myself before blurting out something I didn't really mean. She just laughs at me, seemingly enjoying making me wince in pain. I laugh too, mainly at the look on her face. She seems to take delight in her work, and I begin to wonder how I can exact some revenge.

Over the next few weeks, the exercises get easier and my IT bands have loosened to the point that I almost look forward to Holly digging her elbow into my thighs...almost. We have spent a fair amount of time together, and are now very comfortable with one another. I learn that her time here is coming to an end; she will be headed home soon to finish her degree program. "Who is going to torture me when you are gone?" I ask her one day. She laughs; "I don't know, but I am sure it will not be the same." "That's true...everyone else here seems way nicer than you are" I tease. She slaps my arm, and I give her a playful shove in response. I am ready to follow it up with something else, when I catch myself and remember that she is at work. I don't want to get her in trouble, so I quickly change my mind. She seems to catch on, and turns and walks away before the situation becomes too awkward. I get the feeling that she is warming to me.

The last week of her time here, and I have waited far too long to ask her out. I better do something soon, or she is going to leave and I am going to kick myself for blowing this opportunity. She is a lot younger than I am, but it doesn't seem to be an issue, so I don't bring it up. I am guessing at this point we might go to dinner and that will be about it, we are pretty much out of time. I run quickly through my routine and head for the table. As she is prepping for my bi-weekly elbow grind I make a little joke about maybe needing one of the guys to take over since she can't seem to get into the muscle deep enough. "Oh that's it...lay down! It is so on!" she tells me. I sit there staring at her, a playful look on my face. She grabs my arm and pushes me down onto the table, and yanks my shorts up to expose my hip to her. "And can you cut down on the inappropriate touching this time?" I say in a loud voice, barely able to contain my laughter. I can see her blush a little as she jams her elbow into me, quickly changing the look on my face. I look away from her, steel myself, and look back at her, staring deep into her eyes defiantly. She digs harder, and I just keep looking at her. It is a power struggle, and I do not want to give in. We continue to struggle, fighting for some sort of control over one another. It is painful and delicious and erotic and I am loving every minute of it. She seems to be into it as well or at least playing along. I flip over, and she pinches my ass. I jump and look up at her. The look in her eyes is devilishly sexy, and I am so turned on I want to kiss her right now.

At the conclusion of our session together, I decide I had better find out what is really going on. "So...do you want to go have coffee or something tonight when you are done?" I finally ask. "Oh, I can't tonight, and Wednesday might be kinda tough too" she says, biting her lip nervously. I am starting to think that she is avoiding seeing me outside of the PT clinic. "Maybe we can hang out after the going away party the guys here are having for me" she offers up. "Alright, let's do that" I say, settling for what sounds like a plan B option for her. I left thinking that this would end up with a late night phone call saying something to the effect of "Well I have to get up early, blah, blah, blah..." and that would be the end of things.

Wednesday comes and goes, and Holly seems to be in good spirits. She is practically following me around, checking up on me. I am hard at work on the Bosa ball when I feel a hand on my arm, and then a gentle shove. I jump to the side, catching myself before I crash into the weight equipment. I look up to find Holly standing there laughing at me. "You are such a little shit!" I tell her, smiling back. More foreplay I thought to myself. "Wait 'til I get you on the table" she challenges me. "Bring it girlie" I fire back as she walks away. I hurry through my workout, wanting to get onto the table as soon as possible. I never would have thought a few weeks ago that I would have made that statement, but now it is true, especially since today is the last time with her.

A few moments later and I am headed to the padded table once again. She sees me coming and makes her usual preparations, and I climb onto the table in front of her. She rolls my shorts up my legs, her hand lingering on my ass cheek just a tad longer than necessary or appropriate. "So, what do you have going on tonight?" I ask her. She responds with "Well, I have a little get together with some friends tonight and before that the crew here at work wants to take me out for a drink. How about you?" I am just hanging out at home" I admit, wondering if she is going to invite me out with everyone else. I hope not; I don't think it is a good it is a good idea to give the impression that something has been going on for a while. It is her last day, but I wouldn't want her to.... "Maybe we can hang out after the work thing" she says, cutting my thought off in mid sentence. "Perfect" I tell her, "Grab your phone and I will give you my number." She does, and I hear my phone ring as she dialed the number to save it. She hangs up, and looks at me smiling that cute college girl smile at me once again. God, I can't wait, I think to myself.

My phone rings about 8:30, and I answer "Hello Holly." "Hey...what are you doing?"she asks me. "Like I said earlier today, I am

68

just hanging out" I tell her, which means basically I am waiting around to see if she is actually going to call me or not. She is in a noisy place, and I can tell she is in a hurry to get off the phone. "I am still out with these guys, and it might be a little while before I can break away' she yells into the phone. I am bracing for a "tonight is not a good night" speech to follow her previous statement when she adds "but I really want to see you before I leave. Are you going to be up for a while, or are you going to do the old man thing and go to bed early?" she asks, laughing at her little joke. "I'll be up" I throw back at her, laughing on the inside about her joke, but not showing it for her to see. She ends our conversation with "Cool, I'll call you later." For the most part I believe her, and certainly hope she calls, but I have been through this enough times to know not to count on it until she rings my doorbell.

The clock reads 11:00pm and I am half asleep watching reruns of Seinfeld. My cell phone rings and I practically jump off the couch to get to it. This time it is quiet in the background, and she is speaking more softly into the phone. "OK, how do I get to your place?" she asks. I stay on the phone with her, guiding her through the maze of streets to my house. I am standing out on the driveway when she arrives, and she pulls her car into the driveway and all but screeches to a halt. She gets out of the car, and I lead her into the house. I shut the door behind us and now I am a believer. I skip the obligatory tour of the house and head straight for the bedroom. I turn on the TV but leave the lights off, and she runs and dives onto the bed like a little kid. I follow suit, and land right next to her. We lay side by side, our faces close to one another. I can smell alcohol on her breath, and joke about her getting a little liquid courage in her to be able to do this. She laughs, and admits she is a little bit nervous. I assure her I am too; even though I have been in this situation several times before, being with someone new for the first time always makes me a little nervous. And we are not easing our way into this, it is on right now. No first and second dates, no hanging out away from the PT clinic to get to know a little more about one another. The first kiss and the first time we have sex will be within the same hour of time.

After a few minutes of chit chat, she is beginning to look sleepy. I had better do something soon. I look at her and say "It looks like if you lay here another five minutes you could be asleep....so I guess I had better kiss you now." She smiles, and I lean in to kiss her. She meets me half way, and gently kisses me. She pulls away, and removes her glasses, laying them on the nightstand. She returns to me, only this time she kisses me really hard, almost too hard. Holly is aggressive, biting my lip and sucking my tongue. She rolls over onto me and I feel her weight on me. She is holding me down and kissing me firmly. I am laughing on the inside, thinking to myself that the shy little girl is long gone and the person on top of me is here to fuck. I slide onto my side just a little, shifting her weight to my right. I flip her over in one move, and now I am on top. I return the favor of pinning her down and kissing her. I am on top, dominating....and then suddenly I am not. She flipped me over again. We start laughing and the wrestling match begins. The bed is quickly becoming a wreck as we roll and wrestle and fight for position. She is much stronger than I expect, and it is truly a fair fight. Just when I think I am getting an upper hand she cheats and jams her thumb into my thigh where she knows I am sore. I jump, and she tosses me over, almost off of the bed. I am so turned on by this power struggle I can barely contain myself. It appears she is too, and I dive back into the mix and hook one of her legs under mine. Now I have her; I roll over and trap her arm under my body and suddenly she is helpless. "Ha HA! Victory is mine!" I exclaim. We both burst out laughing.

I relinquish my hold on her, and she seems content to be submissive for now. I begin kissing her again, and this time I am gentler about it. We kiss in long, deep and lingering kisses, exploring one another with hands and tongues. I sit up and pull her up too, and then remove her shirts. She lies back down and I touch her bare stomach, feeling her perfectly tanned skin for the first time. Her nipples are poking through the sheer material of her bra and I want to see them. We start kissing again and I try to reach under her to unhook her bra. I am fighting with it like a high school kid, and she begins to laugh at me. "Seriously?" she asks, making fun of my struggles. I pull her up off of her back once again, and finally get it unhooked. Her breasts are free, and they are glowing white in contrast to the dark tan of the rest of her. They are perky and perfect in their own way, and I cup them in my hands. She arches her back and leans her head back, encouraging my touch. I lean forward and take one, the sensitive skin jumping to attention from the heat of my mouth. I suck it, nibbling and teasing it before moving on to the other one. She leans to meet me, and I look up to see her face. Her eyes are closed and she has her head tilted slightly, and a very sexy look on her face. It is even better than I had been picturing all these weeks.

I slide my hand across her stomach again, tracing over her beautiful smooth skin. I go to unbutton her shorts, and she takes over. I wonder if it was because I struggled with her bra so much, or if she is in a hurry to have me touch her there. Either way, her khaki shorts are off and on the floor before I can finish my thought. I push my hand under the silky material and follow the contours of her body into the folds below. She is hot, and wet, and I can't wait to be inside her. She is trimmed on the top and shaved everywhere else, and I find my way to her clit. I touch it, softly at first and look up to see her face again. She reacts, and I watch her face contort in response to how I touch her. I press firmly, and then softly and back again. I rub it up and down, and in small circles. Holly loves it all, and is now moaning aloud. I feel her arching up, and I take the change in angle to plunge a finger into her as deep as I can. She sucks in a quick breath, holds it, and then exhales in a bursting orgasm. She moans and grips the sheets, tossing her head back and forth as she releases her juices onto my fingers. I lean into her and kiss her hard once again.

I am content to repeat the process, loving pleasuring her like this but she is ready to move on. She rolls over and is yanking at my shorts, tugging them off of me. She has my cock in her mouth immediately, sucking it to full attention. She is working it over good and I am loving every second of it. I am ready to go very soon, and I do my best to hold back as she runs her tongue all over me. The sensation is incredible, and I don't want to stop. She is good, and I want to be a little selfish and have her continue. She is ready for the next step, and lies back down next to me. I smile at her, relishing every second of this exquisite moment. That's the thing about younger girls; even the aggressive ones don't tell you what they what. They seem to think their actions speak loudly enough for men to understand. Now that I am older I get it, but when I was her age the lack of communication lead to some confusing times.

She is lying on her back and I slide between her legs, bending her knees lifting her ass slightly off the bed. I grab my cock at the base and tease her with it, prodding and pushing, rubbing it against her sensitive clit. I push myself into her, just a little at first, enjoying just how tight that young pussy really is. She moans, and I love it. I place my thumb on her clit once again and slowly begin to rub it in clockwise circles. Pushing and pulling my cock in and out of her, I go a little bit deeper each time. I rub her more firmly, and she responds. Her hips are moving in time with my strokes, and we begin to move in unison. Her breathes are coming more and more rapidly, and she is getting close once again. "Oh God yes...that is sooooo good" she moans to me. I am stroking it into her harder and harder, and rubbing her clit vigorously. She is right there, and I push into her, holding myself as deep in her as I can. I rub her hard now, and that sets her off. She is writhing underneath me, groaning out loud as she comes once again. I begin to fuck her hard and fast, releasing the pressure on her most sensitive spot. I go faster and faster until she is unable to match my motion from the bottom any longer. She holds herself still as I pound into her as fast as I can for several strokes. After a few moments I am forced to slow because I too can no longer hold the same pace. I downshift gears, and settle back into a rhythm that she can match. She moves with me, and I love the feeling of the two of us moving as one. I slow my pace even more until it seems more like making love to her than fucking like before.

She is building towards another orgasm, but instead of increasing my strokes and rushing towards the goal, I focus to keep exactly the same pace. It makes the process tortuously slow, agonizing that the euphoria of yet another one is slow close...and yet so far away. I take a deep satisfaction in this delightful scenario. She is panting and squirming underneath me, and I can't help but think back to all those times under her elbow on the table. It finally begins, and she moans a deep sigh, half of relief and half ecstasy. I keep stroking in and out of her, never breaking form as she shudders under me. It seems to last forever, and I love it. "Oh my God that was awesome" she pants to me. I settle down on top of her, kissing her deeply and slowly, wanting to linger in this exact moment as long as possible.

I roll off of her, and she what she said next will be burned in my brain forever. "I don't remember the last time I have come like this." I just laugh a very self-satisfied laugh and tell her "Well...now it's my turn." I get to my knees, trying to decide exactly what I want to do next. "Take me any way you want" she says, and I love it. I roll her over once again, only this time onto her side. I push her right leg to a 90 degree angle, exposing her waiting pussy to me. I position myself behind her, and enter her once again. I push deep, and she arches to meet me. I hit deep inside her, and she loves it. I pull out, and plunge again, and again. I have made the switch for doing this for her, to doing this for me. I hammer her over and over as I built towards my own release. I grab her by the hips and go faster than before. She reaches back grabbing her ass cheek and exposing herself just a little more. "That's it, pound me! God that is fucking hot" she moans. I start to moan more rapidly, and she knows my time is near. She reaches down between her legs and begins to rub her clit, racing me towards the finish line, yet another competitive moment between us. I love it, and continue to plow into her as I close in on what is going to be an amazing release. I hammer her hard three more times, and then it starts.

I stroke her slow and deep, and finally explode. I instinctively push forward, burying my cock deep inside her as I try to extend the extreme pleasure coursing through me. I arch and shudder, feeling the last of it leave my body. I was so lost in my own moment I have no idea if she came or not. It was too late if she didn't as I have peaked and am quickly coming down the other side. I have become super sensitive, and each inch I move is pleasure amplified to the point of near pain. It's too much, and yet I can barely make myself stop moving. Finally I give; pulling out and flopping down on the bed beside her. I wrap my arms around her, pulling her close and holding her there as the waves of pleasure inside me slowly subside. We lay there together, feeling one another breathe, slowly coming down from the high we had produced together.

She looks at the clock, squinting without her glasses on. "Its 12:45" I tell her. "Oh God" she moans, this time in despair. "I have to be up early tomorrow" she informs me. I know what's coming and try to make her departure easy for her. "It's OK, I understand. I am so glad you came to see me." I kiss her once more before rolling over to retrieve her glasses from my nightstand. "Me too...me too" she sighs. She dresses quickly and so do I. We walk outside into the cool night air, and kiss one more time. I watch her drive away and wonder if our paths will ever cross again. I certainly hope so.

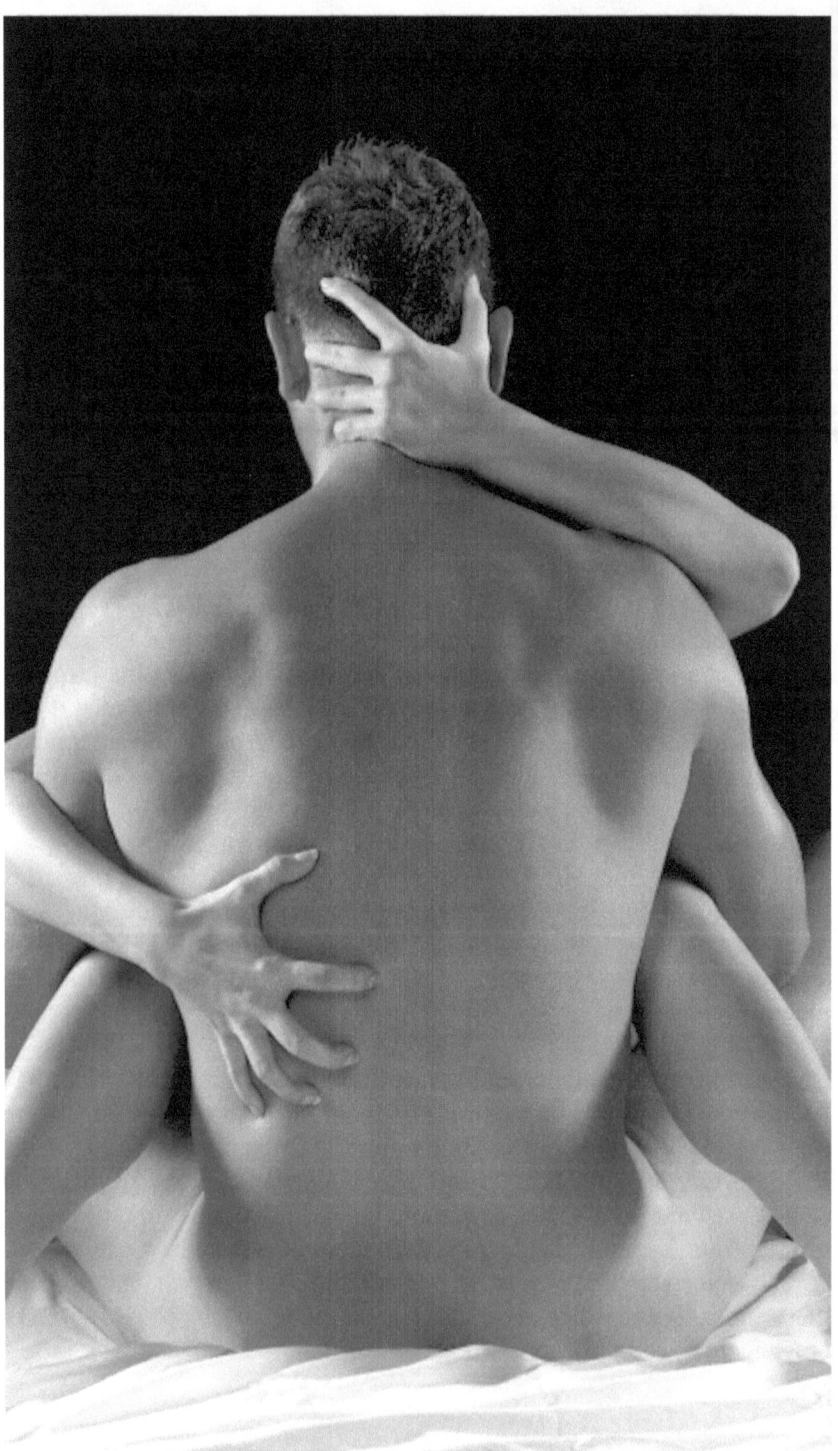

Tracey

I was driving around town the other day with a list of things to do sitting on the seat next to me. The light ahead turns red and I stop at the intersection. Reaching over to grab the list for one more quick review, I suddenly stop and am taken back to several years ago all at once. I look across the street to see the convenience store, and started laughing out loud. I had a flashback to the time I made Tracey do the walk of shame in her Halloween costume the morning after we went to that epic party and ended up spending the night at my place. I can be such an ass when I want to be, but God that was funny. Well, funny to me anyway. Man, what a night that was; I remember it like it was yesterday.....

Steve, Mike and I have worked together for a while now and have become great friends. Between the three of us know most of the staff in every part of the building. Halloween is right around the corner and we are really looking forward to the epic party that Mike is hosting once again. I was out of town last year and missed it, and I know from passed experiences at the party that was a huge mistake on my part. Mike even has a really cool house that is the perfect set up for a huge party; the backyard is nearly an acre. We start spreading the word to everyone in the building, and to everyone the three of us come into contact with over the next two weeks. I made sure to personally invite Tracey, the new manager who just started with the company. We have been flirting with one another at the office since she arrived a few weeks ago, and I really dig her. She seems to be warming to me as well.

Thursday night arrives, and we are making the final arrangements. Mike is a genius at this sort of thing, so Steve and I are just helping out with the final details. The band arrives about six o'clock and starts to set up on the makeshift stage we built on the other side of the pool. I am stocking up the bars on either side of the yard and making sure everything is in place. You can tell we've done this before; everything flows like clockwork, and soon the entire place is decorated in the Halloween theme for this year's epic event. Time for the three of us to change into our respective costumes as well; Mike's choice was that we should go as the three musketeers, especially since one of us was missing from the festivities last year. It does suit us well; the three of us are practically inseparable. So I begrudgingly agree; I secretly hate wearing

75

a costume and doing this sort of thing. But it's important to him, and I certainly don't want to miss out on the fun, so I head upstairs to transform myself in my character for the evening: Aramis. I return downstairs a short while later; fencing sword, stupid floppy hat and 18th century garb from head to toe. After a moment of feeling rather uncomfortable in my new persona I start to lighten up and embrace my role. The ceremonial shot of tequila we did probably helped a little too.

By eight o'clock people are flowing through the door in droves. Everyone is dropping tens and twentys into the donation bucket to help support the cause. I make one more run through the street and chat with the neighbors to make sure everyone is coming or at least not going to have issue with us partying hard through the night. They are used to this annual event, and most have found it easier to join us instead of fighting it. I am three houses away when the band starts their first set, and can hear the music clearly. Steve is friends with a guy who is the lead singer in a great local band, and they play this party for free every year for us. It is one more thing that makes it the party of choice on Halloween night.

By ten o'clock I am buzzing nicely and talking to everyone in sight. Everyone looks awesome in their costumes and I have no idea how we are going to pick a winner in the costume contest. The ladies certainly came dressed to impress tonight; but $200 cash for first prize and bragging rights for the next year are nothing to ignore. I hear Mike on the microphone announcing the contest will start in 15 minutes. Things are about to get interesting.

Suddenly I remember that I have not seen Tracey yet tonight. I am starting to wonder if she is going to show up at all. I was having a great time, but certainly am looking forward to seeing her tonight. I walk out to backyard and am handed yet another beer by someone I barely recognize in their costume. If I drank every that was handed to me tonight I'd be passed out long ago. I re-gift the beer to an empty-handed partier on my way towards the stage. The band finishes up the last song of this set and Mike hops up on stage to start the costume contest. Steve is nowhere to be found, so Mike makes one more loud announcement in hopes he'll appear. I walk up onto the stage, and can see someone pushing his way through the crowd towards Mike and me. It's Steve, and he is smiling ear to ear. I have a vague idea of what was holding him up, and just laugh when he takes his place next to us.

We start the contest with a slightly shy girl who is a little too drunk to realize what she is doing. Girl after girl is lining up to walk on stage to take her shot at the prize and a moment in the spotlight. The costumes range from home made to store bought, but all of them are very sexy. One of the first girls on stage is dressed as a fireman, and her thin white tank top and red suspenders barely contain her ridiculously large fake breasts. She shakes them for the crowd, and pours an entire bottle of water down the front of her. The crowd goes nuts. I look at Mike and laugh; he is mesmerized by her antics. This girl is totally his type, and I think I know who he'll be pulling for in the contest. She is putting on a good show, but is not really my type.

A steady parade of scantily clad women dance and gyrate across the stage, each one trying their best to gain the crowd's support. I am making notes of who to bring back to the stage, and look up to see the next contestant. She is dressed in a belly dancer costume complete with a dark veil hiding her face. She struts across the stage like she owns it, taking center stage right in the middle in front of the crowd. She begins to dance, slowly at first, but quickly increasing the speed and actions of her hips. It is amazingly sexy, and she has the crowd going wild in no time. Dancing around the stage, she extends her time in the spotlight as long as she can. As she takes a bow a flash of blonde hair is revealed from below the head dress. She skips off stage, and just as she passes me, whispers "Hi Darren" as she stares into my eyes. My jaw dropped...it was Tracey!

A few more contestants come and go, one that caught the attention of the crowd and the rest just milking a little time in the spotlight. We round up the five finalists based on crowd applause; four girls who are barely dressed at this point, and one belly dancer who's identity is a secret to almost everyone here. The girls are told to strut their stuff, and are reminded that $200 cash goes to the winner. It seems that was code for "lose the clothing" as four of the five girls upgrade to doing a strip tease for the crowd. Tracey kicks her hips into overdrive, and the veils start flying. She spins in a circle, twirling the thin veils as she goes. It is mesmerizing; the rest of the noise fades and soon I see only her on the stage.   She seemed to dance in slow motion as the rest of the surroundings became a blur. I am suddenly snapped back to reality when I hear Mike's voice on the microphone.

He walks behind the girls, holding his hand over the head of each girl to gauge the crowd's response. The firefighter chick is standing next to Tracey, her top in shreds from her tearing it off of herself in the fray. The crowd went crazy when Mike reaches her. My eyes never left Tracey as she waits her turn. Chants of "lose the mask.....lose the mask" began to echo through the back yard. She takes a step forward, pauses for effect, and then put her hand on the veil covering her face. Instead of pulling it away she simply rolls her hand forward and takes a bow. The tease is met with a chorus of boos, and the contest is over.   The firefighter is handed $200, and she and Mike promptly disappear. Everyone else scatters as well, returning to what they were doing before the contest started. I walk over to Tracey and I can tell by her eyes that she is smiling under the black veil. I love the way her eyes light up when she smiles.

"Can I get you a drink?" I ask her. "Absolutely" she says flatly. "I am parched after that!" she adds. We walk through the crowd together, and she follows me to the bar. I circumvent the line and help myself. "Being co-host has its privileges" I tell her, winking at her. I grab two bottles of water and then take place behind the bar. "What can I get for you ma'am?" In continuing the surprises for the evening, she leans over and replies "I would love a slow comfortable screw upagainst the wall." She looks at me and giggles under her veil. I search for a pithy comeback, and then realize that it is actually a drink. I think for a moment and then go to work trying to fulfill her request. I dig around, surprised to actually find a half a bottle of Galliano behind the bar. I run to the kitchen for some orange juice, and pour a guesstimate about twelve ounces into the metal shaker. Next I add the Sloe Gin, Southern Comfort and top it off with the vodka. I shake the contents and spin the shaker in the palm of my hand before splitting the contents between the two glasses now sitting on the bar. We each grab a glass and raise it to toast. I pause for a moment, thinking, and then say "to what lies ahead." I can see her smile under the veil again. She tilts her head and clinks her glass against mine without saying a word. She didn't have to; I could see it in her eyes. It is on.

It's midnight and the band starts their next set with a loud guitar solo. I lean over to continue talking to her, but I am practically yelling at her. "Why don't we go for a walk?" She nods in agreement; I grab her hand and lead her through the house and into the street out front. We walk down the street into the darkness, talking much more casually. We stop and sit on the curb, hearing the music and the party goers in the distance. I didn't realize until now just how much my ears were ringing. I look over at Tracey and she looks back at me for a moment, her eyes jumping from my eyes to my mouth. "Here it comes" I think to myself. She reaches up and removes the veil from her face. She looks back to me and neither one of us hesitated. We lean in, splitting the distance between us and meeting in a delicious moist kiss. I pull away just briefly to see her reaction, but she follows me. We kiss some more, this time shooting tongues into one another's mouths and kissing with much more force. She tastes like orange juice, and smells like whatever that wonderful perfume she wears is.

After a moment we stop, and still next to one another in silence. She seems very comfortable with me and I don't have any doubt that this will be just the beginning of things to come. I stand up and help her to her feet. We walk back to the party, walking slowly and talking some more. She is still getting settled in at work, but likes the company so far and looks forward to being there a while. I have been there a long time, and to be honest wouldn't mind doing something else. But this job comes easily to me, and offers me a lot of freedom for setting my own schedule so it is tough to leave. We talk about lots of other things as well, and I am learning that the more I know about Tracey the more I like her.

We reach the door at Mike's again, and she quickly puts the veil back on. "By the way, where did you learn to dance like that?" I ask her. She laughs, and responds "Belly dance classes of course. It looked like fun, so I tried it once and loved it. It's a great workout and keeps me in shape." She leans over to me, and adds "It has other benefits, too" and then spins and walks away from me, making me chase after her into the house. I sure as Hell am not letting her get away at this point. I run after her, and catch up to her as she enters the back yard. The party is in full swing; people are dancing and drinking and having a great time as expected. We are near the back of the crowd, but pressed close together because of the flow of traffic in the yard. She starts to dance in front of me; her ass brushes back and forth over my crotch. The thin material of the costume pants are going to do little to contain me before long, and I feel myself swelling from the pressure against me. She speeds up her hips, the veils of her skirt once again flying back and forth at a high rate of speed.

Tracey leans back and puts her arm around my neck, pulling me into her. I am not much of a dancer, but I can move well enough to follow her. We slowly move together, the distance between us disappearing moment by moment. We press together, moving as one. I put my hand around her waist and then slowly let my hand travel up and down her sides. I brush against the side of her breasts, across her stomach, and down the front of her. I look at her, she has her eyes closed as she moves with me. The music pulses, the crowd moves as one giant mass of bodies all on the same frequency. It is a very cool experience, like everyone blended together and became one large thing. It is almost surreal. It went on for the next few songs, and then the band finally said goodnight to everyone and ended the show. Tracey spins around and looks deep into my eyes for a moment. "So...now what?" she asks.

We push our way through the crowd and make our way to my jeep. I am blocked in and have to pull across Mike's lawn to get out. "I am sure he'll understand" I say aloud as we hop the curb and head down the street. We are silent at this point, which concerns me. It seems like we should be talking, but we are not. I fight for something to say, and finally she beats me to it. "I don't usually do this sort of thing" she blurts out. "But I liked you from the moment I saw you, and have been waiting for you to ask me out. I didn't want the first time to end up like this, but I guess I am going with it" she tells me. She seems to be verbalizing her concerns, and I should say something to put her at ease. "I really like you too, and I think we are going to have a lot of fun together. I certainly hope you'll call me after this, and not make me feel like you just got me drunk to take advantage of me" I say to her with a big smile on my face. She reaches over and slaps my arm. I think my cheesy joke did the trick.

Tracey removes the mask she had been hiding behind all night long and lays it aside. "Did you come by yourself tonight?" I ask her, wondering if she is supposed to meet up with someone. "Yes, I was supposed to meet a friend from work here, but I never saw her. She knew about the costume and not to give away my identity tonight. I don't want people at work talking about me; I am supposed to be a manager, remember? The contest was fun, but the two hundred bucks was not worth my dignity and respect at the office" she explains. "Besides, I told her I would probably end up with you tonight." I smiled a huge smile; the ultimate compliment. She was already down for tonight; no alcohol or fancy footwork needed to convince her. Most women are never willing to show their hand so easily, but she is laying her cards on the table. I wish it was always like this, but I am certainly glad Tracey is not playing games. "So....my place?" I ask, looking for confirmation of what I was already doing. She just smiles back at me.

A short drive later we are at my house. The night air is still warm and enveloping, despite the late October date. One of the best things about living in Arizona, I am reminded. We walk towards the door, but I stop suddenly half way there. I turn and quickly grab her in my hands and kiss her firmly. "I couldn't wait any longer" I tell her, smiling. She laughs, and pushes me towards the door. I am wondering if there is any way I can get her to dance for me.....

We walk in and I turn on the lights. "Something to drink?" I offer as I walk to the kitchen. "Water would be great" she fires back, stopping in the living room. I come back a moment later to find her standing in front of the stereo system. I grab the remote off of the counter and turn it on. "Oohh!" she jumps, not expecting the system to seemingly start by itself. She quickly laughs at herself, and so do I. "Anything in particular you'd like?" I ask. "Something to dance to" she replies. "Um, yeah...I don't...uuhhhh......" "Not us....me" she tells me, cutting me off in mid sentence. It takes a second to register, and then I realize that she is thinking the same thing I was hoping for on the ride over. She is going to showcase her belly dancing skills once again. I walk over to the lights and dim them to a more appropriate level, and then walk over to my Sonos stereo system. I lean over the front, looking for some "dance" music, wondering to myself what good belly dancing music sounds like.

Tracey comes and stands right next to me, her arm brushing mine. I feel a rush of excitement because of her proximity, and I look over to her. She looks directly at my mouth, and I know what she wants. I lean to kiss her and she meets me half way. We kiss some more, my tongue finding its way into her mouth after a moment or two. She responds accordingly, and our tongues wrestle and roll. I open one eye to see how far away from the entertainment center we are, and then slowly back her against it. I push her into the structure; it creaks from the pressure. Tracey moans a little as I press my body against hers. I can practically feel her skin through the layers of veils that comprise her costume. I ditched the hat long ago, but I'm still wearing the same three Musketeers costume from earlier. I feel the fake mustache start to peel away from the force of our kisses. I pull away from her, and slowly pull the adhesive-backed mustache from my upper lip. "Thanks...that thing tickles" she says, smiling at me.

I hand Tracey the controls, and she scrolls through the play list in search of music. I turn to her again, and she kisses me once more. This time she is walking me backwards, towards the couch. We stop, and she points for me to sit. Tracey stands before me, looking down at me in my seated position on the couch. She slowly begins to sway back and forth, her hips moving in a wide, slow range of motion. She matches the music perfectly, moving in time with the rhythm of it. As the music increases, so do her shakes and gyrations. "My God this is hot" I think to myself, totally entranced by her. She hides her face behind the veil again, coyly pretending to be shy despite her boldness in joining me tonight.

The dance continues, and Tracey is slowly driving me mad. She is so sexy; the way she moves, the way her athletic shape is disguised under her costume, and when she shakes her hips at a high rate of speed I can't help but think what it would be like to have her on top of me when she does that. I watch her body, my eyes traveling up and down her sleek frame. We make eye contact once in a while, but it is as if she has given me permission not to be as respectful about that as I usually am. She removes the veil covering her face; finally it seems she is no longer hiding from me. Tracey pulls another veil from the costume; soon the layers are diminishing. She wraps it around the back of my neck and pulls me forward into her. Shaking her hips rapidly, she is right in front of my face. I watch her intently for a moment, and then look up at her without moving. In my head I am picturing what it will be like to go down on her, looking up to see the reactions on her face. I give my best sexy smile, as if to convey what I am thinking to her.

She very slowly gets lower and lower until she is on her knees in front of me. She leans back, slowly, still swaying to the music all the while. She is very flexible, and it just adds to the list of things I find so damn sexy about her. We are going to fuck long and hard, it is obvious. My body is having a Pavlovian response to her gyrations. She lays all the way back, her shoulder blades on the carpet. I can see only the bottom of her chin, and her ever gyrating hips. Tracey pulls two more veils from the costume and adds them to the scattered pile on the floor. I can see more and more of her; it is taking forever, and yet it is so tantalizingly sexy I want her to drag this out as long as possible. She pushes the veils between her legs, exposing her bronzed skin to my eyes. I want so badly to reach out and touch her, but I wait. Pulling herself upward, she regains a sitting position in front of me once again. The dance continues, and she pulls two more veils from her costume. These two however seemed to be hiding more than the rest. I can now see the sheer, strapless bra she is wearing despite the dim lighting. We are getting closer, and I thicken in anticipation of it.

Tracey springs to her feet in one deft move. Barely cognizant of it through most of this, I do notice the music is increasing quickly in speed. She follows right along, and the veils begin to fly. She is spinning and gyrating faster than she did on stage; or maybe it just seems that way since this time it is just for me. She is almost down to the flesh colored bra and thong panties she was hiding under all the layers of veils. I am growing antsy, the tension and anticipation almost becoming unbearable to me. Just when I think I can't take any more, she comes forward. She spins around, her perfectly sculpted ass right in front of my face. I reach out and place my hand on her, the flesh warm and glistening under my touch. Her skin is smooth, and I run my hand over her ass and then down her leg. She reaches back and unclips her bra, letting it fall to the floor. I see her hands are now covering her breasts, and she slowly turns around to face me. I am surprised at how big her breasts are; she must hide them on purpose while at work. They are too big to really contain behind her small hands, and I am contemplating helping her when she moves forward again and climbs on top of me. She is now sitting on me on top of the couch. Her hands grasp my face, pulling me into her for a long, deep kiss.

His Eyes

She sits back after a moment, and her hands go to work unbuttoning the myriad of buttons on my costume shirt. I fight to kick off my shoes, and send one flying across the room. She is practically naked at this point, and I am quickly joining her state of dress myself. I put my hands behind her back, touching her warm skin once again. She folds her arms under her tits, pressing them together. I know what she wants, and waste no time. I lean her backwards, and my mouth meets her hard nipple. I kiss and suck it at first, gently. After a brief moment though I slowly begin to bite down on it. She moans in pleasure as I nibble and clamp down on her rigid flesh. She tosses her head back, moaning loudly once again. Her hand finds the back of my neck, holding me in position. She wraps her legs around my lower back, and can hold herself in that position without my help now. My hands are free to travel over her, and I take full advantage of that. I immediately put my hands on her luscious breasts, squeezing them. Her flesh surrenders under my touch; I lift and press them together, feeling the soft skin meld into my fingers. I push them together more and suck on both nipples at once. She shudders at the sensation and squeezes me with her legs even harder. I can feel the heat emanating from between her thighs as she grinds herself into me.

I sit up and kiss her once again. We are kissing forcibly now, and she throws her arms around me. She manages to pull my shirt off of me and now her hot flesh presses into mine unimpeded. We wrestle against each other, moaning and groaning as we kiss. I am growing so hard it is starting to hurt. I slide her over and stand up to remove the baggy costume pants. The velvety material is sweaty and wrinkled, and it feels good to have it off of me. I fling the pants aside and go to sit back down on the couch again. Tracey stops me, and has me stand in front of her. This time it is my hips face level to her. The thin material of my boxer briefs are doing little to mask the desire my body is feeling. She runs her hand over it, stroking my length separated from her only by the thin black material. She looks up at me, and smiles. Her hands find my hips, and in one quick move my boxers are on the floor. My cock flops up and down a little, it too rigid to move much despite her action. Tracey stares at it for a moment, waiting. Reaching over and grabbing a veil that is nearby, she wraps it around my waist. She uses the veil to pull me into her. She uses just her mouth on me, no hands at all. Tracey yanks me back and forth into her hot mouth using the veil she was wearing earlier.

She swirls her tongue around me, running up and down one side and then the other. The heat of her mouth and the suction she is creating is incredible. Finally her hand settles around the base and slowly her hand slides up and down, following her mouth closely. I reach down and pull the veil out of her hand, and place it around the back of her head. I use it to pull her in, making her swallow my cock all the way to the bottom. She can almost do it, and the tip of it touches the back of her throat making her recoil. She is game though, and goes back for more right away. This time she gets a little deeper, and holds it deep in her mouth. I pretend to hold her there with the veil, ready to release her at any second. I throw my head back, the feeling of being all the way into her throat almost too much to bear. By moving I break her hold on her reflexes, and she jerks away quickly. She laughs and then so do I. I grab her hand and lift her to her feet.

I can't wait any longer; I must have her right now. I spin Tracey around to face away from me; my hands grab her and pull her against me. I slide them down to her hips, and repeat what she did to me earlier. I rip her thong off of her, straight to the floor in one move. She steps out of it, and moves closer to the end of the couch. I grab her, and forcefully bend her over the arm of the couch. I am balls deep into her before she knows what hit her. She gasps loudly, arching to meet my thrust. I grab her hips and yank her back and forth, my cock slick with her juices already. "Oh God........Uuuggghhh!" she gasps almost incoherently. Her teeth are clenched and she fights to push back into me, wanting as much of me as she can get. I put one foot up on the arm, and push forward into her. I go so deep like this, and I am bringing it a little rough. I hold myself deep in her for a moment, and then pull out once again. I resume fucking her from behind; hard, deep strokes in a fast rhythm. Tracey groans and clenches her fists, growing close.

She slides her feet together and I feel her pussy clamping down on my cock even more than before. I reach up and grab the base of her ponytail, firmly pulling her head back. It is obvious she likes that; she groans louder than before and starts to buck her hips as only she can. I hold still and let her fuck me; her speed is increasing rapidly and she moans again. She is moving faster than I possibly could, and she gets herself off on my cock. I fight to hold my ground, making sure she gets what she needs. After nearly a full minute her rhythm breaks and she cries out loudly. I grab her hips and thrust into her, parting her deep inside once again. She shudders and squirms against me. I hold her hips firmly, and her hands move to brace herself and hold her body upright. "Ho, oh my God that was hot!" she says after a moment. She looks back at me, her face glossed over in a sexy, spent look.

I withdrawal from her, and walk around her to take a seat on the couch again. Tracey wastes no time in joining me as before. She pushes me back into the cushions, her hands resting on my shoulders. Reaching down, she guides herself onto my hard cock once again. She looks down at me, her eyes half closed in pleasure. We start slower this time, now that we have begun the final act we seem to be cognizant of making it last. I knead her breasts together, loving the feel of them in my hands. Her nipples are rock hard, and I tweak and pinch them as we go. She has her head tilted back and her hands on my shoulders as she slowly starts to take over again. I move with her as best I can, but as her hips begin to do their thing, I can no longer match her moves. I sit still below her, and let Tracey take over.

As I was hoping for, she is putting her talents to use in an entirely different sort of entertainment. Her hips are so flexible she easily glides back and forth and in circles while sitting on top of me. It is incredible. I have stopped watching her face and am now very focused on watching her stomach muscles flex and contort as she swirls herself around my cock. The feeling is intense, and my best description of it would be that she is vibrating. Watching her move like this is turning me on beyond belief. I look up to see her staring at me; she is watching me watch her. She smiles, knowing how much I am getting off on watching her fuck me like this. I think she is really getting off on the idea of me getting off. We continue like this for several more minutes, and I get the feeling that this would never get old.

Finally Tracey stands up and gives her hips a rest; we both need a breather after that session. I walk to the kitchen and return with a bottle of water for each of us. We stand there looking at each other; clothes thrown around the living room, and a big sweat spot on the couch from where I was sitting with her on top of me. I take one more big gulp of water and look over to her. "You ready?" I ask. She doesn't bother replying to my snarky little question. I sit down in the same place, the suede cold against my skin at first. This time she faces away from me. She reaches back and guides herself down onto me once again. Tracey sits on top of me, both of us facing the same direction. I put my hands on her hips and slowly begin to move her up and down once more. She joins in the rhythm and soon my hands are just along for the ride following her moves. I watch her ass travel up and down over me, her bronze skin cleaved by a thong tan line that is bright white. Her skin is so smooth, her flesh glistening from all the hard work she is putting in. Her efforts are not without reward however, and I can hear her moans increasing. She maintains the same steady pace as she climbs towards the top once again.

I reach up and grab her shoulder, jamming her down on it and then pulling her back against me so we are both lying back facing the ceiling. I run my hands all over her, feeling every inch of her amazing body as it slithers and slides all over mine. She turns her head and kisses me, the passion evident in the force with which she kisses me. Her moans grow, and soon her kisses fade off. I brush the hair away from the back of her neck and bite down. Her groan reverberates all through her, and I can taste the salty sting of her sweaty skin. I reach around and squeeze her magnificent tits, smashing them against her. And then it begins again, her hips take over the show. She is spinning and swirling them, gyrating them just like when she danced for me. Mine is building, I can feel it. She fucks me faster and faster, her noises matching her pace. I find myself growing loud as well, and it seems we may finish at the same time.

"Where do you want it?" I ask her. "Not inside me" she blurts out between moans. Her back arches even more, driving my cock deeper into her as she moves on top of me. I pinch her nipples, twisting them roughly. She cries out, as if it caught her off guard. Her body trembles and shakes as she comes. "Don't stop, don't stop!" I practically yell out, begging for my own release. I feel it coming, and I pull her backwards and off of me. Tracey settles back down, rubbing her pussy over the top of my exposed cock. She squeezes her legs together, and it is far more than I can take. I shoot my load all over her stomach, some of it reaching all the way to her tits. She squeezes and shuffles on top of me, making sure I get the full effect. I pump shot after shot of it onto her until I grow so sensitive that I have to ask her to stop. We slump back into the sweat soaked couch, gasping for breath.

After several minutes we stagger towards the bedroom. We crawl into bed together and after a long deep kiss I roll over and am out like a light. I wake in the morning realizing that I had not set the alarm. It is bright outside, and I scramble for the clock. "Jesus...wake up...its 7:00!" I say loudly. "Shit!...we gotta go!" she yells, jumping out of bed. We are up and running before we know it; we are supposed to be at work in an hour, and she is never gonna make it. I run to the shower and rinse off, drying quickly as I can. Thank God it is casual Fridays at our company; I grab some jeans and a collared shirt and I am ready. Tracey is in the other room gathering her costume pieces that were thrown around the room from the night before. "Do you want some clothes to wear?" I shout to the other room. I hear Tracey mumble something, and when I go into the living room she is redressed in her costume. "I have clothes in my car, I'll just wear this until we get back to Mike's" she tells me.

We hop in my Jeep and head down the street. Now that the adrenaline is wearing off, we both start to feel the effects of the night before. Tracey says her headache is growing quickly, and wants me to stop for coffee somewhere before we get to Mike's. My cell phone rings just as we pull in; it's Mike checking up on me. I sit in the car and Tracey looks over at me and then sighs. I ignore the first one, but when she does it again I ask me to wait and then look at her. "We're in a hurry, remember?" she says almost scoldingly. "I don't drink coffee, remember?" I snap back, my patience thin after three hours of sleep. "Fine...I will get it!" she fires back at me and gets out of the car. She slams the door and I continue talking to Mike. She stomps into the convenience store and disappears. I am kind of laughing about the little snit we just had, and get an idea that will either make her laugh or take a swing at me. I am not sure which, but for some reason I seem to be willing to take the chance.

I back my car up, and pull my car almost all the way out to the street and wait for her there. She comes out and looks around, finally seeing where I am now parked. She waves for me to come get her and I just wave back. She hesitates for a moment and then starts across the parking lot. As soon as she steps into the sunlight car horns are blowing and you can hear several whistles and catcall at her expense. She picks up the pace and hurries to the car, scrambling to get in. Tracey hangs her head, hiding her face in embarrassment. I am laughing my ass off when she gets there and she glares at me for a second. Finally she can't help but laugh at herself, seeing the humor in the "walk of shame" that I made her do. We share a good hard laugh, and when we finally wind down she leans over and kisses me. I kiss her back and when she pulls away she looks deep into my eyes and tells me "I will get you back for that" she states flatly. I believe her.

Naomi

I was in the middle of a conversation with the adult book store owner when I notice her. She is obviously listening, and keeps smiling at me. She looks at my book which the owner is waving around as part of his animated hand gestures, so I figure she is interested in the subject matter we are discussing. "That's my book, have you ever seen it?" I ask, inviting her into the conversation. "Seen it...I've read it!" she exclaims, smiling at me bigger than ever. All of the sudden I get where the smile is coming from, and why she is looking at me that way. You'd think that after all these years of trying to attract women's attention that certainly I would recognize it when I do actually see it. You'd think.

She certainly has a different look to her; mid twenties with a bunch of ear piercings, a ring in her nose, several tattoos and a prominent pink streak running through her light blonde hair. All of 5'5" in her platform cork shoes; I look right over the top of her head as I introduce myself. Her beautiful blue eyes sparkle as she tells me her name. A clingy green tank top and a torn up jean skirt round out the look of a girl shunning the conventions of society at every turn. A rocking little body packaged in a different wrapper. I can tell she has both nipples pierced by the bumps visible through her snug fitting shirt. For some reason this girl's look is really turning me on, despite being so different; or maybe because of it.

"What did you think if it?" the store owner asks, hoping to solicit an opinion less biased than my own. "I absolutely loved it...it was very hot" she says to him, but she was looking at me the whole time. I can tell by the gleam in her eye that the stories turned her on, and now that I am standing in front of her she is having a flashback to the readings. Her body turns towards me as I walk over to her. I extend my hand to introduce myself to her, and she reaches for me. Our thumbs catch each other on the way into the handshake, and it becomes a rather awkward exchange. "Real smooth" I think to myself; "I'm Darren" is what I said aloud. "Naomi" is all she offers up. I smile at her, trying to look long enough to let her know that I find her attractive without reaching creeper level. She finally gives first in the staring contest, and shyly looks away. "Are you two about finished?" the store owner asks, effectively killing the vibe we had going between us. It appears he was joking, but Naomi suddenly found the urge to make herself scarce. She put her hand lightly on my back as she walked behind me, saying "It was nice meeting you" on her way by. I am struggling to find a way to engage her once again, to pull her back into the conversation, but am drawing a blank. "Bye" is all I could come up with as I watch her leave. I am right in the middle of the thought that I have no idea where to find her when the shop owner begins to mumble about her "corporate spying". "Does she work around here?" I blurt out unsubtly. "Yeah, she works at the shop right down the street and she is always in here comparison shopping to beat our pricing. "Bingo" I thought.

Three days later I just happened to be in the neighborhood of the other adult book store and decide to stop in and see if Naomi is working. I am not a big fan of these kinds of places, even the nicer ones like this one I always feel a little weird walking through the door. I find the counter amidst a sea of sexy outfits, risqué outfits, and some fetish outfits that make me chuckle a little and look away. I see a girl behind the counter and am disappointed to see it is not Naomi. "Can I help you find something?" the girl asks. "Uh...no, I was looking for, um...is Naomi here?" "Oh My God...you're him, huh?" she practically shouts at me. I had a flash of panic, thinking that I was being mistaken for a stalker that has been hanging around the store or something. "Wait, what do you mean?" I fire back, stopping in my tracks. She reaches under the counter for something, and I freeze thinking I am about to get maced. Instead she pulls a copy of my book out and shows it to me. "This is you, right? She told me she met you the other day, and said you are a total cutie. She is reading your book again, if this is you" she says, making me squirm for a different reason. I was getting ready to run out of the place a second ago, and now she is telling me something I was figuring I would have to discover on my own. "Is Naomi here?" I ask again. She tells me she is in the back of the store.

I follow behind closely as she leads me to the back of the store where Naomi is. "Nay....someone's here to see you!" she yells into the store room. I walk in, and she shuts the door behind herself. There are rows and rows of adult toys on the shelves, and I stand there almost in a weird sense of awe at the quantity and variety of the different items. She walks around the corner, and stops dead in her tracks. I hear her draw in her breath. "HI!" she exclaims in a shocked voice. "Hi Naomi, how are you?" I ask, trying to smooth over the nervous moment. "What are you doing here?" she asks, and I suddenly think this was a bad idea. I may have been wrong about what I thought she was thinking, and now I am going to look like a complete douche bag showing up at where she works. "Um, well you left in a hurry the other day and I didn't get a chance to hear what you really thought about the book" I tell her, figuratively hiding behind the book once again. I notice she is holding several DVDs in her hand, and she sees me looking at them. "New arrivals" she says. Naomi reads through a variety of porn titles all a funny twist on mainstream movie titles or current events. We share a laugh about a few of them. When she laughs, I notice she has her tongue pierced in the middle. The dirty thought of her putting it to use crosses my mind.

I am growing uncomfortable about the fact that she seems rather uncomfortable with me being here. I begin to excuse myself, saying that I should not be intruding while she is working. I look at my watch; it is almost three in the afternoon. "Well, it's my lunch hour soon, do you want to have coffee with me, 'er something?" she nervously asks. "Sure, when can you go?" I respond. "Crystal will cover for me; we can go now if you want." "Cool" is my smiling response.

We walk next door to the sandwich and coffee shop, and the guy behind the counter seems annoyed at me for some reason. She walks up to the counter and orders "the usual" and then turns and asks what I would like. I order just a drink, and then pay for everything. The guy is about Naomi's age, thin and tall with those ridiculous earlobe expander things in both of his ears. The sleeve of tattoos seems to round out his counter culture vibe; I am not sure where the attitude is coming from, but I starting to get concerned that if I had ordered food I may need to look under the bun for something "extra". We sit at a table and begin to chat. Luckily it turns out Naomi is a little older than I thought, all of 26 since her last birthday about a month ago. She seems to be relaxing a little more since we are out of the shop, and her laugh and smile are very engaging. The food is delivered to our table, and he seems to deliberately turn his back to me and stick his ass in my face as he sets her food down gently in front of her. When he does spin around to drop my drink on the table, he leaves with one more parting glare at me. Once he is out of earshot I say out loud "What is that dude's problem?" "Oh, sorry about that...we used to date and he is still rather hung up on me" she informs me.

I fidget with my soda as we begin to talk a little more freely. I am not holding back on the sexual innuendos or my reasons for finding her. She blushes and looks away from me on occasion, but seems to be encouraging my advances. I think she is very sexy for a girl her age, and I totally dig her look for some strange reason. She starts to loosen up and fire some questions and jokes in my direction, and I am glad to see things not be one sided as much as before. The figured that I would be leading the charge given her age in reference to mine, but I am glad to get the impression that if I lead, she will follow.

After lunch we head back to the shop, and I am wondering what my next move should be. Since I am leaning out over my skis here anyway, I begin to formulate a bold idea. My stomach immediately knots up, and I take a couple of deep breathes to make sure I am not going to stumble over my words. "So, how late do you work usually?" I pose the question, ready to lead the conversation where I want it to go. "I close five nights a week, so you can find me here any time" she replies as she clicks her tongue ring against her teeth. I figured that she was thinking the same thing I was, or at least close to it. "Are you guys busy late at night?" I continue. I am already picturing her on her knees in the shop looking up at me, her tongue piercing working its magic. "Not usually, no. And I would love the company" she says with a little hesitation in between sentences. "Cool, then I will come to see you Thursday night" I inform her.

She stops as we reach the front of the store and turns to me. Her arms extended, she steps in and gives me a big hug, pressing her firm young body against mine. I hold her against me, and when she releases her hold on me I only let her pull away from me a little bit. She looks up at me, and I can tell she wants me to kiss her. I waste no time, and lean down just a little to kiss her. It is soft at first, and then we lean into it a little more and start to kiss a little more heavily. Finally we part, and she is smiling at me when I open my eyes. "See you Thursday" she says, and practically skips into the store. Only then did I notice her friend peering out the window at us. As soon as she hit the door I could hear her laughing, and then Naomi giggling right along with her.

Thursday night can't come quickly enough, and when it finally arrives I am trying to map out a game plan for the nights festivities. I think that a large majority of people toy with the idea of having sex at their workplace, but when you work in a sex shop it adds a whole new meaning to that. I hope she is game, because I certainly am. The chance of getting caught, the newness of the two of us and the surroundings are just about an overwhelming combination for my brain to deal with. I look at my watch; it reads 10:30pm. I am only about 15 minutes away from where she works, and so I slowly walk to the car and meander my way to the shop. I pull in and find two cars in the parking lot, and I figure that one of them is hers. I turn off the car and sit for a minute, and sure enough an older gentleman carrying a brown paper bag appears and walks to his car. He seems to be in a hurry and shuffles quickly in the dark. I hear his car start, and then he backs out, enters the street and blends into the traffic. I get out and lock the car, walking towards the front door. I see another car pulling in, and am disappointed to realize that this might be more difficult to pull off than I first thought. I head inside anyway, hoping for a little luck or a suggestion from someone who knows the patterns of the foot traffic in this place.

The door alert dings as I walk in. Naomi turns to see who has entered, and does a half double take when she sees it's me. Her face lights up and she comes running towards me. She practically leaps into my arms, squealing like a little girl in delight. I am happy she is so happy to see me. I kiss her a huge hello, and squeeze her tight against me. I hear the door open behind us, and then the alert sound. We part, and I let her greet the new customer who is intruding on our moment. I walk towards the counter take position there. She joins me a few moments later; now she seems preoccupied with the guy walking around the video section. She watches him on camera, and I search for something to say to recapture the mood just a few moments earlier. "I don't trust this guy; he is in here a lot and I think he steals from us" she informs me. "Anyway...how are you?" she feeds me an opening and we begin to chat freely. She keeps a close eye on the video monitor until he approaches the counter with two movies in his hand. "Ass Bandits 14 and Catholic School Girl Fuckfest...anything else tonight? She says with a straight face. I laugh on the inside at how clinical her approach to her job she has. I guess after you have been here a while not too much phases you. He grabs the brown paper bag from her and walks out, once again leaving us to ourselves in the store.

We stand and talk some more, me leaning against the glass counter with a bunch of dildos in it. I glance downward and my eyes must have widened a little as my reaction draws a laugh out of her. "You're kind of a prude, huh?" she teases. I laugh aloud, and respond "Hardly! I swing with the best of them my dear" quoting a line from Seinfeld that I realize will be wasted on her. She looks at me, tilting her head a little and smiling an inquisitive smile. "That was a line from Seinfeld" I tell her. She blinks like she has no idea what I am talking about. I start in with "There was a TV show in the 90's called Seinfeld that was..." she cuts me off in mid sentence. I am suddenly feeling our age gap, but she saves me by breaking into a huge laugh at my verbal tap dancing. "I know...I just wanted to make you squirm a little that's all" she adds. "You are such a brat" I tell her, and I reach over the counter and grab her shirt, pulling her towards me so I can kiss her again. She is game, and leans in to meet me. We kiss again, and she moans a little. I pull away, and she seems frozen in place, her eyes closed and her head tilted. "Is that all I get?" she asks, holding still. "For now" I state flatly to her, and then breaking into a smile as her eyes open. "Oh I see...who's the brat now?" she asks. I just lift an eyebrow in response, smiling a little longer at her. I hear the door again, followed closely by the alert. My head drops as I exhale an exasperated sigh. She laughs and tells me "Don't worry, I am closing soon and giving you a private tour."

She walks over to greet the couple who has entered, asking if they have been there before. They had, and begin to ask her questions about something they purchased recently. I turn and lean against the counter again, affording them a little privacy if they were in need of it. After a few minutes they are at the counter as well. They leave with some sort of restraint device and a bottle of lube, a sure sign of fun times to come I guess. I glance at my watch; it is 10:58. "Close enough" she says, and she comes around the counter and kisses me in a deep long kiss. She leaves me, heading for the door. She opens it to check the parking lot, and then shuts the door, locking us inside. I turn to look at the monitor, wondering if we are going to end up on security tape. She comes over and stops the recorder, and begins the process of backing up the day's security tape. "There, now I am done for the day" she tells me. I smile at her, waiting to see what is next.

She walks around the counter and heads over to the book section, motioning me to follow her. I do, trailing behind, watching her cute ass shift back and forth in her tight jeans as she walks in front of me. We reach the books, and I see mine prominently displayed in the middle of the rack. "We just got these in today; I got the owner to buy some to sell here" she says proudly. "Wow...that's awesome! How can I thank you, Naomi?" It seemed to be the question she was waiting for. "Oh, you're about to" she says, stepping towards me in an exaggeratedly slow and sexy walk. She comes to me, mouth open ready for action. I lean down and meet her, and we kiss in a deep and sexy kiss. I can feel her piercing inside her mouth with my tongue; it is smooth and hard, and I can't wait to have her put it to use. Her hands find my shoulders, and she grabs them as she kisses me harder. I put my arms around her waist, pulling her against me. We grind into one another, and my excitement is grows exponentially. She seems to be game for whatever, and I am already wondering what items in the shop we should be considering putting to use. It is difficult to let my mind wander too far, as Naomi is holding my attention quite nicely.

I follow her example of letting our hands explore one another's body. She seems to be willing to take the lead so far, and I am happy to follow along as we rapidly get to know one another. Her hands are moving quickly, and she is borderline rough in her exploration. I make a mental note, but continue in a slower and more deliberate pace. She grabs my ass, cupping her hand right where it melds into the back of my leg. I mimic her moves, and we pull each other even closer, just in case there was any space left between us. The heat radiating from her jeans is palpable against my thigh, and I lift my leg into her. The pressure against her crotch makes her moan as she continues to kiss me. I slide down and start kissing her neck, looking for a spot she reacts to. She turns away slightly, exposing it. I chomp down on her neck, two inches from the center and two inches above her collar bone. She tosses her head back, and I follow her to not break the hold on her. "HaaHaa, fuck yeah...right...there" she groans. She grabs the back of my head, letting me know I am not to stop what I am doing. I really start to dig into her flesh and she likes it even more. She is arching into me, grinding her body into mine with increasing force. I finally stop, and look down to see a red mark on her skin. I try not to react, figuring she will see it soon enough and that there is nothing that we can do about it right now.

"Oh my God I am so fucking hot for this" she says, her voice almost rough with desire. "Me too, I wanted you since I laid eyes on you" I fire back, letting her know that the feelings are mutual. She spins me and pushes me back against the book rack. Her hands are on my jeans, and in one quick move she grabs either side of the button fly and yanks it apart. My raging hard on bursts from its confines, and her eyes widen in delight. She is on her knees in front of me immediately, and I see nothing but the top of her head as she gobbles my cock down in one motion. She grabs my hips and goes down again, taking as much as she can. She convulses slightly, and pulls away with a slight gagging noise. She grabs the base and squeezes it, and rams it into her mouth again. She can handle as much as is exposed above her hand, and she sucks slurps my cock furiously. I am pleasantly surprised to realize that I can really feel her tongue ring as much as I had hoped. She is going after my cock like she loves it, and it is a huge turn on watching her do it. She looks up at me with those big blue eyes, watching my face as she sucks my cock. I stare down at her, loving every second of what she is doing to me.

After a moment or two of feverish activity she begins to settle into a slower, more rhythmic motion. She removes her hand from the base of my cock, and for a second it is white from her grip on it. Then she does something that almost buckles my knees. She extends her tongue out, and goes down the shaft again. This time I can feel it, *really* feel it. Her tongue ring is pressing into the sensitive flesh on the underside of my hard cock. She can't go down as far like this, but the sensation is incredible. It is so intense, and is a different feeling entirely from what she was doing before. "How does that feel?" she asks looking up at me. "Fucking Amazing" I praise her. She accepts the compliment and goes right back to work. It is so hot watching my cock slide over her extended tongue, disappearing into her mouth. She alternates back and forth between her hand and her mouth and I am beginning to strain to hold back. I certainly don't want to stop, but if there is more to come I do not want to finish here. I am trying to figure out how to ask that question without sounding pushy if the answer is not what I am hoping for.

Finally I am running out of time too quickly to take any more time and blurt out "You need to stop...right now."

She rocks back away from me and looks up. "Are we gonna, um...continue moving forward or is this the extent of your plans tonight?" I inquire. "Ahh, no...We have all night and the place to ourselves. I am not done with you yet" she tells me, standing as she speaks. "I've read your stories; I want some of that" she adds. She turns and walks away, and I follow behind her. She tears her shirt off and tosses it aside. She seems to be plenty comfortable in the shop. Walking back to the counter she kicks off her shoes. Naomi peels off her jeans as I stand and watch her; that young firm body finally in full view. Holy shit, she is pierced there, too. I remove my shirt as well, dropping it on the floor behind me. I take her in my arms, kissing her deeply once again. I can taste the slight hint of testosterone from my cock, and feel the tongue ring that was working me over just a few moments before. I slide down again, biting the same spot on her neck once more. She reaches behind her and unclips her bra, freeing her small, perky breasts to my touch. I bend down to reach her nipple, sucking it into my mouth. I flick my tongue over the barbell shaped piercing, feeling the cold steel in contrast to her warm skin. Her hand finds the back of my head again, pulling me into her soft flesh. I increase the speed of my tongue, flicking and sucking in a preview of what is to come. She responds, moaning aloud again. I can smell her excitement; the perfume of her lust reminds me of vanilla beans. I want some of that.

I stand again, and grab her hand. I help her step back into her shoes, and she quickly follows along. I doubt she knows what I have in mind, but it does not seem to inhibit her from following my lead. As soon as she has them on her feet and is a few inches taller, she is the perfect height to bend over the counter top. I spin her and push her forward shoving her onto the glass. Her perfect ass is almost tilted slightly upward like this, and I dive into her moist crevice without hesitate. I bury my tongue in her, tasting her. She slams her hands down on the glass, pushing back into me. She arches, exposing enough of her for me to shoot my tongue onto her exposed clit. The piercing is in her hood, and it exposes her clit even more than normal. It is swollen with excitement, and I rub my tongue over it in short, quick strokes. Peeking between her legs I can see her breasts smashed against the glass of the counter, her piercings rubbing the glass. Her face is turned to the side and her eyes are tightly shut, her breath fogging the glass as she exhales.

I notice her fists clench, and she begins to moan my name over and over, faster and faster. She is getting close, and I keep after it. I pull back a little and shove my tongue as far inside of her as I can get it. She bucks her hips slightly, almost involuntarily as she climbs towards the peak. I pull back, and shove forward again, repeating the process over and over, fucking her with the silken fire of my tongue. She reaches back and grabs her ass cheek, pulling herself open for more. I reach up and shove a finger deep inside her, farther than my tongue could reach. I move up, licking her most private hole with a few flicks of my tongue. It is more than she can take; she explodes into a humongous orgasm. She flat out went nuts, clawing at the glass and screaming out loud. Her juices squish out of her, and I remove my finger from her. She squirts again, her juices running onto the glass and down her leg. Her whole body shakes and shudders, and her hips buck wildly seemingly with a mind of their own.

"Holy shit...I have never done that before" she says, gasping for breath. "No one has ever made me squirt before" she adds as she slumps over the glass. It was my first time too, and I liked it. She went crazy from what I was doing to her, and that is the greatest part of this for me. Forget the pleasure I get out of it, it's the ego stroke that is really the best part. But I do enjoy the pleasure part of it as well, and with that thought I put my hand on her lower back and stuff my cock into her. I pull out and thrust again, this time a little deeper. She is soaking wet, and it glides easily into her. I am conscious not to press too deep right away, and so I continue to pull and push in and out of her with about two thirds of my hard length. She puts her hands on top of the counter again and presses back into me. Her back arches and she tosses her head back, looking at the ceiling. Her mouth is open, but no noise escapes for several moments until she gets a deep exhale out. She was holding her breath and finally had to release it. I reach up and run my hand against her head, and then bunch my fist up, grabbing a good handful of hair right at the root. I pull her hair firmly, holding her head back, making her arch even more as I pound away at her.

After a few minutes of this she is ready to burst once again. I let go of her hair and grab her hips. I slam into her really hard, knocking her into the glass. I heard a noise, and then realized what it was. The glass cracked. She pushes herself up off of it carefully, but the spell of another orgasm is broken. She turns to me, and I am waiting to see what is next. "I'll worry about that later" she tells me, and grabs my hand. She leads me towards the back of the store, and the two of us walk in nothing but our shoes to the dungeon section. I am feeling a little hesitation creeping in, wondering if I have finally run into someone who is going to want to do something that I am just not down for. She heads for the sex swing which is set up in the corner, and I breathe a slight sigh of relief. This I am down for.

"I have shown this thing to a bunch of people, but I have never actually used it" she explains. "But I have been dying to try it out" she adds, climbing into the contraption. It has four sturdy legs made of what appears to be two inch thick pipes bent into a U shape and welded together. There is a large spring suspended from the middle, and it has a seat and straps for her arms and legs. She faces me, and puts her limbs in the intended positions. I walk towards her, and stand between her legs. I put my hands on her hips and pull her suspended body towards me. I push myself into her, feeling her warm, wet pussy envelop me once again. She grips the straps, as if readying herself for the pending impact. And then it comes; I begin to pound into her, smashing my body into hers. The position is perfect, and I penetrate her deeply. She is unable to help much, but I am more than happy to drive. "That's it…bang the fuck out of me" she pleads. I pound and pound and pound her until we are getting red skinned from the impact. I feel her piercing against my groin, and know that I am slapping directly against her exposed clit with each thrust. She is building again, and I continue away at her until she reaches the top. Her hands are gripping the straps and she is straining to buck her hips against me in this position. I stop in a deep thrust, pushing inside her. I grab her hips and pull her into me, probing even deeper. Now she has some leverage, and bucks her hips wildly. I do my best just to hold on, letting her do her thing and get hers. She comes hard again, and after a moment or two of spasms, she collapses in the harness, hanging there limp and spent.

His Eyes

After a moment of silence she finally sighs a contented breath. I however, am ready for more. "Can you ride me in this thing?" I ask. A delighted smile crosses her face and I assume the answer is yes. I help her get out of the straps, and unhook two of them removing them from the contraption. Now it is my turn to sit in the seat. I am basically sitting on it like it's a swing set and she climbs onto me, the top of her feet against my thighs. It's not how I was picturing it, but I figured she probably knows what she is doing. Her hands grab the straps supporting the seat above mine, and she settles herself down onto my stiff rod. The suspension is definitely a different sensation, and is only adding to the excitement of fucking Naomi in the porn shop. This is a fantasy that never even crossed my mind until a few days ago when we were at lunch, and here we are going at it like porn stars. She slowly starts to bounce up and down, and the spring in the swing relaxes and contracts, allowing us a far longer stroke for each move than if we were in bed. It is a little tricky catching onto the rhythm at first, but after a moment or two we are off and running. She is rubbing her tits against my mouth, and I suck her delicate flesh skewered by the metal barbells. She is grinding herself into me at the bottom of each stroke, and loving every sensation coursing through her.

Since I am on the bottom, my motion is a little limited. I am trying to help, but to no avail. It seems like she is getting close again, but she may have to do it all herself this time around. I lean back a little, and the move adds a little depth to each thrust. It's all I can contribute at this point, but she seems perfectly happy to ride me like this some more. Our rhythm increases as she tries harder. Soon we are swinging back and forth and almost banging into the support pipes on the side. I start laughing as does she, and we stop moving, slowly settling back to still. She climbs off of me, and I stand up, only then realizing that my legs feel like they are asleep. My feet are tingling like crazy, and I jump up and down a little to speed the recovery of my legs. She turns and looks at me, wondering what the Hell I am doing. "Just getting ready for more" I assure her. "More, huh? Wait here then 'cause you are wearing me out" she says. She disappears only for a moment, and returns with a bottle of warming lube. She comes over to me with a handful of it, slathering it all over my cock. I am red from the friction of her riding me, and just now notice that we both look like we got rubbed with sandpaper. The warming lube is true to its name, and I can feel the heat growing from everywhere she applied it. It is a nice sensation; not too intense, but certainly noticeable.

"Now what?" I ask. She walks towards the other side of the store, and once again I follow behind. We come to a display with two manikins using something called "The Liberator". It is a foam wedge that tilts you at angles enjoyed in favorite positions. She walks over and shoves the manikins out of the way; they break apart as they fall. I laugh at the scene of the scattered bodies, and at Naomi's bravado. "I want you to fuck my ass" she instructs, and she lies down over the wedge. Her ass is tilted up in the air, waiting for me. I grab the bottle of lube, and squish a small dab into my fingers. I rub my thumb into it, and kneel down behind her. I guide my already lubed cock into her waiting pussy, and go to work on her for a little more. She loves it, and so do I. We fuck like animals; hard, fast and rough. I smack her ass, palm flat, and redden the skin. After a few swipes, I can see distinct finger marks acquired during her "punishment". She has her hands on the floor, pushing back into me as I plow into her, and is groaning in delight. I start to get her ass ready for me; I rub the sensitive skin all around the outside. She moans a little more, enjoying the added element our new adventure.

I push my thumb into the gray skin, it disappears inside her. Her ass is so tight I have no idea how she is going to handle my cock, but she seems to think she can. I have faith in her. I press forward, burying my thumb into her without so much as a hint of warning. She squirms in pleasure; I work it back and forth into her, in opposite timing with how my cock strokes her pussy. I reach for the lube, and squish a little more onto us, dousing the whole area in the clear liquid. I switch to my middle finger, and then quickly add in my index finger as well. She flinches at first, and I know I have to go slow. I decrease my thrusts as well, slowing everything down. She relaxes after a moment or two, and encourages me on. I push and pull, twist and turn as I work her into submission. Soon she is moaning loudly again, pleasure having overtaken the pain. "Are you ready?" I ask her, as I reach for the condom she had grabbed earlier. "Yes, I want you to take my ass. Take me now" she growls at me. Passion has consumed her, and the anticipation of this sinful act has excited her to new heights.

His Eyes

I clamp down on the base of my cock, holding the condom in place. She is so tight and I was lubed up when I put it on, so I know it is going to slide around. I push towards her, and she flinches again at the change in size from my fingers. "It's okay, just go slow at first" she tells me. I push again, and after a few seconds of resistance, I breach the outer circle. I am only in about two inches, and I can feel the tightness fighting against my entry. She breathes a sigh of relief, and must have been holding her breath up until then. "OK, now for the fun part" she says. I guess that she has done this before and knows the routine. I have limited experience in this realm, but am smart enough to know it can't be comfortable at first. I start slowly, my cock easing in and out of her. She still seems to be teetering on the brink of pleasure and pain, but it occurs to me that maybe this is what she really wants. She feels the need to be dominated, almost forced to a certain extent. I had a woman tell me she only gets fucked like this when she needs an attitude adjustment. My mind comes back to present, and I focus on Naomi once again.

After a few moments of forced restrain, she is ready to go. I am now stuffing almost all of it into her, and she loves it. In the tilted position she is in it is difficult for me to really touch her anywhere, so I stop for a second and get my feet under me. I am now in kind of a squatting position above her, and the stiffness of my cock is amplified because of the angle from which I am now entering her. I lean forward and kind of lying on top of her; I place my hands on the floor next to hers. I put my mouth on her ear, biting her almost a little too roughly. "Put your hand underneath you and rub your clit" I say to her in a deep, commanding voice. She moans at my command, and doesn't hesitate to lend a helping hand to bring out one more orgasm before we conclude. "That's it...that's my dirty little whore" I whisper into her ear. I fuck her a little deeper, and I can see by the look on her face that it is almost too much to take. Almost. I can feel her hand working over her clit, and then she slides two fingers into her own pussy. I can feel it inside her, the walls of her pussy barely separating me from her fingers. She works them in and out, as do I, and together we push her to the brink.

Her moans come in rapid succession, and I know we are there. I grab a handful of her hair once more, yanking her head to the side, exposing her face to me. "That's it...jerk yourself off while I fuck your ass! Come all over your own fingers while I fuck your ass" I command.

Finally she can take no more, and explodes into a huge orgasm. Her fingers are moving at a blinding speed, and I thrust deeper than I have up until now. She screams out loud, pleasure and pain coursing through her body as she comes. I pull back a little, and fuck her hard and fast for a few strokes. I was so focused on her I didn't realize how close my own orgasm was. As I started to increase my speed I realize that I too am ready. I go at her fast for about 20 strokes, and know that I am going to explode. I pull out of her, and rip the condom off. I grab my cock in my own frenzy of pleasure, and jerk it faster than I can ever remember. It only takes a few second, and I blow. As soon as I start, I lower myself down, and rub my cock in the groove of her ass cheeks. It is wet and warm, and I explode. I shoot streams of it down her back, the angle making it run right down the middle. "Oh fuck yes...come all over me" Naomi cries out. I was so lost in the moment it sounded like she was across the room, her voice coming from far away. It passes too quickly, and soon I am back to present. I slump forward, bracing myself above her.

We roll over, and for a brief moment neither one of us seem to care that we are on the carpet in the porn shop. The reality sets in before long, and I stand and help her to her feet. She disappears without a word to the bathroom to clean up, and I begin the search for my clothing. I gather up all of our clothes, and head back to the counter where this whole thing started. I slide back into my jeans, the denim a reminder of how sensitive my cock is. I carefully button up the fly, and put on my shirt. She returns, naked as she was a moment ago. She suddenly seems a little self conscious, and I toss Naomi her clothes and turn away slightly while she quickly gets redressed. I am not sure what to say after that, so we stand in silence for a moment or two. "Alright...well, do you want help rebuilding the manikins?" I ask, finally breaking the silence. She laughs, and says she'll get to them tomorrow. After a quick trip to the bathroom myself, I return. We head to the door, and she goes to unlock it. The door was slightly ajar, and she realized that she had not locked it properly when she closed earlier. She looks at me in shock, and we both start laughing out loud when we realize that at any moment someone could have walked in on us. What an amazing night.

Vicki

It is 1:30 in the morning and the lines on the road are starting to blur. We made it to Banning, CA and most of the way to San Diego for our weekend road trip. We can crash here and finish the trip in the morning, I think to myself. I see the sign for a Days Inn from the freeway and jerk the car onto the exit ramp. I barely stop at the bottom of the ramp, and head straight for the parking lot.

As cool as the black 350Z looks on the outside, it is proportionally uncomfortable on the inside. Racing seats and a stiff suspension only enhance every bump and turn in the road, and after several hours in the car it begins to wear on us both. We stand for the first time in hours, and stretch our legs and back. My buddy Louis had been fading in and out of sleep for the past hundred miles, and so we are both glad to be off the road for the night. I am surprised to find it has turned a little cooler than I thought, the t shirt and jeans I am wearing are not doing much to stave off the bite of the night air. I walk towards lobby to arrange a room for the night, and reach for the door. I practically yank my arm out of socket expecting to find the door unlocked but quickly learning to the contrary. It made a loud rattling sound and catches the attention of the person working the night shift at the hotel. She sticks her head around the corner and waves me to the window about 15 feet to my left. I walk over and touch the bullet proof glass window and begin to wonder if maybe I should have driven just a little farther. I turn to look around at the cars in the parking lot and try to decide if we are going to stay or not. I get a whiff of perfume, and turn to find a surprisingly attractive girl standing behind the glass smiling at me.

Her name tag reads Victoria and she seems to be very friendly. I am freezing standing out here and ask "It's cold out here, can I come in to do this?" She hesitates for a moment and then replies "No, I'm sorry, I can't let anyone in after 10:00pm." She smiles at me, and is biting her lower lip a little. As tired as I am, I know a sign when I see one. I am trying to make up some small talk to break the ice, but only come up with "So, do you have room for me tonight?" Yikes...nice going I think, as mentally I kick myself. She laughs a little and comes back to me with "Yes, you can practically sleep right next to me. Room 108 is open and it's only two doors away." I laugh, and now suddenly I think I feel a little heat rising in my face. I can't believe it...she caught me off guard with that. She seems to notice and laughs a little at my expense.

I rebound quickly and fire back with "Well good, I am sure I will feel much better sleeping so close to you." I burn my stare deep into her until she finally gives and glances away. Now it's my turn to smile, a small victory won in the exchange. "You smell incredible" I tell her. She blushes and looks away again. She slides the receipt and the key through the small opening between us in the glass, and I reach down to take it from her. Her hand lingers, and I touch her smooth skin as I pull the paper towards me. She smiles and I return the gesture, finally breaking the stare and turning towards my room for the night. Victoria watches me disappear from sight, and I am left wondering if I should have stayed to talk with her a little longer.

We hit the room and I pick the bed farthest from the door as mine. I toss my stuff on the floor and flop down on the bed. I roll over and pick up the phone, calling the front desk. She answers with a giggle like a little girl. "How can I help you Mr. Michaels" she purrs into the phone. I laugh to myself, and respond "Victoria, please call me Darren." She follows with "In that case, call me Vicki" and the conversation flows from there. I tell her we are on the way to San Diego for the weekend and other details relative to our conversation. She grew up here, and is going to school during the day while she works at night. The freedom at night gives her time to do homework and study and still get paid for working. We are on the phone the whole time Louis is in the shower. He comes out and gives me a strange look, wondering who I am talking to at two in the morning. I mouth the words "front desk girl" to him, and he just rolls his eyes and laughs to himself. "Don't forget the wakeup call" he reminds me, and crawls into his bed. We continue to talk as he fidgets with the TV, doing his usual lap through all the channels. Traveling together as much as we have, I know the routine by now.

After about an hour and a half of our conversation I am growing very tired, and as much as I hate to do it, I am going to have to let Vicki go before I rudely fall asleep mid sentence. I say good night, and ask if she will have breakfast with me in the morning. She laughs and agrees. "Cool, call me at 6:45am and wake me up" "It's a deal...sweet dreams" she purrs into the phone and hangs up. My head hits the pillow as I hang up the phone.

The phone rings and it seems that I was only asleep for a moment. It is Vicki, and she is calling to wake me up. "Doesn't this hotel have the automated service that does this?" I ask groggily. "Yes" is her only reply, followed by silence. In my barely awake stage I almost miss the very obvious hint she is giving me. "Are you coming to my room or should I meet you down there?" I clumsily ask her. She hesitates, and my stomach tightens as I realize my question probably sounded different than I intended. "Um...I can't come there. I'll get in trouble" she says. "No, I meant for breakfast....." I reply, but I can hear her talking to someone while she covers the phone. I fear I have just blown the slim chance I was given. "I have to call you back sir" she says into the phone and hangs up the phone. "Damn it!" I practically yell, rousting Louis from his heavy slumber. "What's wrong?" he asks. But he knows the answer, and laughs as he fires back "Crash and Burn, huh Maverick?" I am slightly annoyed, and snap back with "It's a little early for 80's movie quotes, isn't it?"

We gather up our stuff and prepare to finish our trip to San Diego. I walk out and head towards the lobby to turn in my key, and probably apologize. I see Vicki headed towards her car in the parking lot. "Shit, so much for that" I think to myself. She sees me, and throws her hands up in question. I start walking towards her, and she waves me off. She motions that she is moving her car or something, and I stand there confused. "Go back to your room" she yells to me. I am not really sure what she has in mind, but I break the news to Louis he'll be eating his continental breakfast alone. He is fine with that; we have honored "Guy Code" about this sort of thing for the past 20 years. "Work fast, you have one hour" he says, looking at his watch.

I head back to the room, and slide the key in the door. I drop my stuff just inside and sit on the bed, waiting to see what happens next. I hear a key in the lock, and the door opens and quickly shuts behind her. "I could get in so much trouble for this" she says as she turns to face me. "But you came anyway, didn't you?" I try to say as coolly as possible. Inside I am very nervous, but I try to play it off like this happens to me all the time. She stops and is leaning against the door, seemingly waiting for me to do something. I stand and walk towards her. "You didn't bring me breakfast." I state flatly, smiling a wry smile at her and stopping a few feet from her. "We don't have time for that" she responds, and takes one big step towards me. We meet in an embrace, and I continue to move forward until I push her against the door. She is shorter than I am even though she is wearing platform style sandals. I just realized this is my first real look at her as a whole, and I am pleasantly surprised to see just how rocking her body is. Vicki is Spanish and very dark skinned, with light brown eyes and jet black hair that frames her cute face. She is wearing skin tight jeans and a frilly semi low cut shirt that shows just enough cleavage to make you wonder how much more there is. The scent of her perfume hits me again as I lean down to kiss her. I drop my hands down to her ass, and lift her up, pressing her against the door as we devour each other in our first kiss. There is nothing nice about it; it is pure desire.

I smash her against the door, grinding into her as she wraps her legs around me. Her hips buck into me, and she bangs her head on the door as she tosses in back in response to my teeth on her neck. Her arms wrap around me, and her hand finds the back of my head. Her touch encourages me, and I continue to travel downward. My tongue finds the junction between her neck and her shoulder, and marks the spot for my teeth to follow. I sink my teeth into her flesh and her moan echoes through the room. I feel the raspiness of her voice vibrate in her throat as she pulls me into her, wanting, needing more. I bite and chomp on her, changing spots frequently. My arms are growing tired and in one last burst of energy I pick her up and turn, walking to the bed farthest from the door. I reach down and rip the comforter off the bed, sitting her down on the edge. I stand in front of her; looking deep into her eyes, and begin to undress. I pull my shirt over my head, and absorb the look on her face as her eyes travel over me. I reach for my belt, and pull the leather strap to the side and then slowly remove it from the loops in my jeans. I kick off my shoes, growing harder by the second as she sits on the bed, watching me.

I open the top button of my jeans, and look at her. She gets the hint in hurry, and slides to her knees in front of me. Her hands are on the buttons, but stops to rub me through the denim. I catch myself letting a deep moan escape my lips as she presses my hardness against me. In one quick move she yanks the buttons apart and I fall out in front of her. Her eyes widen for the briefest of moments, and I love her for placating me as every man secretly desires. She grabs the base of it, and slowly extends her tongue out of her mouth. She is looking up at me, and I realize she is returning the favor of teasing me like I did to her.

Finally her mouth is on me; her silken tongue rolling around the tip. My mouth drops open and my eyes shut tightly for a moment. The sensation is amazing; especially after the sweet denial she put me through for what seemed like several moments. Vicki looks up at me as she leans forward, engulfing as much of it as she can. She takes it deep into her throat, holding it there. She pulls away, reloads and dives again. Time and time again she bangs her nose into my stomach, never flinching even for a second. Stops for a second, looking up at me, surveying my face to see how much I am enjoying it. I think my look says it all. She goes back at it, and it seems to me she has not lost a bit of enthusiasm. Her hand begins to slide up and down as her mouth follows. Her hand twists and turns and her tongue rolls and caresses. The feeling is amazing and I am suddenly wishing I had more than an hour of time.

On the other hand, I am ready to move forward, and begin that process by reaching down and grabbing the bottom of her shirt. Lifting her arms above her head she makes sure my cock never leaves her mouth until the shirt touches her chin. Vicki dives back after it right away, and picks up the pace. Her own excitement now increasing, she reaches around and unclips her bra, freeing her small perky breasts. They are perfect, and I reach down to cup them in my hands. She moans into my flesh at my touch. She struggles with her jeans, trying not to interrupt her task but not impede our progress either. Finally she relents, standing up and tearing off her shoes and then her pants. She stands in front of me in nothing but a black thong; her bronze skin practically glowing in the morning light which peeks through the heavy hotel curtains. I lean over and help her to her feet, picking her up in my arms again. I hold her against my body, chest to chest, in mid air. She feels it poke into her wet softness, and wants it inside as much as I do. She reaches back and pulls the thong to the side, guiding me inside her moist depths. Her legs are wrapped tightly around me, making it hard for her to move. I tell her to put her feet on the bed, and then the real fun begins. We are standing in the middle of the room, my back to the foot of the bed; her arms around my neck, her feet on the mattress. I put my hands under her ass, and begin to slowly lift her up and down. She tosses her head back again, her moans vibrating in her chest. God she feels so good.

I slowly begin to increase our pace as we fuck like this for several minutes. My fingers sink into the fleshy globes of her ass, and she bucks her hips up and down as she grows close to her first orgasm. Her breathing quickens, her moans become more frequent and much louder. She begins to tilt her hips into me with each stroke, rubbing her clit against my hard stomach as she travels my length. I feel me hitting bottom inside her, filling her up as we go. Her hips buck wildly, and she jams herself down onto it. That seemed to do the trick; she goes crazy with pleasure. Vicki gasps aloud and grips me tightly as it begins. She bucks wildly in my arms and I do my best to hold her against me. Struggling against me only seems to further excite her, and she growls and groans as she fights to move. Her orgasm seems to come in small intense bursts, coinciding with the motion of her hips. She quivers and shakes as it subsides, and I feel her grip on me loosen. I spin around and drop her on the bed, just in time as she goes limp from her climax.

I stand there looking down at her. Her eyes are half closed as she looks up at me. She brushes the hair from her eyes, and starts working her way towards the top of the bed. I walk around the side, and meet her there. She rolls over onto her side, staring at my cock which is right in front of her. She takes it in her mouth again, and I moan loudly. I am twice as sensitive as before after being inside her, and it is almost too much to take...almost. I grab a good handful of hair and tilt her head to the side. I slowly start to move my hips, fucking her mouth. I am careful not to go too deep, remembering how she gagged. I stroke it in and out of her soft, wet mouth indulgently. She jams it into her cheek, rolling her tongue all around it. The better it feels the more I want. The more I want, the deeper I push, testing her resolve. She takes it in, accommodating me for the moment. I try to control my desire, and the speed of my hips. I feel the pressure inside my groin building, and I know I need a moment to recover my composure. I pull away from her; she rolls with me, trying to keep it in her mouth. She puts her hand on my ass and tries to hold me there. "No...don't" I fight to tell her. "I don't want to be done yet" I manage to spit out. She releases me, and looks up at me smiling, and asks "There's more?" "Fuck yeah there's more. Roll over" I command.

I climb onto the bed, taking position behind her. I roughly grab her hips, ready to pound an apology out of her for doubting my stamina. I yank her back into me, stuffing my cock deep into her in one stroke. I put one foot up on the mattress, giving my hips even more range of motion. I increase my grip and slam into her, slapping my thighs into her beautiful ass. She cries out in surprise, my cock cleaving her fleshy folds. I grab her hair and firmly pull her head back, forcing her to arch her back even more. I press forward, probing, stretching, testing her depths. The pressure deep inside her takes her breath away, and after several moments she finally exhales a long overdue breath. It ends in a deep moan of pleasure, and I feel it rattle all through her body. I release my grip in her, and resume my rhythmic strokes in and out of her sopping hole. Vicki collapses forward, ass in the air, chest and face on the mattress. I pound away at her; relentless, fucking her into submission. She grips the sheets, stretching her arms out in front of her, fighting to hold her position on the bed. I cross my arms, holding her ass cheeks in opposite hands. I bang into her body, loving each and every stroke of my cock into her hot, slippery flesh.

I hear my cell phone vibrate in my pants pocket on the floor. "I'm sure Louis will understand" I think to myself. I want just a little more before we conclude this adventure. I withdraw from her, looking down to see it slide out of her. I crawl forward and flop down on the bed next to her, looking over at her. Her hair is covering her face, and I laugh at the disheveled mess I have made her. "I can't move" she says. I laugh a little louder, following it with "Guess again sweetheart, it's your turn to drive." She chuckles a bit and manages to throw an arm over my body. She slowly crawls on top of me, her skin hot against mine. She gets her body onto mine with what seems to be genuine effort, and melts into me. I feel her weight settle onto me, and can feel the heat from her pussy right over top of my cock, just out of reach. I put my arm around her waist, and brush her hair aside so I can see her face. She has that fantastically sexy, sleepy look in her eyes, letting me know it has been good for her. "My work here is almost done" I think to myself. I run my fingers through her hair, settling my hand against the back of her head. I grab her hair again, this time more gently, just enough to turn her head to gain access to her lips. I kiss her deeply, and she moans deeply once again. Or maybe it was me this time.

Her body responds, and she slowly grinds against me. I want to be inside her once more, and I put my free hand on her hip to push her downward. My cock penetrates her soft folds once again, this time with a different intent. I am moving slowly, we are moving together. We have switched from fucking in fifth gear to grinding slowly, almost making love, in second gear. It is different, but no less sexy and erotic. In fact it may be even sexier this way. I feel every part of her with my slow pace, savoring every inch of her entire body instead of all of the focus being solely on one part of me. We kiss and caress one another, grinding our bodies into one molten pile of flesh.

I can feel her hips begin to grind a little harder into me, the downward pressure into me increasing. I am getting close too, but want to make sure she gets one more before I let go. I pull back mentally, somehow holding the reins on my own release. It is a difficult to describe, other than to say it is a feeling that internally I am "puckering" for lack of a better term. I have learned through years of practice to do this for whatever length of time is necessary, but I don't think today will require more than a few minutes of restrain. She puts her hands on my face, holding me as she picks up the pace just a little more. She pulls away from my mouth and sits up, planting her hands on my chest. Her perky breasts glisten from the sweat our friction generated. I reach up and cup them, pinching her nipples a little before squeezing her tits together. I sit up under her, and she wraps her arms around the back of my head, pulling my face into her softest of flesh. My tongue chases back and forth after them, licking and stroking her rosebud nipples. I can taste the salt of our skin on them. She shudders and sighs as her hips shift gears once more.

We are so sweaty from our ride she is easily gliding back and forth on top of my thighs. I can hear her breathing roughen, and the words "Oh yes...Oh God yes" escaping her lips. She is now practically doing stomach crunches on top of me, her clit smashing into my lower abs. I keep them tight so she can get the desired affect; and she takes full advantage. Suddenly she grabs my face and leans down to kiss me, feverishly burying her tongue in my mouth. We kiss harder now than we did at the start of this adventure, climbing towards our own peaks together. Vicki goes first, her hips locking in place, paralyzed by the explosion inside. Moans escape between wet kisses, and then the waves begin. She spasms on top of me, her orgasm once again coming in short, intense bursts. Her pussy clamps down on me, and the feeling intensifies. I had been paying so much attention to her that I realized too late that I was no longer reining in my own release. Now it is me who is moaning aloud.

Just as hers is subsiding, mine begins to rise. "Oh yes...come for me baby!" she whispers to me. "Where do you want it?" I ask, hoping she will answer quickly. "On my stomach, I want to see it, I want to feel you come" she says louder this time. I lean back, putting my hands behind me on the bed. I squeeze my hips about three times and that is all it takes. The feelings start separately, one wave in my head and one at my feet. The waves of pleasure travel through me quickly, and converge in the middle of my body. She grabs my cock, squeezing hard and jerking it firmly. The waves crash over me, and I pull out of her just in time. I shoot stream after hot stream of it out of me and onto her. The feeling is so intense; I have tunnel vision and the world fades away for the briefest of moments. It is over too quickly, and I am back cognizant after only a few seconds. I fall backwards onto the bed and she follows suit, lying on top of me.

I am breathing hard, and feel her rise and fall in time with my breath. She is limp once again, putty in my hands. I look at the clock and know that any moment I am going to have an angry friend banging on the door of the hotel room. I roll her onto her side, and lay next to her for a moment. She must have been able to see it in my eyes. "You have to leave, don't you?" she says softly. "I'm sorry, but I do" I regretfully inform her. "It's OK, I knew that before I came here." I lean into her, kissing her tenderly for the first time today. She kisses me a long, lingering kiss back. And then it was over; I headed for the shower and she began to gather her scattered clothes. I showered quickly, and when I came out she was already half way out the door. "Hey..." I searched for something to say. "Goodbye Victoria......I am glad we met." She smiled, put on her sunglasses, and walked out the door, shutting it behind her. She never said a word.

Meghan

When I began to write my first book, I was not sure where this project would lead. As it grew and began to take on a life of its own, I found myself trying to stretch myself as a writer and really delve into things in an effort to bring the most intimate detail and experiences that I could share. But this was not something I ever thought I would do.

I was invited to do a book signing at a swinger's party that was being held in a very upscale nightclub in Scottsdale, AZ. I have always had a morbid fascination with the whole swinger concept, like the overused analogy of driving passed an auto accident. I just can't wrap my head around the idea of watching someone you are in a relationship with having sex with someone else. Sure, I have the prototypical guy fantasies of a girl I am dating showing up at my house with a female friend to live out a fantasy that we all three share. But the two guys and a girl thing seemed to be something I would swear up and down I would never participate in when it would come up in casual conversation. Yes, maybe that makes me a hypocrite, but I can live with that. We all have our limits. But I guess you should never say never....

I arrive at the club at 9:00pm as instructed by the host and carry a case of books in the door with me. I ask where he wants me to set up and he tells me "wherever you like." I pick a booth in the corner next to the bar, figuring that will be a fairly high traffic zone. I am nervous about this whole thing; I have no clue what this crowd is going to be like, or if I will be walking into an all out orgy in a public venue. I was told it was a "Private Party", but I don't really know what that means. I sit with my back to the wall so I can keep an eye on everything, for better or worse. The waitress comes over and asks if she can bring me anything, and I answer "Yes, a bottle of water...unopened, please." The depths of my own paranoia surprise even me sometimes. Better safe than sorry I guess, but my request made me laugh to myself. "What the Hell am I doing here" keeps rolling around in my head.

About an hour into this event I am starting to relax and even have a little fun. I am always a little nervous in a crowd of people, but I am selling lots of books and signing autographs and seemingly a focal point of the proceedings so far. My ego likes it...a lot. I must admit that I am

117

pleasantly surprised at the crowd itself. The ballroom is littered with members of the 40 and under Scottsdale crowd; slim, fit, tanned girls with fake boobs and veneers, and their spiky-haired, fake Rolex wearing, Ed Hardy adorned douche bag boyfriends. I was anticipating a much less attractive bunch to show up here, but I guess the rumors about the city of Scottsdale ordinance against ugly people is actually true. And then she walked over to the table.

She is easily the hottest woman here, and one of the prettiest faces I have seen in a long, long time. I look up from the table and she is standing there holding one of my books in her hands. "You wrote this?" she asks. "Yes I did" I say to her with a wry smile. "Oh my God, I bought this book like a month ago off Amazon, and I even wrote a review about it! I am JustMeg2008. Oh my God, I can't believe you're here!" Her words grew faster and her voice higher as she went. "I'm Meghan" she says, extending her hand. I shake hands with her, and look up to meet her eyes. She reminds me of Jennifer Aniston but with eyes that are pale blue and piercing. She is burning holes in me with them. I glance at her ring finger, and see a huge flashy diamond that practically screams "I am TAKEN, and taken care of" all on its own. "So, what did you think of the book?" I ask her. "You may have the sexiest mind in the business. I *love* your book" she states flatly. I practically burst out laughing; even my ego has its limits. "Well, I think that is a gross over-statement, but I appreciate it either way" I inform her. "No, seriously...the way you write both sides of the story, I mean...how do you do that? How do you write women so well?" I am tempted by the opportunity to throw out the classic line delivered by Jack Nicholson in the movie As Good as it Gets when his character is asked the same question by a fan and he responds "I think of a man, and then take away logic and reason."

I decide to let the opportunity to look like an arrogant ass slip by. "I have always been a very sensual person, so I try to expand on those feelings and picture what I think the woman in the story is thinking and feeling. Maybe I just end up with what I would want her to be thinking...I don't know" I catch myself flip-flopping from egomaniac to a flashback of an insecure and awkward teenager. "It's like you were in my head" she says, smiling and looking a little star-struck, much to my delight. I catch the scent of her perfume wafting my direction; it is lovely, and fits her well. This is so weird to me; here I am hoping that a few people would want to buy my book after looking at it at this party. Now I have one of the most beautiful women I have ever laid eyes on staring at me like she wants to take me home with her. I know she is married, and maybe even here with her husband. They are obviously swingers...what the Hell am I doing here?

A few other people are in line, and I look to see the next person growing a little impatient. She turns and sees the other people, realizing she is monopolizing my time. "Oh, I'm sorry, I will come back later" she says and turns to walk away. I am caught watching her leave; the curves of her body disappearing into the dark surroundings of the club. I engage the next person, and sign his book, followed by others. I am glad that I am selling books and this did not turn out to be a waste of time, but on the other hand I really wanted to talk with Meghan some more. The image of her face burned in my brain and as if the music wasn't making things difficult enough, now I wasn't really paying attention to what the others were saying to me. I do my best to focus and attend to the people who are gracious enough to buy my book.

After about an hour later the novelty of me seems to have worn off and no one is paying any attention to me sitting in the corner by the bar. All attention is focused on the show that is beginning to take shape on the dance floor. A stripper pole in now firmly planted in the middle of the ballroom, and a few brave souls fortified by some liquid courage are starting to flash some skin while dancing. Some clothing is starting to get removed and the girls in the middle of the circle of people are making out rather heavily. It is quite the spectacle, and I am nervously watching the proceedings. I am not sure where this is going to get cut off, or if this will be the start of people pairing off and heading for the couches lining the perimeter of our private little haven. I see Meghan dancing on the other side of the room; she is looking my direction. I wonder how long she has been watching me. I had lost sight of her while signing books, and managed to push the thought of her to the back of my mind. Now that I am an afterthought to the group I find myself with plenty of time on my hands to be able to sit and wonder about her. In just a few moments time several different guys and girls have tried to dance with her, all to be politely rebuffed. She looks at me and motions for me to join her on the dance floor, but I shake my head. I do not dance, and the last thing I want to do is show her just how true that is.

I don't want her to think that I am not interested in her, so I motion for her to come my way. If she had not already shown some interest in me there in no way I would even think of trying to get a woman like this come to me. But I am not going onto the dance floor, this I know for sure. I glance downward, a little shy about the stare she is sending my way, hoping to indicate that I am out of my element here. I look up to find her walking through the crowd right towards me. I smile at her as she approaches. "Dance with me?" she asks. "Oh I can't...I don't dance" I tell her, once again kicking myself for never learning how. "Oh come on, you can't be that bad" she fires back with a sexy smile, biting her lip slightly. "Seriously, I don't have any rhythm unless I am lying down" I inform her, trying to make light of the situation. "Come on" she says, rolling her eyes at me. She grabs my hand and leads me to the dance floor. I am not happy about this, but I find it hard to believe that I am going to turn this woman down.

She leads me to an open spot on the floor and turns to face me. "I don't dance" I tell her once again, feeling like all eyes are on me. "No one is watching" she says, trying to reassure me. "Meghan...everyone is watching you" I offer, contradicting her last statement. "Close your eyes, put your hands on my hips, and feel me move. Just follow my hips." "Sounds easy enough" I thought to myself, and suddenly seem willing to at least give it a try. Always a sucker for a beautiful woman and her demands. I keep my eyes open slightly, watching her feet, trying to be careful and not step on them. I am awkward and stiff at first, and am blatantly aware that I have no rhythm whatsoever. I try to relax and follow her, but it is tough for me. The music is too fast and I can't keep up. She seems to sense my dilemma and waves to the DJ, making a motion to him to slow things down a little.

The next tune is a fair amount slower, and she looks into my eyes. "Just follow my hips" she says, wrapping her arms around my neck. I put my hands on her hips, closing my eyes this time. I focus on her movements; reacting, following, feeling her body move to the music. I concentrate on my center, feeling the music vibrating through me, ringing in my ears. I open my eyes to find Meghan looking at me and smiling. She says to me "I love your book. I have read each story several times, and loved every bit of them. I so wanted to meet the man behind the words, and here you are." "Did you envision me as this bad of a dancer?" I ask jokingly. "I am not sure what I was picturing, but I like what I see" she confesses. She is neither bold nor shy, somehow striking a balance in between. Her words are firm yet unassuming. I have to assume she has been here before, and I begin to wonder if I am going to be able to handle an adventure in this uncharted territory. She leans forward, her lips brushing against my ear. Her hair smells amazing, and I drink in the delicious scent. "Kiss me" she says, and pulls away to face me once again. I stop moving, suddenly frozen by her words.

"Is he here?" I ask, wondering about her husband. "Yes, he is watching. He knows I want you, that I picked you" she whispers to me. "So it's OK?...I have never done..." my thought trails off as she leans towards me. "God she is beautiful" I think to myself, and lay the best kiss I can conjure up on her. She stops moving, her body closing the gap between us. She leans against me, those delightful curves firmly pressing against me. I put my hand behind her head, pulling her mouth into mine as we linger in a soft and delicious kiss in the corner of the dance floor. After a moment I realize that I can no longer hear the music, and that realization snaps me back into reality. Suddenly I am present again, back from wherever I had drifted to. I stand there looking at her, searching her eyes for some clue as to what I should do next. Lucky for me, she grabs my hand and leads me off the dance floor.

We sit down at a table, ordering drinks as soon as the waitress comes by. We sit and chat for a while, learning a little about one another. Finally I can't take it anymore and have to ask a question that has been on my mind since I walked in here. "So...how did you get into this, um, lifestyle?" I was dying to hear her answer, I think. I braced myself for something I had not considered, hoping that she wasn't going to say something I just couldn't handle. "The man I married was into this sort of thing before we met. He was honest enough to discuss it while we were dating, and I have always had a wild side trapped inside me. I had a close girl friend who I found out had an interest in me, and so one night when my husband was out of town we had a few drinks and she walked me through that door. It was wonderful, and I wanted more. So we began seeing each other when we could until I finally asked her if he could join us. She agreed, and the three of us had an ongoing relationship for about two years until she moved away. After that we decided to explore our own sexual fantasies together and eventually we ended up at one of these parties" she shares with me. "So do you do this sort of thing all the time?" I inquire, hoping the answer is no. "Oh no, we rarely do this. We decided to have a little fun this weekend, that's all. It keeps our marriage interesting, you know...sexually."

"Well, I have never known a swinger to my knowledge, nor been to a party like this. What usually happens here?" I ask. She tells me "For the most part it is just a place to meet people, and then if you find a person or couple you like you invite them to a hotel room or to you place. We never have anyone at our house, just to be safe." "OK, now for the real pressing question. How do you learn to deal with watching your husband having sex with someone else?" I ask, hoping to gain some understanding on all of this. "Deal with? No, you are looking at this the wrong way. We are not in an open relationship; we are sharing the experience with each other. It is about us sharing someone for our pleasure and fun, so it is a mutual desire, not something to put up with until it is the other person's turn" she tells me. I am not sure that was enough information to convince me, but it did change my perception a little bit. "So where is your husband anyway?" I ask. I am curious to see this guy, and how he landed such a beautiful and confident woman. "He is the guy in the black shirt at the bar, talking to the pretty Asian woman" she says, kind of motioning with a nod so as not be too obvious. I slowly turn around to look, and he looks right at me. I suddenly feel guilty, or like I got busted talking to another man's wife. Then he did something I did not expect; he smiled, and lifted his beer as if to say hello and what I am doing is okay. It is hard to describe, but it was just the feeling I got.

"So how do you decide who, I mean which one of you chooses someone?" I ask, wishing I would have thought that questions through a little better first. She smiles and says "I always choose; sometimes it's a man, sometimes a woman, sometimes another couple. It is really about who I want us to share, because as a woman I have to feel comfortable with who I am going to be with. He is a little more flexible about that than I am. So I am the 'screener' as we call it; I find someone I may like and get to know them a little, and decide where we go from here." I was getting insight into a world I never knew, and am still wavering on whether or not I want to know more. Feeling a little bold, I ask "So, am I getting screened right now?" She laughs a little, and tells me "Yes, but you seem a little nervous about all of this, so I am not sure it is going to work out." I am crushed; I feel such an empty feeling inside. "No, no...I want to know what it is like" The words practically spewed out of me. I caught myself, surprised at my reaction, my willingness to press forward. We sat in agonizing silence for a moment until she finally broke it with "OK, we'll see how things go. I really want it to be you; I feel like we have a connection already. While reading your stories, I would touch myself and try to picture what you look like. I never imagined this might actually come true, that I could actually have you. I am getting slippery just thinking about it."

Wow, this is so surreal, I thought. I am sitting in a nightclub watching half naked people dance while talking to a beautiful woman about going home with her and her husband...What the Hell am I doing here? We sit and chat for a while longer, getting more comfortable with one another. My stomach is no longer feeling tight, and I am enjoying just sitting and talking with Meghan. I notice she looks up, and find him standing behind me. I stand quickly, extending my hand. He shakes it, and motions for me to sit down. "We loved your book, and I figured you would be the one" he tells me. I stammer for something to say. "I take it you're new to this?" he says, half laughing at me suddenly looking nervous again. "Uh, yeah, you could say that" I admit. He smiles, and places what seems to me to be a condescending hand on my shoulder. "It'll be fun, just try and relax and you'll be fine" he coaches me. Now all of the sudden I am not so sure about any of this. Can I really do this? Can I be in the same room with another man while I am with Meghan, let alone actually sharing someone, especially someone who is his wife? "Oh John, quit it...you're going to scare him off. Go play, I'll let you know when I am ready to leave" she tells him. I am nervous all over again. I look Jonathan over; he is about six feet tall, broad shoulders and his tight shirt reveals just about every muscle he obviously works at to keep so fit. I feel a wave of inferiority crash over me; this guy is better looking and way bigger than I am...what would she want with me?

I try to put him out of my mind as Meghan and I sit and talk some more. She is sipping a tall shot of very expensive tequila, and I ask her about it. "Here, try it" she says, pushing it towards me. I hesitate at first, but decide if I am going to do this, I had better start showing a little trust. I take the shot glass in my hand, and like the feel of it. It is heavy, and for some strange reason I feel cool just having it in front of me. I take a small sip, testing it. It is surprisingly smooth, and finishes with an almost smoky aftertaste. "Wow, how interesting" I conclude. She waves at the waitress, and before long two more are delivered to us. Seems that even women jump to Meghan's commands. I fiddle with my own shot glass, and find the contents to be going down rather quickly. I order two more before even thinking about the fact that I rarely if ever drink. I had better pace myself if I have any hope of making it through tonight.

About an hour later I can no longer feel my teeth. I am too buzzed to drive, but I haven't changed my mind about the fact that I can't dance, so I am probably at a comfortable stage of numb. I see eight empty shot glasses in pyramid formation on our table, but only remember drinking three of them. I hope that Meghan was responsible for a five to three ratio and that I am still coherent enough to remember that correctly. I glance at my watch; it is about 1:30AM and I have been here far longer than I had ever planned on. Staring into the eyes of a beautiful woman does tend to make me forget details like that. I am curious if I have passed Meghan's screening process enough for stage two...whatever that may be. I smile inside realizing that internally I just agreed to possibly break my own rule.

The party is in full groove at this point, but nothing too raunchy like some of my friends were speculating I would see. I may have missed a few things since I am fully engrossed in my conversation with Meghan. She turns out to be well educated, well traveled and quite the humanitarian. Two years in the Peace Corps has taught her what to really value in life and the self discipline necessary to be successful. She owns her own business, and yet travels six weeks a year for her own mental wellness as she calls it. It still seems like such a dichotomy that this woman is here at this party, doing something that I consider so out of the norm. I may be coming to realize my own rigid view of the world is not the only path to be followed. Am I trying to convince myself to break my own rules just because of her, or am I on the verge of an actual shift in my perception of the world I live. Wow...I must have had a little too much to drink. I am trying to turn compromising my ideals so I can have sex with a beautiful woman into a perceptual shift of consciousness. My flair for the dramatic is running rampant once again.

The next thing I know the three of us are sitting in a cab headed for the hotel. The world seems to smear a little if I turn my head too fast, and I conclude that I have had too much to drink. I am thinking this is happening faster than I want, but if I am actually going to do this I surmise that I can't analyze anything and just go with it. For some strange reason I find myself trusting Meghan; maybe it's my overwhelming desire for her that is clouding my judgment. That coupled with several shots of tequila could probably do the trick. I am glad the remorse gene generally skips most men, and I am even gladder that I am one of them. If this goes badly or I get too uncomfortable, I will just leave. I always have that safety valve...I can walk away if I want. OK, deep breath...exhale. I look over to find Jonathan's hand on Meghan's thigh and a flash of jealousy and possessiveness rips through me. I laugh to myself, realizing my reaction was not only ridiculous but also backwards. I am not going to be able to do this.

The cab slows, and we all pile out in front of the hotel. The short ride did little to sober me up, and I feel like I am wobbly while I walk into the lobby. "If this goes bad, I can walk" I remind myself as we enter the elevator. Meghan leans over and purrs into my ear "Mmm...God I want you." I look into the shiny gold door and see Jonathan's reflection as he watches his wife whisper in my ear. "What the Hell am I doing here?" flashes through my mind again. He looks even bigger now that we are standing side by side. It is not helping my confidence any. If he has a huge cock to top it off, I am outta here. I hear the elevator ding, and the car comes to a stop. "Go to the bar and have one more drink" Meghan turns and says to Jonathan. She grabs my arm, interlocking her elbow with mine and we head for the room at the end of the hall.

My brain is screaming "RUN" but my body is walking down the hall. I am so nervous, I am not even sure I can...well, you know...do this. But I must admit that part of me really does want to push forward, to see what happens. Meghan and I reach the door, and she turns and smiles at me. "Last chance" she says teasing me. I laugh, and I reach out to touch her face. Her skin is as smooth as it looks, and I cradle her face in my hand as I lean in to kiss her. We end up pressed against the door, kissing each other feverishly. Suddenly I am swept up in the moment, oblivious to anything around me other than the feel of Meghan's tongue in my mouth. We kiss hard and long, and gently jockey for position against the door. She feels for the card slot, and inserts the key without ever breaking her kiss. The door opens and she pulls away from me, following the door into the room. I stand in the doorway looking at her. I know this is the point of no return, and, to my surprise, I step over the door jamb without a moment's hesitation. I am in, literally and figuratively speaking.

She smiles, knowing that I am game. Meghan comes to me, shutting the door behind us. Pushing me back against the door, she kisses me once again. She purrs in my ear once again "Oh God I want you! I have been dreaming of this moment for a month, and I can't believe this is going to happen." Her hands are all over me; grabbing me, feeling me through my clothes. I put my hands on her stomach, and slowly slide them upward until I am lifting and squeezing her deliciously firm, full breasts in my hands. She lets out a moan as she breaks from my mouth, and her tongue travels down my neck. She nibbles and kisses my neck as I continue to squeeze and knead her breasts in my hands. I taste her skin, and feel the slightest sting of salt on my tongue. I guess she really was glistening on the dance floor and it was not my imagination. It is not a turn off...far from it. I look forward to tasting more of her soon. I pinch her nipples through the sheer fabric of her dress and the slight padding of her bra. She reaches back and unhooks it through her dress, and I carefully reach inside the shoulders and pull the dress down to her waist in one quick move. She is naked from the waist up, her bra falling down in front of her. I stare at her in amazement of her exquisite beauty. She is perfect, and I want her. It is dark in the hotel room except for the light in the bathroom, and it silhouettes her in front of me.

"Take them in your mouth" she tells me, and I jump at the offer. I cup one gently, lifting it to meet my extended tongue. I touch it gently, adding the slightest bit of moisture to her nipple. It is bulging with excitement, and seems to beckon my mouth. I swirl my tongue around it once more before I engulf as much of her soft flesh as I can. She tosses her had back, grabbing me by the back of my neck as if to keep herself from going over backwards. I clamp the tender, rigid flesh between my teeth; gently at first, but slowly adding to the amount of pressure until I think I have hit her limit. I switch to the other, and travel back and forth between the two for several moments, enjoying them both. I pull her back to a standing position, and we kiss once again. She grabs my hand, and spins away from me. She leans back into me, and I kiss her neck. I squeeze her breasts again, smashing them into her. Her ass grinds me like on the dance floor. I was too focused on trying to keep up with her to enjoy the pressure of her body against mine then, but now is a different story. She can feel me rising, and changes to sliding up and down against it. I run my hands all over her, feeling every inch I can reach.

After another moment or two of the heavy petting and grinding, she breaks free and heads towards the bathroom. I stand in place, not really sure what I should be doing next. Then I hear water running. I see her dress land in the middle of the floor, and figure that is an invitation to join her. I walk towards the light of the bathroom, and find her with her back to me, completely naked. I look her over before she realizes I am there. She looks back over her shoulder and then slides the door open and steps in. I begin to undress, expecting to continue the fun in the shower. She is already lathered up by the time I get there, and she rinses off quickly and steps out of my way. I get under the water and do the same, assuming this is the proper thing to do before a threesome. Damn...I had almost forgotten about him. I had lived the last few moments of my life thinking that it was just the two of us. I turn the water off and reach for a towel. I dry off quickly and wrap the towel around my waist before venturing out of the bathroom. I wander out to find Meghan standing next to the bed. I walk over to meet her and kiss her once again. She has her towel wrapped around her the way women do, and I pull the tuck from in between her breasts and it falls to the floor. She stands before me naked as the day she was born, and I allow my eyes to travel up and down her body in a long, lingering look. I smile once again at her amazing beauty.

"My turn" she tells me, reaching for my towel. I grab her hand in a moment of shyness, pulling her towards me. We kiss once again, and I can feel the rush of heat rush to my groin. I am growing thicker by the moment, and so I pull from her mouth and step back. She reaches for me again, and this time she reaches her goal. Tugging at the towel, she frees me from the cheap terrycloth confines. My cock surges forward, wanting her attention immediately. I am aching for her to touch me, and she does. I almost shudder as her hand runs up and down the length of my swollen cock. She explores it, running her fingers over the tip and the cut of my circumcised flesh. She kisses my chest, and slowly works her way down my stomach. Her chin brushes against it, and I am so hard it feels like I have run out of skin. Finally, after what seems like an agonizing wait, her mouth settles over my cock. I feel like I am going to explode almost instantly, but catch myself and mentally step away from the edge. She starts slow, running her tongue underneath and around the bottom. It feels incredible, and I put my hand behind her head, encouraging her for more. She takes it deep, smashing her nose against my stomach and making herself gag in response. "You are so hard" she moans between mouthfuls of me. Meghan goes back down again, this time pulling away quickly before reacting to it touches the back of her throat. She repeats the process, going over the full length each time, down to the bottom and back up. My buzz is wearing a little thin and I am cognizant of every single sensation she is creating in me.

I reach down and feel the smooth, creamy skin of her breasts again. She groans in approval as I pinch her nipples once again. I squeeze her soft flesh, feeling them give under my hands. She increases her speed, sucking me more and more furiously with each passing moment. I have to make her stop soon or I will not last much longer. I think she can sense my dilemma, and she stands and turns to the bed. Pulling the covers back, we climb into bed. The sheets feel cool against my skin as we settle into them. We kiss and touch one another some more, enjoying the moment together just a little longer. A thought crosses my mind. I am waiting for Jonathan's grand entrance, mainly to see my reaction to it. I am not sure what to expect, and at this moment I can honestly say I have no idea what I am going to do when that moment arrives. Until then, I am enjoying my time with Meghan.

She climbs on top of me, and I am hesitant for a second. I start to say something, but she beats me to it. "Don't go inside me just yet, I want to taste you again." She spins around and settles down on top of me, allowing me access to free pussy for the first time. I put my hands on her ass, and I dive in. She is shaved slick and wet from the activity so far. I flick my tongue over her clit; it seems to be straining with excitement. I gently suck it into my mouth, and she jams my cock into hers in response. She is moaning loudly with me in her mouth, and the sensation is incredible. Her moans reverberate down through me. She begins to buck her hips against my face, and I can tell she is going to cum quickly. Meghan pulls her mouth away from me, and the room begins to echo with her cries of ecstasy. I shove two fingers into her, and I suck her clit as I move in unison with her. She releases, her whole body shuddering as she comes. I hear a voice from the corner of the room. "That-a girl...let it out" he says. It's Jonathan; he had been sitting in the corner the whole time. He must have come in while we were in the shower, and he has been watching us the whole time. A sense of panic runs through me as I realize that he has been in the room watching us, watching me fuck his wife. He stands up out the chair in the corner. I can barely see around Meghan, but I am searching for him, trying to locate where he is, to read his intentions. She sits up, sliding down onto my stomach and I can see him. He is naked, and walking towards the bed.

"Having a good time, dear?" he asks in his raspy masculine voice. "Oh God yes...he is wonderful" she says. "Come over here and get on the bed" she adds. I am ready to freak out, but before I can even protest she grabs my cock and plants herself down onto it. She takes it all the way in, and is grinding herself against the root of it. Jonathan walks over to the bed and, much to my temporary relief, climbs up and is standing on the bed in front of her. Jesus...his cock is huge. She grabs it at the base, squeezing it. It looks like her hand barely reaches around his girth, and I am feeling very inadequate all of the sudden. She looks back over her shoulder at me quickly, a devilishly sexy grin on her face. Somehow I find encouragement in her look, knowing that she is enjoying me as well. I grab her hips, and she tosses her head back for a moment before leaning forward and going to work on him. She keeps perfect timing with her hips, assisted by my grip on her. I raise and lower underneath her; she moans, a mouthful of cock muffling her noises. The scene is something right out of a porn movie; Jonathan is standing on the bed looking down at us while Meghan rides me. What the Hell am I doing here?

She feels so good sliding up and down my cock that for a moment I almost forget about the Jonathan factor. I close my eyes, focusing on the heat and moisture emanating from Meghan on top of me. In spite of what she is doing to him she never breaks her rhythm on top of me. She rides me like this for several minutes, all while sucking his massive cock. After a while I find myself watching her, mesmerized by what she is doing. It is just like in the porn movies you see on line. Both of her hands are on his shaft and she is sliding them up and down, twisting them in unison. It looks like that coupled with her mouth on it would be the most amazing feeling ever. I am, unfortunately, not blessed with a cock that warrants both hands at the same time, so I guess I will just have to settle for speculation. She is really into this, moaning and groaning as she grinds into me, slurping and sucking her husband's cock. She is getting close again, and I want to push her over the edge once more. I push myself up so that I am sitting underneath her, and place one hand behind me to keep myself there. I can hear her working him over since I am closer to the source of the noise. I reach around and slide my hand down her stomach, finding her swollen clit once again.

She pulls away from his thick member, and her hand slaps down on top of mine. I thought for a second she was going to stop me, but she just held it there. Her fingers rest on top of mine, feeling how I am touching her. "Oh yes...right there....RIGHT THERE!" she cries out. Her hips shift gears and she is grinding fast on top of me. She grabs her tits, pinching her nipples, ignoring Jonathan for a brief moment. She arches back and within seconds she erupts in a huge orgasm. She bucks and grinds on top of me as I push into the soft flesh between her thighs. Her moans deepen into animal-like growls as she rides it out for as long as possible. There is nothing romantic about it...it is all need, pure carnal desire. And it is sexy as Hell.

Instead of slumping against me and needing a break, her orgasm seems to have only heightened her level of desire. She climbs off of me, and practically commands me to get behind her. She grabs his cock once again, giving him the attention I am sure he badly wants. He springs back to life quickly, and is at full salute once again. I put my hand in the middle of her back, and she arches to give me entrance into her. I drive deep into her once again, being careful not to shove her forward into him. Her body reacts as I touch her deep inside. In this position I can go deeper into her, and she gives me an unspoken warning to be careful with my strokes. She takes some of the arch out of her back, and adjusts the depth of my next stroke for me. She has one hand planted on the bed and is jerking Jonathan like crazy with the other. I continue to push in and out of her as I try not to make eye contact with him. I don't like this position because we are facing each other. I can see his broad shoulders and perfectly sculpted chest just above Meghan's head as it bobs up and down. I look down at her, trying to focus on the fact that I did get chosen by her for this adventure. That is something...that should be enough. But I still can't help but wonder why she wants me when she has that guy for a husband.

I decide to up the ante a little bit, and do something really naughty to her. I spit on my thumb, getting it nice and wet, and then place it on top of her private hole. I gently swirl it in tiny circles, apply more pressure moment by moment. The tip of my thumb slips into her, and I hear her moan into his cock. I leave it there as I stroke my cock in and out of her a little slower now, teasing her with it. I get into a rhythm of pulling my cock out and pushing my thumb and then reversing the process. She continues to jerk his cock but she can't contain the verbal outpour any longer. Her cries reach their peak as does her body, and I break pattern and push forward with both of my implements of pleasure. She glances back over her shoulder, staring hazily into my eyes before the overwhelming pleasure floods her and forces them closed. She pushes back into me, filling herself completely. I look up to see Jonathan grabbing two handfuls of her hair, forcing her to look at him, staring deep into her eyes, stealing her focus from me. He is pulling her head back, making her look at him until he can tell she is finished. He releases his grip on her. She slumps forward into him, away from me, spent. I feel cheated, like he did it on purpose. I am jealous of her husband, as ridiculous as that sounds.

I walk to the bathroom to wash my hands. I look into the mirror to see Jonathan take position behind her. She arches her back, welcoming his cock into her. She is looking forward, but glancing sideways at me. I realize that when I return he and I will have switched positions. I clean up a little, and then turn to watch the proceedings. His big hands are holding her by the waist, and he is stuffing as much of his huge manhood into her as she can take. She winces every once in a while, trying to take more but unable. Her hands are gripping the sheets as she braces herself for each stroke. She looks very small on her hands and knees in front of him. He also is looking at me; grinning an indignant grin. I take his look as a reminder of who is boss, and I don't like it. I am once again questioning my decision to be here. I look back to Meghan, finding her looking at me. I see the look of pure pleasure on her face, enjoying what she is getting at the moment. I find myself watching them, suddenly realizing that I have never been in a room with two people having sex. I watch them from a third person point of view, seeing the looks on her face change, his hands on her, bodies arching to meet each other all on the edge of the bed in the dimly lit room. I stand alone, watching, waiting, not knowing if she is finished with me. Feelings of discomfort and exclusion float through me as I wait for a sign from them. I watch for a while until she motions for me.

I walk over to her, and she overtly licks her lips while staring at my cock. I stand in front of her, putting one foot on the bed. She greedily goes after my cock, wanting it in her mouth as soon as I am near her. I am not rock solid at the moment, but feel the rush of sensation quickly reawakens me. She puts her hand between my legs, hooking under and pulls me a little closer. She works it back to my usual stiffness, no give in it what so ever. She jams it into the back of her throat, holding it there, fighting. Jonathan keeps slowly pumping away at her from behind as I try to ignore him. I focus on Meghan right in front of me, her beautiful face contorting in effort to not gag. She pulls away and smiles, her eyes watering slightly. "Whew...can't do that with his dick, that's for sure!" she says, gasping. She sees by the look on my face that I am insulted, hurt by the thought mine is not enough. "I fucking love going all the way down on it" she tells me with a dirty glint in her eyes. Suddenly it hits me that in some ways she likes my cock just as much as his. A rush of power and confidence surge through me as her words ring in my head. I am all of the sudden not intimidated by Jonathan at all; he is different but not necessarily better. I grab a handful of hair, pulling her into me, smashing her face against my stomach as I hold her there. I feel her convulse before ever letting her up. Jonathan's wife gasps for breath as she pulls away. She laughs a little, encouraging me for more. I oblige, grabbing her and repeating the process over and over as she gets fucked from behind by her husband. The three of us go at it like this for a while, sandwiching Meghan in between us. Once in a while I even look up to see Jonathan's face.

Meghan

It appears he is getting close, as his pace increases and his voice roughens. She pushes herself away from me, and then turns to him. "No way, mister...you're in time out." She points to the corner of the bed, and the half serious scolding tone in her voice lets him know that she has not gotten her fill just yet. Jonathan returns to the chair where he was, only this time pulling it right next to the bed. He has a front row seat to watch me fuck his wife. Meghan turns to me, and hears exactly what I wanted to hear her say. "Pound me hard and fast" I smile at her, the words like music to my ears. She lies back, and I take position on my knees in between her legs. I lift her legs, putting one over each shoulder and I climb forward until I lift her ass off of the mattress. I slowly push into her, teasing her. She bucks her hips a little, partly in time with mine and partly out of frustration of not getting exactly what she wants just yet. Without warning I rear back and drive deep into her, slapping my body into hers. She shudders from the impact of my body into hers. I pull almost all the way out of her, until just the tip is inside of her, and slam into her again. This time she is ready for it and moans deep as the reverb of the collision ripples through her body. This is what she wants, so I give it to her over and over. I pound into her relentlessly, fucking her harder and harder until one orgasm seems to blend into another. I go and go until I feel I am getting sick to my stomach and finally have to stop. I slow my pace, finally surrendering to the cramp in hip-flexors and the spasms in my lower back. She writhes; spasming, aftershocks and heavy breathing continue for several minutes while lying next to me. "Fuck yeah...that was what I wanted" was the only thought she seemed to be able to vocalize.

After a moment of well earned rest, we are ready to go at it again. Jonathan stands up, his cock in his hand and walks to the bed to join us. It occurs to me that this time I am much less concerned about him joining us. "The grand finale?" he asks her. "Oh God yes...absolutely!" she emphatically responds. I have no idea what that means, but I assume I am about to find out. She jumps off the bed and runs to the sink, leaving him and me waiting for her. OK, a little weird being here without her, that's for sure, I think to myself. She returns with a bottle of lube in her hand and a fresh condom for me. Jonathan lies down on the bed as Meghan clicks open the top on the bottle of Astroglide. She squeezes some onto the palm of her hand as she leans forward and takes his cock into her mouth. Her hand reaches over her arched back and begins to rub

133

lube on her most private opening. "You're gonna have to go slow, I haven't done this in a long time" she informs me. Part of me really wants to believe her.

Jonathan lies down on the bed, and she is quick to mount him again. She slides up and down that huge shaft of his, growing accustom to it as she goes. She plants her hands in his chest, and scoots her feet under herself until she is squatting above him. She increases her pace in this position, able to control the depth of his penetration. I watch, waiting for her to let me know what she wants me to do. After a few more moments of her attention focused solely on him, she turns to me and, without saying a word, lets me know it is time. I am not that thrilled about being intertwined with the both of them, but if I want one I have to accept the other. I move behind her, trying to find room for both of my knees between Jonathan's legs. I jump the first time I touch him. I step my right leg up and over both of them, planting it on the mattress next to them. It frees me up, giving me more space to move and not be rubbing against his legs. I slide the condom over me, its snug fit clinging to me. A quick whiff reminds me of how much I hate the smell of latex. I grab the base of my cock, holding the rubber in place as I push the tip against her opening. She is waiting for it, but still jumps a little when I touch her there. She gets down on her knees once more, straddling him underneath her in a more comfortable and accessible position. I slowly push forward into her, easing it in her. Her flesh finally relents to my swollen head, granting access to her back door.

She is now sandwiched between to two of us, held there by four hands and her desire for anything and everything the three of us are doing. We let her move on us instead of fighting over rhythm ourselves. I put my hand on her lower back, watching my cock slide in and out of her puckering hole. Each stroke seems to build the fire inside of her, and she loves every second of it. She digs her nails into Jonathan's chest, her rocking motion increasing in speed and length. She is slowly working me deeper into her ass, and riding his cock in the process. I can feel him inside her, the thin walls inside barely separating us from one another. My knee is already beginning to hurt from bearing all my weight on its own. I shift a little to the side to relieve the strain and change my angle into her just a little bit. She approves, and I must be hitting a slightly different spot now because she is getting ready to come once again.

"That's right baby, take those cocks in you" Jonathan growls to her. She moans faster and louder as she climbs. Her hips buck faster and harder, and I push forward in effort just to stay inside her. "Oh my God....OH MY GOD!!!!!" Meghan screams at the top of her lungs. He grabs her and pulls her down onto him, yanking me forward in the process. She is now smashed between us, unable to move under my weight yet still convulsing in her intense orgasm. "Fuck her hard...do it......fuck her now!" Jonathan commands me. Meghan is breathing so hard she can only groan in agreement.

I raise back away from her, putting my hands on her hips and go to town. I pound her as fast as I can, slapping into her firm ass cheeks. He holds still and lets me take over, fucking his wife and pushing the both of them back and forth on the bed with my thrusts. She is squirming and whimpering under her breath, seemingly lost in pleasure. Her sounds deepen, her voice roughened by desire and pleasure. I am getting close to my own, and I continue to hammer her ass for all I am worth. I am only conscious of the noises in the room sporadically as I focus on pushing myself over the top. Jonathan's voice catches my attention once again, and this time he is the one getting off. She pushes down on top of him, and the shift in position breaks my rhythm. I can feel his hard member inside of her, and he spasms and explodes, filling her with his seed.

I try to regain my form, so close to my own that I am nearly frenzied with desire. I grab her hair, yanking her head back and ram forward. I take over, fucking her once again as his pleasure subsides and he dutifully stays with her as she seems to be readying herself again. I find my release point, seeing it almost viscerally in the distance. I run towards it, gaining ground, getting closer. I sprint to the finish line, my hips going faster than I thought possible as my cock burns the edges of her in the process. My orgasm explodes in me like a stick of dynamite, it suddenness and force completely out of my control at that point. I am not sure how loud my voice is or what the ecstasy I am experiencing is making me say. I am hollow for a moment, trapped inside looking out before I regain consciousness. Meghan has started again and soon her voice takes over as mine subsides. I let go of her hair, finally realizing that I was holding her off of him with a handful of hair. She grinds it out, her sweaty body easily gliding back and forth between us. The three of us collapse in a heap of exhaustion.

I quickly realize that I am once again touching Jonathan and carefully remove myself from her. I clamp my hand around the bottom of the condom and pull out of her, heading straight for the toilet without ever looking at it. I flush it and turn to the sink to clean up. I walk back into the room to find them still clinging to one another. I lie down away from the two of them, and after a while realize that my part here is done. They embrace and kiss, and I am left alone. Eventually she slides off of him and they seem content to drift off to sleep just like they are. I quietly gather my clothes and get dressed. I put on my shoes and head for the door. I pause, looking back at the two of them in the bed. And then I leave. I stand in the elevator, looking at my reflection in the shiny finish on the door once again. It was an amazing experience, and I am interested to see how I feel about this tomorrow. For now, I need to find a cab and get back to my car. I am in desperate need of a shower and sleep. I laugh to myself as I walk out of the hotel and get into a cab, thinking that maybe I should never say never again.

FLIPSIDE EROTICA
both sides of the story

Volume 2

Darren Michaels

ISBN: 978-0-615-44232-7

Printed in USA

www.flipside-erotica.com

This book is dedicated to those who are
smart enough to *dream*, brave enough to *act*,
and confident enough to know that life is all about the
experiences you have along the way.

A special thank you to HyperDonkey.com
for the technical assistance on this book project and the
www.flipside-erotica.com website. Without your help,
this project would not have been possible.

Table of Contents — Her Eyes

Introduction

I hope you enjoy the unique twist this book presents. I have written each and every story; I do "research" with some of the people in the stories, and have certainly asked questions regarding thoughts and feelings to gain a better understanding of both sides of the story. These stories are a mixture of experiences I have had. All are based on fact, at least concerning the person(s) involved. Some are true to the letter and some are the way I wished things worked out, these being total fabrications built around someone I've met. As the reader, you will have to decide which is which. If you are looking for a romance novel, put this book back where you found it. This is a book about classy adults doing erotic things. This is a nightstand book more so than a coffee table book. Enjoy the stories one or two at a time, whether by yourself or with someone you are close to.

As an advocate for safe sex, I strongly encourage you to take the necessary precautions in your own adventures. Although I do not make reference to the use of condoms in every story, I assure you I do my part to protect myself and my partner. You should be sure to do the same.

Please log onto my website at www.flipside-erotica.com and let me know what you think of this project. Enjoy the free preview of the audio downloads that is offered. Some of the voices in the audio files are the actual people in the stories; some are just friends of mine. Again, you will have to decide for yourself who's who. ☺

Jennifer

My cell phone vibrates in my purse and I try to keep my eyes on the road while I feel around for it. I stop at the light and open the text message from Darren. It reads "The door is unlocked, come inside. There is a blindfold hanging on the doorknob, put it on and wait for me." Oh God...he is doing it again. He knows it makes me ache deep inside when he does this. As if I wasn't amped up enough already; the thought of his touch, the taste of his skin, has been omnipresent in my mind since yesterday when he called to invite me over. Regardless of how busy my day is, I would hang up the phone with an angry client and still think about him. The thought never leaves me; like it is hanging just to the side and I can see it with my peripheral vision. It is delightful, and yet I get so worked up I almost find it painful when he plays with me like this. The light turns green and I hammer the pedal to the floor, passing the slow car on the left and squealing the tires a little as I turn down the street to his house.

I pull into the driveway and can see the shades are drawn. We must be starting in the living room today, I think to myself. I feel a jolt hit me from the inside, my thighs clenching involuntarily at the mere sight of his house. It's show time, and my body knows it. I get a whiff of my body lotion, and quickly reflect back on the preparation I did this morning: extra time in the bathtub, shaving as slick as I can. I save the good Bath and Bodyworks lotion for him and I rub it all over me; everywhere -- between my toes, on my feet, up my legs and even where I want his mouth the most. It is an exquisite routine, like an athlete going through his pregame rituals before taking the field. Only I have to wait, all-day-long, until I get to perform. Despite my lack of patience, the waiting, the anticipation, and the torture he makes me feel before finally giving me what I want is one of the things that separates him from every other man I've ever known.

My feet hit the driveway and I feel my stomach tense a little. After all this time I still get nervous and excited about walking through that door. And knowing that there is a blindfold hanging on the door handle, waiting for me, just makes it that much more exciting. I open the door and peek in, never sure what I will find. I do not see him. "Hello?" He does not answer. I walk in and put my keys on the glass table near the

9

door and drop my purse at my feet. I put the blindfold on and back against the door, announcing that I am ready for him. I wait a few moments, but grow impatient as I always do. I shout "I'm ready!" once again and then jump when I realize that he is already standing in front of me. I laugh a little, embarrassed that my lack of patience got the better of me again and that he snuck up on me like that.

I can feel him in front of me now, as if his body heat permeates my skin. I feel his breath on me; his lips brush my skin gently. He pushes me against the door and I know the fun is about to begin. I can feel myself ready for him; my inner thighs taut with desire. Moisture soaks my lacey black thong, and I ache for him to touch me there. I lean forward, trying to find his mouth with mine. The blindfold is hiding him from me, and it adds to my excitement. For all I know he may be standing naked in front of me; at least that is how I am picturing it in my mind. I can't find him, but soon I feel his lips on my neck. He kisses my flesh, moistening the spot before sinking his teeth into me. A ripple courses through me, my skin prickling under his bite. My legs nearly collapse out from under me and I push back into the door to hold my ground. A deep groan escapes my lips as I reach for him. I can't take it anymore; I need.....something.

I feel his hands on my wrists, and I know right away what is coming. He pushes my hands down to my sides and once again I am forced to wait and follow his lead. His pace is excruciatingly slow; his lips brushing over the little bit of exposed flesh my shirt allows. I feel him next to my ear, his voice rough with excitement. He tells me he has something special planned for us today, and his words make me tremble to the core. He begins to unbutton my blouse one button at a time. His hands slide into my shirt, pushing the silky material back over my shoulders. He kisses my neck and down towards my breasts; my nipples are hard already despite the fact that he has yet to touch them. His hands cup my breasts, pressing them against me. He works them over just short of being rough. His touch is firm and yet still gentle.

I bite my lip in effort to control my desire to tear off the blindfold and my clothes right now. His fingers brush back and forth over my nipples, heightening their sensitivity. His pace increases and he pulls one of them free from my bra. His tongue is on my rigid flesh, his teeth

10

biting, nibbling. Instinctively I grab the back of his head, pulling him into me. He grabs my hand once more, pushing it back to my side again. I want to take a swing at him, but I don't. As frustrating as it is, he is doing it because he knows I love it. He is teasing me for me as much as he is for himself. Suddenly he pulls me away from the wall and finds the hooks in the back of my bra. The lacey black material gives way, freeing my breasts from their confines. My nipples jump to attention, almost as if to salute their master. His tongue finds them again; first one and then the other, teasing, sucking them.

I moan aloud once again and feel his hands working their way downward towards my aching pussy. I am so wet already his fingers would slide right in. If only he would move faster! I think to myself. I hear him lean down in front of me, his hand on me. He pushes upward into me, the heel of his hand pressing into my slick flesh. I press the back of my head into the door, moaning in relief as he finally touches me. I can feel the rough material of my lacey panties rubbing against my soft flesh as he readies me for the first one. I reach for him again, and this time he grabs my wrists and pushes them above my head against the door. The idea of him restraining me is such a turn on, and I fight the pressure of his hands on mine just to add to it. His lips find my nipple again, and he sucks in my sensitive rosy flesh into mouth once more.

Suddenly my hands are free, but his hand is already on my belt, removing it hastily. His excitement is growing as well, and I can hear his breathing change. He grabs the sides of my pants, pulling them apart. His fingers fumble for my zipper, jerking it downward, exposing me. My pants slide off of me, bunching around my ankles. I step out of them with a little help, and he tosses them aside. I hear him step back, sighing in approval of what he sees. I wish I could see that looks in his eyes at this moment. I hear him move again, and this time he kneels in front of me. I feel his breath on my thighs, and I want so badly for him to taste me. He is teasing me again, kissing my thighs and pushing his hand into me. I lean forward towards him, applying pressure down to meet his upward push. Finally he is going to give me what I want, what I need so desperately. He pulls my panties aside and plunges a finger deep into me. I moan loudly, finally feeling a sense of relief in my pre-orgasm pleasure.

Her Eyes

I can feel it gliding in and out of me, his pace increasing. Suddenly he yanks my panties to my feet in one swift motion. His silken tongue is on me; swirling, flicking. He adds another finger, increasing the tension and friction inside. "Oh Jesus...Oh My God!" I hear myself cry out. The thoughts and words pour out of me without filter or cognition. I arch, bearing my weight onto him. I feel myself start to lean to the side, almost falling. I am clutching at the wall, trying to find something to hang on to so I can focus on what he is doing to me. He pushes me against the door, bracing me, holding me in place. Finally I can let go. It hits me, like standing waist deep in water and then a huge wave crashing over top of me. I drift off, swept away by an ethereal tide.

He leaves me against the door. I begin to feel my feet once again, cognizant of just how long I have been on them today. He moves something towards me and then grabs my hand leading me towards it. He gently pushes me into the chair, and I recognize it to be the high-back chair from the bar in his home. I sit down in it, and he places my leg over the arm of the chair. The blindfold has moved a little, and I can sort of see under it. I see him on his knees in front of me, staring at me. He leans forward, kissing my thighs, teasing me once again. His tongue finds my sensitive clit, still quivering from a moment ago. His tongue travels over the length of me, down threateningly close to my most private hole that even he has never dared to tread. His mouth covers me, sucking my soft flesh in and out. The sensation is amazing, totally different than any other kind of pleasure I feel. His fingers invade me once again, turning and twisting as they enter and withdraw. I feel myself moving instinctively; I want to hold still, to make it easier for him, but I can't help it. The feeling is too intense. My cries grow louder as I edge closer and closer to another. He keeps after it, never letting up. It rushes up from within the depths of me, exploding to the surface. I shudder and shake as I cry out in ecstasy once again. I melt like chocolate into the chair on which I am seated.

I am coherent enough to hear him removing his clothing. I know more is coming, but I am still reveling in the last one. He tosses his clothes aside, likely scattering them around the room as he usually does at times like this. Most of his life is organized, buttoned down, but at times like this he truly lets go. It is the ultimate compliment and turn on. He reaches for my hand, and places it on his throbbing hard cock. He is

12

up to the task, as always. I squeeze it, feeling just how hard it is. Suddenly my focus is switched from myself to him, and it sobers me instantly. Time to go to work. I slide off the chair, falling to my knees in front of him. I swirl my tongue around the top, readying it to be engulfed.

I go down on it, deep as I can before pulling back. The next trip I follow my mouth with my hand, squeezing, twisting. I feel a moan reverberate through him. I cannot see him, but I picture the look on his face, the scene as a whole. I watch me suck his cock from afar, mesmerized by my own actions. My focus returns to him, and I suck and squeeze him even harder than I did before. His hand is in my hair, brushing it aside, holding it out of the way. I love it when he takes the lead and "makes" me suck it. He slowly adds pressure into his grip, and soon he is gently forcing my head to bob up and down on him. I can feel him swelling in my mouth, growing closer by the moment. His breathing changes, becoming labored and raspy. His grip on my hair tightens, and I know that he is debating what to do. Part of me wants him to cum right now, but I also want so much more of what we started.

"You alright?" I ask him, knowing full well I have pushed him to the brink once again. He doesn't answer, which means that he is closer than he wants to be. Suddenly he grabs my wrists and pulls me to my feet. I am spun in a half circle, and shoved forward over the chair. I find the back of it, placing my hand on it, bracing. He teases me, brushing his cock against my swollen clit which has been feeling neglected for the last several minutes. I don't want any more teasing, I want him inside me. I move, trying to help him enter me. He laughs at my struggles. "You in a hurry?" he asks almost spitefully. I cave, not wanting to, but my growing desire now leading the charge. "God yes, fuck me....fuck me hard" I plead. He grants my wish, and I one stroke is deep inside me. I grunt in response, getting filled like that nearly knocking the breath out of my body. He pulls almost all the way out of my, and rams it deep inside once again. I feel the chair wobble underneath me from the impact. He grabs my hips and begins to hammer away at me, much to my delight.

His hands find my breasts again, squeezing them, pulling them against me. Fingers clamp down on my nipples and I nearly yell out

13

from the surge that it causes to run through me. His pace slows into a nice rhythm and I feel every inch of him on each and every stroke. He continues at this pace for a few moments, until I feel his hand on my shoulder. I know what is coming, and my body tenses a little in automatic response. He continues at the same pace, and just when I begin to relax a little he hits me with it. His hand clamps down on my shoulder and pulls me towards his upward, deep thrust. Our bodies slam together, the impact echoing down to my bones. He touches me deep inside when he does this, and the internal tension is exquisite. He stays in place; pushing, stretching me to my limits. I look back at him, despite the blindfold blocking my view of him, my mouth open in a silent scream.

I feel his hand in my hair, and my head is jerked backward with a forceful tug. He withdraws just a little bit, only to push what feels like even deeper the second time. "Oh God...fuck yeah!" I cry out, forcing the words through gritted teeth. I like it a tad on the rough side and he never disappoints. I arch into him, wanting more. I am growing close, and he knows it. He lets go of my hair and grabs my waist again. He sets a furious pace right from the start, slapping his skin against mine. The feelings mount, the friction increasing, and my brain begins to shut down. Thoughts of anything other than my desire dissipate into thin air. I hear his voice, as if from across the room say "That's it, take my cock you dirty little whore." His words release me and I explode in a hard, deep orgasm once again. "Oh yes, fuck me....FUCK ME!!!" I scream at the top of my lungs. I grip the chair as I push back into him, wanting more. He doesn't stop, letting me get every bit of it and more until I can no longer fight back. I slump forward into the chair, exhausted once again. I feel like I can't go on anymore. I want to sit here and absorb the feelings cascading through me.

After too brief of a moment he takes my hand and leads me to another room. I can barely walk; my legs rubbery. I feel like I am drunk as he leads me into the bedroom. He sits me down on the edge of his bed, and I hear him fidgeting with something nearby. I can see his feet under the bottom of the blindfold but not much else. He places something under my nose, and the smell seems foreign to me. I recoil, not sure what is was. He laughs a little, and does it again. This time I recognize it....strawberry. What the Hell is he up to now? I think to myself. "Open your mouth" he tells me. I obey, waiting for it to hit my tongue. He brushes it against my lips, and I stick out my tongue as if to reach for it. He is taking too long again, playing games with me. I feel the strawberry against my lips and lurch forward taking a bite of it. "Hey! You cheater!" he yells out. I laugh in defiance, thinking somehow that I won this round.

A moment later I feel him scoot forward and I can see his feet between mine. I reach for him, and put my hands on his hips. I know what he wants, and I go for it. I slide my hand down his stomach and find his rock hard cock once more. I take it in my mouth and suck it again. I can faintly taste myself on him, but I don't even care at this point. I am lost in the moment, ready for anything. His hand slides into my hair again, and I am ready for another good session of him in my mouth. Just as this thought enters my mind he pulls me away from it. After a few seconds he lets go, and I want it in my mouth again. He likes to tease me so much I have grown used to being denied, even at his own expense. I grab him, and feel the base of his cock is wet. As soon as my mouth hits him I know what he has done. I suck it furiously, loving the taste of the strawberry and his flesh. "MmmohhGod....you taste so good" I tell him between mouthfuls of it.

I grab its hardness in my hand, my grip fighting it, trying to make it give even a little. I lean down and run my tongue over his balls. The juice runs down him as he replenishes the strawberry on himself. I slurp it in, tasting the combination of him, me and the strawberries all at once. I suck him as if my life depended on it, with more fervor than I than I think ever before. I love it, and everything he has created for today's adventure. I could do this all day I think to myself. Just as the words flash through my head I feel his hands on mine again, pulling me upwards. I get to my feet and he pushes me backwards onto the bed. I love the feel of his silk sheets against my skin; cool at first but quickly warming under me. I lie on my back, and I can see him for the first time today under the blindfold. He is on his knees next to the bed, and I see him bite into a strawberry. He looks at me, and then I feel him spread me open. "Oh my God...he isn't" I think to myself. I feel the cold strawberry push inside me, and realize that yes, he is.

Her Eyes

His hot tongue is on me once again; I feel it stroke my pussy up and down. The juices run out of me, trickling down to my private spot. His tongue ventures close to it once again, and I secretly yearn for him to explore just a little farther. He returns to the top, licking my clit with short, firm strokes of his tongue. My hips are beginning to buck again, and I grab the back of his head to brace myself in effort to hold still. Despite the fact that I have only one foot on the bed I thrash about as it hits again, the blood leaving my brain. I feel as though I am going to pass out at any moment; I can't take any more pleasure and I beg him to stop. After a few more strokes he finally relents and lets me settle back onto the sheets.

I feel him climb onto the bed, and know what he wants. He wants his, and he is coming to get it. He throws one of my legs over his shoulder and before I know it he is deep inside me once again. I am a quivering mass of flesh, and offer no help other than to let him have his way with me. He pushes into me, hitting bottom slightly on the first stroke and firmly on the next. He holds himself there, so deep, and makes me feel every inch of him. My mouth opens to scream, but no noise escapes me. I feel him withdraw, only to drive into me again. The process repeats, he hesitates and I never know when it's coming. The suspense is delightful, and the impact ripples all through me. I moan in ecstasy as I lie there and take it. He begins to pound into me; I am trapped in his hold as he stretches my legs to their limit. My cries increase and despite my expended state I may have one more in me. My strength slowly returns, and my will to carry on powers me. He slams into me over and over, and the impacts finally jar one more orgasm loose from its hiding place deep within. I moan and groan as it rips through me once more.

He finally relents, and despite the typical spent feeling my orgasms produce, I am empowered by this one. He lies down on the bed, and I feel around to find him. I crawl towards him, and climb on top of him. I guide it into me; he is still so hard. Pushing down onto it, I take it all the way inside. I slowly grind on it, setting my own pace for the first time today. Planting my hands on his chest, I enjoy the first dose of control I have had in a long time. I angle my hips back just a bit, changing the angle inside me to hit an even better spot. I begin to moan aloud, and each move of my hips brings more and more pleasure to me. His hands are on my breasts, lifting, squeezing. He pinches my nipples and I jump in response. "Oh God...yes...put your mouth on them" I beg of him. He sits up under me, and I wrap my arm around his head, pulling him into me. He takes one in his mouth, clamping his teeth down on it. "Eeeasyyyy" I remind him, my nipples already sensitive from all the rough play today.

I feel his hand smack down onto my ass, the sting taking a second to rise through me. I am sure that one left a welt that I will be able to see later. I moan in response anyway, loving the sting of his hand on me. I move a little bit and he hits a new and even better spot inside me. It springs me forward in the process, as if skipping over the buildup and pushing me right to the edge immediately. My mind focuses on it, and suddenly my only goal is to squeeze one more out of me today. I move my hips faster and faster. Soon my body is thrashing around on top of his; my tits are bouncing everywhere. I grab them and keep them from jostling so much they hurt. I keep after it, my hips doing their thing until I reach the top one last time. I always come hardest when I am on top and in control; despite how many times I have already gotten off today. He grabs my hips and takes over when I begin to lose momentum, helping extend it just a little more.

I fall forward onto him, my chest heaving. I am done; I have no more to give. He rolls me over onto my side, and takes position behind me. Cradling my right leg, he holds it up in the air as he penetrates me from behind. I am nearly numb from it all today; barely able to even discern what he is doing to me anymore. I feel his hand on my face; he slides the blindfold off of me. I turn to look at him behind me. His eyes are filled with hungry desire. I reach back and place my hand on his neck, pulling him into me. Our bodies are glistening with sweat, and we slides back and forth with no friction between us. I can feel his breathing change, and I know he is growing close. He pace quickens, and he is closing in on it. He wraps his arms around me, pulling me into him, squeezing the air out of me. I feel him explode inside me, pumping stream after stream of it into me. After a few brief moments he relaxes, growing still as he lies behind me.

I am exhausted, and already beginning to feel sore from the fucking I received today. It was amazing; another incredible afternoon of sex with him. As I drift off to sleep I recall what he did today and also flash forward to what the next time between us will bring. I fall asleep in his arms, feeling more safe and relaxed than I do in my own home. My brain is still as I slide into a deep slumber.

Chloe

I am in the middle of packing my luggage for my last trip to the company's world headquarters in the States. I have made this long trip two other times in the past 8 months, and have yet to meet an American boy that I like. Throwing some of my favorite boyshorts into the suitcase, I wonder if this is the trip that someone besides me will finally see them. "One more time" I say aloud amidst a big exhale. I shut the case and drag it off the bed towards the door. I glance at the clock on the wall; it is 5:00AM my time. I do not relish the idea of changing time zones and fighting jet lag once again. Hearing the taxi pull up outside I button my jacket and head for the door. I am tired already.

I check in at the airport and find a chair to wait for my flight to arrive. I am falling asleep in my seat as I wait for the passengers to deplane. Finding my way to my assigned seat I flop down, grabbing a pillow and blanket on the way down the aisle. I lean against the window and I am out like a light. I don't even remember the plane taking off. I awake in America, just a few minutes before touching down in New York. One more leg to my trip and I will once again be back at the corporate headquarters for a week of training. Another deep sigh leaves me as I think of the week spent trapped in a chair listening to lectures. I change planes and leave New York, headed to my destination traveling at 30,000 feet. I am growing restless just sitting here, so I reach for my book to pass the time. I soon find myself engrossed in the story, seeing things through the main characters eyes. I am absorbing the details, pouring over the pages as the story of two people in a chance meeting throw caution to the wind and run away to live happily ever after. A nice thought, a fairytale ending, but I think by now I know better. I'd settle for a little adventure at this point.

I arrive at my destination and collect my bags. I find the shuttle to the hotel and once again sit in a seat for an aggravating length of time. Arriving at the hotel I am irritated, road weary, and in need of a shower. As soon as I enter the lobby I see familiar faces and am happy to know a few people to endure the week with. We begin to chat and exchange pleasantries when I notice a guy standing at the hotel desk checking in. He is staring at me and smiling, but he does not look familiar. He smiles, and I smile back, nervously brushing my hair behind my ear. I look

21

away, and then look back a moment later to find him still looking at me. He finally jumps ever so slightly, and I realize that the woman behind the desk said something to him. He turned to face her, and she seemed to say something and smile at him. I can see him laughing. I look him over from head to toe, wondering if he is the adventure I have been searching for. Time will tell.

I get in que to register at the hotel and continue chatting with everyone, bearing the constant barrage of jokes about my accent. If I have to utter the phrase "stro burry low lee pop" one more time I am going to go crazy. I do my best to comply with a smile, liking the attention but laughing at the ease with which everyone here is so entertained. I look for him, but he is gone. I wonder if he is here for week that I am, or if he was checking out while at the desk earlier. I check in and scurry to my room. I want to take a long shower and get something to eat. I open the door and sigh, yet another hotel room to live in for the next week.

I am now famished and throw on some clothes that will pass for decent. The door bangs shut with the heavy thud that hotel doors do, one more reminder of my time away from home. I walk into the elevator, arrive on the first floor and make a beeline for the bar. I hate to eat alone, so I will get my food to go and eat in my room. At least at the conference I will be with people I know. I walk to the hostess stand and ask if the menu is the same in the bar and the restaurant alike. As I look around I catch eyes with him; it's the guy from the check in line earlier today. I feel my stomach knot immediately and I smile back in response to his. I see the chair in front of him slowly push back from the table, inviting me to join him. I lean over to the hostess and inform her I will be joining the gentleman seated at that table. I walk towards him, feeling completely exposed as I make my way through the empty tables and chairs until I finally reach him.

He stands and introduces himself "Hi, my name is Darren, and I'd love for you to join me." I relax under his warm smile, "Chloe...and I would be delighted" I tell him. We sit at the table and seem to instantly pick up conversation as if we had already met. He makes me feel comfortable in my decision to join him, and we talk like we are old friends who haven't seen one another in a while. Suddenly the waiter arrives, and asks what I would like to order. I grab the menu and jump right the steaks; eating on the company dime has its rewards. "A Ribeye steak, medium rare, a bake potato with everything on the side and a Corona with lime" I rattle off. I see a devilish look emanating from him..."Corona? They have that crappy Mexican beer where you're from?" "I happen to like a bit of the amber nectar, and I can't always get it where I live" I shoot back at him with a flash of a smile. "Speaking of which, where are you from anyway?" he inquires. "I am from just outside London in the UK" I tell him.

The waiter appears from behind me again with two beers on a tray. He sets them down in front of us and hurries off for some unknown reason. The place is empty; I have no idea why he pretends to be so busy. "What brings you to St. Louis?" he asks, snapping me out of my internal conversation. "I am here for a conference my company sent me to" I answer. He reaches for his beer, and I grab mine, pushing the lime down into the neck of the bottle. I turn it over as anyone who drinks Corona knows you should do. "Well then here is a toast to...the fun that lies ahead." I touch my bottle to his glass, acknowledging the underlying message of his toast. "I am enjoying things so far, we'll see" I think to myself. I glance away from his stare; suddenly a little shy feeling creeps in. "How is it you find yourself here today?" I ask, trying to break the tension. He chuckles a little before answering "I am here for a conference as well, maybe we are here for the same reason...where are you headed tomorrow?" "My company's headquarters is here, and I am going for some sales training" I respond, hopeful he is in fact part of the same company. "Me too" he confirms. The waiter arrives with our dinners, setting the plates down in front of us. I pick up my knife and fork and looking at his plate, realizing that he has ordered the exact same dinner as I before I joined him. We both break into a loud laugh at this coincidence, and I am starting to think this is meant to be.

Dinner conversation bounces from topic to topic, and although I have been to the States before, I am learning just how many little differences there really are, and yet how much we are all the same. It turns out he is a fan of tennis as am I, and he asks if I have been to Wimbledon. "Oh yes, everyone goes to Wimbledon if they have the chance. It is difficult to get tickets, so we usually just wait in que for ground passes to open up" I state. "Que? You mean wait in line?" he asks me, another playful smile on his face. "Yes, you snobby American...in line." I fire back, not backing down from his teasing. We exchange another stare, the attraction between us growing. I see him looking at the bottle in my hand, and he gestures without saying anything for me to look. I see a chunk of lime sliding down the bottle neck, and without thinking about it lick it off of the side of the bottle. I see his eyes widen and realize what I had just done. I feel a wave of heat and embarrassment rush through me. I am blushing and self conscious about both what I did and about being embarrassed about it. I have to change the subject, and fast. "So...how long have you been with the company?"

We take our time eating our dinner, but I am drinking far more quickly than he is. I have noticed that most of the Americans I have met do not drink as much as we Brits, so I guess he is no different. It is getting on in hours and I look at my watch. I don't want to leave, but I don't want to rush things either. We likely have all week together in one way or another, and I want to enjoy the time. He orders one more round, and I decide that if things continue in the same manner we will be having a snog in the hallway for sure. I don't have any clue what American customs are when it comes to these sort of things, but I want to find out. In the UK a proper lady would not rush into bed with a man, but we are not in the UK. I may decide that I want to play by American rules for a change. I laugh at the conversation in my head while he and I converse as if that was the only conversation I was involved in. I want to know if he has done this before, if he is one of those guys who picks up women and sleeps with them every chance he gets. I don't want to be with a guy like that. I inquire about what dating in America is like. "What would you like to know?" he asks. "OK, so when two people start dating, how long is it before they, um...you know?" I didn't want to finish my sentence for some reason. "Know what?" he asks, making me finish my thought any way. "How long do people wait before they kiss?" The expression on his face changed, and he answers "Oh, well usually no more than 20 minutes if you like someone...so I guess you're not really that interested in me" he says. For some reason I panic, thinking I had offended him or something. "No, no...I like you. Er, I mean...bullocks!" I realize halfway through that I had fallen for his trap. I can feel myself turning bright red. He sits there laughing at me. Finally he says something..."It's ok...I am really digging you, too." We are locked in a stare, the moment of silence growing uncomfortably longer by the second. Finally the waiter comes, unwittingly rescuing me from this moment which is both so uncomfortable and yet so stimulating all at once. "Just the check, please" he tells the waiter.

He starts, and then stops, and starts again with a question. "Well, at the risk of misreading you, I am going to ask you a question. I would love for you to come back to my room with me, would you be comfortable with that?" I fidget with the empty bottle in my hand, trying to appear calm on the outside. Inside I am freaking out; thoughts are racing through my head. Can I do this? Can I do this tonight? What if he tells everyone at the company? What kind of underwear am I wearing? Am I ready for a chuffing this soon into the trip? Everything rushes at once, and I swim through the current of thoughts. "I would like to..." I start out, but he cuts me off. "...but we just met and it's too soon" he adds, thinking he is getting shot down. "You didn't let me finish" I reply quickly, trying to answer before I lose my nerve. "What I was going to say was that I would feel better if you came to my room instead." I hear the words leave my mouth but I barely remember thinking them. "Hahhahaha...what's the difference? They are the same rooms!" he says back, thinking my answer was strange. I want things on my own terms, even if it is the same hotel rooms, it is my room and that matters to me. I decide to keep things light, and finish the exchange with "Yes, but if you leave my room in the middle of the night, you'll be the one spotted in the hallway with your shoes in your hand" He charges dinner to his room and we head for the stairs and to my room. My mind is racing, wondering if I really know him well enough for this, is he going to want to have sex tonight, or just get to know one another a little bit the first night together. We climb the stairs to the second floor, and I feel myself slowing down as we walk to the door. Part of me is ready to turn and run, but part of me wants this so badly I can taste it.

We reach my door, and I am waiting for him to do something, say something, lead so I can follow. I pull the keycard out of my back pocket and slide it into the door. He reaches for the door handle, keeping it closed for a moment. "Wait....I want to kiss you before we walk through the door." "Thank God" I think to myself. I look at him for a moment, and then lean in to taste his lips. His kiss is tender and warm, delightful, memorable. For the moment I am lost, warm and safe. Then we part and instantly I am brought back to the reality of our situation. "I can't sleep with you tonight" I blurt in a panic. "I mean we can have fun, but I don't want to sleep with someone I just met. I never have slept with someone on the first date, and I don't want to break that" I feel like I am standing behind myself, watching me say the things I just said. I don't want to ruin this, but I don't to feel pressured either. It's out there now, maybe he'll be OK with it. "HA! What makes you think I am that easy?" he says in a loud voice, pretending to be put off. I practically sigh in relief, laughing at his surprise response. He opens the door and I give him a shove, only to have him grab my wrists and spin me. He hits the bed first, and I land on top of him.

He rolls me over, and I feel his weight bear down on me. I love that feeling; it makes me feel small and somehow vulnerable under him. He puts his hands on the bed, lifting himself off of me a little. He leans over and kisses me again; I reach up and wrap my arms around him, pulling him down on top of me. We kiss long and deep kisses, sweet and sensual. Our tongues play and twist, intertwining as we pet and feel on another. I am conscious of a deep ache beginning to rise within me. I want him, all of him. But I don't want to rush into things. Then again I will not be here in the States again anytime soon. Do I want to wait and not enjoy every moment we have together? I hear myself moan a little as he kisses my neck, his teeth sinking slowly but deliberately into my flesh. I arch away from him in spite of the fact that I want more. He comes back up and kisses me again. "It has been so long...." I think to myself.

He stops kissing me; I open my eyes to find him standing up from our position on the bed. He extends a hand, helping me to my feet as well. He grabs the covers and yanks them back, revealing the dingy gray sheets underneath. In spite of my desires I hear myself say the words "Hold your knickers...we are going slow, remember?" He looks concerned, and I laugh as he fumbles for something to say. "I know, I don't know how it works where you are from, but here we do not trust that the comforters in hotels are clean" I make him squirm for a moment until I roll my eyes and let him off the hook.

He directs his attention back to me. He leans in to kiss me, and once again my mouth welcomes his. I close my eyes again, lost in his kisses. While I am unaware he quickly slides one arm under my knees and the other behind my back. He jerks me off of my feet, and I let out a surprised yell in response. He lifts me and holds me for a second, and then sits me on the edge of the bed. He stands there, looking down at me. He hasn't left himself any room to climb into bed, and is now going to have to crawl over me or walk around to the other side. I laugh a little about it, and suddenly find him sitting on top of me. He is tickling me, and I am gasping for breath in no time. Bullocks!...I hate it that I am so ticklish I scold myself, but am laughing so hard my flash of anger dissipates quickly.

He stops for a moment, and I try to catch my breath. My eyes are watering from laughing so hard, and my sides ache. He is hovering above me again, and I look deep into his eyes. His piercing stare seems to be questioning, and I know what it is he wants. I want it too. I surrender to him, pulling him down onto me again. I wrap my legs around him, beckoning, inviting him. He accepts my invitation and begins to slowly grind himself against me. I can feel his excitement for the first time, and it is wondrous. He pushes me into the mattress, and I arch my back to meld our bodies together. The pressure against my sex is exquisite, and I kiss him even harder. His mouth leaves mine and travels to my neck again. A moan escapes me; exhaling in pleasure. I grind back against him, urging him onward. I feel it through our clothes, and I want him even more. I reach around and place my hands on his bum; feeling, squeezing. It is firm and round and I feel it flex as he grinds into me with more force. I dig my nails into it, loving everything he is making me feel.

I am getting so close already I can't believe it. I want to pop, and my body feels like it is on fire. I feel my hips increase in speed, my desire getting the best of me. I am so wet I feel it all over me. He pushes down into me, and it feels so good. My hips fight against him, bucking in spite of his weight on me. "Yes, keep doing that....just like that...." I command. I feel it bubble to the surface, and I explode into a toe-curling orgasm. It comes in wave after wave, seeming to go on forever. I feel as If I am looking inside myself, lost in a dark room, vibrating from within. Finally it passes, and I realize what just happened. I am suddenly self conscious as I lay under him. I couldn't move if I wanted to, so I lie still for a moment. He looks at me, smiling. He leans in and kisses me again, tenderly this time. "Wow, that was...unusual" I whisper. He pauses for a moment. "Um, thank you?" he says to me, pulling back to look at me. I laugh nervously "what I meant was I have never had an orgasm like that before, you know, without someone...touching me" I confess. "It was quite cool" he says, smiling at me.

He removes himself from the tangle of limbs we have become and walks across the room. I am ready for more and he seems to be distracted. "What is with this guy?" I ask myself. "Where are you going?" I ask aloud. "I am thirsty" he states, not pausing for a second at my question. "I can't believe this, is he going to leave?" I want him to stay, all night long. "DO SOMETHING!" I tell myself. I get up and start tearing my clothes off, tossing them aside. He reaches into the fridge and grabs a bottle of water, twisting the top and throwing the cap aside. He takes a long drink before he turns around to see me. He is very surprised to see me standing there naked, and almost chokes on his drink. After a second he seems to compose himself, and looks me over with a smile. It makes me feel confident in my bold move, and I am growing more moist by the moment in anticipation of what is to come. "I wanted to make sure you weren't going to drink my expensive water and walk out of here" I tell him with a devilish smile." He pauses for a moment and then offers "And you thought this would do the trick?" he says, finishing in a laugh. "Smartass." I think to myself.

Instead of coming towards me, he steps backwards and leans against the wall. He signals for me to come to him. I decide it will be okay to indulge him, thinking I will also be rewarded. I feel the urge to be a dirty little girl, and I get down on my hands and knees and crawl across the floor to him. I reach his feet, and straighten up to reach for my prize. His jeans are doing little to contain him at this point, and I grab his zipper and pull it all the way down. I reach in and release his balls from their confines as well. It is all there in front of me, and I can't wait to have it in my mouth. The combination of his musky scent and mine fill my nostrils. I waste no time, and jam it deep into my mouth. My tongue swirls around it at the base and I flick it over the top of his sack. His hand finds the back of my head, cradling me, holding me in place as he moans in delight. I would do the same if I wasn't straining not to gag. He lets go of me, and I pull back, my eyes watering as I look up at him. I squeeze the base of it, amazed at how hard he is. I run my tongue up and down the length of it. He watches me, and I look up at him as I service him. His hands find my breasts; my nipples so hard they would scratch glass. I moan at his touch; firm yet gentle at the same time. He has magnificent hands, strong but gentle all at once.

He straightens and pulls his t-shirt over his head while I continue to work him over. I look and see his carved abs and reach to touch them. I don't want to pull his cock from my mouth long enough to approve. After a moment or two of trips up one side and down the other with my tongue, he has had as much as he can stand. He helps me to my feet. I walk to the bed and he follows. He pulls at the bottom of his jeans, removing them as he reaches the side of the bed. I lie on my back, ready to be taken. He comes to me, but stops as his face reaches my thighs. "Thank God I trimmed the bushes before I left" I think. I am ready for him to be inside me, the overwhelming desire almost enough to protest his delay. He kisses the inside of my knee, and suddenly I too am on board with his idea. His soft kisses and flicking tongue on my thighs are making me ache for it.

He is taking too long; I am too wound up for the slow and steady pace he is setting. He finally reaches his goal, only to skip over it and kisses up towards my stomach. I groan, aggravated that I will have to endure a little more of this torture. Suddenly I feel his fingers pierce my soft flesh below. I arch instantly, the relief of pleasure rushing through me. I grab the sheets trying not to buck wildly as I feel the sensation deep inside me. I lift my hips off the mattress, silently begging for his mouth on me. I feel it, and let out a deep growl as he now works his fingers into me while delivering a proper tongue lashing. Bridging off the bed completely now, his hand hold my bum to steady me. I throw my leg over his back, pulling him into me as my desire climbs to maddening heights. I feel my orgasm rising again, and I feel my breath leave my body in short quick bursts. I groan aloud, and get louder with each stroke of his tongue. His mouth is all over me, and I can take no more. I scream in desire, explosions firing through me as my body convulses in orgasm after orgasm. I cannot tell when one stops and another starts. My strength diminishes, and I can longer hold myself up in this position. He is still standing next to the bed, and lets me crumble back to the mattress. I am paralyzed as he climbs into bed with me.

I lie still for a moment; I feel like every cell in my body is vibrating.

29

Her Eyes

The feeling in my body slowly returns, and only then do I become conscious that he is next to me. I open my eyes to find him looking at me, smiling. "Wipe that smile off your face, you arrogant Yankee" I tell him, smiling back. He laughs to himself, and comes back with "Why don't you try to wipe the smile off my face." He already knows how to get to me. I take his words as the challenge they are, and roll over on top of him. I feel his hardness between my legs, and want it in me. I reach down and grab it at the base. I slowly push down onto it, feeling it slide inch by inch into my depths. He lets out a groan as I slowly envelop him. I push down, sliding back and forth on it, making sure I get it all the way inside. I am filled to the hilt. I lean over to put my mouth on his; I kiss him deeply. I love being on top and in control. "Let me do it" I whisper to him.

I begin slowly at first, grinding our bodies together. It is so deep it almost hurts...almost. I kiss him again, our passion growing as our fervor for one another intensifies. We kiss like lovers long separated, together at last. I feel my hips moving faster as my mind shuts down and my body takes over. I glide back and forth over him with ease; our bodies glistened with sweat and fluid. I am close. I feel the internal signal and know what I need. I push down, thrusting him into me. His hands reach for me and I grab them, putting where I want them most. His hands firmly grab the soft flesh of my breasts, holding them in place as I grind faster and faster, closing in on it. I slap my hands onto his chest, digging my nails in as I feel the huge bubble inside me begin to burst. I am frozen with pleasure, my breath trapped inside me. Suddenly it happens, the bubble breaks and I explode. I hear myself cry out, my hips at instantly at full speed as I ride him into the skies. I can feel my own juices leave me, running down his leg. I collapse on top of him, spasming, convulsing as I drift back to Earth.

After what seems like a long time I feel him push me off onto the mattress. I slide off of him, face down on the sheets, unable to lift myself if I wanted to; Jell-O. He bends me into a new position, my leg up against my chest. I feel him inside me again, the spike of pleasure restoring some of my equilibrium. I push back into him, suddenly desiring more. I moan again, arching to get more of him. Soon he is pounding into me, seemingly close to his own. He is slamming himself into me, slapping my ass with his thighs. His hands grip my hips roughly, pulling me with even more force into him. His groans grow rapid, and I feel him tense up. I squeeze for all I am worth, pushing back, urging him on. I feel him expand inside me, feeling the stream of hot liquid released into me. He expends himself, holding above me.

I look back at him; he kisses me, tenderly this time. He lies down next to me, his arm pulling me close to him. We lay still, spooning, breathing and savoring. I drift off to sleep in his arms, although it seems only for a moment. We jump as the phone rings for the wakeup call. I look at the clock; it is 6:00am already. I grumble and head for the shower. He jumps up to meet me at the door. He kisses me a small kiss, saying goodbye. As much as I want to spend the entire day in bed with him, we are going to be late if we even think about it. He heads to his room to shower.

I walk into the lobby, searching for him. I walk over and introduce myself to him in front of everyone, absolving my sins with feigned unfamiliarity. He catches onto my desire for secrecy and plays along. We get on the bus once it arrives, and sit together chatting about business. He taps my arm and signals for me to listen to the people behind us. I tune in, and hear a woman complaining she could not sleep last night. "Why not?" her friend asks. She replies "Oh my God, you should have heard the people next to me going at it...they were having a good old time." We look at one another and are fighting not to laugh aloud and give ourselves away. We barely contain ourselves as we pull into company headquarters. I am so glad the third trip to the states finally has the adventure I have been looking for.

Deidre

I hear his voice outside the door and for some reason it catches my attention. I hear the door handle rattle, and am holding my breath to see who walks through the door. I have no idea why, but suddenly I am really nervous. He steps through and our eyes meet, and then I know why. I am instantly attracted to him. It was as if I knew it was coming, like he voice tipped me off that lightning was about to strike. I stand and take a step towards him, introducing myself with a handshake. His grip is firm yet not overbearing, and it seems just to linger a tiny little bit than necessary. He is taller than I am by a few inches, enough to wear heels with. I smile at my thought, knowing we are a long way away from that point. He looks like he is fit under his work attire, and I like his shoes. I can't believe after all this time someone has finally gotten my attention. I was starting to think that maybe it would never happen again.

From time to time I reflect back to my last relationship, and how it ended many years ago. It took me a long, long time to get over Eddie, and part of me never wants to go through that again. And yet this man has given me a spark of hope, a glimmer of a chance that I could love again. It seems crazy to think that in an instant I could feel and think so much, but it is true. It was as if one look at him was all it took.

Several weeks have gone by and I find myself looking forward to our meetings more so than when we began. Things are winding down and I cringe at the thought of not having a reason to see him once we are finished with this. I find myself rehearsing asking him out for a drink sometime, trying to find the words to not sound desperate or too forward. I am praying he will ask me so I will not have to, but I am prepared if necessary because I do want to see him socially. I feel too much to have this end now. I have spent the last few weeks getting to know him, to love his smile and the way he makes me feel just being around him. I take time to make sure I look nicer than usual when it is my day to see him, just so he'll hopefully notice. One more week to go; I can hardly stand the fact that I don't know what is going to happen next. I want to ask him just so the suspense doesn't kill me. We have become more friendly over the weeks, so I hope he will want to continue at least that part. Maybe we'll there, I console myself.

Her Eyes

Another week passes and this is it. We know that today is the last meeting we have scheduled. I exhale deeply as I brush my eyelashes with my mascara. I chose my outfit for today carefully; something that makes me feel confident and sexy and still looks very classy. I enter his office after taking what will probably be the last deep breath for a while. I walk into the room, and turn to shut the door behind me. I spin and start across the room, smiling a huge smile as soon as I see him. "Today is the least day, huh?" I ask him, trying to make it sound like I haven't been thinking about this moment for weeks now. "I believe it is" he says coolly. Suddenly I feel like maybe he wasn't worried about it, like it wasn't going to matter to him that next week I won't be here. I feel the color leaving my face as I quickly ponder him comment. He seems to notice, and rescues me from my dilemma. "Don't worry, I have a feeling we may be seeing more of each other soon" he informs me. "If you were to agree to that" he adds. "Are you asking me out?" I ask, trying to hide my sheer delight and relief. He hesitates for just a moment, making me sweat it just a little more before answering "Yes, I am asking you out. I would love it if you joined me for dinner sometime." I smile back at him, so happy to hear the words. "I would really like that" I reply, trying my best not to jump up and down in front of him. I am so relieved I feel like a huge weight has been lifted from me. I turn and walk to the chair where we always sit, eager to move on now that the suspense is behind us.

Our discussion begins, and we both seem to be relaxed and having fun today. We are going over the details of our time together, making sure all the details are covered. We pour through the information and the hour passes by far too quickly. Before I am ready, we are finished. We both stand and he extends his hand to conclude our business together. I return the gesture, and our time and client and professional conclude. We give one another a lingering look, and then he turns as walks towards his office.

Two days later my phone rings with a number I do not recognize. I hope that it is him as I answer the call. As soon as I he says hello I know it is him. I can hear the excitement in my own voice as I accept his invitation. I immediately start to mentally scan my wardrobe and think that I have got to find a dress for this occasion. I have not been on a date in a long time. Suddenly I am very nervous about this pending date on

Saturday night. Despite how much I wanted this to happen, I am really worried about what will happen.

Saturday rolls around and I have lots to do. I start by cleaning the house even though we are going out tonight. I skip lunch in favor of more time at the mall to find the right dress for tonight. I go from store to store looking for the right little black dress. Finally I find the perfect dress, and fortunately it is also on sale. I am very happy to have found something I like and not have to pay full price for it. I look at my watch and see that it is already four o'clock. I had better get moving, he will be at my place before I know it. I pay for the dress and head for the car.

I arrive back at the house at 4:30, and am already feeling like I am running out of time. I head for the shower, making all the preparations needed for a first date. I realize just how long it's been since I had a first date, and I get nervous all over again. I start the process of doing my hair, hoping I get it to look right the first time through. I fight with it, cursing at myself for making this harder than it needs to be. I check the time, and it is 6:30 already. I decide to leave it the way it is and move on. I begin putting make up on, standing in the bathroom in my black lacey bra and underwear. I open the door and walk out, going to the stereo to put on some music. I hear a car slowing down on the street and nearly have a panic attack until I realize that it is not him. I go back to the bathroom to finish getting ready, praying I can make it through the evening without dumping food on either one of us or saying something that is totally off base for the conversation.

I go to the closet door to retrieve my new dress, carefully pulling it over my head to avoid messing up my hair or getting makeup on the black fabric. I sort through my eight pairs of black heels looking for the right ones to complete the outfit. I dump everything out of my purse onto the bed and shove it into the smaller black purse needed for the occasion. I grab my heels and head to the living room to wait for his arrival. I glance at the clock and it appears I may not have long to wait. I sit on the edge of the couch, fidgety and nervous, waiting. After a few moments I hear a car pull up in the driveway. I look at the clock again; it is exactly 7:30pm. I am going to have to remember this, as I have a bad habit of being late for everything. I hear him approach the door and knock, and my heart jumps. I leap off the couch at the noise, and slip on my stiletto heels before walking to the door. My feet hurt in the first few steps, but they are perfect for the dress so I will ignore it.

I open the door and find him very well dress and smiling ear to ear at me. He is hiding something behind his back, and I have to assume he brought me flowers. He accepts my invitation into the house, and follows me to the kitchen. He makes a cute production of presenting the flowers to me, and I love it. I am flattered that he went to the trouble for me. "Roses….they are beautiful" I compliment him on his selection. I retrieve a vase from the cupboard and put the roses in water and display them on the counter. I lead him around the house for an obligatory tour, feeling like a real estate agent as we walk from room to room. I am heading for the door when I hear his voice several steps behind me. "Doing your best Pat Benetar impression?" I jerk around, stunned to hear his question. He is standing in front of the bookshelf with the photo of me on stage at the Roxy. "How did you know that?" I exclaim, shocked that he could tell what I was doing in that photo. "I don't know…just a feeling I had" he tells me, shrugging it off like it was no big deal. I am floored; I can't believe that he could intuit so much with just a glance. "I was singing Fire and Ice in this shot. That is freaky that you knew that" I tell him, totally perplexed. I look at him quizzically, and then turn for the door. I am totally freaked out.

He opens the car door for me and I settle in, trying to put that rattling experience behind me. We drive down the street to a nice restaurant where he made reservations. We chat freely over dinner, talking and enjoying each other's company. I find myself more relaxed with him than I expected to be, and soon I quit worrying so much about what I say and how I say it. Dinner was wonderful and I am so full I think I might burst out of my dress. The waiter approaches and asks "Would you two care for some dessert?" I begin to protest the idea, but he asks for the check before I can answer. He looks over at me with that boyish smile of his, and asks "How does ice cream strike you?" I smile at him, thinking it is a nice idea but I am not sure I could stuff any more food into me tonight.

He pays for dinner and leaves a healthy tip and we leave the restaurant. I didn't realize just how noisy it was in there until we stepped outside. We get back in the car and head down the street, pulling into the ice cream shop in a strip mall nearby. I already ate more tonight than is lady-like, and now I am eating ice cream too? I am going to have to spend four hours at the gym tomorrow to burn all this off. I follow him into the shop, and as soon as we enter I feel my teeth ache. "I don't really eat ice cream" I tell him in a feeble protest. "You don't like ice cream?" he asks, looking at me like I am crazy. "That is not the problem, I like it too much. If I want to fit into this dress, I don't eat ice cream" I tell him, pleading my case. "Well you're already in that dress, so come on" he says, grabbing my hand and pulling me forward.. "You can get a child size if it makes you feel better. Besides, you ate like a pound of pasta at dinner" he says accusingly but with a playful smile. "I did not!" I protest loudly, smacking his arm. We both laugh out loud and then order from the acne-riddles kid behind the counter. "Let's go for a walk" he suggested. My feet are killing me, but it seems like such an old fashioned, charming thing to do that I agree.

He seems to know where we are headed, and I follow him around the corner to a park that is right next to the strip mall. I can smell the lake that is nearby, the pungent odor of water with a slight tinge of fish to it. But the atmosphere is perfect; it is a nice night and it is very quiet as we walk along talking. I am so impressed by his considerate manner and his old fashion approach to our date. He makes me feel like the center of the whole world tonight. We walk towards a table and stop there. He leans against the edge of the table, and I stand in front of him. I am wondering if his kiss will be as good as everything else so far tonight. I look up him, hoping he will get the hint that I am dying for him to kiss me. He looks at me for a moment and then looks at the ground. Oh my God, he is shy too. I can't believe this guy! He is so amazing.

"Can I have a bite of that?" he asks me softly. I lift the cone to his mouth and he takes a bite of the ice cream. He holds his up for me to do the same, and I lean forward to take a bite. He moves it, like he is tease me with it. He shoots me that delightful boyish grin of his again, and holds the ice cream up for me again. I lean forward to take a bite, but to my surprise he pulls it away and leans in to kiss me. I am surprised and it takes me a second to realize what happened. I start to kiss him back but he stops and pulls away. A moment later he is back, and I kiss him like I meant to the first time. I put my arms around him and hold myself against him, drinking in the moment. My head is spinning, and I feel like I am floating off the ground. He pulls away from me again, and I open my eyes after a moment to look at him. He is staring at me, smiling. He tosses the rest of his cone into the trashcan a few feet away. I try to be cool and copy his move, but I miss. "Nice shot" he tells me, laughing at me a little. "Shut up and kiss me again" I tell him, smiling a huge smile. He does, pulling me close and holding me firm as his mouth devours mine. It is wonderful.

We walk towards the car and I know the evening is going to conclude soon. I can't invite him back to my place so soon, even if we don't do anything it just seems too soon for that. But I don't want him to think I do not like him or want to, its just too soon for me. It's been too long. My mind wanders as I deliberate my situation. Finally I decide to verbalize my thoughts. "Look, its been a long time since I have been in this situation. I hope you can be patient with me as I get used to dating someone again" I plead, hoping he will understand. "How long has it been?" he asks gently. I decide to come clean and tell him the whole story. "I used to date someone who was in a band; he traveled a lot and I stayed home living my life around the brief visits from him. It went on like that for eight years, and I finally gave up and ended it. I haven't dated anyone since." He is quiet for a moment, and he delay in responding is making me rethink my decision to tell him. "Wow, how long ago was that?" he asks finally. "Six years ago, hmm, more like six and a half" I confess. He has another agonizingly long pause and then breaks into a smile. "How am I doing so far?" he asks. I breath a huge sigh of relief and inform him "Not bad....not too bad" I say laughing. His well thought question has calmed my internal storm. I climb into the car feeling much better about everything. He drives me home and walks me to the door. I kiss him heavily at the door and bid him a good night. All I want to do now is still by the phone until he calls me for the next time we can see each other.

As time progresses we see more and more of each other. We talk on the phone almost daily and spend every weekend together. I am letting my guard down finally, and my desire for him is ever increasing. I love the way he kisses me, holds me, touches me. Being that intimate with someone again after all this time scares me, but it excites me as well. I am going to have to make a decision soon. We make dinner plans for Saturday night, dinner at my brother's place. I am house-sitting for the summer and love his home. It is perfect for a romantic dinner and an intimate evening together. I think that Saturday will be the day, our first time together. It will be easier for more on my own terms, at my own place. I am envisioning an elaborate evening; complete with dinner, wine, rose petals on the floor to the bedroom, and maybe even a sexy new negligee just for the occasion.

I call him and we make plans for Saturday night. I tell him we will be spending the night in, and "dessert" will be served as well. Ever since our first date when we had ice cream the term "dessert" has become synonymous with sex. At first it made me nervous, but he has proven patient and deserving of my trust. I tell him to arrive at 7:00, and be sure to go to the door by the garage, knowing the front door is too close to the bedroom and will give away the rose petal surprise. I know the next three days will be spent in preparation, hoping to make every single detail right and try to plan everything that happens to a tee. "I have a surprise for you" I whisper in the phone to him, hoping he catches on.

Friday rolls around and I run to Victoria's Secret at the mall to find something appropriate to wear for our "after dinner" fun. God I am so nervous about this. Everything is laid out to plan; I will make dinner and we will make love all night long. I want this to be as special as if it is my first time; and in some ways it is. It has been so long since I have been with someone. At least this time around I know what I am doing, I laugh to myself. My brother's house is so much nicer than mine; I am glad I am house sitting again this summer. A sprawling floor plan, pool, Jacuzzi, and a huge master bedroom with the greatest bed in the world. It will be the perfect scene for our first time together, and I will remember this night forever.

My next stop is my friend's flower shop; picking up the rose petals she has been gathering for me the past week. When she hands me the bag and asks what these are for, she could tell by the look on my face what I had planned in the near future. "Have a good time, honey. And do call me to tell me all about it the day after" she says, beaming a huge smile at me. I feel the heat rising in my face as I feel strangely embarrassed about what I am doing. "Thanks" I tell her, grabbing the bag and heading for the car. I check the time; it is later than I thought. I rush into the store and grab everything on my list for dinner and run for the car. I speed home and turn on the oven, start the salad preparations while it heats up. I put the brisket in the oven, browning it on all sides before adding everything else. My grandmother would be proud I think to myself as I slide the giant pan into the oven. I set the timer for three hours and I tend to the rest. I roll out the dough for the dinner rolls and make a mental note of 6:45 to put them in the oven. I skip through the house, grabbing the last few items that need picked up. I head to the stereo and put in my favorite six CDs and program it to play randomly throughout the night.

As I walk through the house lighting candles and dimming lights, I look at the carpet, and realize I have not vacuumed yet. I run to the closet and grab the vacuum cleaner. Plugging it in, I beg the process of vacuuming the entire house. I can't believe that I forgot to do this until right now. I am in a panic as this oversight is throwing off everything. I wonder what else I have forgotten…Oh my God, the rose petals!!! I stop in the middle of vacuuming and run to the car. Damn, the door is locked. I run back into the house, and catch myself once I enter the house. "Calm down, everything is going to be fine" I tell myself aloud. I see the bottle of wine on the counter next to my purse and decide that might help calm my nerves a little. I open the bottle with my brother's fancy air injector cork screw and pour myself a tall glass of red. I take two big swallows, one deep breath, and them calmly walk to the car to get the rose petals.

I have two big bags of rose petals in one hand and a half full glass of wine in the other as well as the car keys. Just as I enter the house again one of the bas slips out of my hand. I reach to grab it, and in the process tip my glass towards the floor. Red wine spills out, dousing the white carpet right in front of the door. "AAAGGGHHHH!" I scream out loud. Frozen, I stare at the stain on my brother's white carpet. My brain is on overload as I try to think how to handle this. I run into the house and grab a pot, filling it with water. I run back to the wine stain and dump the water all over it, diluting the mess. I go to the garage to find the carpet cleaner and drag the big heavy thing into the house. I plug it in and look behind me, only to find the wheels have left dirt marks all over the carpet. "Dammit!" I yell. What next?!?!" I am getting so frustrated I feel like I could cry. I collect myself and slowly start to run the carpet cleaner over the wet spot just inside the door. Slowly the red stain disappears, but the carpet is still very wet. I try to get the vacuum cleaner to erase the dirt marks from the carpet cleaner, but to no avail. I am going to have to use the carpet cleaner on that too. I look at the clock on the wall, it read 6:25pm. Shit! Grab the vacuum and stuff it into the closet and pick up the carpet as best I can, running with it to the garage. I scramble upstairs to get ready, jumping in the shower. I quickly rinse off and shampoo my hair. Turning off the water I rub baby oil all over me and then dry off, wiping the residue from my skin. I wipe the mirror off and quickly put on makeup as my hair starts to curl from the steam. Grabbing the hair dryer and opening the door, I start to style my hair, praying I can get it right on the first try.

I walk into the bedroom and see the black dress laid out on the bed, and the Victoria Secret bag next to it. I dump the contents of the bag out, tearing off the tags and slipping into the silky thong and bra. I jump into the dress and grab a pair of heels out of the closet. I check the time....6:45! As I approach the kitchen I can smell something burning and realize it is the roast. I break into a sprint, yanking open the oven door. Oh my God....No!!! The brisket is burnt to a crisp. I slam the door in disgust, mad at myself for being so stupid. I look at the counter top to see the rolls still sitting on the baking sheet. Everything is falling apart, I had all of this planned out perfectly and it is falling apart! I feel myself starting to break down, wanting to cry. I catch myself, shaking it off, trying to come up with a plan. I grab the phone and call the Italian place down the street and make a reservation. I hear a car pull up out front, and run to the window to see if it is him. I hear a knock on the door. Shit! I yell aloud. I am not really ready, but I don't have a choice. I grab the garage door opener, my jacket, and my heels. "Be right there!" I shout towards the door. Opening the door as little as possible, I step over the wet spot on the carpet and squeeze out. "Change in plans, we are going out" I explain. "Alright, where are we going?" he asks. He is cool and calm as usual, and I am a wreck on the inside, trying my best to hide it. We climb in the car and I guide him to the restaurant.

We walk in and the Maître D seats us in a corner away from everyone else. The room is dark and filled with couples talking quietly to one another. The atmosphere is nice, and after a few moments I begin to calm down and enjoy the moment. Dinner is wonderful, and he puts me at ease once again. I look at him in the dimly light restaurant and think to myself "Yes, tonight is the night." The waiter comes over and asks if we would like dessert, interrupting my thoughts. I stammer for an answer, but he jumps in and saves me, asking just for the check. I feel myself blushing again, as if the waiter could read my thoughts when he walked to the table.

Once again in the car, we head for the house. After several moments of silence, he asks "Everything OK?" "Yeah, I am just a little nervous" I confess. I am also worried about the mess I left behind and how I am going to explain my way around it. "Look, we don't have to...you know, tonight. It's okay, I understand" he says softly. I look over at him, my eyes almost welling up with tears at his consideration for me. "Thanks" I tell him. We pull into the driveway and I open the garage door. We walk through the garage and into the house, avoiding the mess by the door. It still smells slightly of burned pot roast and the doughy rolls are now flat from sitting in the air for quite some time. I grab the tray and jam it into the oven before he notices. I have an idea; we should get into the Jacuzzi and start things there. He is walking around the big kitchen, admiring it. "Wow...I've always wanted a kitchen like this" he says aloud. "Me too" I agree. "Wait here" I add, going to the bedroom on this side of the house.

I rummage through the drawers and find a pair of swim trunks that he can wear. I return to the kitchen and suggest "Change and I'll meet you in the Jacuzzi" as I point to the door that leads out back. He turns and walks into the bathroom to change and I run to the master bedroom. I grab the bag of flower petals and create a trail of rose petals from the door to the bed, a perfect S curve if I do say so myself. Lighting candles all around the room, I then quickly change into my bikini and run back to the kitchen. I grab two bottles of beer and head outside, grabbing pool towels out of the hall closet on the way. I turn on the backyard lights on a dim setting and walk outside. He is already in the water waiting for me. As I enter the Jacuzzi he stands to meet me. I stop on the stairs and look at him for a moment, the greenish glow of the water highlighting his athletic build, his broad shoulders. I smile in approval and then lean down to kiss him, melting into his arms. His warm, wet flesh envelops me as we kiss. After moment we part and he steps back letting his eyes take a long look at me. It makes me shiver to have him look at me that way. He seems to be searching for something to say, and finally "Wow" escapes his lips. Not poetic, but good enough I think to myself.

We sit down in the water right next to one another, and I feel his leg next to mine. I feel like a little girl in the back of a movie theater on a first date, giddy and nervous. He reaches over to find my hand, and we hold hands underwater. His touch relaxes me, and I look up to me his gaze. His eyes say it all; he wants me as much as I do him. He leans over and kisses me with a warm soft kiss. I am lost in it, swimming in the feeling, floating. He stops and stands; the steam is rising off of his body like he is smoldering. I drink in a long look at him and then reach to touch his rippling stomach. I am mesmerized at the way the drops of water bead on his skin, and I trace my fingers over his hot flesh. I run my finger down the groove in the middle of his stomach, and then lean forward to touch my tongue to his skin. The switch has flipped, I am no longer treading lightly; I am down for tonight to happen.

I look up at him while I gently kiss my way up his stomach and towards his face. I gently drag my lips up his neck, kissing the water away as I go. I stand on my toes and whisper into his ear "I want you to make love to me tonight." I hear him groan in approval and his arms surround me, holding me, making me feel safe and secure. I feel his hand on the side of my face and I pull back to look at him once more. "I have wanted you since the moment I saw you" he tells me. We kiss again, more passionately this time. Despite how hot the water is the cool air is making me cold and I can feel the goosebumps growing on me. I reach for his hand and lead him to the stairs again, wrapping myself in a towel in effort to try and stop my chills. He does the same, and I lead him into the living room. I slide back the glass door and shut it behind us and then lead him to the far door of the bathroom, careful not to reveal the surprise of the flowers just yet.

We walk into the bathroom and I step into the huge shower to turn on the water. "Watch this" I tell him, loving the rainfall shower. I get under the water and he follows, and suddenly I realize that we are going to start here. His body presses against mine. I lean back to slick my hair back under the water and he holds my hand so I can linger there. He pulls me back up and then spins me around so he is now under the water. He washes the chlorine smell from his skin, and I watch as his hands travel over his own body. He touches me under my chin and lifts my mouth to meet his again, and I throw my arms around his neck, wanting him to take me right here in the shower. He leans back, picking me up off the ground and holds me there. I can feel his growing excitement pressing against my leg, and it makes me ache so deep in anticipation of him inside me.

He puts me back down on the hard floor, my feet feeling lighter than ever before. He turns me around, pulling me against him. I feel his mouth on my neck, gently nibbling and biting my flesh. It sends shivers all through me and I arch my back to press into him even harder. I feel him slowly tug at the string of my bikini top. He moves slowly, taking his time despite my rising desire. His hands are on my stomach, and they slowly drift upward until he is cupping my breasts in his hands. I put my head back on his shoulder, the feeling of being touched after all this time almost too much to bear. His fingers gently play with my nipples, making them grow ever harder with each brush of his fingertips.

His hands explore me, gently running over my body under the warm water. His teeth bite deep into my neck, and my knees nearly buckle from the feeling. I arch my back more in response, feeling his hardness against my lower back as I do. I want to touch it, to taste it, I want it inside me. I want everything all at once. I grind against it, pressing it between us. I lean back and kiss him again as I reach down and grab the string for the bottom of my bathing suit. I want him now; the desire growing out of control. I need him inside me before I burst into pieces. I pull the string and feel it release, and do the same with the other one as well. I wriggle my hips a little and it slides out from between us. The only thing separating us is the thin material of the suit he is wearing, and it is doing little to contain him at this point. His hands run down my thighs and then back up. He brushes his fingers over my waiting mound, only to move on once again. I am dying to be touched, to be released but he continues to tease me, to take his time.

I reach behind me, feeling it for the first time. I grab it, squeezing it, feeling its length. I want it now. I reach into his waistband and find the drawstring, pulling it upward. I release the material, the only thing separating us drops to the floor. Now we are both naked under the water, our bodies pressing firmly against one another. I rub against him, feeling his cock rub against my ass. After a brief moment he quickly spins me around, pressing me into the wall. His hands grab my breasts, rougher this time, desiring and almost uncontrolled. I gasp, surprised at the sudden burst but then moan in delight as he is moving us closer to what I so desperately need right now. His hand parts my legs, and I feel his fingers touch me down there. Suddenly one of them is inside me, and I toss my head back in a deep moan. My body surrounds him as he slowly works it in and out of me.

His mouth is on my nipple, sucking it firmly. He is growing rougher but the moment, his desire for me rising as well. I put my hand on the back of his head to let him know I like it, to encourage his actions. He drops down to his knees in the shower, his face even with where his finger was. "What are you....?" I can't even finish my sentence before his face is between my thighs. I feel his silky hot tongue slide up and over my pulsating clit. My legs can no longer support me; I feel myself falling and yet and more concerned about the heat and pleasure radiating through me from below. I reach out to the wall, trying to brace myself. His hands find my hips, and they help steady me. I throw a leg over his shoulder and grab the back of his head to hang on to. His tongue shoots into me, and I feel it boil up inside me. "Oh God!" I cry out, and it is the last thought through my head for several moments. Everything is feeling; intense, pleasured, and explosive. I dig my nails into his shoulder as my body convulses in a tremendous orgasm. It was what I pictured, like it had been trapped inside me for so long, finally released. It ripples through me, wave after wave until it slowly subsides. I slump forward against him, incapable of standing on my own from what he did to me.

A hazy moment later we are out of the shower, drying our bodies. I barely remember leaving the water, but am growing more sober by the moment. He grabs my hand and leads me towards the other door into the bedroom. He opens it, finding the rose petals on the floor and the candles burning all around the room. He freezes in his tracks, stunned as he looks at me. "When did you do this?" he asks in surprise. I smile a huge smile at him, proud of the affect my surprise had and thankful of his appreciation of my efforts. "When you were waiting for me in the Jacuzzi" I answer. He is hesitating for some reason, but I have grown tired of waiting. He has opened the door, and a flood of emotions and desire has taken me. I grab his hand, stepping around the flowers and leading him to the bed.

We reach the side of the bed, and suddenly I stop. I am fighting myself; parting of me wanting to make love all night long and part of me afraid to take the last step. I need reassuring; I want him to remind me everything will be ok. I turn and look at him, searching his eyes for an answer. He looks back at me, smiles, and says to me "If I forget to tell you, later, I had a really good time tonight." I don't know how he does it, but once again he read me perfectly. I smile and sigh in relief. He puts his hands on my face and kisses me tenderly, slow and controlled once again. I relax against him, feeling comfort in his arms once again. I reach my arms around his back, squeezing myself against him, our naked bodies pressing into one another once more. I feel him moving and open one eye to see him pulling back the covers. He climbs into bed and holds the sheets back for me. Always the gentleman, I think to myself.

I climb into the silky sheets and the comforter falls around me. I am enveloped in his arms and the feel of skin against my skin. He rolls towards me, wrapping his arms around me and then rolls away, pulling me on top of him. I feel small on top of him, his body large under mine. He kisses me again, his hands slowly traveling over me. I can feel a thread of moisture run out of me, and my desire to be touched is increasing again. I feel his hard stomach against me and I open myself to rub against him. I break from our kiss as I toss my head back in pleasure again. His hard stomach and smooth skin having much more affect on me than I anticipated. I plant my hands on the bed and lift myself up, slightly changing the angle of my body into his. I grind against him, gaining speed and force, his skin slick with my creamy juices. I go farther with each stroke, and soon can feel his hard cock pressing into me on my downward stroke. It pushes into my soft, silky folds, almost entering me.

His arm is over my shoulder and he guides me down on his hard cock. His flesh is so stiff, penetrating me in one smooth stroke. The feeling is amazing, and he is inside me as I desired. I close my eyes, lost in sensation, feeling nothing but the unison of our bodies. I press my face against his chest. It builds and builds inside me. I continue my steady pace, the climb to the top delicious and frustrating at the same time. I want it; I want him to release me again. I feel his hips tilt up into me and I freeze. He touched me so deep inside; I am paralyzed by it. He does it again and this time the effect is different. I explode in a huge orgasm, as if everything bottled up inside me released at once. I become lost in it once again. I lose my rhythm and he takes over, extending it that much more. I slowly go limp on top of him, melting my body into is. We lay as one, entwined in one another.

After a few moments he rolls me over and is now on top of me. I have given myself over, welcoming him to do as he pleases with me. He starts slowly again, sliding in and out of me in short gentle strokes. The feeling is incredible; he probes deep into me with some strokes, never letting me forget how deep inside he can touch me. I put my hand in his ass, wanting to feel him work. I move my hips, timing his strokes into me as best I can. I feel it building again, another one on its way. As I moan and wriggle under him his pace increases. He kisses me again, my mouth never getting enough of him. He moans a little as we kiss, and I can feel him growing inside me. As he increases I feel more and more friction between us. I wrap my leg around him, bucking my hips harder as we climb together. I arch into him, allowing him even deeper into me. It feels amazing and I am going to come again. His groans of desire increase, and we may finish together. My begins first; I freeze for just a second, my mouth open but no noise coming out. Then the release comes, cascading through me. I feel me deep moan rattling through me as my nails dig into his flesh. He is growing closer and I feel his strokes go deeper. He pushes deep, holds, and then explodes into me. I feel it all through him, his body shaking all over as he comes for me.

It was amazing, and I almost feel like I could cry. My emotions almost getting the better of me, trapped for so long, finally released. My body is warm and vibrating, and I lay under him. He is breathing heavy but quickly his body calms. He looks at me, and has the same look in his eyes that I do. "That was…." He starts, but drifts off, not able to find the words. "Yeah….I start, but also unable to complete my thought. He kisses me once more, this time as tender as ever. We wrap in each others arms, and eventually fall asleep like this. The next thing I realize it is morning. I awake in his arms, his body warm against mine. I feel something touch my lips and I jump in reaction. I laugh at myself, the old walls in place for just a moment until I realize….its him.

"Mmmm, I slept so good" I tell him, purring like a cat. I am ready for more, my body feeling his so close. We kiss, and then I slide down, kissing his chest and feeling his body come to life once again. I slide back up to kiss him again and slowly climb on top of him once again. Our kisses grow deeper as our bodies become one once again. We make love once again, this time tender and gentle. It is perfect, despite its contract to the passion last night. I feel safe and small in his arms, and want to spend the rest of my life there.

Donna

"God I am so bored being back here at home. I am so glad I went away to college and got out of this crappy little town, even if it was just for a little while. Nothing exciting happens here, ever." Flopped on the couch with the remote in hand I know my Friday night will be spent here instead of doing something fun. My brother is coming up from Phoenix this weekend, which means we will be playing happy family for the next few days. Dad will be his usual cheery self, and Paul will be telling stories about whatever he is up to these days. I don't know if I can take two whole days of that. I wonder what Paul will think of my new look; I am sure that I have at least one of his usual lectures in my near future. Dad certainly hasn't let up since I've been home.

I see lights approaching and soon I will no longer be alone in the house. I can't tell if it is Dad or Paul as I look out the window from the den. I sit back on the couch figuring I will find out soon enough. I hear a car door shut, so it must be Paul because Dad would have pulled in the garage. I hear someone knock on the front door, who the Hell is here? I get up and walk to the front door curious as to who would be coming by the house on a Friday night. I look through the peephole and see a familiar face. Oh my God its Darren; my brother's friend who practically grew up with us. I haven't seen him in years; my stomach tightens up knowing how much I liked him all this time. He was my first crush, and he teased me relentlessly. No wonder I have so many issues with men.

I take a deep breath and open the door. I pull the door open and am still surprised to see him standing in front of me. However the look on his face is much more animated than mine. He stares at me in disbelief, looking me over as if to confirm that it is really me under all the metal and makeup. After a moment of silence he finally says "Wow, you look a little different since the last time we saw each other!" I play it cool and snicker at his comment, replying "In spite of what you may have thought, I did not remain twelve years old." I break into a smile and give him a big hug, suddenly feeling like the same little girl I used to be standing in front of him.

Her Eyes

I turn and walk back into the house, leading us back to the den. We talk just like old times, but I am uncomfortable in front of him. "Six years! I can't believe it's been over six years!" he exclaims, nearly making me jump at the suddenness of his words. I fidget with my hair and squirm in my seat, flip flopping back and forth between college girl and insecure pre-teen little girl when I last saw him. He has been frozen in time for me as well; his eyes look a little older, tired maybe. His college days of partying and hanging out with my brother are long gone. Now he has a busy job and a real life. And yet I see flashes of the old him as well, picking on me every chance he gets. If he only knew how many times I cried in my room after he and Paul would make fun of me. And yet I still wanted to spend every second of every summer with him. I would tag along with them any time I could, begging Dad to make them include me. And people wonder why girls grow up with such poor self esteem.

Our conversation dwindles and soon we are just watching TV together. I can't believe after six years we don't have more to talk about, and the silence makes me uncomfortable. I find myself fidgeting with my hair again, a nervous habit of mine. I keep sneaking glances at him and find him already looking at me some of the times I do. I smile nervously and my mind races through thoughts of kissing him, seeing him, touching him. I used to dream about him at night, touching myself in my bed, thinking of him. I long so much for him to notice me, to see me as a woman and not a little girl. But he never would. But now he is looking at me differently and I am dying to know what he is thinking. He makes a comment about the show we are watching, and it snaps me out of my thoughts. I laugh, and reveal that I hope I still will like my tattoos when I get to be his age. "Thanks a lot!" he says, catching on to my joke about our age differences. "Wait, you have a tattoo?" he asks. "Not a tattoo, three" I reply matter-of-factly. His eyes light up as he looks at me. It makes me feel warm inside. "Really? Can I see them?" he asks, sounding a little unsure. What a turn of events; now he is the one who is nervous in front of me. The feeling empowers me, and for the first time ever with him I feel like I am the one leading the conversation. I stand, turning away from him and begin to pull my shirt up over my back. I am trying to reach far enough to show him, but my arm won't bend that way. His voice startles me; he has stepped closer to me and it is lower than before. He offers to help and all of the sudden I realize exactly what situation I have created. I hesitate, trying to decide, to pick a side in my head as the voices all begin to speak at once. I shouldn't, I want to, I can't, we don't have time, I can't all firing at the same time. I hear myself agree, allowing him to help me. I feel him step closer, his hand grabbing the back of my shirt and pulling it up over me. I begin to describe what he is looking at; the spider on my shoulder and the web that extends down my side and across my lower back. I designed it, drew it myself and spent hours in the chair enduring the needle to create this. His fingertips brush my skin, and shudder at his touch and then jump in realization of what just happened. I turn to look at him. The look on his face says volumes.

I laugh nervously at the guilty look on his face. "Don't panic, it just tickled, that's all" I tell him. But it seems obvious that when he touched me things changed. His look is burning through me and I am grabbing the floor with my toes in effort to not turn and run away. I am waiting, and waiting. I am waiting for him to do something, to kiss me, to touch me again, anything. The moments pass and I grow more and more uncomfortable by the second. I can't take it anymore, and I start to think he doesn't want to kiss me. And then he reaches for me, touching my face tenderly, running his fingers along my ear. "Guess that little girl I used to know has grown up" he says, smiling down at me. I laugh nervously again, watching him looking at me multi-pierced ears. "That's true...and actually that's not all of my piercings" I hear myself say aloud. I can't believe it when I hear, but the words couldn't have come from anywhere but me. "You wanna see?" I ask, baiting him. "I did them myself" I tell him, proud of the fact that I could take the pain enough to do it. I turn away again and pull my shirt over my head, tossing it aside and covering my breasts shyly in my hands. I draw a breath and turn to face him.

I stand there in front of him, more exposed than I have ever been before. I feel so vulnerable; like his words could literally break me into pieces if he disapproves. My stomach is in knots, and I wait for some sign that he likes me, that he likes what he sees. He reaches for me, touching my stomach, tracing the lines of the tattoo there. He smiles what seems to be an approving smile, and my heart flutters. His touch warms my skin, the ache inside me growing. I want him to take me, right here right now. "We shouldn't be doing this" I hear myself say.

Her Eyes

Why did I say that?...cover, cover!!!! "But....." I start, stalling while I think. "Yes?" he asks, leaving me an opening. "I've had a crush on you for as long as I can remember. How much time do we have?" I ask, plunging head first into the pool of my trepidation. He looks at his watch, frowning a little. "Not much" he tells me, and my heart sinks momentarily. I've come this far... I tell myself. "Then we better get started!" I blurt out lifting my hands away and show them to him. His eyes widen in surprise and he looks me over for a brief second, as if to reassure himself this is going to happen right here, right now. He leans towards me, and I meet his advances, diving into his kiss. Our mouths meet and I groan; a lifetime of desire and curiosity finally satisfied. His tongue is strong and forceful, and it invades my mouth as we kiss harder. He spins me around and backs me towards the desk. He pushes me towards the edge, but I have something better in mind, especially if this is going to get cut short by my brother's untimely arrival.

I grab his arms and turn him, backing him against the desk as he did me. I reach down and grab his belt, my nervous hands shaking as I pull the leather through the loops. "Oh God I have always wanted to do this" I confess. I can feel his cock through his pants and it excites me that much more. I unzip his pants, dying to see what's inside. His cock plops out in front of me. I get on my knees to worship him as I have been dreaming all these years. I reach out and grab it, dying to taste him. I engulf as much of it as I can, sliding my mouth down it until I can feel my lips touch my fingers. I hear him moan and revel in his unspoken approval. I run my tongue all over it, over the side and down to his balls. I jerk it, feeling how hard it is in my hand. I am so into it I barely notice his hands on my shoulders until he pushes me away. I start to protest, wanting more but he grabs my hand and lifts me to my feet.

He kisses me deeply once again and runs his hands all over me. I feel him touch my nipple ring, and then pinch it. It sends shock waves of pleasure through me. I can hear is breathing is heavy and he seems very excited by our encounter. He pinches me again, this time a little too rough. I jump in reaction, telling him "Easy now, they are more sensitive than ever since I pierced them." He smiles at me, realizing the pain was not that bad. "Oh, I'm sorry; I'll kiss them and make them feel better. He takes it in his mouth, his tongue flicking over it. I grab the back of his head, tossing mine back in pleasure. It feels so good I never want him to stop.   Suddenly I feel his hand grab the top of my jeans, and he pulls them upward into me.   The tightness against my body sends a wave of shock and pleasure upward through me.   He holds it there, continuing the pressure against my clit.   After a moment he lets go and I relax, realizing only then that my toes were curling inside my shoes.   He kisses my breasts, flicking his tongue over one and then the other as he struggles to undo my jeans.   He looks down to see I am shaved and smiles. "Nnniccceee" is all he says.   And all he needed to.

He picks me up and sits me up on the edge of the desk.   I lean back on my elbows, waiting to see what he is going to do to me.   I open my legs slightly, offering myself to him.   He looks me in the eyes and I am lost in gaze.   Suddenly I feel something inside me down there and my eyes open wide in surprise.   I realize what happened and I close my eyes, feeling the sensation of his finger inside me echoing through my body. He moves it in and out of me; I feel it rubbing me inside.   He leans forward and I know what's coming.   I want his mouth on me and he gives it to me.   He expertly flicks his tongue over me and for a brief moment I wonder how many times he has done this.   I refocus, concentrating on the feeling as I close my eyes tightly.   I can hear myself moaning out loud as he runs his tongue up and down over me.   He pulls his fingers out and I feel empty all the sudden.   Then his tongue enters me, his mouth sealing over my pink pussy.   I slam my hands down on the desk and arch my back, exploding instantly at the sensation of his tongue inside me.   I scream his name, desperate for it to continue, wanting more, wanting it to never stop.   I grab the back of his head, bucking my hips into his face, grinding against him.   I am lost in it as I ride wave after wave of my orgasm.   I feel his fingers back inside me; different, stiff and rough instead of the languid softness of his tongue.   The change spurs my release onward, and I feel my juices squish out of me and he works his magic.

I am left breathless and weak after it.   I feel the hard desk under me, realizing I felt like I was floating only moments ago.   He removes his fingers from me and I look up to see him standing over me.   I feel it touch me, and then slide inside.   It is firm and commanding, forcing my body to accept it.   He pushes it halfway into me and stops.   I want it all, and convey my desires by grabbing his ass and pulling him towards me. He understands and pushes onward, filling me completely and then some. I jump in reaction to it touching my so deep. My body gives, taking it all within just a few moments. He increases his pace, and begins fucking me hard on top of the desk. I tilt my hips to meet his thrusts, gaining confidence in helping as we go. I look down to see it disappear inside me. The image of what he is doing to me will be burned in my mind forever.

His pace increases again, and the new gear is even better than before. I dig my nails into his back, my cries of ecstasy echoing through the house. His body slams into mine and I hang onto him for dear life and he fucks me into oblivion. I grow lost in it; inside my head, picturing it, feeling it. It is better than anything I have ever had. I feel his hands behind my back and he picks me up off the desk. His hands are locked behind me, and my legs are wrapped around his waist. It opens me even further to him, and I am anticipating the feeling of him impaling me with his cock like this. I wrap my arms around his neck to hold on while I arch my back and lift myself off of it. He pulls downward and rams me onto it, stuffing it deep into me.

He turns us around and I put my feet on the edge of the desk where I was sitting. I can now control my own leverage and I move up and down on him quickly. It is perfect; the feelings coursing through me as he fucks me. It only takes a few strokes and I explode all over him, my body shaking in his arms. I hear myself crying out "Oh God, Oh Fuck!" over and over as it crashes through me a few more times. He is straining to hold me and is growing close to his own. I climb off of him avoiding the desk as he seemed to be aiming for. I stand in front of him and notice headlights on the road in the distance when I look out the window. The excitement of nearly getting caught gets the better of me, and I want him to finish. I get down in front of him, taking his slick cock in my hand. I start jerking it as fast as I can. I look up to see him looking out the window. "I'd better swallow the evidence" I tell him like a dirty little whore. I jam his cock into my throat, tasting my own cum all over him. He groans aloud and I feel his hand in my hair. He grabs my head and yanks me away from him. I jerk it and jerk it, wanting it. I open my mouth, ready for it. I hear a car door slam. His begins, shooting streams of it into my mouth. I swallow it up, jerking his cock the whole time. He stares down at me; the look of sheer pleasure on his face burned in my brain forever. I hear another noise outside and figure we are out of time.

I gather up my clothes and run for my room. I hear the door open just as I reach the top of the stairs, cutting it closer than I realized. I hear Darren ask him "How was the trip up? I can tell by their conversation that he covered the situation and Paul will be none the wiser to our adventure in the den. I fix my makeup and get redressed before heading downstairs. I wonder how long he is staying, and if we will ever do that again. I can't believe after all these years we finally did. It was amazing. I knew it would be; a fantasy comes true after all this time. I shudder as an aftershock ripples through me at the thought of it.

Emily

"I don't get it. We seem to get along great, I think he is funny and always laugh at his jokes, I even showed him my tongue piercing! Maybe he just doesn't like me" I tell Sarah. She and I have a two hour overlap until the evening rush slows down and she goes home. It's nice to have someone to talk to; this job gets so boring at times. "Maybe he is just shy" she offers as a possible answer to my dilemma. "I looked at his file; he's older than I thought" I confess. "What!?!?! Are you crazy? You could get fired for that!" Sarah exclaims. "Oh stop it, I was careful. Besides, it was exciting to be sneaky like that. It's almost like I am stalking him or something" I tell her, feeling a twinge of excitement ripple through me. "Maybe that's it, maybe he thinks he's too old for you, that you wouldn't be into him" she poses. "I don't know, but if I don't hook up with that guy soon I am going to go crazy!' I inform her. The exasperated look on my face makes her laugh, and then I join in too.

About two hours later Sarah is preparing to leave for the day. "Well, good night! Hopefully he comes in tonight; maybe if you flash him your boobs he will realize that you are actually into him." "Sarah!" I exclaim. "Well...we'll see how many people are around" I admit, smiling a devilish smile. "See ya tomorrow girl." The rest of the evening drags on and since I haven't seen him in a while I am not too hopeful that tonight will be any different. The gym is dead tonight, even for a Friday. I look around to see three people in the weight room and one in the cardio area. I grab my book and sit down; might be a long two hours until close I think to myself. I get to one of the good parts, and try to picture him and me in the scene. What would he be like? Would he make love to me like a princess, or fuck me like a dirty whore? Maybe he would do both. Oh God I hope he comes in tonight!

I read on, squirming in my seat, dying to touch myself again. I can't seem to ever get enough these days, it's all I think about. I hear the door open, and jump up. Two people walk in looking for a tour of the place. "Sorry, you'll have to come back tomorrow between eight and five when Mark or Jeff are here. I can't leave the desk, and I can't allow you to walk around by yourselves either" I inform them. They leave, and as they exit they are holding the door for someone. It's him, he's here. My heart jumps, and my stomach flutters. I try to look busy, not wanting to look too desperate when he comes in. He walks towards the desk, smiling a tired smile at me. "Rough day?" I ask cheerfully. "Rough month" he responds with a heavy sigh. He stops and chats with me like always. He notices my book, the cover a typical scene of the hero with long flowing hair holding the damsel in distress in his arms. "So, is that what you do with all your free time here?" he asks me. I feel myself blush, the excitement of him so close to me just barely contained under the surface. I stumble for something to say; he pauses for a moment but I can't find the words. He turns and walks away, and I feel my fingers clench into fists as the frustration of him still not asking me out sets in.

I am sitting at the desk, pouting. I pick up my book and start where I left off, only to be annoyed by the woman in the scene making love to her man and I am obviously not going to ever do that with the one I want. I look at the clock; it is about 45 minutes until closing. Maybe I can catch him on the way out. I start the process of closing; counting the drawer of money and sort through paperwork. Definitely a slow day. I finish quickly and then start my walk through. I hate re-racking the weights and cleaning up the free weight room, I should hang a sign that says "Your mother doesn't work here, clean up after yourself." I wipe down the benches and straighten up as best my attention will allow. I keep glancing at the door, hoping I don't miss him on the way out. I hear the front desk phone ring and I run to answer it. It's him. "What can I do for you?" I blurt out, cringing instantly afterwards thinking how that must have sounded. He pauses, and I am thinking that was bad, I shouldn't have said that. He asks me if someone can bring the spray stuff for the steam room in to the locker room for him. I tell him I am the only one here, wondering if he has any idea how much I have thought of him lately. He asks if I can bring it to the door, and he'll meet me there. I agree, wondering if I will get a glimpse of him.

I walk back to the men's locker room, knocking on the door, waiting for him to open the door. He does, but he doesn't step out to meet me. He leans out the door, and I can only see part of him. I hold the bottle out and then pull it away from him playfully. He steps forward; I look up and realize that he is in a towel. I look at his chest and shoulders, and downward from there. He is very fit for a guy who works out so sporadically. He catches me looking at him and smiling. I smiles back, and I think I finally got his attention. He seems to be searching for something to say, but I get nervous and turn and walk away before he says anything. I practically run back the desk, nervous and excited at the same time.

I try to keep myself busy, waiting for the time to pass and he comes out of the locker room. I am nervous, but I want to go out with him so bad my excitement outweighs my nerves. I fiddle with things to do, becoming more and more engrossed in what I am doing. Before I know it the clock reads 10:30pm, and I jump to lock the door. I pull off my ugly club shirt, tossing it aside. I realize that I never saw him leave. The place is empty, and I am here by myself. I still haven't gotten used to that idea. I look around, walking through the whole building to be sure. I go through the women's locker room but no one is there. The guys who were here I saw leave, everyone but him. Maybe he is in the locker room still. I crack the door open, dying to peek inside but fighting the urge. "Hello?" I say loudly, waiting for answer. "I'm coming in!" I warn, propping the door open. I walk in, hesitantly, not sure if I should be doing this. Maybe he's not even here anymore. Maybe I am being silly. I creep in, sticking my head around the corner, looking into the locker area. "Helll—ooooo?!?!?" I say, louder this time. Nothing. Its empty, he left without saying goodbye once again. I walk towards the showers and reside myself to the fact that he left. I turn the handles in the shower, making sure the water is off before I leave. I walk into the Jacuzzi area, and hear the steam room running. I walk over to the window, peering into the steamy room. I see someone laying there on the bench, wrapped in a towel. It's him. He's here.

I go to the door, nervously grabbing the handle and then letting go and grabbing it again before pulling the door open. I announce myself, hoping not to scare him when I walk in. I pull the door open, and he jumps at the noise. He is surprised to see me. "Are you OK? It's almost 10:30! I was about to close up when I realized that you are still in here" I explain, my presence in the locker room still seeming to baffle him. Oh my God, I can see the bulge in his towel, he is totally turned on and I can see it under his towel. Oh my God, should I say something. I want to see it. No, I have to go. My internal dialog runs wild as he fidgets with the towel trying to hide himself. I take a step towards him, only to chicken out. I want to see it, touch it, taste it. My glasses are fogging up, and I can no longer see. I take them off, waving them in the steamy air, but to no avail. I get a funny idea, and ask "Hey, can I borrow your towel? My glasses are fogging up." He pauses for a second, making me question my bold move. "Sure, come and get it" he tells me. I figure it is now or never, and I go for it.

I walk over to him, finally getting to realize the desires I have been harboring for so many weeks. All the desire within me boils over, and I feel like I am being pulled towards him. I climb on top of him, straddling him on the bench. I can already feel it against my leg, but I focus on kissing him first. We start to kiss, slow at first but quickly gaining speed and force. He grabs me in his arms, holding me against him. My wife beater t shirt is already soaked from the steam in the air, and I can feel the heat from his body through it. He keeps banging into my glasses as we kiss and I feel him pull away. He reaches for them, pulling them off of me and setting them aside on the bench. We go back at it, kissing one another boldly once again. He pulls away once again, looking at me. "Are you sure want..." I kiss him again, answering his question with my lips instead of words. After a moment I confess "I have wanted to do this for a long time." I start to grind into him, my body taking over and moving on its own. He scoots down a little, and I can feel it through my shorts. I want to tear my clothes off and jump on him, but I resist. His hands find the bottom of my wet shirt and he pulls it over my head. He unclips my bra and it falls onto the wet tile floor. He looks at me, surveying my body. I am dying for him to touch me, and I lean towards him just a little to let him know.

Finally he reaches for my breasts, his strong yet gentle hands squeezing them. A shiver of pleasure runs through me, and I lean forward to taste his kiss once again. His hands glide over my slippery flesh, the air thick with moisture. He pinches my nipples and squeezes my breasts, making the ache inside me deepen. He is kissing and sucking my flesh and I am mad with desire. I feel his hand slide up my back, his wet flesh sliding over mine. His hand finds my hair, and he pulls a firm handful of it, making me stare at the ceiling in the sauna. A moan escapes me, as if the breath rises out of me, freed from my body in this position. His kisses, move to my chin, down my neck, and slowly towards my aching nipples. He leans me backwards, and I arch my back to accommodate our mutual desire of his mouth on my breasts. "Oh God yes!" I beg, my hand grabbing the back of his head, pulling him into my soft flesh. His tongue is hot and silky, and it flicks over my hardened flesh with devious intent. A deep moan echoes in the tiled room.

Jesus that feels so good; I grind myself against him, the fire inside fanned by his mouth on my flesh. I am growing dizzy from desire and the hot air in the steam room. I toss my head back, lost in the pleasure of his mouth on me. My body is tingling with desire and I want more. Suddenly I feel a shock, a jolt of pleasure rips through me like a shot. He is pulling my shorts against my hyper-sensitive clit, and the sensation is incredible. No one has ever made me feel so much desire before; he is amazing. I am dating older men from now on. I need him now. I stand up and tear my clothes off, standing in front of him, ready for the taking. I want him inside me immediately.

I climb back on top of him, hoping he will take his cock and shove it into me right away. He is looking at me, a devilish grin on his face. "Say please" he tells me. Are you kidding me? I want to fuck him and he wants me to say please? "No!" I respond defiantly. My head is spinning in confusion, what the Hell is going on here? I feel a sting on my ass, and then the sound echoing in the steam room registers in my brain. He smacked my ass like a little girl. "OK, OK, you win." I concede. I lean forward to hide my face from him, but decide instead to fight back. I bite into his shoulder, making him jump in surprise. He moves and suddenly his fingers are inside me. Oh my God it is so good, it feels so good. I gasp in surprise and toss my head back, feeling like I am going to fall over backwards. I feel his arm around me, and I relax again, focused on the intense pleasure between my thighs. He is touching me on a spot so sensitive it almost tickles, but so much better. I feel my body rise, the tension in me peaking for just a moment, and then....release. My cries echo as my whole body shakes and convulses; I explode under the touch of his hand. I melt in his arms for a moment; my head spinning, my body shaking.

Finally my senses return, and I want to return the favor of how he made me feel. I grab a towel off the bench next to him, and drop it on the floor at his feet. I grab the towel around his waist and pull it aside, freeing him. It is rock hard and staring straight up at me. I touch it, confirming it is as hard as it looks to be. I don't think I have ever felt one this hard before. I begin to move my hand back and forth, his slick flesh barely moving under my touch. I look up at him, trying to be as sexy as I can and tell him "I have been waiting to try this thing out." I dive forward, taking all of it in my mouth. I can taste the mix of testosterone and eucalyptus on his skin. I press the metal ball into him as hard as I can, hoping he can feel it. I slide my tongue all over him, working it in and out of my mouth. I can feel his groans of pleasure, his chest vibrating as my mouth works him over. I love the fact that I am getting to him, that I now have control. "Do you like it?" I ask, stopping what I am doing. "Oh yes" he confirms. "Do you want some more?" I playfully tease him. "Uh huh!" he blurts out. "Say please" I tell him, stretching my won limits of comfort, playing this game. "No" he says back in a firm, almost scolding tone. I am shocked, and I stand up thinking maybe he is serious. "OK" I mumble back. "Alright, alright….PPPLLEEEAAAASSSSSSEEEEEE????!!!!!" he pleads, reversing my thoughts from a moment ago. I was winning.

I lean over him and swallow his cock once again. It is easier at this angle, his stiff rod not rubbing the back of my throat like this. I love sucking cock; I would do this all night long if he wanted me to. He begins to move on the bench and I am wondering what he is thinking. He slowly lies down on his side on the bench, and I quickly catch on. I shudder at the thought of his mouth on me while I do the same to him. He rolls to his back and I climb onto him, my now aching pussy right above his face. Oh God his tongue is on me; it feels so good, so fucking good! I attack his cock, my pace increasing as he works me over on the other end. He teases and rubs my clit with it, his tongue soft and forceful at the same time. I am….Oh GOD! His tongue is inside me. It freezes me; I have to stop what I am doing to him in. I pull away from him, moaning loudly. I arch to meet his mouth, my body craving more and more of what he is doing to me. Damn, he is going to make me come again. I jerk his stiff cock in my hand, soon I am sucking it furiously once again. My frenzied state is building and I am going to explode even harder than the first time. I am growing numb with pleasure, no longer able to decipher what he is doing to me. I no longer care; it all feels so good I don't care what he is doing as long as he doesn't stop. His tongue is shooting in and out of me again and he is rubbing my clit. I erupt; my body shaking and convulsing as wave after wave of it washes over me. It seems to last forever.

Finally it subsides. I am paralyzed, limp on top of him for the moment. "Give me a minute" I beg of him, unable to move even if I had to. He ignores my request, sliding out from under me. He sits me up on the bench, and takes place in front of me on the towel I laid there before. I open myself to him, ready, wanting more of how he is making me feel. He guides it into me, parting my slick walls all the way up into me. A different pleasure hits me; deep inside me, in my core instead of on the surface. My eyes widen as he fills me completely. He starts slow, and I gain my strength back as he goes. Soon he is pounding me into the tiled bench. The noises our bodies make only add to the excitement, and amazingly I am close again within just a few minutes of this. God, this guy is fucking like no one ever has. I am close, and he can sense it. He knows me, feels what I feel. He reaches down with his hand, and rubs his thumb on my clit. It is almost too much to take; I flinch at first but soon the pleasure takes over. My hips start bucking on their own, my body taking over once again. Another orgasm bursts from down deep inside me, surfacing after mere seconds. I am breathing so hard I think I am going to pass out. He pulls away from me, standing up as I melt into a puddle atop the bench.

I feel his hand on mine, lifting me, encouraging me to my feet. I am not sure I can stand; my legs weak from my body's output so far. He guides me forward onto the towel on the bench, and I get on my knees in front of him, facing away. He wants to take me from behind, and I want him to as well. I arch my back as he positions himself for the next round. His hard cock goes right into me, into my depths. I feel more of him this way, his cock going very deeper than before. I push back into him despite my hands slipping on the slick tile. His hands are around my waist and I feel his grip slipping as we move. I feel his hand in my hair again, and he yanks my hand back once more adding to the fun. He pulls my head back to his mouth, making me arch more than ever. I hear him whisper in a rough voice "Oh God Emily, you feel so good. I have wanted you for so long." I shudder at his words, his actions, the thought that we have wasted so much time not knowing what the other thought. His words trigger another orgasm; this one seemingly starts in my brain and rushes downward through my body. I buck into him, my sweaty body gliding against his. It keeps rolling and rolling in me, the feeling taking several moments to subside. I slump forward into the towels, exhausted.

Her Eyes

I have no idea how he is holding out so long. My feet are starting to cramp from so many toe curling orgasms. And yet I am aching for more. He sits down on the bench next to me and pulls me over on top of him again. My body responds, wanting him inside me once again. I am sitting on his lap and we are facing the same direction. I rise up a little and guide myself down on it one more time. With my feet together there is even more friction between us. My legs are weak and I struggle to bounce up and down on him. I settle for moving my hips, grinding into him and sliding over his wet skin. He runs his hands all over me, feeling my skin, touching me everywhere. I love his touch. I begin to move more, feeling him deeper inside me as I do. He grabs my hair and turns my head so he can kiss me. I whimper a little as I lean back into him, into his kiss. His hands stop on my breasts, kneading them, pinching my nipples back to life.

I feel his hand travel down my chest, across my stomach and towards my most sensitive spot. He stops, I wait, hoping, begging him inside to touch me there. I move instinctively towards his hand, trying to get him to touch me. He holds, teasing me, taunting me. Just as I am about to cry out and beg for it he grants my wish. His fingers touch my folds and I explode almost instantly. I grind myself onto him, loving the feeling of pleasure from him inside and out. I hear him groaning, realizing it is his turn very soon. I want to taste it; I go to get off of him but he pushes me down onto it, driving it deep inside me once more. I shudder in pleasure as I feel him fill me up. He pushes and struggles against me until he can give no more. Finally he is done, spent, had his fill.

I have no idea how long we sat there together, the two of us breathless and weary from our adventure. Finally he moves to get up and I join him, suddenly feeling uncomfortable in front of him. I reach for my clothes only to realize they are all soaking wet. I put on my t shirt; it is cold and clings to me. I squeeze into my shorts, hating the feeling of the wet material on my skin. We walk out towards the locker room and I hear him mention something about a shower. Are you crazy? I think to myself. Suddenly I hear voices and realize we are not alone. "The cleaning crew!" I gasp in surprise. I leave him behind, running for the other door, embarrassed. I take the long way around to my car in the front of the building. He meets me there after a few moments. We laugh about almost getting caught before he kisses me once more and tell me goodbye. I fumble with my keys as I sit in the car watching him drive away.

I can't believe that just happened. But I am so glad it did. I hope to see him again soon, but right now all I want to do is get out of these wet clothes. I start the car and drive home, smiling all the way.

Holly

I saw him walking towards the door towards the Physical Therapy clinic; I happened to be standing close to the row of exercise bikes near the front of the building. I am not sure what I notice about him, but something catches my attention. I guess I am not dead after all, despite working constantly while I am here in Phoenix. Thinking I would be bored and have nothing to do, I have once again over committed myself and am running around like my hair is on hair most of the time. I smile at him when he enters, but he doesn't really look my direction. I go back to what I was doing, sighing. It seems it has been a while since I have attracted someone's attention anyway.

I escort Mrs. Anderson back to the therapy table for her ultrasound work. I help her onto the table, and gather a pillow to slide under arm while Mitch goes to work on her shoulder. I hear Warren's booming voice, and I jump again. You'd think after two months I would relax a little. "Holly, Can you blast his IT bands? My next patient is here." He is already walking away from...Oh my gosh...its the guy I saw at the door. I am suddenly nervous as I walk to the table. He is really cute, but older than I first thought. I look at him for a moment, and then shyly look away as he looks up to meet my gaze. I arrive at the table where he is standing. My professional side takes over, saving the rest of me from this uncomfortable introduction. "Hop up on the table and lay on your side" I tell him. He is shorter than I thought, too.

I reach between his legs, placing the pillow so his hips are angled correctly for this procedure. I reach under the table and grab the jar and jam my fingers into the congealed gel. More of it gets crammed under my nails, and I am going to have to give up the dream of ever having my nails done again. I grease up my elbow for the tenth time today, and start to feel around for the greater trocanter to begin. "Try and hold still" I say to him, smiling down at him on the table. I roll his shorts up and out of my way, standard procedure for this exercise. "He is cute" flashes through my head just before I begin. I get a weird flash of embarrassment cascade through me as I look down at his black boxer briefs his has on under his shorts. I press hard down into his flesh, my elbow digging into the tendon that is the source of his problem. He tenses, going almost completely stiff as I slowly run my elbow down his leg towards his knee. He is trying his best not to scream in pain, too macho for that I guess. Or trying to be anyway. I know this hurts, and try to temper the pressure as best I can. "Breathe" I remind him. He exhales, realizing that he has been holding his breath all this time.

I reach his knee after the standard 10 seconds it should take to massage the tendon. "Good, that's one" I tell him, as I watch his face melt into a look of what I would best describe as nausea. "How many of those are we doing?" he pleads, his voice almost cracking. "Usually six times" I tell him. "Per leg" I follow quickly. He looks as if he is going to get up and run away. I start over, beginning at the hip and slowly working my way down to his knee. I am staying in clinical mode as best I can, but I can't help but wonder what he is thinking, what he thinks of me. I instruct him to flip over, and start the process on the other side. I hike his shorts up again, this time just a little higher. He has a cute little butt. Focus! I remind myself. I run through the six repetitions one this side as well. "OK, you are done" I tell him. "See you Wednesday." I hear him mumble something as he walks away from me.

It is finally nearing the end of the day, and I can breathe. Crazy morning blended into a crazy busy afternoon, but it is almost time to go home. I wonder who is left on the schedule? I ask myself. Oh yeah I realize, smiling in recognition of the name on the list. I look up just in time to see him coming through the door again. He heads to the locker room, and after a few minutes returns to begin his exercises. I keep tabs on him, watching him. I don't usually pay attention to my patients like this, but for some reason I can't seem to help it. I am drawn to him. I keep myself busy so Warren doesn't yell at me. He is so intense; I wish he would lighten up once in a while. I see he is almost finished, and I walk over behind him. "Is it almost table time?" I ask, beaming a smile at him. He turns to face me. "You enjoy your job a little too much" he tells me, smiling back. We look into each others eyes for what seems like a long time, finally I break the visual lock he has on me, turning and heading for the tables in the back.

He follows along behind me, and I feel his eyes on me. I wish I had done something with my hair. He climbs up on the table and lies down, used to the routine already. I grease my arm up, and begin the task of grinding his IT Bands into submission. I can tell a difference already, and the first time is typically the worst. I want to make the most of his treatment time, so I dig in a little deeper. He snaps his head around, mock glaring at me and squealing in pain under the pressure from my elbow. I laugh a little at him, sympathizing having been through this myself. He looks at me accusingly, like I am trying to hurt him on purpose. I laugh at him a little more. "You sadistic bi..." he catches himself before letting it slip. Now I really laugh at him, and dig in even harder. He keeps smiling at me despite moaning and groaning, looking at me while I run my arm up and down his leg.

Over the next few weeks we get to talking and learning about one another. He is a really cool guy and used to be a athlete. I get the impression he is trying to hide his age from me. He gets vague when he talks about stuff that happened a while ago. I think to myself that I am going to have to sneak a look at his medical chart to be sure of his age. He has traveled, has a real job now and is settling into a busy corporate lifestyle. I listen to his stories of his past, seemingly hanging on every word. He is funny and charismatic, and my fondness of him is growing by the day. I hope he asks me out, but then again I really should since he is a patient. I am leaving before the end of summer, and I am afraid I will not get the chance to see him outside of work.

It is almost the last week of my internship, and I am looking forward to returning home and my life getting back to normal. However, I am running out of time, and have a million things to do before I leave. I hope he is on that list; I laugh at my own dorky little joke. He still hasn't even asked me out yet, what is he waiting for? I have made it so obvious that I like him, I don't understand. I am giving him signal after signal, maybe he doesn't like me that way. He probably thinks I am too young for him. Just as I am in the middle of my own conversation he walks through the door. He sees me and smiles, waving as he heads for the locker room. He quickly returns, and goes to work. I walk over to him, wondering what to say to get the point across that I want to see him before I leave. He looks up and smiles, asking me "So...who is going to torture me when you are gone?" I laugh a little, and respond "I don't know, but I am sure it won't be the same!" He gets that playful smile on his face and comes back with "That's true...everyone else here seems really nice" he barely gets out before laughing at me. I feel myself turning red with a mix of embarrassment and excitement. Nothing gets me going like playful banter. I slap his arm, an obvious sign I approve of his tactics. He gives me a quick shove, and takes a step towards me like he is going to grab me. He quickly turns, and I walk away from him hoping no one saw our little exchange. God I so want him right now. How am I going to focus on work now? This will seem like the longest hour of my life.

OK, this is ridiculous, it is my last week here and I so want to see him it is not even funny. I am going to ask him out. No, I can't...what if he says no. That would be embarrassing. Dammit! What am I gonna do? Once again he walks through the door just as I am thinking about him. It has become routine that he waves on his way in and hurries to change out of his work clothes. He comes back, and I take a deep breath and ready myself, and then start walking towards him. I get within earshot and he turns and asks how my day has been. We start chitchatting and it has broken my momentum. I chicken out, and never ask him out for coffee. I walk away from him, letting him finish his routine and mentally abusing myself all the way back to the office. I walk away from everyone and kick the leg on my desk, the anxiety of this getting the better of me. Maybe I can ask him when he is on the table.

I return to the floor and watch him from across the room. He is finishing, and will be headed my way. I feel my stomach knot up. He is smiling at me the whole way over, and when he gets to me we are both smiling ear to ear at one another. He asks "Do you need one of the guys to do this since you can't seem to get deep enough into the muscle?" I react to his challenge. "Oh that's it...lay down! It is so on!" I fire back, my lower jaw jutting out defiantly like when I was a kid. I grab the bottom of his shorts and yank them up, exposing his hip a little more than necessary to me. I am so worked up I can barely contain myself. "And can you cut down on the inappropriate touching this time?" he says in a loud voice. I feel myself flush all over, my face beat red as everyone looks at the two of us. I am so embarrassed, and that just makes me blush even more. I retaliate, jamming my elbow deep into his thigh. He lets out a moan, and his eyes widen in pain. He looks away for a brief second, and then looks back at me. I can see him straining not to react, so I dig deeper. He is burning holes in me with his stare, and the delicious power struggle is on. I step up on the shelf under the table for more leverage, and leaning further over him. Then I see it, he looks at my mouth. He is thinking it too. The exchange between us is so hot; I can feel the moisture in my shorts, and it is in the middle of a room full of people. This is so inappropriate and dangerous, and yet that only adds to the appeal. I want to climb onto him right here and now.

He flips over, and just to make sure we understand each other, I grab his ass. It is as firm as I thought it would be. He turns quickly and looks at me, a surprised look on his face. Then he breaks into a smile, a knowing smile. It's on.

At the end of the session, I know I no longer have to ask. I know he is going to, so I wait for him. We continue with the small talk, and finally he asks "So...do you wan to go for coffee or something tonight when you are done?" Oh God, not tonight I thought. "Oh, I can't tonight, and Wednesday might be kinda tough too. Suddenly he looks concerned, like I am blowing him off. "Maybe we can hang out after the going away party the guys here are having for me" I offer hoping he gets the implication of a late night call to visit. "Alright, let's do that" he says, looking a little more enthused than a moment ago. God do I wish it was Wednesday already.

My last day! I know it is going to be a long day, and hopefully a long night. I am running late as usual, so much for doing something different with my hair today. I work through my day, busier than usual and also saying goodbye to people who I have worked with the short time I have been here. It is the best part of my job, for sure. The end of the day finally nears, and I look up just in time to see him walking towards the door; I feel a tingle run through me. I am done with everyone except for him, so I sit and wait in the office. I enjoy being off my feet for the first time today, but I know he is out there and I want to talk to him, to be near him. I leave the office to find him. He is going through his routines as usual, and I find him in the free weight area. He greets me as warmly as usual, and we talk while he is quickly going through his workout. I follow him over to the bosa ball, watching him carefully try to balance on top of it. Just when he gets settled and the ball is almost still I give him a little push, nearly sending him flying off of it. It was more than intended, and he almost crashes into the weight machine next to him. "You are such a little shit!" he scolds me. I giggle like a child standing there in front of him. We are picking up right where we left off on Monday, and I like it. "Wait til I get you on the table" I tell him. I turn and walk away, and her him chase me with "Bring it girlie."

A few moments later I am leaning against the table waiting for him. He comes my direction and I reach for the white gel one last time. I rub it on my elbow as he hops up on the table. He smells sweaty, but not in a bad way. I can smell how his skin will taste, and I twinge just a little bit deep inside. He lays down in front of me, and I grab his shorts like I have done twice a week for the last 6 weeks now. This time, I help myself to a good squeeze of his ass. He pretends not to notice, but it was too obvious not to. "So what do you have going on tonight?" he inquires. "Well, I have a little get together with some friends tonight and before that the crew here at work wants to take me out for a drink. How about you?" I answer, hoping. "I am just hanging out at home" he tells me. I know I can't invite him out, I want this to be out little secret. "Maybe we can hang out after my work thing" I offer up, practically saying "I will be over to sex you up and down" directly to him. "Perfect" he responds, and I guess it is set. "Grab your phone and I will give you my number" he says. I discretely retrieve my phone, and he tells me his number. I dial it and hear his phone ring, giving him mine as well. I smile at him, a knowing smile. We part without another word, not wanting to blow our cover.

It is 8:30 and I am having fun but can't wait for it to be over so I can go meet him. I am so distracted; I am so looking forward to this, it has been a long while since I have had fun. What a perfect way to end my time here in Phoenix. I dial his number, just checking to make sure he is still planning on seeing me. "Hello Holly" I hear his voice on the other end. I can hear him smiling through the phone. It is loud here in the bar, and I realize I should have walked outside before I called. "Hey!...What are you doing?" I ask. "Like I said earlier today, just hanging out." I can barely hear him over the background noise. "I am still out with these guys, and it might be a while before I cab break away." He is quiet on the other end. "But I really want to see you before I leave. Are you going to be up for a while, or are you going to do the old man thing and go to bed early?" I say laughing, trying to break what suddenly feels like an uncomfortable mood. "I'll be up" he says, and it sounds like he is smiling again. "Cool, I will call you later" I tell him, and hang up. I rejoin the group, but mentally I have already checked out.

It is about 11:00pm and I am getting tired. I am still in my work clothes, and I want desperately to take a shower before I go to see him. I know there is no way I can make it all the way to my place, shower and back to his before midnight, so I am going to go as is. I call his cell phone again, and he answers sounding a little sleepy. We chat as I pull out of the parking lot. I know he lives close to work, so I head that direction before asking directions. He leads me through the back streets of his neighborhood, and I see him walk out into the street halfway down the block. I speed up, and turn abruptly into the driveway. I had more to drink than I realized, and I notice at the last second that his car is in the driveway as well. I hit the brakes, and the tires squeal as I skid to a stop. He laughs and I pile out of the car. He grabs my hand and leads me into the house without a word.

We head straight for his bedroom, and he turns on the TV. I was hoping for pitch dark but this is close enough I guess. I am buzzed enough to not care too much about it. I am growing a little nervous as we enter the bedroom, and in a burst of energy I run and jump into bed. Much to my delight he follows along, and lands in bed right next to me. We lay facing each other, and he jokes about me having to get drunk before coming to see him like this. I laugh nervously, and admit that I am a little scared about this, but I am out of time, and I want to be right where I am. He makes me feel better by admitting he is nervous as well, which had not occurred to me until he said it.

I am feeling my buzz start to fade and I am getting tired. "What is he waiting for?" I keep thinking to myself. The small talk continues for another moment or two until he finally says " It looks like if you lay here another five minutes you could be asleep....so I guess I had better kiss you now" "Finally! I shout inside. He starts to move towards me and I lean in to kiss him. I feel my glasses rub his face, and I pull away to remove them and put them on the nightstand. I want more of his kisses, and I go back to his mouth, wanting, needing more. I rollover onto him, and I bite his lip, sucking it into my mouth. Our tongues wrestle around as we turn up the heat of our kisses. I like being on top of him, feeling like I am in control. I feel him shifting underneath me, like he is trying to squirm free. I bear my weight down on him, trying to keep him in place. Suddenly he yanks me to the side and rolls me over. I am now on the bottom, quicker than I could react to do anything about it. He grabs my wrists and pins me down, pressing into me. I let him have his sense of control for a moment, enjoying kissing him and play fighting. I slowly begin to grind my hips upward into him. The friction feels so good, but that can wait. I seize an opportunity to flip him off of me and onto his back, and I quickly regain my top position.

That did it; we break into a full blown wrestling match. Sheets are tearing loose and clothes are getting disheveled as we wrestle and fight on top of the bed. Just when he thinks he has me I jam my thumb into the tender flesh in his upper thigh. He jumps, and I nearly toss him off the bed as I flip him over once again. This is the hottest foreplay I have ever had; I want him to pin me down and fuck me right now. I feel his arm slide under my leg, and he puts me in a cradle move like my brother used to when we were kids. He rolls me over and despite how I struggle against him I cannot get away or flip him over. I fight and fight to no avail. He has won. "Ha HA!...Victory is mine!" he yells out, celebrating his win. We both burst out laughing and falls forward on top of me.

He kisses me gently now, long deep kisses like I have been picturing all this time. Our hands begin to explore one another, feeling each other through wrinkled clothes. He grabs my hands and pulls me up, and then takes off my work shirt and the shirt underneath. I lay back down, feeling self conscious all of the sudden. His warm hand touches my stomach, and it flutters on the inside. His hand runs across my bra, the sheer material barely hiding my hard nipples. He reaches around under me to try and unhook it, and I know he wont be able to from this angle. He struggles for a moment, and I can't help but laugh. "Seriously?" I poke fun at him. He yanks me upwards again and reaches behind me to unhook it. I slide it off, and flop back onto the bed again. His mouth is quickly on them, and I arch my back in response to the warm and wet feeling my nipple. He licks and flicks his tongue, and the jolts of pleasure course through me. He looks up at me, smiling, as he kisses his way from one to the other. I lean to meet his mouth, wanting the feeling again. I close my eyes and toss my head back, drinking in the sensations his mouth is creating. God he is driving me crazy!

I feel his hand slide across my stomach, and I am ready to burst. Just so we don't have another clumsy repeat of the bra situation, and I push his hand aside and I tear my shorts off, tossing them onto the floor. I am so wet, and as soon as his fingers touch me I am ready to explode. I am aching for release. He touches my clit, and I feel like I am going to come within seconds. He works it over, teasing, testing to see what I like. I love it all, and moan accordingly. I arch my back again, wanting his fingers inside me. He gets the message and buries one deep inside me. That was all it took; I suck in a breath, hold until I am about to pass out, and explode in a huge orgasm as I exhale a deep breath. I grab at the sheets, gripping handfuls of the material as I try to ride it out. He leans over me, and kisses me hard once again. I am paralyzed, and kiss him back as best I can.

After a moment or two I am ready to proceed. I want to taste his cock, and I yank his shorts out of my way, freeing him. It is growing hard already, and I want my mouth on it. I dive at it, wrapping my lips around its length. I slide my mouth up and down over it, loving the sensations. I taste him, my tongue running over every inch of it. His scent is reminiscent of the preview I would get at the clinic; salty and very masculine. I devour him, moaning as I go. I want to suck him forever, but I must quench this need I feel deep in my soul. I need him inside me. I stop what I am doing, and lay down next to him. He understands what I need, and he gets onto his knees and climbs between my legs. I lift my legs for him, offering myself for the taking. I want it hard, and long and deep. He teases me with it, rubbing it against my sensitive clit and all around my pussy lips. I moan a little, desperate for him to bury it inside me. He enters me, slowly pushing it in. He pulls out, only to push in a little farther. God I want to scream. He is rubbing my clit while he does this, and I love it. I feel my hips move to meet him, trying to match his rhythm. "Oh God yes...that is soooo good" I hear someone say. After a moment I realize it was me after all. I am so close, and he knows it. He begins to fuck me harder, rubbing my clit under his thumb roughly. I tense again, holding my breath. He responds, and shove himself deep into me, holding it there, filling me. I explode twice as hard as the first one; I feel like every part of me is lit up with electricity all at once. It is amazing, and I want this perfect moment to last forever. I am frozen, paralyzed once again by my own intense orgasm. He thrusts into me over and over, the sensations flashing through me with every stroke. He slows his pace, until he is slowly moving in and out of me. He feels so good inside me.

After a few minutes of this, I can feel me building towards another. The constant pace is pushing me nearer the edge. It comes from deep down inside, and as it slowly makes its way to the surface inside of me, I ache for it to arrive. Finally, I tense up, bracing for it. I exhale, and it comes...slowly, steadily it rises within. It is like a bubble rising to the surface, fighting, struggling to break through. It is driving me crazy. I let out a low, deep moan, and it seems to release it from inside. I relax, and out of me pours a long, slow, deep and spicy orgasm. It seems to go on forever; I shudder and shake underneath him, feeling his weight on top of me. "Oh my God that was awesome" I praise, finally able to speak.

He lies next to me, allowing me to recover from the best orgasm I have ever had. "I don't remember the last time I have come like this" I admit to him. I hear him laugh a little as he rolls to his side. He lies still, looking at me as I regain my senses. "Well...now it is my turn" he says with a grin. He gets to his knees, and I am waiting to see what he wants me to do. "Take me any way you want" I tell him, urging him to be back inside me. He climbs off the bed, and I know what he wants. I get on my knees, and arch my back, offering it to him for the taking. I feel him part my lips, and soon he is deep inside me once again. I grab the sheets in effort to not give an inch under his thrusts. I feel each and every impact of his body into mine, the shock waves of pleasure echoing throughout my body. He fucks me hard and fast, grunting as he goes. I reach back and grab my ass, prying myself open even more for him. "That's it, pound me!" I tell him, encouraging him for more. "God that is fucking hot" I follow.

I can feel another growing inside, and I want it. I lick my fingers, and slide my hand between my thighs. I can feels his balls slap against my hand and I begin to rub my own clit. It is different than when he did it, but it is good. I am closing in, almost like once again we are competing. I rub it faster and harder, and I feel it rise. I tense my whole body, readying myself. I can hear him groaning louder and faster as we both grow near the end. Mine begins, but he is close behind. I exhale, and another delicious orgasm pours out of me. I feel him hit me with three hard thrusts, the final one holding himself deep inside me. I feel him grow, and the flex over and over as he pours himself into me. I lose all thought and feeling, going numb with pleasure and faint with fatigue. We collapse on the bed together. I can feel his heavy breathing against me.

I squint to try and see the clock. I know it is late, and that I have to go. I can barely make out the outline of numbers. "Its 12:45" he informs me. "Oh God" I moan. "I have to be up early tomorrow" I tell him. "Its OK, I understand. I am so glad you came to see me" he says, pulling me in for one more kiss. "Me too" I sigh, reaching for my glasses. I put them on, and in the darkness take one final look at him, burning it into my brain forever. What an amazing night I think to myself. I gather my clothes and quickly dress, walking towards the door. I sneak out quietly, locking the door behind me. I sit in my car for a moment, savoring the last remnants of tonight before driving away.

Tracey

I arrive bright and early Monday at my new job, ready to begin my role as manager at the new firm. I am hoping to be able to fit in and get along with everyone quickly; I hate being the new girl. I stroll into Ms. Walker's office and take a seat in front of her large wood desk. After a moment she turns away from her computer and acknowledges me. "Let's take the tour" she says flatly. We get up and I fall in line behind her; the tone for our relationship seems to be already set in stone. She escorts me around and introduces me to everyone in the office, and as soon as we are out of earshot of the person we just met she fills me in on that person's brief life story. I am surprised to find that she pays so much attention to everyone's life given her "arm's length" approach to management.

We continue the tour of the place meeting people along the way. We turn the corner and I lock eyes with a guy sitting on the edge of a desk across the room. I look away after a moment, and then quickly look back. It seems his eyes never left me, and I feel myself flush just a little bit. He has that look that I find hard to resist; shaved head, goatee, and his demeanor just reeks of bad boy. My thoughts about him are interrupted by Ms. Walker saying "Stay away from that one...he's trouble, if you know what I mean." "Yes ma'am, I do" I tell her, nodding obediently. In my mind, that statement all but seals the deal.

A week later and I am settling in to my new role. I am glad to see that although Ms. Walker has not lightened up one bit that everyone else seems to be comfortable with me. I have been the consummate professional in the office, having exchanged only a knowing glance or two to Darren as he passes by my office. He tries to be cute and funny when we chat, and I do my best to be professional but yet give the hint that I am interested. Office romances are so tricky; I have done it before and they can go really badly if you are not careful. But he doesn't strike me as the relationship type so it should be less of a problem. I just have to make sure I am not going to be the target of office gossip. If I can find a way to feel that he will keep it our secret, I am on board. He is sexy as Hell, and the tension is getting to me.

Her Eyes

Audrey from account and I have become fast friends, having lunch together a few times and talking frequently at the office. I stop by her desk to say hi and see a flyer for a party lying on her desk. How high school I thought to myself. She grabs the paper and excited starts talking about it. "You have to go with me...it will be the party of the year! Steve and Mike throw the best parties ever, and last year this was epic! And I am sure Darren will be there...." she adds. "Who?" I ask, trying to play it cool. "Hahahaha; oh don't even, girl! I see the way you look at each other. It is so on" she laughs, making me break into a guilty smile. Once in a while Audrey reminds me that I am in fact five years older than she is, and that her college days are not as far behind her as mine are. "I don't think I should, being a manager and all, I just don't think it would be a good idea" I inform her, my professional side shining through. "Oh God....alright fine, here, take this in case you change your mind" she sighs, handing me the flyer. I look at it a little more closely. It's a costume party of Halloween. "Bingo" I thought to myself. A devilishly clever idea crosses my mind, and I suddenly can't wait for the night to arrive.

As the week wears on Darren has been upping the frequency of his visits. He finally mentions to party, inviting me in a non-committal way. I tell him I'll think about it, not indicating one way or another just yet. He seems to be unsure of how to approach our situation; although technically I am not his boss I am farther up the food chain than he is. Knowing the delicate nature of this dance, so far he has been proceeding with caution. I see him flirting with other girls in the office, and the girls who flirt with him. He seems to spread his attention around quite a bit, so I am guessing he is quite the player. Hmm, maybe this is not such a good idea after all. But then again...

Thursday rolls around and everyone in the office seems to be talking about the party tonight. I guess this might be a bigger deal than I realized which is even worse. I am not sure I can pull off my plan of showing up in disguise if everyone from the building is there. It is almost five o'clock and I am still sitting at my desk. Everyone I hear talking is discussing this party, what they are going to wear, and when they will arrive. That's it, I decide, I am going. I told no one of my plans, so I can show up and hide my identity from everyone until the right time. Or the whole night for that matter. I refocus on the report I am finishing when I hear a knock on my open door. I look up; its Darren leaning in my door with a huge grin on his face. "You coming tonight? Or are you going to sit here and work you life away?" he asks, that smarmy sales guy grin on his face. "Maybe" I reply, sticking to my vague answers. He shakes his head and looks a little peeved. "Maybe is all I get, huh?" he fires back. "Yes, it is" I reply, breaking into a smile. His eyes are burning right through me as he searches for something to say. The silence is growing uncomfortable but I hold my proverbial ground. He cracks first, finishing with "OK then, hopefully I'll see you tonight." He turns and walks away, and my stomach is in a knot from the exchange.

It's nine o'clock and I am in full costume, a veiled belly dancer. I added an extra veil to the mask, making sure that you cannot see my face. I finish my glass of wine in one big swallow and grab my purse. I head for the car, nervous and excited about what I am going to attempt to do. I am not really sure how I am not going to reveal my identity and yet still talk to Darren. I guess I will figure it out as it happens. I get into the car and drive towards Mike's house. I get within two blocks of the place and there are cars everywhere. This can't be for this party, can it? I keep driving, locating the house as laid out on the map. There are people everywhere, and I can hear a band playing. Seriously? Holy shit! This is the biggest party I have ever been to, and my trepidation increases. I sit outside for a moment, and then hear the crowd inside roar over something. I decide I am going to join the fun, and begin looking for a parking space. I drive around the neighborhood until I find a spot and park my car. I get out and can still clearly here the music. I follow the sound back to the party, and soon am inside the house where everyone else is. The place is packed, and there are people in various stages of intoxicated all over the house. I see Darren across the room; he is dressed in a funny 17th century costume, sword included. I laugh a little to myself, watching him work the room and making sure everyone is having a good time.

I hear someone on the microphone making an announcement. The crowd quiets as if on cue and I see Steve on the stage with the mic in his hand telling everyone the costume contest will begin in 15 minutes. I bump into a girl with two drinks in her hand, and she offers me one of them. "I don't know where my friend is...drink this" she slurs. It looks fruity enough so I do. It has a ton of alcohol in it and it burns all the way down. I should have tested that out a little first, but I did not have the foresight for that. A few moment s later I feel the drink hit me. The mystery concoction seems to have re-activated the glass of wine I had earlier; they have joined forces and I have a pretty good buzz going already. I work my way towards the stage, joining the crowd in the festivities. Girl after girl goes on stage to strut their stuff and although some of them are hot, none of them can move like I can. I am seriously considering running up on stage and showing everyone what's up.

After two more mediocre contestants and another swig of liquid courage I decide to get in line to go on stage. This crowd seems easily impressed; that $200 bucks should be mine no sweat. I walk up the steps and the stage is mine. I do my thing, shaking my hips as fast as I can, swirling in a circle as I use the whole platform for my show. I take a bow and exit the stage, and just as I pass him standing on the edge of the stage and say just loud enough for him to hear "Hi Darren." I keep going, but am dying to see the look on his face when he realizes it is me. I stand around for a few moments, waiting to see if I get called back for the final round. I glance at him, to see if he is still looking. I see him; his eyes burning through me like never before. I feel his stare on me. I like it.

A few more girls go on stage and then they announce the finalists. I am the second to last person called back, but by far the most dressed. I see that to win this contest I am going to have to shed some clothes. I am thinking that the two hundred bucks is not worth my dignity; this is the kind of thing that never dies within the office rumor mill. If I can't win it shaking my ass then so be it. I wait my turn and when it comes, I pull out all the stops. I shake my hips hard than I can ever remember; and I look at Darren every chance I get. He is watching me again, his eyes glued to my hips. My time is up, and I go stand next to the other girls as the last one does her thing. She is wearing a thin white t shirt and has a bottle of water in hand. I know I am about to lose. She dumps the water over herself and proceeds to tear the t shirt off of her body. The only thing covering her boobs are red suspenders and the crowd is going crazy. It's over, and I know it.

A moment later the finalists are lined up on stage. Steve walks behind each of us, and despite the respectful rounds of applause for each of us, as soon as he gets to the girl with the big fake boobs the place erupts. He moves behind me and the crowd begins to chant "Lose the mask...lose the mask." I take a step forward, pretend to reach for the mask, only to take a bow and shuffle back into line. I concede to the girl in the red suspenders, not willing to reveal my identity to so many of my coworkers. My actions are met with a chorus of boos and I know that it is over. I glance over at Darren, and he smiles at me again. I think he is beginning to catch on.

I walk off the stage towards him, and he greets me with "Can I get you a drink?" "Absolutely, I am parched after that!" I respond. I follow him closely through the crowd as we make our way to the bar. It is packed, but we go to the side and he steps in behind the bar. "Being co-host has its privileges" he says, winking at me. He hands me a bottle of water and I tear into it, drinking half of it in what was most likely unlady-like fashion. The cold water cools me and I am now ready to kick this party into gear. "What can I get for you ma'am?" he says, practically yelling at me to overcome the noise in the house. I think for a moment, trying to come up with something sexy and funny to say. "I would love a slow comfortable screw against the wall" I whisper as I lean towards him. I pull back to see the look in his eyes as I break into a laugh at his surprised reaction. I have no idea what is in the drink, but I thought the request was appropriate for the moment. He searches my eyes, trying to think of a reply. I didn't expect to have outplayed him so easily, and it's funny to watch him squirm a little.

He goes to work making the drink, and I am impressed that he knows what's in it. Then again, I could totally see him working his way through college as a bartender, so maybe I shouldn't be so surprised. He runs to the kitchen and comes back with orange juice and puts everything into a shaker bottle. He pours each of us a drink, and raises his glass to make a toast. "To what lies ahead" he proposes, and I clink his glass with mine in agreement. I can see that burning look in his eyes again, and it makes me tingle inside. I try to find something to say, but the moment passes so I just smile under the mask. I think he understands. Just then the band starts to play again, and the crowd noise elevates to another level. He leans forward to say something, but it is too loud to hear. I read his lips as best I can, and I think he said we should go for a walk. I agree, and he grabs my hand to lead me through the crowd once again.

We walk outside and across the street, and can now speak in normal voices to one another. We sit on the curb and talk for a moment, and I am still feeling the buzz from before. He is looking at me like he wants to kiss me, and I realize I still have the veil on. I look away for a second and remove the veil. As soon as I look back we lean in to kiss. He pulls away too soon, and I lean into him trying to keep going. He comes back for more and this time we really start to kiss one another like we mean it. The moustache from his costume tickles. After a moment we decide to cool things for now and we start talking again. He is much more interesting than I think I gave him credit for at first. A pleasant surprise to say the least. We walk back towards the house and right before we enter I put the veil back on. "By the way, where did you learn to dance like that?" he asks. I turn around and tell him "Belly dance classes of course" I tell him. "It looked like fun, so I tried it once and loved it. It's a great workout and keeps me in shape." I lean forward, close to him, and add "It has other benefits, too" and then quickly turn and walk into the house.

He follows after me, and I love that I got him once again with my comment. We work our way towards the back of the house and go outside to join the crowd in front of the stage. The band is playing and the crowd is dancing and moving all in rhythm to the music. It is a very cool scene. As more people file in we get pressed closer together. I start dancing to the music, and decide to have a little fun at his expense. I shake my hips like I did when I was on stage, grinding against him a little. I lean backwards and put my arm around his neck, pulling him against me. His hands find my hips, and he does his best to keep up with my movement. I feel his hands tracing up and down my sides, gently touching me, making me shiver in anticipation of us doing this later with nothing between us. The moment is amazing; flipping back and forth between the feel of the crowd and the loud music to totally focus on his hands on my body. We continue to move together for the last few songs until the band ends their set and disappears into the crowd. I spin around to look at him again, ready to move things forward.

"So...now what?" I ask him, hoping he has a good answer. He grabs my hand and we make our way through the crowd once again. We walk outside and get into his Jeep which is parked on the grass of Mike's lawn. We are blocked in, and I am wondering what he is going to do. He starts it and we pull straight forward over the grass and up over the curb. He looks at me and laughs, saying "I'm sure he'll understand." We drive in silence, and I am growing more and more nervous by the minute. Finally I can't take it anymore and I blurt out "I don't usually do this sort of thing, but I liked you from the first moment I saw you, and I have been waiting for you to ask me out. I didn't want the first time to end up like this, but I guess I am going with it" all in one breath. He looks over at me and smiles, and suddenly I feel like an insecure little girl sitting next to him. Finally he says something, "I really like you too, and I think you and I are going to have a lot of fun together. I certainly hope you'll call me after this, and not make me feel like you got me drunk to take advantage of me." I break into a big smile and slap his arm playfully. I think he understands.

The uncomfortable moment seems to have passed and we talk more freely now that we both know what we are in for. I pull the veil off and set it aside. "So, did you come by yourself tonight?" he asks. "Yes, I was supposed to meet a friend from work here, but I never saw her. She knew about the costume and not to give away my identity tonight. I don't want people at work talking about me; I am supposed to be a manager, remember? The contest was fun, but the two hundred bucks was not worth my dignity and respect at the office" I inform him. "Besides, I told her I was probably going to end up with you tonight" I add. He pauses for a moment once again, and then looks over at me, "So...my place?" he asks, already knowing the answer. I just smile back at him.

We arrive at his place in a short time and park in the drive. As we are walking to the door he stops suddenly and turns to face me. He comes forward, kissing me, catching me off guard with his sudden move. "I couldn't wait any longer" he says with a big smile on his face. I laugh, not realizing just how cute he can be when he wants until that moment. I push him towards the door, growing antsy to get things started. We walk in and I quickly look around to see how he lives. The place is very neat and clean, and I am surprised. I kind of expected to watch him run around picking things up in a hurry and apologizing for some reason, but that is not the case. He walks into the kitchen and asks "Something to drink?" "Water would be great" I answer, not needing any more liquid encouragement for tonight. I walk over to the stereo and try to figure out how it works. It is a new and compact version, and I have no idea... "Oohh!" I am startled as it comes on by itself, and then laugh realizing that he turned it on with the remote. He laughs at me, too. "Anything in particular you'd like?" he inquires. "Something to dance to" I respond, thinking that a private dance session sounds like a great way to start things off. "Um, yeah...I don't...uuhhh..." "Not us...me" I tell him, putting his mind at ease that I am not going to make his dance in his living room with me. He walks over and dims the lights in the living room, and then comes to the stereo where I am. God I want him, I think to myself. As soon as he looks at me I look at his mouth. We begin to kiss again, and I love the way he kisses me.

He turns me and slowly backs me up into the entertainment center. I feel it behind me, and I like the mild roughness he is bringing. Our bodies press together as we slowly grind into one another. He pulls away and rips off the fake moustache of his costume. "Thanks...that thing tickles" I tell him, laughing a little. He hands me the controls and I start searching for something to dance to. I pick a random CD that should do the trick and then turn to face him. This time I kiss him, and slowly walk him backwards towards the couch. I break from the kiss, and point for him to sit down. I stand in front of him and slowly begin to dance a very slow version of what I was doing earlier tonight. My movements are slow and swaying, very sensual. I match the rhythm of the music, and as it increases in speed so do I. He watches me as he did before, his eyes glued to me. His stare is so enticing.

I remove the veil that I was hiding behind. I can feel my excitement growing as I slowly pull veil after veil out of the costume. I grab one and put it behind his neck, pulling him into me. I shake my hips right in front of his face and he watches me. His eyes slowly trace their way up my body and soon he is looking me in the eyes. His face is looking up at me from seemingly between my legs, and I feel myself squish a little bit at the sight of it. He has a dirty smile on his face and I know he is thinking the same thing I am. I am having trouble containing myself, and want to move things forward faster. I slowly work my way lower and lower until I am on my knees in front of him. I lean back very slowly, moving as much as I can in this position. I pull some more of the veils from the costume, tossing them aside. I grab two more and know that these two are the point of no return because of where they are placed. I yank them out, not hesitating for a second that this is what I want.

As the music increases I follow and I leap back to my feet. I begin to dance faster, shaking my hips and spinning quickly as I pull veil after veil out of the costume. I am down to wearing nothing but the fleshtone bra and thong that I had on under the layers of veils. I spin around and stick my ass in his face for him to touch. He reaches for me, and I tremble at him finally touching me. His hand runs over my ass cheek and down my leg. I reach back and unclip the bra, letting it fall to the floor. I cover my breasts with my hands, waiting a moment more before revealing them. I know my tits are great, but I hide them at the office so they are not a focal point for everyone. I turn to face him and slowly climb on top of him in his seated position on the couch. I release them, and grab his face to kiss him hard once again. I am so turned on at this point I can barely stand it. I need his touch, and I need it now.

We go to work on his clothes, struggling with the buttons of the costume. He wriggles out of his shoes and I unbutton his costume shirt. His strong hands grab my back, pulling me forward into him once again. We kiss even harder this time, the desire growing exponentially. I place my arms under my breasts, lifting them against his warm skin. He leans me backwards and takes one in his mouth. It is rock hard but quickly softens under the warmth of his mouth. He gently bites down on it, and it springs back to life in response. He clamps down a little more, and I toss my head back in a silent scream. I moan loudly as I wrap my legs around him, holding myself there. My hands clasp behind his neck, allowing his hands to roam freely over me. I am aching for his touch, and he seems to know it. His hands squeeze my tits, cupping them and squeezing them as he bites and licks away at them. He presses them together, and fits both of my rosy nipples into his mouth at the same time. He is driving me crazy, and so far this bad boy player is everything I was hoping he would be.

I begin to grind myself against him, my thong panties soaked with desire and doing little to separate us. After a few more seconds of this I am going to explode all over him, I think to myself. He pulls me up and we kiss again; our bodies press together as well moan and groan. I am beyond turned on, ready to explode at any second. I need to slow down just a bit or I am going to go crazy. And there is something I want to do first before we get around to focusing on me. I reach down and feel him through his baggy pants and find him to be at full attention. He slides me off of him and stands up, practically ripping his pants off of him. He goes to sit back down but I stop him; he is exactly where I want him, right in front of my face. His boxers look like they are straining to contain it, and I run my hand over it. I look up at him and smile like he did to me earlier, hoping it had the same effect as it did on me. I put my hands on his hips and yank the boxers to the floor, seeing it its full glory. I stare at it for a moment and then lean down and grab a veil off the floor. I put it around his waist and pull him forward, taking it into my mouth. His skin tastes salty from us grinding earlier but it quickly wears off and I can taste his skin. I pull him back and forth using the veil as leverage.

I work him up and down, running my tongue over his hard flesh and sucking as hard as I can. I grab the base and squeeze, seeing if I can make it give. I slide my hand up and down his cock, following my mouth with it. He moans as I do it, and it turns me on that much more. I feel him pulling the veil out of my hand, and I release it. I expect it to end up on the floor, but instead he puts it in his hands and wraps it behind my head, pulling me towards him, mimicking my move from earlier. He pulls me forward, and I take as much of it as I can into my mouth. It touches my throat and I flinch a little but go right back after it. He holds me in place, so deep in my throat I think I am going to gag at any second. He lets out a deep groan and moves a little bit forward. I pull away, coughing just a bit. I laugh a little bit and then he does too. He grabs my hands and pulls me to my feet.

He turns me to face the couch and I am about to protest him not following through on his implied promise earlier when looking up at me from between my legs. He grabs my thong by the sides and rips it straight to the floor. I step out of it and move closer to the end of the couch. I know what is coming and I think I want it as badly as he does. He grabs me forcefully and bends me over the couch. He is deep inside me before I can even squeal in delight at his roughness. I cry out loudly, the pleasure so intense so quickly. I arch to meet his next thrust and it seems to go even deeper than the first. It hits my core, and I shudder in delight. His hands grab my waist and yank me back and forth into it. I hang onto the couch, arching, bracing and crying out loudly. "Oh God! ....Uuugghhh!" I hear myself exclaim. I see his foot on the arm of the couch next to me, and I know it will go even deeper like this. He pushes deep, holds it there, pressing, stretching, until he withdraws, only to repeat the process again. I am getting close after thirty seconds of this, and I grab onto the cushions of the couch in effort to brace myself for the coming storm.

I slide my feet together to gain a little space inside. I squeeze him for all I am worth and the increased friction will push me over the edge in no time, I can feel it. He grabs my ponytail and pulls my head back, taking control of me. I moan in approval; feeling him push forward and hold still. I know what he wants, and I want it too. I move my hips like before, grinding and fucking him back. It is incredible, and I go faster and faster as it feels better and better. After a moment I feel it start; my body seizes up and my rhythm breaks. I cry out loudly, fighting to keep going, to not let it end. He holds my hips and slowly takes over as I can no longer keep the pace I set earlier. "Ho, oh my God that was hot!" I say loudly, looking back at him behind me.

He leaves me and walks over to the couch and has a seat. I am ready for more of that, and I quickly climb on top of him. I put my hands on his shoulders to gain some leverage. I lower myself onto it, and it goes right into me with ease. I look down at him, half drunk with pleasure. We begin more slowly this time, grinding and kissing gently as we go. His hands, oh God his luscious hands are on my breasts again, feeling me. My nipples grow hard and he teases them with his fingertips. The pleasure is pulsing through me and I start to work my hips once again. He is so hard I feel like I could spin in a circle on him. He moves with me at first, but soon lets me take over. I grind and slide all over him, my hips working their magic. I watch him as he stares at my hips, watching me move on him. It feels so good and I love the look in his eyes as he watches me work. He looks up at me, and the look in his eyes is so intense. This is so fucking hot I think to myself. We fuck like animals for several more minutes before my calf starts to cramp and I have to stand up.

Her Eyes

He walks to the kitchen bare assed, retrieving another bottle of water for each of us. We both survey the room and then look at one another, laughing. It is obvious we are both into this, and very compatible as lovers. We are both breathing hard and have redden skin from the session. He takes another drink and then tosses the bottle aside in semi-dramatic fashion and asks "You ready?" I just smile back at him, knowing I can take anything he wants to dish out tonight. He sits back in the same spot and signals for me to turn around and face away from him this time. I reach down and guide it back into me once more. I put my hands on his knees and start to move, and he moves under me. I quickly take over, sliding myself up and down on him, working his stiff cock in and out of my depths. I am getting closer to another orgasm, and I begin to move faster as I close in.

He catches me off guard by yanking me backwards onto him. Now I am lying on top of him and we are both facing the ceiling. His hands run all over me and our sweaty bodies slide easily over one another. I turn my head to the side and he brushes the hair out of my face. We kiss again, and despite the minor interruption to my groove I am getting close once again. He bites down on the back of my neck and that did the trick. My hips go into high gear and I grind into him as hard and fast as I can. He smashes my tits against me as I come all over his cock again. I am left breathless and limp on top of him.

I can hear him groaning and know he must be close. I fight my way to the surface, trying to focus. "Where do you want it?" I hear him ask. His words snap me out of my fog, and I respond "Not inside me." I keep going, sliding up and down on him as he begs me "Don't stop, don't stop!" I thrust my hips upwards and remove him from inside me, clamping him between my thighs. I move up and down a little and it is more than he can handle. He moans loudly as he empties his load onto my stomach. So. Fucking. Hot I think to myself, loving the feeling of his warm liquid on me. We both collapse on the couch, breathless and spent from the awesome romp we just had. Holy shit, what a way to start this I think.

After several minutes on the couch we walk like zombies to the bedroom. It is very late and neither one of us wants to do anything but sleep. We crawl into his bed, kiss, and I roll over and fall right to sleep.

In what seems like only a few moments later I hear him yell "Jesus...wake up...its 7:00!" I am instantly wide awake, my feet on the floor. "Shit...we gotta go! I yell, running to the living room to gather my clothes. I realize that I have a ton of veils scattered everywhere, but in my haste start to piece the costume back together instead of just borrowing some clothes. My car is still at Mike's house, all of my stuff is inside...shit! I am supposed to be at work in an hour, how am I going to pull that off? I ask myself internally. Why is he in the shower, we don't have time for that! I hear the water shut off soon after that, and I am half way dressed in the veils again. He yells from the bedroom "Do you want some clothes to wear?" I tell him I am almost ready to go, but I don't think he hears me. He comes into the living room with clothes in hand, but sees me redressed and tosses them aside. "I have clothes in my car; I'll just wear this until we get back to Mike's" I tell him, and head for the door.

We get into his jeep and head for Mike's. As the scare of the abrupt wake up wears off I am starting to feel the effects of last night. A headache starts creeping in and I am in desperate need of coffee. His cell phone rings and I hear Mike's voice on the line. He is talking loud and my head starts to hurt even more. I point at the convenience store and mouth the word COFFEE to him, and he pulls over. He sits there talking to Mike, and I sigh in disapproval, figuring there is no way I am getting out of the car dressed like this. He ignores me further, and finally I snap at him "We're in a hurry, remember?" He looks over at me, and looks pissed. I immediately think I shouldn't have been so harsh in my tone. "I don't drink coffee, remember?" he says, glaring at me. "Fine...I will get it!" I hear Mike say "Who is that?" just before I slam the car door. I stomp into the store, ignoring the obvious stares I am getting.

When I come out of the store I am calmed down a bit and start to feel bad about being a bitch to him. I look for his Jeep and it is not where he parked it. I look around for it and see that he is now parked out by the corner. I can't believe he did that! I start to get mad, but realize that I probably deserve it for being such a bitch. I am embarrassed to be seen the morning after Halloween in my costume; I feel like a slut. I hesitate for a second, but it is obvious he is not going to come and get me. I take a deep breath and steel myself, and then head for the Jeep. As soon as I clear the first row of cars I can hear car horns blowing and people whistling. I am so embarrassed! I run to the Jeep and climb in. I flop down in the car and he is just sitting there laughing at me. I start to glare at him, but I can't help but join in his laughter. "I will get you back for that" I vow to him.

Naomi

I have to get out of this store; the late nights, the crappy pay, and not to mention the constant stream of dysfunctional weirdos, perverts, and uncategorized nutjobs that frequent this place. I knew I should have gone to college. Climbing in the car I look at the clock and find that I am about twenty minutes earlier than I thought. I decide that I should stop by the other shop that is right down the street from us and see if they are hiring. Maybe a change of scenery would do me some good. I head down the street and pull into their parking lot. It is about empty as I would expect this time of day. It will be a good time for me to speak with the manager and find out what's up.

I pull the door open and walk in. The smell of incense hits me; it is warm and pleasant, and a far cry from my store. The place I work in smells....plastic. The girl at the counter greets me, and I walk in, pretending to be browsing. I can't help but comparison shop a little, and am surprised to find their pricing to be less than ours. No wonder they are always busier than we are. I walk around flipping over tags, shaking my head. "Can I help you find something?" a voice from behind me asks. It is the girl from the counter. "Actually, is the manager in?" I ask. She responds "He is, but he is speaking with someone right now. That's him in the black shirt." I lean forward to see him; I can only see the guy he appears to be talking to. I walk their direction, trying to see who it is I want to speak with soon. The two guys are standing there talking about a book the manager is holding. I walk to the counter and stop a polite distance away from them but close enough to hear their conversation.

I look over at them and see the book he is holding. It is the same one we have in my store that I took home and read. It was so hot. The cute guy looks at me and I smile back at him. I hear him ask the manager if they would consider selling his book. Wait, his book? Oh my God...did he write that book? I look at the book in his hands; I would know it anywhere. He looks at me, and asks "That's my book, have you ever seen it?" Seen it? I've read it! I exclaim with a huge smile. I feel my face flush with excitement. He was good looking enough for me to notice earlier, but I had no idea he was that guy. Oh my God. I look him up and down in obvious fashion; not my usual type that is for sure. Probably mid thirties, looks like he is in shape, wearing jeans, a nice

97

shirt, and those eyes. He looks right into me it seems. I swear I feel myself twinge with excitement as soon as he smiles.

The store owner snaps me out of my momentary dream, "What did you think of it?" he barks in my direction. He seems irritated with me; he knows where I work and probably thinks I am price checking. " I answer him, but I look to the man standing next to him when I speak. "I absolutely loved it...it was very hot!" I tell him with a gleam in my eye. I bite my lip a little on purpose. He turns and walks towards me, and suddenly I am very nervous. He extends his hand to introduce himself; I nervously reach out my hand, hoping I am not shaking so much he notices. I try to look him in the eye, but when I do I hit my thumb into his and make the handshake rather awkward. "I'm Darren" he says. "Naomi" is all I can respond with. I am sure this happens to him all the time, but I am feeling rather intimidated by this whole situation. He is burning holes in me again with that stare, and I want to run away and hide. I look away, and hear the store manager gruffly interject "Are you two about finished?" He is blocking the only way out, and so I walk over and slide passed him, trying not to touch him. I put my hand lightly on his back as I pass; his cologne hits me and almost freezes me in my tracks. It is musky and warm, and inviting. I catch myself and press onward, pushing passed him and heading straight for the door. "It was nice to meet you" I say, shooting him one more glance, stealing one more picture for my mind. "Bye" is all I hear him say as I swing open the door and step into the bright sun.

Several days later I am back into my usual routine at work when I hear the door chime, and then hear Crystal greet the customer. I hear her squeal in that childish way she does when she is excited, and look to see what the commotion is about. I see a man standing talking to her, and right away I know it is him. I can feel him viscerally. I turn and run into the back in a panic. I am practically hyperventilating, my stomach in knots. "Nay...someone's here to see you!" I can hear Crystal yelling from the front. I can't answer her, I am suddenly frozen. I hear her walking towards the back room and decide I better look surprised when I see him. Crystal leads him to the back room and shuts the door behind him. Bitch, she knows I like this guy and she is not helping me here. I walk around the corner, and pretend to be startled to see him. "Hi!" I blurt out, the sight of him still catching me off guard even though I knew he was here. "Hi Naomi, how are you?" he asks in his usual casual voice. "What are you doing here?" I ask, hoping its why I think, and yet scared it will be. "Um, well you left in a hurry the other day and I didn't get a chance to hear what you really thought about the book" he says, suddenly sounding a little unsure of himself. It's charming, and makes me realize that he is a little nervous too. I suddenly don't feel so out of place. He is looking at the handful of DVDs I am holding, "New arrivals" I tell him. We share a laugh about the titles, and the tension seems to melt away from my body. The laughter between us relaxes me. And the attraction is obvious.

He on the other hand seems fidgety, and I almost laugh to myself about how quickly things have changed. It appears now he is the one that wants to run and hide. He looks at his watch, and starts to say goodbye. I decide I don't want this to be over just yet, and grow bold enough to say "Well, its my lunch hour soon, do you want to have coffee with me, er something?

We head to the only place close by, even though I know we will run into Bryce there. Maybe this will finally get him to leave me alone. We walk in and he smiles until he sees that I have someone with me. He looks angry, and turns away. We walk to the counter and I order my usual, and Darren orders just a drink. I feel bad making him pay since he didn't really order any food and I dig into my purse for my wallet. But he waves me off, paying for my lunch anyway. We go sit in the corner table and pick up chatting where we left off. Bryce comes over a few minutes later and drops off the sandwich and the drinks we ordered, and is rather rude and immature about it. He looks at Darren and then rolls his eyes in an obvious fashion to me. Ha, if he only knew what this guy was about. He turns and walks away in a huff, and Darren asks "What is that dude's problem?" "Oh, sorry about that...we used to date and he is still rather hung up on me" I answer, and quickly try to change the subject. I keep an eye on the time and before long we have to head back to the store.

We walk back to the store and I am hoping he is going to ask me out. I laugh at the thought that flashes through my head about him being a "first-dater". I know Crystal keeps telling me I need to quite that, but he is too yummy to wait on. "So how late do you usually work?" he asks, snapping my out of the conversation in my head. I tell him "I close five nights a week, so you can find me here any time." Hoping he gets the hint. "Are you guys busy late at night?" he asks, and I am looking at the hi9nt of a dirty smile on his face and wonder if he is thinking what I am thinking. "No, not usually.....and I would love the company" I tell him. "Cool, then I will come see you Thursday night" he states. I already can't wait to see him again. I reach out and give him a big hug, getting a preview of what he will feel like. His body is firm, and his cologne is only noticeable with my nose in his chest. I squeeze him tight, and feel myself ache slightly with desire. I go to pull away, but he stops me. He looks at me, and I can tell he wants to kiss me. He moves in before I even have time to protest, not that I would have. His mouth is on mine; he kisses me first, then I feel his mouth open and his tongue flick against mine. I follow his lead, twisting and twirling mine into his. It is brief, but said volumes. We stop, and I open my eyes to see him. "See you Thursday" he says, and I just smile at him. I turn and practically float to the door. As soon as I open it I hear Crystal laughing, and I burst out to join her. She runs over to me, and suddenly we are 12 year olds at a sleep over. She wants details, and fast. "The first words out of my mouth are "Oh My God!......"

It is Thursday night and I am practically pacing around the store. I still have three hours to go and I am clenching already. I am never going to make it I think to myself. I am going to fuck him in the store I decide. I am quitting this job anyway, so I have nothing to lose. And God do I want him. We barely know each other, but there is something about him...I hear the door alarm and practically jump out of my chair. It's not him, and the disappointment rips through me. I pray the next three hours go by fast.

After a steady parade of customers a fair amount of time has passed. It is almost 10:30 and I am starting to think maybe he is not going to show. I close in half an hour, where is he? I start the process of shutting things down for the night, knowing that a few stragglers will still come through the door. This sucks...I so want to see if this guy is as good as he pretends to be in the book. I was so turned on reading about how he takes control; a far cry from the boys I dated recently. If I have one more guy apologize to me afterwards I swear I am going to become a lesbian! I might as well put back the condoms I took off the counter earlier; it seems I am not going to need them.

I hear the door alert and turn half-heartedly to see who it is. I do a double take when I see that its him! Oh my God!!! I run towards him, so happy he didn't let me down. I am smiling inside and out as I rush to him, grabbing him and squeezing him tight.   I feel so....relieved. I stand on my toes to kiss him. His tongue touches mine as we mouths openly kiss. It is as delicious as I remember from the other day, and I want more of it. Right now. I hear the door ding again, and he turns to see someone entering the store. I turn and walk towards the counter, only to see that the customer is that creepy guy who is always hanging around here. I am disappointed that he is here when the man I have been waiting for tonight has finally arrived.

I do a loop through the store to let him know I am watching him, and then return back to the counter. I am focused on the security camera monitors so I can keep track of him. "I don't trust this guy; here is here a lot and I think he steals from us" I tell him. "Anyway...how are you?" I ask, hoping he will take my mind off of that guy. We begin to talk and laugh again, just like before when we met. He is funny and quick with his comebacks, and I find him entertaining as well as attractive. Once again with bad timing the guy walks to the counter with two movies in his hand. I try not to sound annoyed at the interruption. "<u>Ass Bandits 14</u> and <u>Catholic School Girl Fuckfest</u>...anything else tonight? I ask, not hiding my bitchiness very well. I stuff them in our obligatory plain brown bag and he grabs them and hurries out the door.

We stand at the counter and talk some more. I really should go lock the door, but it is still a few minutes before closing time. But I don't want to cut our conversation short. He looks down at the collection inside the counter display and his eyes widen in surprise. I laugh at him, poking fun at him with "You're kind of a prude, huh?" He laughs aloud and fires back "Hardly! I swing with the best of them my dear" I look at him blankly, not getting what seemed to be a joke he was making. "That was a line from Seinfeld" he clues me in. Oh, now I get it, my mom used to watch that show all the time I tell him "There was a TV show in the 90's called Seinfeld that was..." he blurts out. "I smile a big smile at him, and interrupt him by saying I know...I just wanted to make you squirm a little, that's all" He laughs again, sighing in relief that he is not

101

that much older than I am, I assume. "You are such a brat" he tells me, smirking. He reaches over the counter that separates us and grabs my shirt, pulling me towards him. He leans in to kiss me, and I meet him half way. We kiss again, and his mouth is quickly becoming an addiction. He pulls away, but I don't want him to. "Is that all I get?" I ask. "For now" he says firmly, then breaking into a smile. "Oh I see...who is the brat now?" Someone else walks in, the door banging shut behind them. My lean forward and sigh, irritated that we are intruded upon once again. I laugh at the situation, and then say to him with a dirty smile "Don't worry, I am closing soon and I am giving you a private tour."

I recognize the couple who came in, and walk over to greet them. They have a few questions, and then want to buy a set of our SportSheets that have the restraints built into them. We chat for a moment, but I am aching to get back to the guy waiting for me at the counter. I do my best to hurry them along and escort them to the counter to ring them up. They pay and head for the door, and I look over at him, waiting patiently for me. He looks at his watch, and I inform him "Close enough" regardless of what time it really is. I can't wait any longer. I go to him, and deliver a long deep kiss before heading for the door. I peek outside to see if anyone is there, and then shut the door, locking it behind me. I remember to start backing up the security tape, and wonder if I should have been more careful about that so far. Oh well, too late now. Besides, no one looks at those tapes unless something is missing anyway. "There, now I am done for the day" I announce. I turn to him, waiting to see what he has in mind for tonight. I am tingling with excitement; the anticipation of whatever is about to happen is making me dance with excitement.

I want to show him the books of his we have on the shelf. I still can't believe that I am here with him, it blows my mind that we met, and that he is here with me tonight. I can't wait to see what he is like. I motion for him to follow me back the aisle to the book section. I stop in front of the display I created for them. God I cannot stop looking at his mouth. "We just got these in today; I got the owner to buy some to sell here." His eyes open wide and he smiles wide. "Wow...that's awesome! How can I thank you, Naomi?" It seemed like a loaded question, but I was searching for the right way to get things started, so I am taking this one. My stomach is one big knot, but I am doing it anyway. I take a step towards him, and say as boldly as I can "Oh, you're about to."

I walk towards him until my toes are practically touching his. He reaches for me, putting his hand on my hip as we kiss. I kiss me hard and deep, the desire within finally overtaking the nerves. I click my tongue ring against his teeth, reminding him of what I am going to do to him very soon. I reach up and run my hands over his shoulders, feeling the muscles under his shirt. I pull myself up into him, kissing him even harder. His arm is around my waist and he pulls me in like he is trying to push us into one. Our bodies grind against each other. I have been thinking about this since we parted ways the other day. I want to bang him right here in the store, just like I have been picturing all week.

My hands follow the lines of his body, traveling over the ripples and bulges of his form. I grab and clutch at him, being rough in hopes he'll return the favor. I am growing bolder by the second within the confines of the store. It feels safe here, safe to be a dirty little girl. Hell, what better place to be a dirty girl than here? I ask myself. I grab his firm ass, filling my hands with his flesh. He does the same, and we squeeze ourselves together. I can feel his cock pressing into me, and my body's own preparations have already begun. My underwear is sliding against my skin already. His thigh is between my legs, and he lifts it into me, pressing into me. I moan inside, enjoying the pressure against my sex. He breaks our kiss and goes to work on my neck, sending shivers all through me. He explores, and finds the spot with the slightest of hints from me. He goes after it, knowing in this case more is better. "HaaHaa, fuck yeah...right...there" I gasp slowly. I grab the back of his head making sure he continues. I arch my body into his, grinding, rubbing. It feels so good I don't want it to stop. Finally he comes up for air, looking down at me.

"Oh my God I am so fucking hot for this" I tell him, confessing my body's desires. "Me too, I wanted you since I first laid eyes on you" he informs me, confirming my thoughts. I delight at the thought of catching this man's attention, and I aim to keep it. I spin us around and press him against the book shelf with his books on it. I am going to suck him off right here, right in the spot many a woman will stand and see his book. I want that...to know, to know that I did this with him. I fumble with his

103

jeans and finally tear them open. His cock flops out in full view for me, and I want it in my mouth. I squat down in front of him and swallow it whole in one motion. I pull back and go again, this time feeling it a little more. I try not to show it, but he made me gag. I want him to know I can take it, and so I don't stop. I grab it and squeeze, "Christ is he hard" I think to myself. I use just my mouth at first, sucking it hard and rubbing it against the inside of my cheek. He likes it, and moans a little. I like that he likes it, and I start doing it harder and faster. He moans more, and I really like it...and I haven't even pulled out my secret weapon yet. He looks down at me, and I meet his stare, confidently, knowing he is totally into what I am doing to him.

After a few moments of this I finally release my grip on it and change things up a bit. I look up at him, wanting to see the look on his face when I do it; I stick my tongue out and slowly engulf his cock. I can feel it pressing down into my tongue ring, and am sure he can feel it too. I run my tongue all over it, putting my favorite accessory to work. I run the smooth ball of the tongue ring underneath the entire length of his cock, up and down, rubbing it as hard as I can. It is more difficult to go deep like this, but I think he is enjoying it just fine. I do another run through and finally ask "How does that feel?" He looks into my eyes and tells me "Fucking amazing". His words make me smile, and I take satisfaction that despite his experiences that I have read about I am getting to him.

After a few minutes of this he suddenly blurts out "You need to stop that....right now." I sit back and look up at him, a little confused. "Are we gonna, um...continue moving forward or is this the extent of your plans tonight?" he asks me. I laugh a little, thinking it's funny that he isn't convinced that we are here to do the deed. I have read his stories; I want to see what it's like, what he's like. "Ahh, no...we have all night and the place to ourselves. I am not done with you yet" I tell him, meaning that he better not be done with me yet. "I've read your stories; I want some of that" I add, smiling devilishly up at him. I stand and turn away from him, walking towards the other side of the store. I have pictured in my mind getting fucked on the counter, and that is where we are going to start. I pull off my shirt en route, dropping it on the floor. I reach the counter and turn to see him. He watches as I remove my jeans, tossing them aside as well. I stand before him in nothing but my bra, which will have to come off next. I reach behind and unclip it as he removes his shirt.

He comes to me, taking me in his arms and kissing me deeply once again. He tongue invades me and I return the favor. We kiss and touch as we lean against the counter. He reaches for my tits, his hands traveling across my skin until he reaches his goal. He kisses my neck, biting and nibbling his way downward until he takes my nipple in his mouth. His tongue rubs and rolls over my piercing, and the feeling makes me tremble. They are so much more sensitive since I had that done. I love having them sucked and played with now more than ever. I start moaning aloud, loving the feeling on it in his mouth. God his tongue is so good, I hope he goes down on me and does it there too. I feel his hand start to slide down my stomach and I start to ache to be touched. Just when I think I am going to get some relief he stops.

He grabs my hand and leads me back over to my shoes. I don't know what he wants my shoes on for, but I don't want to delay things any more so I obey. I am now closer to his height again. Maybe it will make it easier for us......He spins me around and pushes me over the counter before I can finish my thought. He crouches behind me and I feel his tongue on me instantly. I slam my hands down on the glass, gasping for breath as he licks my folds from behind. I lean my weight down on the counter, my piercings clicking against the glass. I arch my back, giving him more access to me. I push into his face, loving it so much. His tongue searches for my clit, running all over me. He flicks it over the barbell, and then right onto my super sensitive clit. I am throbbing with excitement by the time he finally gives me what I want. The short quick strokes and driving me crazy, and I close my eyes, picturing what is looks like, what he is doing down there. I can feel it begin, the rise of the wave, and I moan his name. He hears me, and suddenly his tongue is inside me again, like he knew what I wanted, what I needed right then. He withdraws and plunges again, doing it over and over, fucking me with his tongue.

I reach back and grab my ass, prying it open for him. I look at him, watching him for a moment until his tongue forces my eyes closed again. He drives it into me again and I cannot keep my eyes open in the blinding pleasure. I feel something more firm than his tongue in me and realize it it his finger that is now sliding in and out of me. It feels different, but no less good. His mouth goes back to focusing on my clit as his finger probes my depths. He is working around his hand in this position and it feels so good. I am so close and I....Oh God! I feel his tongue on my ass and I instantly explode. It is too much to take and I feel my hips buck and my juices gush out of me. I groan so loud as he continues to finger fuck me. My hips buck and grind in the air as I feel it slide in and out of me. His touch is amazing and it feels like it is going to go on forever. I can feel myself running down my leg from what he did to me. I collapse forward onto the counter, limp...spent from coming so hard.

"Holy shit...I have never done that before" I tell him, gasping for breath. "No one has ever made me squirt before" I confess. This was so hot, doing it in the store like this, and what he did to me. It felt so good. My thoughts slowly reform as I come back to conscious after the best orgasm I have ever had. I feel his hand on my back and then I feel him enter me. I can feel it sliding in and out of me, and I squeeze it as much as I can, making it feel even better for both of us. He continues his pace, stuffing a little more into me moment by moment until it feels like I am taking all of him inside me. His hand slides up the back of my head, and I feel the tension in my scalp as he pulls my head back. I love it, and he seems to know without ever asking. His other hand is on my hip, and he pulls me back into him by using my body as leverage.

I can feel it start again, my body tingling from my toes all the way up to my head. He senses it as well, and grabs my waist with both hands and really starts pounding into me. His body impacting mine like this is jarring me into the glass. Just as I start to think this I hear the last thing I want to hear...the glass cracking. I am instantly sober, snapped out of my near orgasm haze by the damage we just did. I carefully lift myself off the glass counter top, making sure not to make things worse. I don't want this to be over, so I act quickly and grab his hand, leading him away from the counter. "I'll worry about that later" I tell him, dismissing it as best I can for now. A delightful thought comes to mind, and we turn towards the bondage section. I am heading for the swing.

"I have shown this thing to a bunch of people, but I have never actually used it, but I have been dying to try it out" I confess. I climb into the straps just like before, but this time without clothes and only one intention. I motion to him with my eyes, and he comes forward, standing between my legs as intended. I grab the straps, bracing myself for another good hard fucking. He pushes himself inside me again, this time slowly at first. He works me back into form, and soon it is gliding in and out of me in rapid fashion." After a few moments of being slow and steady he grabs my hips and thrusts himself deep into me in one move. The impact nearly knocks the breath out of me, and before I can draw a breath he does it again. "That's it…bang the fuck out of me" I encourage him. And oh my God does he; pounding into me, powered on by his desire. My cries echo through the store, my body tip toeing the line between just enough and too much. I can feel each impact smash my piercing into me, and I know that I am going to be sore tomorrow. God, what a story this will be.

My body wants to help, and in spite of my suspended state I manage to buck my hips into him. I groan a deep groan as I grow ever closer, just needing a little more to reach the goal. He grabs the straps right above my hands and thrusts into me, holding himself so deep as he can. I arch into him, pulling myself upward and throwing my head back all at the same time. The feeling of him so deep inside is incredible, and I explode once again in an intense orgasm. My body bucks and shakes as I draw it out as long as possible. I collapse back into the harness, thankful for it holding me intact as I feel if I could literally fall into pieces on the floor after that one.

I am hanging there in the straps for a moment before I hear him ask "Can you ride me in this thing?" His question brings a surge of energy back to me, and I sit up and begin to remove the harness from me. We trade places, and I eagerly put him into the harness. He sits down in the swing and I quickly climb on top of him, placing one foot on each thigh just like I saw in the video for this thing. I am not sure if it will work, but it looked like fun when I watched it. I lower myself down on him again, loving the feeling of his hardness penetrating my pink softness. With two of us in it, the swing travels a long distanced down before starting to rebound upward. We do our best to find a rhythm, and slowly settle into a slow, long stroke as our ride. My tits are in his face, and I brush them against his mouth. He gets the hint, and start to suck one of them will squeezing the other. His tongue goes to work just like before, and the feeling of it coupled with him being inside me start the process once again. It seems as if he can't move much from underneath me, so I take over and begin riding him briskly. He leans back and it forces him deeper into me. I clutch the straps and my hips go to work, grinding back and forth on top of him quickly. I am getting close and soon I feel it burst inside me once again. I throw my head back and it jerks us out of our rhythm. Soon we are swinging wildly inside the frame, nearly banging into the sides. I break into a laugh as we slowly swing back to stop.

We stand up and he seems to be having some sort of issue; he is jumping up and down. I look at feel sideways, and then ask what he is doing. "Just getting ready for more" he assures me. "More huh?" I ask, and think I better recruit a little help if I want to keep going."Wait here then, 'cause you're wearing me out!" I tell him. He is getting rubbed raw in a bunch of places, and I sure feel the same way. I walk to the counter and grab a bottle of lube and more condoms from the shelf. I love this stuff and I keep stealing bottles of it to take home. I squish some of it into my hand, and after a few seconds feel the warming sensation in my hand. I walk towards him, and gently apply a thick coat of it to his reddened cock. He smiles at me, and asks "Now what?"

I turn and walk towards the other side of the store to find the Liberator display. I walk to it and shove the manikins out of our way. It was a little more forceful than I planned, and the bodies break apart and scatter in different directions. I hear him laughing out loud before I even turn around. I grab the lube and take a small amount in my hand again and then tell him "I want you to fuck my ass." I lie down over the foam wedge and stick my ass in the air for the taking. He comes forward, positioning himself behind me once again. I brace myself for his intrusion, but instead his slips it into my pussy instead. I groan, half in pleasure and half in relief of not having it in my ass just yet. His hand smacks my ass, and the sting is hot against my flesh. I was surprised to hear the words come out of my mouth, but he is making me want to be dirty than I have ever been. His strokes build from slow and steady to pound me hard and fast. I fucking love it, and the desire to push my boundaries returns.

I feel something starting to rub around my most sensitive spot, and the sensation sends chills of pleasure rippling through me. It must be his thumb, and soon I feel its lubed tip enter my most private place. I moan in approval, glad to see he knows to ease me into this uncharted territory. I have done it myself a few times with my toy, but it is different when I am the one with the controls. I am turning myself over to him, hoping he reads me well enough to make it alright. He hand slaps my ass again, the sound echoing through the store. It pushes deeper into me, and I like it. He matches the strokes of his cock into me with the withdraw of his thumb, contrasting the two. It is amazingly intense, and I crave the full brunt of him in my ass. I want to feel it; to take it all, to wince and moan, to feel the blend of pleasure and pain. I want to be owned by him. He pushes deeper and I love the feeling of him stretching me. He removes his thumb, and I feel the cool liquid hit my ass; it is more lube. Here it comes I tell myself, bracing for it. I feel it enter me, and realize it is not his cock, not yet. His finger penetrates me, and I take it with no problem. Then comes the second one, and it is big difference. "I am not ready for this" shoots through my mind. He feels me flinch, and slows his pace a little. I relax a little and before long I can handle this new width as well. He slides them in and out of me with growing intensity, and my cries match his pace. His cock is still stroking me with every inch he has, and I am growing close to exploding all over him once again. He is fucking me like mad again, his cock and fingers nearly burning me with friction. I am growling and groaning in time with his thrusts, as if he is knocking the air right out of me with each impact. I am climbing, growing closer, so close to coming once again. His voice snaps me out of it; "Are you ready?" he asks me.

"Yes, I want you to take my ass. Take me now" I say without hesitation. My body is burning for it. I want it now, I want it all now. I hear him tear the condom wrapper and in a moment it is pressing into the soft flesh where his fingers were. He presses into me, more than I am ready for at first, and my body reacts. He stops, freezing in place. Once again my excitement has outweighed my sensibility. "It's okay, just go slow" I tell him. And he does; he is tuned into what I need. My body begins to grow accustom to him, and he pushes in and out more rapidly without going any deeper for several moments. The feeling is so intense; different and yet still exquisite. I love that I am taking it, that I can handle it. I can't tell how much of it is in me, but it feels like more than half. As I get as comfortable as I can with this amount, I decide I want more. It is going to be more than I can handle at first, but I figure I will grow used to it like I have done with each stage of this so far. "OK, now for the fun part" I tell him, letting him know I am ready for more.

I grit my teeth, bracing for more of it. He pushes forward, down into me from his position above me. He is driving down into me like his body is a hammer and I am the nail. I wince and cringe, and then relax and breathe my way into comfort once again. He paces himself based on my reactions, and is pulling me along into this new ground. I am his; his for the taking, his fuck toy, and I am loving every second of it. He leans forward and puts his hands on the floor next to mine. Now I feel his full weight on top of me, and it reminds me of my position underneath him. His weight presses him into me, his cock traveling deeper than before. I have to be taking all of it at this point. I have to be. It feels so big in me, so tight, stretching me unlike anything ever before. I feel his breath on my neck, and then he bites me ear. His voice echoes in my head, like I was wearing headphones. "Put your hand underneath you and rub your clit" he commands to his slave.

I comply eagerly; the missing link to one more epic orgasm tonight. As good as he feels in my ass, it is not enough to push me over the edge for one more. I touch myself and my pussy throbs in response, jealous that it has been ignored all this time. I rub it hard, rough against my own soft skin. "That's it...that's my dirty little whore" he says, verbally rewarding my efforts. My hand increases in speed, and I am quickly on the brink of the one orgasm I have wanted more than any ever before. I moan aloud, growing louder with each shove of his cock into my depths. He is growing larger by the moment, and his voice roughens with desire. He grabs my hair and yanks my head to the side. I shove my fingers inside my drenched pussy, finger-fucking myself with three of my own fingers. "That's it, jerk yourself off while I fuck your ass" he bellows in uncontained lust. He fucks me harder and I do the same. "Come all over your own fingers while I fuck your ass" he commands, and I explode as he utters the sentence. He did it once again, and I feel my own juices squirt and pulsing out of me, running down my leg. I shudder and scream as I continue fucking myself all the way through it. I lose track of sense and time, blinded by my own passion.

I hear him groaning, and slowly become aware that he is sliding his cock in and out of me faster and faster. He fucks away at me, his desire for his own overtaking his concern for me. He groans and pulls out of me in one quick move. I hear the condom snap off of him; his cock is in between my ass cheeks, and he is fucking the groove. He squeezes my cheeks together, and I feel it hit my back. He shoots stream after stream of it onto me. "Oh Fuck Yes...Come all over me" I beg him. I look back over my shoulder and see him jerking his cock furiously, getting the most out of it. He empties himself onto me, and I feel each thread of it hit my skin. A sense of overwhelming satisfaction fans through me. We roll over onto the floor, embracing one another.

We stand up after a few minutes, and I walk towards the bathroom ready to remove the remnants of our session together. I shut the door behind me, seeing the hand print on my ass in the full length mirror and the glistening streaks on my back. I grab a hand towel and wipe it off of me. I pull my clothes on and walk back out into the store. He is mostly dressed by the time I return. I am embarrassed, and he seems to realize it. He tosses me my clothes and I quickly turn away to put them back on. After a moment of awkward silence, he asks "Well, do you want help rebuilding the manikins?" I laugh out loud, and it breaks the tense feeling that was building inside me. "I'll get to it tomorrow" I tell him. He walks to the bathroom and I watch him leave. One more reminder of just how hot this night was. He returns and we walk together towards the door. I reach for my keys and push on the door handle, only then to realize that it was never locked. At any moment someone could have walked in on us. We look at one another, and just start laughing.

Vicki

I walk into work just like I do every night at this time. My life has become so routine lately, and I am just aching for some excitement. The daily grind of school, work, and homework blends together into one big monotonous blur. I chat with Jeff, asking how buy his shift was and if there is anything going on I need to know about. He gives me the rundown of the day's happenings, but I find my mind wandering worse than usual. I am so bored with this job.

I glance at the clock, somehow hoping it will be far later than it really is. Working the late shift at a hotel is not exactly an interesting job, but it does allow me to do my get all my homework done as I close in on my degree. I can't wait to get a job and start working a normal schedule. I never see my friends working a night shift like this. I remind myself that while they are out partying and whatever I am gaining ground and soon I will be much better off because of it. I see a car roll into the parking lot as the conversation in my head continues. It is a cool looking sports car; black, shiny and fast looking. I see the guys step out of the car and draw a breath. Oh my God that guy is cute! I feel a twinge of nervousness shoot through me. As they approach the door the phone rings, and I realize I left the wireless receiver in the back room. I hear the door rattle loudly as I answer the phone. I know it is locked, as I did it myself just an hour ago.

After programming a wakeup call for someone I walk into the small office with the glass window. He is standing there waiting for someone to help him. I smile as soon as our eyes meet, and he smiles back. He looks like he is cold, standing there rubbing his arms in his thin t shirt. "it's cold out here, can I come in to do this?" he pleads. Oh God how I wish I could let him in. But I know the security camera is on, and I would get in trouble. "No, I'm sorry, I can't let anyone in after 10:00pm" I inform him. I glance downward, feeling bad about telling him he can't come in. I look up again, wishing there was a way we could talk. He hesitates for a moment, and then asks "So do you have room for me tonight?" I giggle a little bit, glad he is playing along. "Yes, you can practically sleep right next to me. Room 108 is open and its only two doors away" I shoot back at him playfully. I said it quickly and with confidence, and he seems caught off guard, searching for something to

113

say back to me. I smile inside, knowing that I got to him just a little bit. "Well good, I am sure I will feel much better sleeping so close to you" he rebounds with, and looks deep into my eyes. I flinch a little, and then feel the heat rise in my face. I slide the paperwork through the opening and ask for his initials and signature.

"You smell incredible" he continues. I giggle again, thankful for the compliment and his attention. He slides the paperwork back through the opening and our hands touch. It caught me by surprise and I look up at him to see him smiling once again. He takes the keys to the room and walks away, disappearing around the corner. I hate to see him go, but I am enjoying the view of watching him walk away from me. I sigh out loud, wondering if I will ever see him again. I finish with his paperwork and file it away for the day shift to process after check out. I sit down again in front of my books, not wanting to face the reality of grinding through another nights worth of homework. I try to find where I had left off when the phone rings; the monitor flashes room 108. I pick up the receiver and click the button, greeting the caller in as sexy a voice as I can muster on short notice. "Good evening Mr. Michaels, how can I help you?" I ask playfully. He laughs quietly and says "Victoria please, call me Darren." "In that case, call me Vicki" I tell him.

Our conversation quickly jumps from one topic to another; he tells me how he and his friend are on their way to San Diego for a long weekend and other things about him that seem interesting. He asks about my life, and I tell him that is it pretty boring here in Banning, CA. I run through my typical week and cringe at the thought of how dull I must sound. I gotta get a life I think to myself. I can hear the TV in the background and wonder if he is listening to me or just barely paying attention. I hope it is his friend who is flipping channels. I ask him a questions and he responds right away, so I guess he is listening after all. I close my book, figuring this conversation may last a while. He makes me laugh and is very entertaining despite sounding really tired. Time flies by as we talk, and before I know it
it is 3AM.

He finally gives in and says he needs to get some sleep. To my delight he asks me to have breakfast with him. "Cool, call me at 6:45 and wake me up" he says. "It's a deal...sweet dreams" I whisper into the phone before I hang up. I set my cell phone to remind me to call him personally for his wake up call. I am hoping and praying he is going to stay for more than one night. I hate the thought of saying goodbye over breakfast a few hours from now.

I find myself looking at the clock almost every half hour all night long. I cannot wait to see him again; even though we just met I feel so...connected with him. Talking on the phone with me for so long last night just made me feel like we've known one another for a long time. Finally its 6:45 and I pick up the phone and dial his room. He answers in a sleepy voice and asks "Doesn't this hotel have an automated service for this?" "Yes" is all I can reply, suddenly nervous to hear his voice again. I don't understand why I was so comfortable earlier and now I am nervous. My stomach is tight and I feel myself breathing quickly. "Are you coming to my room or should I meet you down there?" he asks, and I feel my stomach contract in response. "Um...I can't come there. I'll get in trouble." Suddenly I hear someone behind me, and realize Vanessa from the day shift is here. She doesn't like me anyway, and always gets me in trouble. If she catches me meeting with him I am going to get fired for sure. "No, I meant for breakfast..." he says, but I cut him off. "I will have to call you back sir" and quickly hang up the phone. I look busy while Vanessa is in the office, but I am dying to call him back and let him know I want to see him.

I finally get the chance to call his room about half an hour later. The phone rings, and rings......and rings. He is not answering. Oh God, I've blown it! He's mad at me and I blew it. Dammit! It is time to clock out, so I grab my stuff and run to the back room to clock out. I rush to my car, hoping I can pull around back and go to his room without being seen by Vanessa. I throw my stuff onto the passenger seat and then I see him and his friend walking towards the office. "What are you doing?" I say out loud. I wave to him to go back to his room, but he doesn't understand me. He starts walking towards my car and I panic. I wave him away excitedly, hoping no one in the office is watching all this. Finally I step out of the car again and yell "Go back to your room" to him. Not a good idea, I think to myself, but it's too late now. I jump in the car and pull around to the back of the hotel. I am so keyed up from all of this I feel like I am going to burst.

Her Eyes

I sit in my car for a moment collecting myself. My hands are shaking with excitement. What the Hell am I doing? I ask myself. Then I am reminded that just an hour before he rolled in here that I was begging for some adventure in my life. Well, be careful what you wish for, you just might get it was what my mom used to say. This is a bad time to think about mom, what would she say about this? "OK.....enough, get out of the car" I command myself. I look around and find the parking lot empty, so I go for it. I am running towards the hallway where his room is when I hear the maid cart coming. I reach into my purse and grab my master room key and sprint for his door. I jam the key in and throw the door open. I quickly jump inside and shut the door behind me. He is sitting on the bed, waiting for me.

"I could get in so much trouble for this" I tell him, feeling a naughty delight to the situation begin to overtake my trepidation. "But you came anyway, didn't you?" he asks. He's right I think to myself, I do want this. He stands up and walks towards me, and I want him to take me in his arms and kiss me. "You didn't bring me breakfast." he says, finally breaking into a sexy smile. He stops a few feet from me. I take half a breath and exhale while saying back "We don't have time for that" I hear myself say it, but am still surprised at my response. My body aches for him, and it is putting words in my mouth. My pussy is a traitor in situations like this, always winning out and getting what it wants regardless of how bad an idea it may be. I take one big step towards him, closing the gap between us.

He steps forward and we meet half way in an impassioned kiss. He is taller than I am, and I reach up to put my arms around his neck and press my body into his. He feels so good against me, and I realize just how long it has been since I have touched a man. Far too long. Kiss warm kisses envelop me, and I feel like he is lifting me of my feet. I feel my heart pounding in my chest, my animal desire growing from within. His hands are exploring me, and I welcome his touch. His hand is on my ass, and he leans into me, pushing me backwards towards the door. I settle against it with a thud; not enough to hurt but certainly enough to know he tried it. We continue kissing and groping one another in the doorway of his hotel room. One last fleeting thought of "I shouldn't be here" disappears into the recesses of my mind.

116

He grinds against me and I wrap one of my legs around him. I love to feel the pressure of him against my hot mound. It feels so good, and soon my hips are grinding back into him. A flash of pleasure courses through me as his teeth sink into my neck. I throw my head back instinctively, smacking my head on the door. I put my hand behind his neck, pulling him into me even harder. He continues a delicious mix of biting and kissing my neck and shoulders, each one sending shivers of delight through me. Suddenly I am off my feet; he grabs my legs and lifts me up in his arms. We are walking towards the bed across the room, and I can tell I am drenched with excitement already. He reaches down and pulls the comforter away and sets me down on the bed. He looks down at me sitting on the bed, his eyes staring deep into me. He pulls his shirt slowly over his head, and I get my first look at his chest. I bite my lip in anticipation; I can't wait to run my tongue over every inch of him. Next comes his belt, he pulls it through the loops and tosses it aside. He kicks off his shoes, pushing them aside.

I look up to meet his eyes, mine drawn to all of him I can now see. He is athletically built, not too big but definitely in good shape. I can't wait to see the rest. As if reading my mind he pulls at the top button on his jeans. It gives, and I am waiting just for a moment for the rest to follow. He slides his hand away, and I know what he wants me to do. I know what I want to do; I fall to me knees in front of him. It is now my turn to take over the process of undoing the buttons on his jeans. I am trembling with excitement and anticipation of seeing it, feeling it, touching him. I yank the flaps apart, and the buttons release his hostage inside. It plops out in front of my face, almost staring up at me. He is very hard already, seemingly as turned on as I am. I want to ram it into the back of my throat, but I resist the urge, barely. I wrap my hand around the base of it, feeling it pulsate in my hand. I look up at him, and slowly move towards it, teasing him before diving in.

I begin slowly, rolling my tongue around the tip of him. I open my mouth and slowly engulf as much of him as I can. I slide back and forth over him, pushing and pulling while swirling my tongue all around him. I am growing more excited by the second, and my pace increases. I grab his hips and lunge forward at him. He touches the back of my throat and I gag and cough. My eyes instantly cloud with tears, my body reacting to the invasion. "Woops, getting a little over excited there." I say, laughing

117

at my unbridled enthusiasm getting the best of me once again. I go right back to it. This time I place my hand on him, and slide my slippery flesh up and down him as my mouth follows. I stroke and suck his cock like a dirty whore should.

He leans forward and grabs the bottom of my shirt, pulling it up over my head. I pull him out of my mouth for the briefest of moments, and dive right back after it once my shirt is off of me. I am aching from inside out, and I want to expedite the process of my own pleasure. I reach back and unclip my bra, it falling to the floor beside me. My tits are finally free of their confines, my breasts swollen with excitement. My nipples are so hard as he touches my soft flesh in his rough-skinned hands. I moan, my mouth still full of his cock. God I feel like I am going to explode if he doesn't touch me there soon! I struggle to get my jeans off without stopping what I am doing. I can't wait any more, and I stand up, tearing my shoes off and then my jeans. I stand before him in just my favorite black thong. My skin is prickling up from the cool room and the excitement coursing through me.

He picks me up again, this time holding me face to face with him. I wrap my arm around his neck and reach back to pull the lacey panties aside and expose my waiting pussy to his hardness. It slides into me easily; I am so wet I can feel it practically running down my leg. He slowly turns in a circle until my feet are against the bed. He instructs me to put my feet on the bed, and I obey. I can now control my movement against him, but still get held in the air and fucked. It is so hot; I am swollen with excitement and my pussy grips him as he slides in and out of me. His hand slide under me, squeezing my ass as he begins to drive me down onto his stiff cock. I moan aloud, growing close to exploding already. I dig my toes into the mattress as I fight for traction, trying my best to fuck him back. I hear my voice growing louder and I want to be quiet but I can't. I want to scream out. He is fucking me so good, my clit rubbing against his stomach as he slides me up and down.

His strokes lengthen and soon he is impaling me on this cock. It hits bottom and sends wave after wave of pleasure through me. I join in the fray, and am practically jumping up and down on him. He is squeezing me so tightly I can barely move against him, and the frustration and delight are too much to take. It starts, and I feel the jolts of electricity shoot through me. My hips take over, grinding against him in effort to make it continue on. I clench in spasm after spasm until I can no longer hold myself against him. He quickly spins me around and drops me onto the bed. I am spent; my eyes are closed as the room swirls around me.

After a moment I can finally feel my hair in my face. I brush it aside and look up at him. He is still standing next to the bed looking down at me. I muster the energy to climb towards the head of the bed, and he walks around the edge to meet me there. His cock is right in front of my face again, reddened and straining with desire for more. I know the feeling; I put it in my mouth again, tasting myself on him. He groans loudly after only a second and I feel his hand slide into my hair. He turns my head to the side and pushes forward, traveling deeper into my mouth. He withdraws, and pushes again. He does it over and over, now fucking my mouth. I jam it into my cheek and then back into my throat. It excites me, like he is making me do it. He tries to pull away but I move with him, grabbing his ass in effort to keep him in my mouth. "No...don't" he mumbles. "I don't want to be done yet" he adds. I am delighted to hear we are not done. "There's more?" I ask him, already knowing the answer. "Fuck yeah there's more. Roll over" he says firmly.

He joins me in bed, on his knees behind me. I love getting hit from behind I think to myself as he enters me once again. His hands are on my hips, and he jerks me backwards onto him. He is so deep inside in one stroke and yet my body arches trying to get even more inside. I gasp in delight and surprise. I look down, and see his right foot on the mattress next to me. He grips my love handles and jams himself into me. It steals my breath; I grip the sheets as I try to hold my ground against his body's thrust. After a moment he withdraws and I can finally breathe again. My head is spinning from holding my breath and the thrashing he is giving me. Finally a long deep moan draws from me and I am back to present suddenly. It drains me, and I fall forward onto the bed. I stick my ass in the air like a cat, ready for more but not able to help much at the moment. I grab the sheets and try to hang on as he moves forward and begins to pound into me once again. I feel his hands on my ass again, and my flesh ripples as he slams into me over and over. I am growing numb with pleasure as he has his way with me. I have no idea how long he does this before he finally gives up and settles down on the

119

bed beside me. He crawls forward and flops down on the bed next to me, brushing the hair out of my eyes once again.

"I can't move" I confess. He has literally pounded the life out of me. "Guess again sweetheart, it's your turn to drive" he tells me. I groan, a combined desire for more and a protest of the effort it will take. He pulls me onto him, our flesh pressing into one another once again. I climb onto him, willing myself to push through the exhausted feeling running through me. I lay on top of him, hoping he can take over from here. He is rubbing the outside of me, and I feel a spark of desire and energy kick in. He grabs my hair again, turning me to meet his mouth. We kiss deeply again, and he moans like he's missed my kisses for months. His hands slide down to my hips and slowly push me downward. I feel him poke my soft flesh, and then slip inside my velvety folds. I shudder like it is for the first time today, but it is far from it. I can't believe that this guy is still going, and that I am keeping up with him. I crunch forward, pushing my hips down into him and taking it deeper into me.

I can't go fast again, I don't have it in me. He seems to know, and we slowly move together as one. We are now making love to one another, soft and slow. It is amazing, and maybe better than anything else today. I feel so close to him; we kiss and pet one another as we meld into one. I never want this feeling to end.

After a few moments I am growing close again, and I think he is too. I muster the strength to sit up on him, pushing my hands into his chest to rise above him. I feel the chill on my skin; sweaty skin now exposed to the air-chilled room. My nipples grow hard instantly and he reaches up to grab them. He pushes and plays with them, pressing them into me. He sits up under me, and I wrap my arms around him, pulling myself against him. My breasts smash into his face, and his tongue flicks over my hard nipple. I toss my head back again, and hips seem to find new life. Despite the cool room we are still sweaty where our bodies meet. I rock back and forth over him with ease. I reach down and put my hands on his face, kissing him as we move together. My body responds, and I hear myself saying "Oh yes...oh God yes!"out loud.

I kiss him harder and harder as it builds inside me. Finally I reach the peak and explode inside and out. My hips grind, my eyes close, and our mouths kiss as I shudder through another delightful orgasm. It carries on and on; washing away slowly like water lapping the sand on a beach. I an so deep inside myself I barely notice that he is starting his. He moans and tightens his body's hold on me. I fight to the surface, trying to focus. "Oh yes...come for me baby!" I encourage him. He is growing inside me, I can feel it. "Where do you want it?" he asks me, the urgency in his voice evident. "Right where you are. I want to feel it in me, I want to feel you come" plead. He leans back, putting his hands behind him on the bed. I feel his quick thrusts into me, lifting me off the bed slightly. I watch his face as his eyes shut tightly and he throws his head back. He spasms time after time inside me, and it feels so good I swear I could almost come again. I feel it swell and subside a few more times before he slumps backwards onto the bed. I lay down on top of him, feeling his chest heaving under me.

After a few minutes I open my eyes and look at the clock. He sees me and lets out a big sigh. He seems to be searching for the words to tell me what I already know. "You have to leave don't you?" I ask, saving him the trouble. "I'm sorry, but I do" he informs me. My heart drops, but I catch myself. "It's OK, I knew that before I came here" I tell him. He kisses me more softly than any time before, and I melt into him.

He gets up and heads for the shower, and I search the room for my scattered clothing. I get dressed, feeling a mix of emotions about what I just did. I knew he would leave, and yet I went into this hoping it would be fun and quick, and I would not over think this. But he got to me, and now I have to live with the thoughts consuming me for a while. I hear him grab a towel off the rack and I hurry towards the door. He came out of the bathroom as I am half way out the door; I wanted to leave before he saw me again. "Hey...Goodbye Victoria. I am glad we met" he smiles at me. I quickly put on my sunglasses, hiding my eyes from him. I wanted to say goodbye, but I could tell my voice would give me away. I muster a smile and shut the door behind me.

Meghan

It has been a little while since we have decided to venture out to a party; Jonathan and I have a great sex life, but we both have always desired more. It's not that we don't satisfy one another completely, but we have learned that in order for us to be faithful to one another we need to allow one another some liberties once in a while. I turn the handle and slip into the hot water filling the marble bath tub. Jonathan has done well for himself, as have I and the two of us live bordering on a luxurious lifestyle; huge home and lots of toys to play with. But once in a while even we want to spark things up a bit.

I sit and relax for a while, picturing what tonight might hold for us. Will it be another woman, or a man this time? I love either, but the last time he chose a woman to come home with us. I think I might want to be the focus of attention from two men. It is a gloriously delicious and naughty thing to pleasure someone while another is pleasuring you. I shudder a little just thinking about it. I grab my razor and go to work, making appropriate preparations for the night's activities. I pull the plug and drain the water from the tub; grabbing the bottle of lotion from the shelf, I rub baby oil all over my skin. I love the feel of the oil on my skin; it is warm and sensual and my hands travel all over my body. I enjoy rubbing my tits, pinching my nipples and squeezing them together. I look at myself in the mirror; I can see myself from the waist up. I see my hands massaging my breasts and feel the heat emanating from my pores. I slide one hand down my stomach and into my waiting, wanting lips below. My hand is slick from the oil, but my pussy is already wet from my own touch. I part my pouting lips with my middle finger, sliding it over the soft pink flesh. Jolts of electricity shoot through me as I brush over my clit. I put one foot on the edge of the tub, giving myself access inside. I gently slide one finger in, and then another. I work them in and out of me, watching my face in the mirror. My mouth is open, but no noise escapes me. My nipples are hard, and I rub them with my free hand. I know tonight will be full of rough play, and I am taking this moment to live the other side, sensual pleasure. I can feel it building, knowing myself better than another ever could, and I watch my expression in the mirror as my fingers disappear inside me. I am so close, and I slide my other hand down to push the release valve. I touch my clit, and I am ready to explode. I circle it a few times, and then press

123

it against the soft folds.

It starts from deep inside me, slowly swimming towards the surface from within. It is sweet and gentle and comforting; enough to take the edge off of my mounting desire for tonight....for now. I work it back and forth as I slide in and out, drawing the most out of it before I realize that my eyes had closed. I had seen the last thirty seconds in my head instead of in the mirror. It looked the same to me, so much so that I do not know exactly when I closed my eyes. I look at myself one more time in the mirror before grabbing a towel and drying off, removing the excess baby oil from my skin. Now I need a drink.

I slide on my favorite purple dress and head downstairs, shoes in hand. I am ready and I am sure Jonathan is too. I look at the clock on the wall; it is about 9:30 and time to leave. I guess I will get that drink at the bar. The party we are going to is not a typical party, it is for swingers. We found a group of friends who share our philosophy on marriage and on occasion we all meet at a designated spot. This particular night will be in an upscale nightclub in Scottsdale. The crowd we travel with is certainly more attractive than most, and the Scottsdale zip code will be certain to bring out some new talent as well. I feel a twinge of anticipation run through me.

We hop in the car and head to the club. Upon entering I notice a book lying on the table next to the bar. It is the same book that I have at home; I look to see who else had ordered the same one when I see there is a line of people in front of the table and someone is there signing books. Oh my God...could it be? Is he really here? I ask myself. I grab the book off the table and interrupt the person speaking, yelling over the music "You wrote this?" He looks up from the book he is signing and tells me "Yes I did" in a matter-of-fact tone. "Oh my God, I bought this book like a month ago off Amazon, and I even wrote a review about it! I am JustMeg2008. Oh my God, I can't believe you're here!" I am nervous and flushed with excitement...as if my body remembered how his words resonate within me. A hundred thoughts run through my head, but I can't pick the right one to say, so I stand there in front of him smiling. He looks at me and smiles, and then looks at the person at the table in front of him as if to silently apologize for the interruption. "So, what did you think of the book?" he asks me. "You may have the sexiest mind in the business. I love your book" I state to him. It was true, nothing I have ever read has ever gotten me hotter than his book. He laughs aloud at my statement, and I am slightly taken aback. "Well, I think that is a gross over-statement, but I appreciate it either way" he offers with an incredulous smile.. "No, seriously...the way you write both sides of the story, I mean...how do you do that? How do you write women so well?" I am trying to compose myself a little bit by now, the initial shock wearing off of finding him here. He is surprisingly attractive and I decide right then and there who my choice for tonight will be.

"I have always been a very sensual person, so I try to expand on those feelings and picture what I think the woman in the story is thinking and feeling. Maybe I just end up with what I would want her to be thinking...I don't know" he says over the music. He seems to be kind of shy and I find it so appealing compared to the usual guys I meet at these events. "It's like you were in my head" I inform him. After a moment I realize that I have butted in line in front of several people, and look up to apologize. "Oh I'm sorry, I will come back later" I say in front of everyone. I turn and walk away, flushed with nervous excitement.

About an hour later Jonathan and I part ways, and goes off to tease the ladies as he loves to do. His ego gets off on the idea of "parading his fine ass in front of women who can't have him" to directly quote him. He was only half-kidding when he said it; but I find his healthy dose of self confidence sexy. I head to the dance floor; the DJ playing some good grooves to dance to. I will get him to dance with me, and see if he can move as well as he describes in his stories. The onslaught begins as the party starts to amp up; guys and girls both approaching me to dance, but I only have my eyes on one person. As for everyone else, the clothes are beginning to loosen and so are the inhibitions. The standard issue stripper pole practically has a waiting line, and there are several girls who are kissing on the dance floor. I can see him through the crowd, sitting at the bar by himself. I stare at him, hoping he will notice me. He finally looks my way, and I signal to him to join me. He shakes his head no, much to my disbelief. People are lining up to party with me and he says no. "Who is this guy?" I ask myself, the intrigue growing. He raises his hand and motions for me to join him. Who the Hell does he think he is? Then he looks shyly away again, and I flash back to the moment at the table. I decide to take another approach.

Her Eyes

I walk across the dance floor, defiantly pushing my way through the crowd to get to the bar where he is sitting. I walk right up to him, determined to get what I want. "Dance with me?" I ask in a loud voice. "Oh, I can't...I don't dance" he responds. I laugh a little, not believing him. "Come on, you can't be that bad" I shoot back, biting my lip trying to entice him. "Seriously, I don't have any rhythm unless I am lying down" he says, laughing slightly and trying to be cute. I roll my eyes at him, forgiving the cheesy line. I grab his hand and drag him forcefully out of the chair. "Come on." I am determined to get what I want, and I don't know why he is being so resistant. We reach the floor, and I can see the nervous look on his face. "I don't dance" he says again. "No one is watching" I tell him, trying to put him at ease. "Meghan...everyone is watching you" he protests. I guess he really is serious, and I am starting to second guess my choice. "Close your eyes, put your hands on my hips, and feel me move" I instruct him. If he is this awkward on the dance floor I can't see him being any good in bed. He is trying, I'll give him credit for that. I wave to the DJ and ask him to slow things down a little. The next track starts and it is definitely slower. "Just follow my hips" I whisper at him. I put my arms around his neck, and feel his hands slide down to my hips. He follows my moves, pressing himself against me. I look at his face, his eyes closed as he concentrates on what he is doing. He opens his eyes and I smile at him. "I love your book" I tell him again, much more collected than my first attempt. "I have read each story several times, and loved every bit of them. I so wanted to meet the man behind the words, and here you are". I am coming around again to the idea of being with him tonight. He is able to match my moves on the dance floor, and I am hopeful he can do the same elsewhere. "Did you envision me as this bad of a dancer?" he asks playfully, poking fun at himself. He is different than Jonathan, and different is what I want tonight. He is smaller in stature, but fit and firm. "I am not sure what I was picturing, but I like what I see" I inform him. I lean into him, brushing my lips against his ear, and then whisper "Kiss me" to him. Suddenly he freezes.

"Is he here?" he asks, wondering about Jonathan. "Yes, he is watching. He knows I want you, that I picked you" I say, granting him permission. "So it's OK?...I've never done...." I am tired of waiting, and I lean in to kiss him. He meets me half way, and presents a wonderfully sensual kiss. I feel his hand on the back of my head, pressing me into him even more. I like the intensity level the kiss builds to, and I push myself against him. I like the way his body feels against mine, and how he is now taking charge. We kiss for a moment more before I pull back from him. He is looking at me, waiting for something. I need a drink; I take his hand and lead him to a table in the back of the bar. I motion to the waitress and order two beers. We talk freely now that we are off the dance floor. He is very interesting; having traveled like me and seemed to be fairly successful in most of his pursuits. Eventually he asks the inevitable, having the same difficulty everyone else does about my relationship. "So...how did you get into this, um...lifestyle?" he asks hesitantly.

I start my well rehearsed speech: "The man I married was into this sort of thing before we met. He was honest enough to discuss it while we were dating, and I have always had a wild side trapped inside me. I had a close girl friend who I found out had an interest in me, and so one night when my husband was out of town we had a few drinks and she walked me through that door. It was wonderful, and I wanted more. So we began seeing each other when we could until I finally asked her if he could join us. She agreed, and the three of us had an ongoing relationship for about two years until she moved away. After that we decided to explore our own sexual fantasies together and eventually we ended up at one of these parties" I finish. "So, you do this sort of thing all the time?" he inquires. "Oh no, we rarely do this. We decided to have a little fun this weekend, that's all. It keeps our marriage interesting, you know...sexually" I reply, watching him breathe a sigh of relief. I would love to know what he is thinking right now; was what I told him a turn on? Or is he going to bow out now and not see through what we have started? So many questions....."Well I have never known a swinger to my knowledge, nor been to a party like this. What usually happens here?" he interrupts my thoughts.

"For the most part it is just a place to meet people, and then if you find a person or couple you like you invite them to a hotel room or to your place. We never have anyone at our house, just to be safe" I tell him. He draws a breath and starts to say something, and then stops. He starts again, "OK, now for the real pressing question. How do you learn to deal with watching your husband having sex with someone else?" I chuckle to myself realizing he, like most people, do not quite understand.

"Deal with? No, you are looking at this the wrong way. We are not in an open relationship, we are sharing the experience with each other. It is about us sharing someone for our pleasure and fun, so it is a mutual desire, not something to put up with until it is the other person's turn" I explain. He nods his head, seeming to understand a little better. "So where is your husband anyway?" he asks, looking around the bar. "He is the guy in the black shirt at the bar, talking to the pretty Asian woman" I tell him, pointing him out with a nod of my head. He smiles and lifts his beer in a mock toast, acknowledging the two of us together. "So how do you decide who, I mean which one of you chooses someone?" he asks me. I smile, confessing that I get my way with that, too. I always choose; sometimes it's a man, sometimes a woman, sometimes another couple. It is really about who I want us to share, because as a woman I have to feel comfortable with who I am going to be with. He is a little more flexible about that than I am. So I am the 'screener' as we call it; I find someone I may like and get to know them a little, and decide where we go from here.

"So am I getting screened right now?" he asks with a look of sudden realization on his face. "Yes, but you seem a little nervous about all of this so I am not sure if it is all going to work out" I say to him, laughing. The look on his face changes; I think I hurt his feelings. "No, no...I want to know what it is like" he blurts out. I laugh a little harder this time and say "OK, we'll see how things go. I really want it to be you; I feel like we have a connection already. While reading your stories, I would touch myself and try to picture what you look like. I never imagined this might actually come true, that I could actually have you. I am getting excited just thinking about it."

We sit and talk for a while longer, and nursing the beer in front of me. I see Jonathan approaching, much to the dismay of the Asian chick at the bar watching him walk away. He comes to the table and stands, waiting to be introduced. He notices my looking behind him, and turns to face Jonathan. He politely extends his hand, and Jonathan and he shake hands. "We loved your book, and I figured you would be the one tonight" Jonathan says in his deep voice. Jonathan sees him nervously searching for something to say, beats him to it. "I take it your new to this?" he teases. I jump in "Oh John, quit it...you're going to scare him off. Go play, I'll let you know when I am ready to leave."

The longer we sit and talk, the more his ability to match me intellectually is a huge turn on for me. If Jonathan has one weak spot, that would be it. I decide to up the ante a little, and order a shot of tequila. The waitress comes back with a tall skinny shot glass and I see him looking at it. "Here, try it" I say, sliding the glass over the table towards him. He picks it up and looks at it, and then at me. He seems a little untrusting, and I wondering once again if he is going to make it through this. He takes a small sip, testing it. "Wow, how interesting" he concludes. I love the silky smooth liquid; the smell, the taste, and the smoky aftertaste that lingers behind. I wave at the waitress, and before long she returns with two more. After a shot or two, he really begins to loosen up. It may be getting close to the time we should leave. I have a nice mellow buzz going, but one more wouldn't hurt.

About an hour later, there is a pyramid of dead soldiers in front of us, and I feel fuzzy. I haven't seen Jonathan in a while, but I have been engrossed in our conversation. He started out writing as a hobby, and worked a day job that he enjoyed. After a while things really started to roll along, and he is now juggling two careers as best he can. He shares that the dream of being a full time writer would provide him a lifestyle he has always desired; money providing the ultimate freedom: time. I understand completely, its like we are kindred souls. My career has consumed me, and only recently have I reached the point where I can steal some time away when I feel like it. I see Jonathan approaching, and I let him know with a quick nod that we are ready to leave. He heads out the front door to hail a cab, and I drop two fifty dollar bills on the table to cover the tab and a generous tip. I stand, and take a moment to steady myself before heading to the door. I lock my arm through his, partly to control my wobbly gait and partly to make sure he doesn't run the other way now that it is show time.

We pour ourselves into the cab; Jonathan appears far more sober than the two of us. I sandwich myself between the two of them, a preview of what is to come. I twinge in anticipation as well as we make the short trip to the hotel. We never have someone at our home, this is a suspension of reality and a different location only adds to the fantasy of the moment. I put my hand on Jonathan's leg, reminding him know that he is the one, that this is fun and nothing ever comes between us. We are quickly at the W Hotel, our palace for the weekend. It is gorgeous and luxurious and I love this place. We walk through the lobby, my heels clicking on the marble floor. I push the button for the elevator, and I look over at him. Despite my level of intoxication I can tell he is nervous. The three of us step into the elevator and the doors close. I see him looking at Jonathan in the reflection, and the blood draining from his face. It appears I am going to have to lead him through this after all. I lean over and purr "Mmm...God I want you" into his ear. We reach the fifth floor, and I catch Jonathan before he steps out of the elevator. "Go to the bar and have one more drink" I tell him. He isn't happy about the idea of us starting without him, but he complies. The doors shut behind us and now there are two.

We reach the door to our room I turn and look him in the eyes. "Last chance" I say. He laughs a little, and then leans in and gives me a long, soft kiss. His hand touches my cheek, and then cradles my face as we kiss some more. I can feel the passion rise between us, crash over us like a wave as he pushes me against the door. His tongue shoots into my mouth and I return the favor, unsure if the tequila taste is from him or me. I spin him around, letting him know that I am not one to submit. I fumble for the key, and open the door. I put the key in, and quickly pull it out. I hear the electronic lock release and I push the door open. I walk in, and he follows me without a moment's hesitation. I smile at him, knowing that I am in fact going to get what I so desire.

I go to him, pushing him backwards into the door with a thump. We kiss with a fever I have not known in quite some time. He kisses my neck and I say aloud "Oh God I want you! I have been dreaming of being with you for a month, and I can't believe this is going to happen." I begin to explore him, my hands running all over him. I feel his hands on my stomach, and he is moving them achingly slowly towards my breasts. My nipples would cut glass at this point, and I am begging on the inside for him to touch them. Finally his hands reach them, and he cradles one in each hand. He squeezes and pushes them against me and a wave of pleasure cascades over me. I am in the moment, more present in time than I have been all night. Every sense is heightened, his every move and touch amplified. I want his mouth on them, so I push him back and unzip my dress. It falls around my waist, and my sexy lace bra follows close behind. He looks at me, drinking in a long look at me standing before him.

His eyes travel downward and he is staring at my breasts. "Take them in your mouth" I tell him, growing impatient. He sticks out his tongue and touches it, and I feel like I am going to shatter in anticipation. Finally he sucks it in, swirling his tongue around it, flicking it rapidly over my rock hard nipple. He uses his whole mouth and sucks more of my soft flesh in. I arch my back, falling away from him as I beg for more. His teeth clamp down on it, and I tense up, bracing myself. He is towing the line between pleasure and pain but seems to know when it is too much. He goes to the other one, treating it with the same gentle roughness. I love it; it is just like I read about, just like I imagined. I am lost in the feeling, drunk with pleasure until he slides a hand under my back and lifts me to face him once again. I can taste the salt of my own skin on his lips as we kiss once again. After a moment I spin away from him, leaning back against him.

I feel his hardness through his pants, and I push back into it. His hands find my breasts again, and he holds me tighter against him by pulling them into me. I grind into him, stroking his cock up and down, readying the both of us for the fun about to come. His hands travel all over me, touching, teasing me. I love every moment of it, and am ready for more. I pull away from him, heading straight for the shower. I turn on the water, and look to find that he has not followed me. I wriggle out of my dress and throw it into the room where I left him. A few seconds later he is with me, but I continue to face away from him. I look over my shoulder at him, and then slide the glass shower door. I step in as he removes his clothes, dropping them on the floor. I hurry through cleaning up, and move out of his way as he enters the shower. I grab one of the thick, plush towels and dry off. I walk out into the room, finding Jonathan sneaking into the room. I point to the chair in the corner, and Jonathan takes a seat quickly. I walk over to the edge of the bed and wait for him. He comes to me, and kisses me once again. He pulls the towel from its folds, and it falls away from me in almost ceremonious fashion. I am naked in front of him, and growing impatient once again. I reach for his towel, wanting to tear it away and devour him. He grabs my hand and pulls me towards him once again. I kiss him, allowing him to signal when he is ready. I feel it once again, and try once more. This time he allows me to fulfill my desire. I yank the towel from around his waist, and his cock is staring straight up at me, beckoning.

Her Eyes

I kiss his chest, never taking my eyes off of it. I work my way downward, across his stomach and I fall to my knees in front of him, and run my hands all over his hard cock. It is a more manageable size than Jonathan's, but is powerful nonetheless. I open my mouth and take it in. Settling my lips around him, I begin slowly, taking my time, caressing, tasting, feeling every inch of it with my mouth. His skin is shaved slick, and I delight in the taste of it. His moans echo inside him, and I feel his hand on the back of my head pushing me, urging me forward, downward. I flatten my tongue, extending it, engulfing him. It is so hard it does not give, and it touches the back of my throat. I fight the urge to withdrawal, water building in my eyes. I take it all in, and hold it there. I want every inch of him inside me in every way possible. "You are so hard" I praise him. I know Jonathan is watching, waiting for my signal. He is sitting in the dark, watching me with him. I have always wondered what goes through his mind at times like this. Does he truly enjoy watching me with another man, or does he simply do this because he knows I may leave if I can't indulge my desires?

His hands find my breasts, kneading them, pinching my excited flesh. His touch elevates my desire, and increase the fervor of me sucking his cock. I grab the base, squeezing, jerking, twisting in time with my mouth. I am quickly working myself into a frenzy, and I finally decide to break the cycle and make this first one really last. I stop in the midst of what I am doing, expecting him to protest but he does not. I turn towards the bed and pull back the sheets. He climbs in first, and settle in beside him. We kiss again, and begin slowly exploring one another with gentle hands. I climb on top of him, wanting to slide all over him before I take it in my mouth again. "I am not done having you in my mouth; I want to taste you again" I tell him. I decide to let him return the favor, and I spin around and back into him. I feel his hands on my ass, pulling me towards his mouth. His tongue is like silken fire against me, and I moan deeply as I slide his cock into my throat.

He is working me over so well, I am ready to burst within just a few seconds. Fuck I am so turned on, I say to myself. I continue to jam him into the back of my throat, slurping and cradling his cock with my tongue. My moans escape once in a while, and I know that Jonathan is watching me, waiting, stroking that big cock of his. So fucking hot. My hips begin to move, and I feel it building. I am rising, falling, spinning, frozen. I feel something penetrate me, and I can no longer hold the rushing waters back. The dam breaks, and I buck my hips and press downward into him. I want more, want it all, and want it right now. I ride it out as long as I can, and then I hear Jonathan's voice. It is like a beacon in the dark, calling me back to the present from wherever I had drifted. "Atta girl, let it out" he says. I feel him stiffen underneath me, reacting to the trap I had set.

I sit up facing away from new lover, and see Jonathan walking towards us. "Having a good time Dear?" he asks, a playful smile plastered on his face. "Oh God yes, he is wonderful" I commend. I look over to him and add "Come over and join us" and just to make sure he doesn't get up and run away I climb on top of his cock. I plant it deep inside me, wriggling and riding it all the way to the bottom. I am sitting reverse cowgirl-style, and I want Jonathan's cock in my mouth. He climbs on the bed, knowing me, knowing what I want. I grab it; it seems even bigger than usual since I have been handling one that is not as large. I force it into my mouth, trying to get as much of it as I can. It is difficult, but I manage as best I can while I shift my focus to the one I am sitting on. God this is fucking hot. I look back over my shoulder at him, wanting to see his face as I ride his cock. It feels so good, so hard. His hands find my hips and he begins grinding me into him, pushing downward with more force than I can muster on my own from this angle. It touches me deep inside and I toss my head back in response.

I go back to work on Jonathan as I ride and grind. There is nothing like the feeling of two men inside you at the same time. As crazy as it sounds, it is so empowering. Controlling them, making them serve me is the greatest turn-on I have ever known, and why I continue to seek it out. I slide my hands onto his cock, my mouth following close behind as I go up and down the entire length. I jerk and grind and twist his tool as I slide my mouth all over it. I totally focus on him for a moment, blindly riding away. I have trouble staying evenly focused on each of them, so they will have to play nice and take turns at receiving my attention. After several minutes of this I feel him sit up underneath me. His hand slides around from behind me, and finds its way to my aching clit.

I yank my head away from Jonathan, feeling suddenly like I am going to blow to pieces. I had no idea I was that close. I grab his hand with mine, ensuring he is going to take me there. "Oh yes...right there...RIGHT THERE! I cry out. My hips take off, grinding against him furiously. I squeeze my tits with my free hand, pinching my rock hard nipples. I am lost in my own process; my hips bucking, my hand feeling his fingers touch me, moaning and groaning and I arch my back to get just a little more pressure inside. Finally it comes; it seemed so close and yet feels overdue when it arrives. I explode all over him, cumming all over his cock. I feel myself shuddering on top of him as the pleasure courses through me.

The only thought in my head is that I want more. I am insatiable once I get going, and tonight is no exception. I climb off of him, hating the fact he is not inside of me. The animal is uncaged, and pure desire overrides my every thought. I climb off of him, wanting to reposition myself for further pleasuring. I shoot him a look and a quick command to get behind me. I go back to work on Jonathan, his cock growing firm once again in my mouth. He is smart not to smash me forward, and instead waits for me to move. I push back and forth, timing jamming the cock in my mouth deeper as I pull away from the one behind me. It is an exquisite rhythm, most indulgent and I delight in every stroke I control. He is so deep inside, filling me completely and just a little more, and I adjust so I can handle it better. I push into the mattress with one hand, balancing myself while I squeeze the base of Jonathan's cock with the other.

I feel something on my ass; he is rubbing me in small, wet circles and it is sending shivers through me. I moan deeply in spite of the mouthful I have. He is teasing me, prodding and pushing making my desire increase to new heights. We settle into a delicious rhythm of his thumb pushing into my most private hole while his cock withdraws from my sopping wet pussy. His timing is good, and he really starting to make me a believer in the tales his book tells. Another orgasms rises, and I begin to lose feeling and specific sensation. Everything blurs into one, and it is perfect, and I want this feeling to last forever. Finally it breaks, and I hear myself cry out like I am across the room watching the three of us. It seems to come from somewhere outside of me, and the deep moans seem to carry on forever, echoing. Jonathan grabs me, making me look at him; swallowed up by his gaze I can only stare back. The moment seems frozen in time, I have no Earthly idea how long it lasted.

It seemed forever and not nearly enough in the same moment. I slump forward, resting against Jonathan as I feel it all subside.

Jonathan moves behind me, and I feel him climb off the bed. Jonathan's cock parts my waiting lips, and I arch into him taking as much as I can. He slides it in to the hilt, knowing when to stop. It stretches me and I wince a little at first, still not totally used to his size after all this time. I grab handfuls of the sheets showing I am ready for it. I do not want to give an inch of ground, and I brace myself for the onslaught I know is coming. He fucks me, and I love it; I love him. There is nothing that feels better than the emotional connection we have. But his size doesn't exactly detract from it either. His hands find my waist, and he stuffs me full of his cock over and over. I look over to see Darren standing, watching us. Jonathan is tearing me up, and I am close to explosion once again. I growl at him, encouraging him to push me to another one. Knowing me almost as well as I do, he knows want I want. He shoves forward until he hits bottom, and holds me there in his big strong hands. I struggle and fight against him, almost as if I were trying to escape. But away is the last thing I want. The struggle triggers me, and I come hard. I shudder and shake, grinding back into him as I yell out. I look through the haze of my orgasm to see Darren watching me. It only adds to it that he is witness to yet another orgasm.

He seems to sense my next desire, and walks towards me. I stare at him, his cock. I want it in my mouth again; I reach under his legs and yank him towards me. In seconds he is back to full stride, and is so hard I doesn't seem real. I am in the mood to play rough, I want to be dominated. I jam his cock into the back of my throat, holding on as long as I can until he wins and I have to give. I pull away, my eyes watering. "Whew....can't do that with his dick, that's for sure!" I tell him gasping for breath. I look up at him smiling, but quickly see he misread my statement. "I fucking love going all the way down on it" I assure him with a dirty smile. He smiles back, seemingly understanding that bigger is not necessarily better. I am enjoying them both, they are each bringing me pleasure. He grabs a handful of my hair, brushing it aside so he can watch me. He shoves it into me, burying his cock in my throat. I am getting what I want, being smashed between the two of them. I struggle against it, trying to hold out as long as possible before giving in and coming up for air. Jonathan is stroking in and out of me, taking his time, trying to pace himself. I hear him begin to groan, and I know he is getting close. I turn around and shove him away from me. "No way mister, you're in time out" I command, pointing to the edge of the bed. I have one more itch that needs to be scratched before tonight is done.

As Jonathan pulls up a chair for a front row seat, I lay down on my back. "Pound me...hard and fast" is the next command I deliver. He smiles at me, and takes position on top of me. He is just the right size for this, and I want it. I lift my legs, settling my calves onto each shoulder so my legs are in the air. He moves forward into me, lifting my butt of the mattress. He pushes it into me, slowly at first, testing. I am growing impatient in spite of the number of times I have gotten off tonight. Suddenly he lurches forward, driving deep inside me. My mouth opens to scream out, but I drew in a breath in surprise. He withdrawals almost the entire way out, only to slap his firm body against mine again. I shudder in delight, and my moans encourage him for more. He increases his speed and force, almost crushing the air out of me with each impact. I love every one of them. I can tell I am going to go multiple this time, and I buck my hips and thrash around under him begging for it to happen. I am losing clarity again, and it begins with a hard, almost violent impact from within. They follow closely together, or blend into one long one, I can no longer discern the difference. He fucks me and fucks me, and I dig my nails into his arms and hang on for dear life. It is amazing, and I feel myself going soft, limp from the energy spent and the explosions within. Finally he releases me from his grip, and I melt back into the mattress. "Fuck yeah...that was what I wanted"

After lying beside one another for several moments, we are both breathing normally once again. I cannot believe the stamina he has. I had to send Jonathan to wait, but he was ready for more at a moment's notice. I hear Jonathan stand from the chair, and walk over to the counter. He returns with the bottle of lube and a condom. I practically squeal inside at the thought of both of them inside me at once. Jonathan lies down in front of me, his cock straining in its own skin. He must have been "priming the pump" as he likes to call it while he watched us, because he is rock hard. I devour him once again, still cock hungry after all this. I am such a dirty whore when I want to be. And I am about to do something so, so dirty. I haven't done this in a long time, but tonight is the time. I squeeze some lube into my hand, and rub it on my ass. I slide a finger all over it, even slightly inside just to make sure I am ready. I look back and tell him "You're gonna have to go slow, I haven't done this in a long time."

Jonathan lies down on the bed, and I climb on top of him. I impale myself on his staff, and slowly go up and down as I revel in his thickness. I squat above him, dropping down on it at a pace and force I create. It is so good inside me, I could do just this forever. But there is more to be had, and I want that, too. After a moment or two I look back at him and he is ready. I turn to try and see it slide into me, but cannot. He grabs the base of his sheathed cock and pushed it into my ass. It resists at first, not letting him in. He is persistent, slowly but surely inching forward until I give and relent to the pressure. Once the tip is inside the rest is easier to take. I begin to move again slowly, Jonathan waiting for me to restart our motion. The pain is beginning to give way to the pleasure, and I can breathe again. I increase my stride, taking more in with each passing moment. It is the most intense feeling ever, nothing compares to having two men inside you at the same time.

Jonathan encourages me onward, his hands on my hips help me move in between the two of them. We are sweaty with desire and gliding back and forth comes easier now. Jonathan must be getting close, I can feel the tension in his body. "That's right baby, take those cocks in you" he mutters at me through gritted teeth. His desire fuels mine, and I increase my pace just a little more. I am climbing as well, but this time I seem to stay present. I am totally conscious of every little move and sensation the two of them are creating in me. "Oh my God...OH MY GOD!!!" I can hear myself practically screaming as it begins. Jonathan yanks me down on top of him as his begins as well. He follows close behind and the two of us come together in an exquisite exchange of pleasure. I feel Darren's weight on top of me, and I am smashed in between my lovers, convulsing in pleasure. "Fuck her hard...do it...fuck her now!" I hear Jonathan bellow. I am paralyzed, and can only moan in agreement as my orgasm begins to subside.

I feel him lift off of me as Jonathan's hands grip my waist. He is bracing me for it, knowing I am almost incapacitated at this moment. He begins to pound into me, and to my surprise my body takes it. His body meets mine, and over and over I hear the slap of skin echo in the room. I squirm under his onslaught, trying to fuck back but almost unable to move. My voice doesn't sound like my own as my groans deepen. My head gets yanked backwards, and the tension in his grip sends me flying over the edge once again. I can feel him expanding, growing ever so close to his own as he pounds me. He is pulling my hair so hard it is lifting me off of Jonathan. He seems to notice and holds me up so we can finish. I grind as best I can as I feel him shudder so deep inside me I am not sure where he was. He grows louder with each final stroke, his stiff cock invading me, pumping his load into my ass. Finally the two of us are finished, and we collapse in union forward onto Jonathan. The three of us lie motionless for many minutes in a sweaty, exhausted tangle of limbs.

He gets up and excuses himself, heading for the bathroom. I hear the toilet flush, followed by the water running in the sink. I can't possibly move, and so I stay right where I am at, in my husband's arms. I kiss him tenderly, as if to thank him for the freedom to be who I want with him, no matter what that may bring out. Eventually I slide off of him, and fall fast asleep. I have no idea where Darren is, but at the moment I can't muster the energy to look for him. "I will speak to him in the morning" is the last thought that drifts across my mind before the world is blank and I am asleep. I sleep the sleep of the dead, and awaken to find that Darren has gone. I do not know when he left. I roll over to find the clock reading ten o'clock and I reach for the phone to order some coffee from room service. I head to the shower, washing away the remnants of last night's encounter....